The Annotated Supernatural Horror in Literature

H. P. Lovecraft

The Annotated Supernatural Horror in Literature

Edited, with Introduction and Commentary, by S. T. Joshi

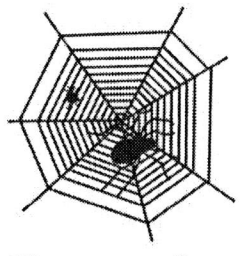

Hippocampus Press
New York
2000

Copyright © 2000 by Hippocampus Press
Introduction and editorial matter copyright © 2000 by S. T. Joshi

Published by Hippocampus Press, P.O. Box 641, New York, NY 10156.
http://www.hippocampuspress.com

All rights reserved. No part of this work may be reproduced in any form or by any means without the written permission of the publisher.

Cover design by Barbara Briggs Silbert.
Cover illustration by Vrest Orton from *The Recluse* (W. Paul Cook, 1927).
Hippocampus Press logo designed by Anastasia Damianakos.

First Edition
3 5 7 9 8 6 4 2

Contents

Preface	7
Introduction	9
Supernatural Horror in Literature	21
I. Introduction	21
II. The Dawn of the Horror-Tale	23
III. The Early Gothic Novel	26
IV. The Apex of Gothic Romance	30
V. The Aftermath of Gothic Fiction	33
VI. Spectral Literature on the Continent	38
VII. Edgar Allan Poe	42
VIII. The Weird Tradition in America	46
IX. The Weird Tradition in the British Isles	55
X. The Modern Masters	61
Appendix	73
The Favourite Weird Stories of H. P. Lovecraft	73
Notes	75
Bibliography of Authors and Works	111
Index	163

Preface

H. P. Lovecraft's "Supernatural Horror in Literature" has been widely acknowledged as the finest historical treatment of the field, and yet both Lovecraft scholars and scholars of weird fiction do not seem to me to have made as full use of this document as they could have. This edition is an attempt to show to both groups of scholars—and to general readers as well—how much we can learn from Lovecraft.

In the preparation of the text I have departed somewhat from the principles I followed in editing Lovecraft's fiction (Arkham House, 1984–89; 4 vols.). Although I have collated all relevant texts—the *Recluse* (1927); the serialisation in the *Fantasy Fan* (1933–35); the first book appearance (*The Outsider and Others*, 1939)—I have amended Lovecraft's citation of titles to conform with modern usage. Hence, all books, long poems, and plays (of whatever length) are printed in italics; all short stories, short poems, and articles are printed in double quotation marks. I have indicated in square brackets the significant additions Lovecraft made to the essay following its first appearance.

The bibliography at the end of the volume gives detailed information on all authors (save those mentioned merely in passing) and works cited in Lovecraft's treatise. I have attempted in nearly all cases to locate 1) the first appearance of the work in question; 2) convenient modern or critical editions; and 3) criticism of the work or (if there is none such) of the author. Only for Lovecraft's "modern masters" (Arthur Machen, Algernon Blackwood, Lord Dunsany, and M. R. James) and for Clark Ashton Smith have I taken the liberty of supplying bibliographical information on works not mentioned by Lovecraft; citations of other weird works by other authors are given in the notes. For foreign works I have tried to list both appearances of the original text and of translations. The designation "*LL*" placed after an entry indicates that Lovecraft possessed some version of the text in his own library.

There are several persons and institutions deserving of thanks for their assistance in the compilation of this volume. I did most of my work at the John Hay and John D. Rockefeller Libraries of Brown University, and have also made use of the Providence Public Library, the Muncie (Indiana) Public libraries, the Bracken Library of Ball State University, the New York University Library, and the New York Public Library. The following individuals have contributed information: Barry L. Bender; Donald R. Burleson; Peter Cannon; Jason C. Eckhardt; Steve Eng; William Fulwiler; Jeffrey Greenbaum; T. E. D. Klein; Robert M. Price; and David E. Schultz.

—S. T. JOSHI

New York City

Abbreviations Used in the Notes

AHT	=	Arkham House transcripts of Lovecraft's letters
D	=	*Dagon and Other Macabre Tales* (rev. ed. Arkham House, 1986)
DH	=	*The Dunwich Horror and Others* (rev. ed. Arkham House, 1984)
FDOC	=	S. T. Joshi, ed., *H. P. Lovecraft: Four Decades of Criticism* (Ohio University Press, 1980)
IDOD	=	*In Defence of Dagon* (Necronomicon Press, 1985)
JHL	=	John Hay Library, Brown University (Providence, RI)
LAL	=	*Lovecraft at Last* by Lovecraft and Willis Conover (1975)
LL	=	S. T. Joshi, *Lovecraft's Library: A Catalogue,* rev. ed. (New York: Hippocampus Press, 2002)
MM	=	*At the Mountains of Madness and Other Novels* (rev. ed. Arkham House, 1985)
MW	=	*Miscellaneous Writings* (Arkham House, 1995)
SHL	=	"Supernatural Horror in Literature"
SHSW	=	State Historical Society of Wisconsin (Madison, WI)
SL	=	*Selected Letters* (Arkham House, 1965–76; 5 vols.)

Introduction

In November 1925, when Lovecraft was living alone at 169 Clinton Street in Brooklyn, he received an offer from his friend W. Paul Cook to write "an article . . . on the element of terror & weirdness in literature"[1] for publication in Cook's legendary amateur journal, *The Recluse*. In this innocent and almost incidental way was born probably one of the most significant—certainly one of the longest—essays ever written by Lovecraft; a work of criticism which even today has no rivals in keenness of historical analysis and in the pithy and penetrating studies of such modern titans of weird fiction as Arthur Machen, Algernon Blackwood, Lord Dunsany, M. R. James, William Hope Hodgson, Ambrose Bierce, and many others. It is a sad fact that most of the better studies of the weird tale—Edith Birkhead's *The Tale of Terror* (1921), Eino Railo's *The Haunted Castle* (1927), Maurice Lévy's *Le Roman "gothique" anglais* (1968)—are solely or largely concerned with the Gothic novels of the late eighteenth and early nineteenth centuries; modern criticism has been unusually slow in exploring the enormous quantities of superb weird fiction written from the middle nineteenth century to the present. But Lovecraft's treatise gains its importance not merely from its discussion of the whole spectrum of horror literature from antiquity to the 1930s, but from the insight it can provide into Lovecraft's own theory and practice of weird writing.

Lovecraft admitted that "I shall take my time about preparing"[2] the treatise, and such proved to be the case. By 1925 he had, of course, read many of the significant works of weird fiction written up to his day, but knew that an extensive course of rereading would be necessary for proper execution of the task. It was, in fact, only in December 1925 that Lovecraft seems first to have come across the work of M. R. James,[3] and he had encountered Blackwood's "The Willows"—which he ultimately ranked as the finest weird tale in all literature—only about a year previously.[4] Machen he had discovered in 1923 (cf. *SL* I.228, 233f.) and Bierce and Dunsany in 1919.[5]

Once he received the request from Cook, therefore, Lovecraft at once abandoned his desultory reading of weird fiction and undertook a more thorough and systematic course of absorbing the weird classics, doing much work at the New York Public Library and the Brooklyn Public Library. It appears that he began writing the essay very late in 1925: by early January he had already written the first four chapters (on the Gothic school up to and including Maturin's *Melmoth the Wanderer*) and was reading Emily Brontë's *Wuthering Heights* preparatory to writing about it at the end of Chapter V;[6] by March he had written Chapter VII, on Poe;[7] and by the middle of April he had gotten "half through Arthur Machen" (Chapter X).[8] The work was probably finished in essence by May, for at that time Lovecraft remarks that he has not yet read the work of Walter de la Mare—whom he ultimately ranked only just below the "modern masters" (Machen, Blackwood, Dunsany, and James) among living fantaisistes—but that he "really ought to [read him] before giving my article a final form" (*SL* II.53). This surely means—given

Lovecraft's disinclination for using the typewriter—that the article was still in autograph manuscript and that he was merely making random inclusions into the holograph text. Indeed, in early June, when he had read de la Mare, he not only "made space" (*SL* II.57) for him in the essay, but was adding "paragraphs here & there" (*SL* II.57–58) as well as continuing random readings. By the middle of October 1926 Lovecraft announces that he has "delayed typing my now finished sketch of weird fiction because of some new source material discovered at the Providence Public Library" (*SL* II.77). (Lovecraft had returned to Providence from New York in April 1926.) What this new material was we do not know, but it appears that Lovecraft must have prepared the typescript by the end of the year and sent it to Cook. Even this, however, did not end the history of the first publication of "Supernatural Horror in Literature": as late as May 1927, when the essay had already been set in type, Lovecraft continued to make last-minute additions on the proofs—chiefly to take note of the work of F. Marion Crawford (whose "The Upper Berth" alone had been cited in the text theretofore) and Robert W. Chambers (*SL* II.122, 127). *The Recluse*—only one issue was ever published—came out in August 1927,[9] nearly half of it devoted to Lovecraft's essay.

But Lovecraft continued to take notes for additions to his essay for some future republication. A list of "Books to mention in new edition of weird article" survives at the end of his *Commonplace Book*,[10] and most of the works on the list—John Buchan's *Witch Wood* (1927), Leonard Cline's *The Dark Chamber* (1927), H. B. Drake's *The Shadowy Thing* (1928), etc.—were in fact discussed in the revised version of the essay. Several items, however, were not discussed; they are as follows (brackets in the text are Lovecraft's):

    R. E. Spencer—*The Lady Who Came to Stay* (1931)
    [Hogg—*Memoirs of a Justified Sinner?*] and others
    Blackwood—"Chemical" <from Asquith's *Ghost Book* [1927]>
    "The Undying Thing" by Barry Pain (in *Stories in the Dark* 1901)

Lovecraft frequently made note in letters of the worthiness—or lack of it—of this or that weird writer for inclusion in his treatise. But the chance for revision did not come until late 1933, when Charles D. Hornig wished to serialise the essay in his fanzine, *The Fantasy Fan*. Lovecraft evidently revised the essay all at once, not piecemeal over the course of the serialisation (October 1933–February 1935); indeed, he seems simply to have sent Hornig an annotated copy of *The Recluse*, with separate typed sheets for the major additions.[11] This is borne out by the nature of the revisions: aside from random revisions in phraseology, there is almost no change in the text save the following additions:

    Chapter VI: the small paragraph on H. H. Ewers and part of the concluding paragraph (on Meyrink's *The Golem*);

Chapter VIII: the section beginning with the discussion of Cram's "The Dead Valley" up to that discussing the tales of Edward Lucas White; the last paragraph, on Clark Ashton Smith, is augmented;
Chapter IX: the paragraph on Buchan, much of the long paragraph discussing "the weird short story", and the long section on Hodgson.

Of these, the section on Hodgson was added separately in August 1934[12] (this is an earlier version of the essay later published as "The Weird Work of William Hope Hodgson"[13]), while the section on *The Golem* was revised after April 1935, when Lovecraft (who had based his note on the film version) read the actual novel and disconcertedly observed its enormous difference from the film.

The serialisation in *The Fantasy Fan* ended, however, in the middle of Chapter VIII, as the magazine folded in February 1935. In late summer 1936 Willis Conover conceived the idea of reprinting the text in his *Science-Fantasy Correspondent* from the point where it had left off in *The Fantasy Fan;* the project never came to fruition, although in anticipation of it Lovecraft sent to Conover the annotated copy of *The Recluse* which Hornig had returned to him (*LAL* 86, 97) and also prepared a condensation of the first eight chapters of the text for Conover to print prior to resuming the serialisation.[14]

The first publication of the complete revised text of "Supernatural Horror in Literature" was in *The Outsider and Others* (1939), edited by August Derleth. There is some mystery as to which text Derleth used in the preparation of his text: he could not have used the abortive *Fantasy Fan* serialisation, for he fails to include some minor revisions in wording Lovecraft made there. He similarly could not have used Conover's copy of *The Recluse,* for this was still in Conover's possession as late as 1975 (cf. *LAL* 110 and 259). Conover did, however, retype "about half" (*LAL* 213) of the entire essay, incorporating all the changes, and sent the typescript to Lovecraft. Lovecraft acknowledged receiving the text and made a few final corrections (*LAL* 219), but his terminal illness prevented him from returning the typescript to Conover. It is possible that Derleth found this typescript amongst Lovecraft's papers after R. H. Barlow had donated them to the John Hay Library, and so based his text upon it and the *Recluse* appearance. If so, he never returned the typescript to the library, for its whereabouts are now unknown.

Assuming that Derleth printed Lovecraft's additions as he intended them (and we have no authority to doubt it, however reluctant we may be to rely upon Derleth's recension of the text), we must note that Lovecraft did not take very great care in the revision of his essay. The additions are made sporadically with no especial attempt to incorporate the new material into the historic progression of the weird tale, and certainly no systematic or comprehensive revision of the entire text (a task which would presumably have entailed that most horrible of tasks for Lovecraft, retyping) was even considered. It is particularly surprising that the last chapter took no regard of the later fantastic work of Blackwood, Machen (only *The Green Round* [1933], read by Lovecraft very soon after publication [*SL* IV.397]), and Dunsany (especially such novels as *The King of Elfland's Daughter, The Blessing of Pan,* and *The Curse of the Wise Woman,* all of which he read [*SL* I.356; II.277; IV.390; V.268, 353–54]). It is true that Lovecraft did not much care for the later work of Dunsany, but surely at least a brief summary of this and other work would have been appropriate.

At this point it might be well to discuss in general how complete Lovecraft's treatise is. Critics have not been inclined to agree with Fred Lewis Pattee's dictum that the essay "has omitted nothing important":[15] Peter Penzoldt chided Lovecraft for not even mentioning Oliver Onions and Robert Hichens,[16] while Jack Sullivan has quite rightly taken Lovecraft to task for his very scanty mention of LeFanu.[17] E. F. Bleiler has remarked:

> Lovecraft had an excellent knowledge of Edwardian and contemporary supernatural fiction, but his knowledge of earlier material was limited. What he knew of Gothic fiction he picked up from Edith Birkhead and Montague Summers, and went little beyond them. He was very weak on Victorian literature. He dismisses Le Fanu with a brief comment and seems to have been unaware of the work of Mrs. J. H. Riddell, Mrs. Henry Wood, Mary Braddon, Rhoda Broughton and others.[18]

This statement contains much that is true, some that is false—Lovecraft did not know of Montague Summers' criticism until relatively late in life—and some that is irrelevant. Lovecraft in fact displays his knowledge of the best Victorian weird writing in his remark that "the Victorians went in strongly for weird fiction—Bulwer-Lytton, Dickens, Wilkie Collins, Harrison Ainsworth, Mrs Oliphant, George W. M. Reynolds, H. Rider Haggard, R. L. Stevenson and countless others turned out reams of it" (*SL* IV.239), and his omission of the writers cited by Bleiler—none of whom have been at all influential in the history of weird writing—cannot be considered significant. It is true that Lovecraft's readings in the Gothics were none too comprehensive, but it is equally true that most of the several hundred Gothic novels written in the late eighteenth and early nineteenth century fully deserve his label of a "dreary plethora of trash." Lovecraft is certainly to be commended for his brief citations of fantasy in ancient literature (even though some of these were derived from second-hand sources[19]), although I find it a little surprising that he does not cite Greek epic (the various descents into the Underworld by Homer,[20] Vergil,[21] Ovid,[22] and others), Greek and Roman tragedy (especially such things as the grisly conclusion of Euripides' *Medea*[23] and the bloodthirstiness of Seneca's dramas, which led directly to the Elizabethan tragedy cited by Lovecraft), and other random works such as Lucian's *True History* or Catullus 63 (the "Attis" poem), which he must have read.[24] Perhaps he did not wish to give too much emphasis to this very early material, since he was clearly correct in stating that "the typical weird tale of standard literature is a child of the eighteenth century".

One of the most interesting features of the text, from the perspective of our understanding of Lovecraft, is the degree to which Lovecraft attributes to other writers qualities that are manifestly found in his own work. In particular, he points out the "cosmicism"—the central principle in his fiction, involving the suggestion of the vast gulfs of space and time and the consequent triviality of the human race—of many authors whose actual sense of the cosmic was probably very small. Hence *Melmoth the Wanderer* is said to reveal "an understanding of the profoundest sources of actual cosmic fear". Machen is hailed as the best "of living creators of cosmic fear". The word "cosmic" here may be no more than a rhetorical ornament, for as early as 1930 Lovecraft was coming to "suspect the cosmicism of Bierce, [M. R.] James, & even Machen" (*SL* III.196), while in 1932 he stated bluntly that Machen's "imagination is not cosmic" (*SL* IV.4). Of Dunsany we are told: "His point of view is the most truly cosmic of any held in the literature of any period." But by 1936 Lovecraft had come to revise his estimate: "What I miss in Machen, James, de la Mare, Shiel, & even Blackwood and Poe, is a sense of the *cosmic*. Dunsany . . . is the most cosmic of them all, but he gets only a little way" (*SL* V.341). Most remarkable, however, is his assessment of Poe:

> Poe . . . perceived the essential impersonality of the real artist; and knew that the function of creative fiction is merely to express and interpret events and sensations as they are, regardless of how they tend or what they prove—good and evil, attractive or repulsive, stimulating or depressing—with the author always acting as a vivid and detached chronicler rather than as a teacher, sympathiser, or vendor of opinion.

Poe scholars may raise their eyebrows at the claim for Poe's "impersonality" and "detachment", although it is surely true that Poe scorned the moral didacticism of the prevailing Victorian temper; but let us recall Lovecraft's statement of his own aesthetic of weird fiction, written in 1927:

> Now all my tales are based on the fundamental premise that common human laws & interests have no validity or significance in the vast cosmos-at-large. . . . To achieve the essence of real externality [i.e. cosmicism], whether of time or space or dimension, one must forget that such things as organic life, good & evil, love & hate, & all such local attributes of a negligible & temporary race called mankind, have any existence at all. (*SL* II.150)

It is, however, unjust to think that Lovecraft's analyses are vitiated in this way. In fact, in both his specific comments on individual writers and in his general remarks on the aesthetic foundations of weird literature—the importance of "atmosphere", the cosmic point of view, the superiority of impressions and images over the "mere mechanics of plot"—his essay has stood the test of time and has been little improved upon by subsequent scholarship.

It is, then, easy to second-guess Lovecraft, and to complain of the relative praise given to this or that author;[25] but no one can deny (nor has anyone yet done so) that Lovecraft's work remains, as Bleiler noted, "the finest historical discussion of supernatural fiction".[26] Jack Sullivan similarly finds that "Lovecraft's essay remains the most empathetic and original study of the genre to date".[27] And Bleiler is correct in emphasising the value of Lovecraft's work as an *historical* study; for—granting any omissions of particular authors or works, important or otherwise—Lovecraft never loses sight of the historical development of the field, and it is precisely in this regard—as well as in its analysis of certain authors whom he read "empathetically" and perceptively—that the essay gains its primary value. The central place given to Poe—as both the summation of the Gothic movement (recall that "Ms. Found in a Bottle" [1831] was written only eleven years after the publication of *Melmoth*) and as forger of an entirely new tradition in fantastic writing and in short fiction as a whole—is surely a sound historical decision, for all Lovecraft's adulation of Poe. The subsequent history of weird fiction, both in Europe and in America, was, as Lovecraft knew, either an attempt to imitate Poe's psychological realism or to escape from his influence and continue the now enfeebled Gothic tradition. Lovecraft was particularly acute in selecting, from the vast torrents of weird fiction produced in the latter half of the nineteenth and the first decades of the twentieth centuries, the four "modern masters" who, as we now clearly see, have—with the inclusion of Lovecraft himself—shaped contemporary fantastic writing. The fact is still more remarkable when we reflect that three of these four "modern masters" (Machen, Blackwood, and Dunsany) outlived Lovecraft by anywhere from ten to twenty years. M. R. James' last collection of stories, *A Warning to the Curious,* was published in the year Lovecraft began his treatise, so that his analysis of James' work could, chronologically speaking, almost qualify as a book review.

Bleiler has already noted one of the important sources of the essay; and the work is—in spite of Derleth's statements to the contrary[28]—rather embarrassingly reliant in its first five chapters upon Edith Birkhead's *The Tale of Terror* (1921). The fact that Lovecraft had at the time not even read the whole of *Melmoth the Wanderer,* but only those excerpts of it printed in George Saintsbury's *Tales of Mystery* (1891) and Julian Hawthorne's *Lock and Key Library* (1912) (cf. *SL* II.36), testifies to his dependence upon other critics for the Gothic tradition. Lovecraft does not, certainly, conceal his debt to Birkhead—he cites her and Saintsbury at the conclusion of chapter IV—but he does not go out of his way to proclaim it, either.[29] The chapter on continental weird fiction seems to be fairly original, and is the more valuable as this body of work is still generally ignored by Anglo-American critics. The Poe chapter was also an early breakthrough in criticism, although the information on Poe's life and background was probably derived from George E. Woodberry's biography of 1885.[30] But it is in the last three chapters—particularly chapter X—that the work gains its chief scholarly value. Here Lovecraft had almost no previous criticism upon which to work—save in the cases of Hawthorne and Bierce—and it is interesting that these chapters are given over almost entirely to critical analysis rather than to biographical or historical criticism. If we must carp we may say that Lovecraft paradoxically cites too many works rather than too few—works which, while perhaps worthy ventures in their own right, are hardly central to the development of the field: the disproportionately lengthy analysis of Cline's admittedly brilliant *Dark Chamber* (1927) is an example, as are mentions of such exceedingly obscure works as Gorman's *The Place Called Dagon*, Leland Hall's *Sinister House*, the tales of Mrs H. D. Everett (*The Death Mask* [1920]), Drake's *The Shadowy Thing*, and the like.

The general value of Lovecraft's remarks on the nature and function of weird fiction—or, rather, his type of weird fiction—is perhaps beyond the scope of this essay, but some notes can perhaps be added, specifically in reference to their relevance to contemporary horror fiction. Aside from many random but very perspicacious remarks in letters, one of the first occasions in which Lovecraft defended his theory of the weird was in the so-called *In Defence of Dagon* essays, written in 1921 as part of a discussion with the Transatlantic Circulator, an Anglo-American group of amateur journalists who exchanged works in manuscript and commented upon them. Lovecraft sent several of his stories—"Dagon", "The White Ship", "The Nameless City"—through the Circulator, and the generally unfavourable remarks by other members led him to articulate his theory of the weird in terms remarkably similar to those found in the introduction to "Supernatural Horror in Literature". Consider the opening paragraphs:

> In replying to the adverse criticisms of my weird tale "Dagon", I must begin by conceding that all such work is necessarily directed to a very limited section of the public. Fiction falls generally into three major divisions; romantic, realistic, and imaginative. The first is for those who value action and emotion for their own sake; who are interested in striking events which conform to a preconceived artificial pattern. . . .
>
> The second fictional school—the realism which rules the public today—is for those who are intellectual and analytical rather than poetical or emotional. It is scientific and literal, and laughs both at the romanticist and the myth-maker. It has the virtue of being close to life, but has the disadvantage of sinking into the commonplace and the unpleasant at times. Both romanticism and realism have the common quality of dealing almost wholly with the objective world—with things rather than with what things suggest. The poetic element is wanting. Romanticism calls on emotion, realism on pure reason; both ignore the *imagination,* which groups isolated impressions into gorgeous patterns and finds strange relations and associations among the objects of visible and invisible Nature. (*IDOD* 11)

This very unorthodox division of literature into three categories—romantic, realistic, and imaginative—allows Lovecraft to stress the importance of the last by maintaining that it draws upon the best features of the other two: like romanticism, imaginative fiction bases its appeal on emotions (the emotions of fear, wonder, and terror); from realism it derives the important principle of truth—not truth to fact, as in realism, but truth to human feeling. As a result, Lovecraft comes up with the somewhat startling deduction that "The imaginative writer devotes himself to art in its most essential sense" (*IDOD* 11).

In defending himself, and his writing, from charges of "unwholesomeness" and immorality (charges still made today against weird fiction), Lovecraft states that the weird, the fantastic, and even the horrible are as deserving of artistic treatment as the wholesome and the ordinary. No realm of human existence can be denied to the artist; everything depends upon the treatment, not the subject matter. Lovecraft cites Wilde's pretty paradox that

> a healthy work of art is one the choice of whose subject is conditioned by the temperament of the artist, and comes directly out of it.... An unhealthy work of art, on the other hand, is a work ... whose subject is deliberately chosen, not because the artist has any pleasure in it, but because he thinks that the public will pay him for it. In fact, the popular novel that the public calls healthy is always a thoroughly unhealthy production; and what the public calls an unhealthy novel is always a beautiful and healthy work of art. (Cited in *IDOD* 35)

In this way Lovecraft neatly justifies his unusual subject-matter while simultaneously condemning the popular best-seller as a product of insincere hackwork. And yet, because Lovecraft realises that weird fiction is necessarily a cultivated taste, he is compelled to note repeatedly that he writes only for the "sensitive"—the select few whose imaginations are sufficiently liberated from the mundanities of daily life to appreciate images, moods, and incidents that do not exist in the world as we know and experience it. This leads to the following amusing declaration, in response to a Circulator member's assertion that Lovecraft's stories would gain a wider following if he wrote about "ordinary people":

> I could not write about "ordinary people" because I am not in the least interested in them. Without interest there can be no art. Man's relations to man do not captivate my fancy. It is man's relation to the cosmos—to the unknown—which alone arouses in me the spark of creative imagination. The humanocentric pose is impossible to me, for I cannot acquire the primitive myopia which magnifies the earth and ignores the background. (*IDOD* 21)

What Lovecraft is really saying is that his disinclination to write for or about "ordinary people" is derived not only from his own lack of "interest" in them, but from the fact that such people in turn have no particular interest in his imaginative work.

Lovecraft's defence of weird fiction as the literature of pure imagination and as the preserve of a select few is a very compelling one, and we can see how well it justifies the work of such of his contemporaries and successors as Lord Dunsany, E. R. Eddison, Arthur Machen, Clark Ashton Smith, Ramsey Campbell, T. E. D. Klein, and Thomas Ligotti. The bestsellerdom of Stephen King, Clive Barker, and Anne Rice, on the other hand, seem motivated by exactly that sort of "unhealthiness" that Wilde detected in the popular novel, and there can hardly be a doubt as to which group of writers will survive as exponents of genuine literature and which will be banished to the oblivion of superficial, if lucrative, hackdom.

Another area in which Lovecraft's theory of the weird may gain significant contemporary relevance is in his remarks on the aesthetic status of non-supernatural horror—a subgenre that has become very popular of late, under the various terms "psychological suspense", "dark suspense", or "dark mystery". Is this type of fiction—from Bloch's *Psycho* to Thomas Harris' *The Silence of the Lambs*—genuinely a branch of weird fiction? Lovecraft is somewhat ambiguous on the matter, but in the end he decides in the negative. His discussion, in "Supernatural Horror in Literature", of such things as Poe's "The Man of the Crowd" and several of Bierce's non-supernatural tales may suggest that he is not intrinsically opposed to the notion of a weird tale based on "abnormal psychology and monomania" (his designation for a certain group of Poe's tales); but the general tone of his remarks leads one to believe that very few such works could pass his muster. A critical passage in "Supernatural Horror in Literature" attempts to distinguish between the weird and the merely grisly: "This type of fear-literature must not be confounded with a type externally similar but psychologically widely different; the literature of mere physical fear and the mundanely gruesome." This distinction sounds good on paper, but it seems very hard to apply in actual cases. Is there a point at which the "mundanely gruesome" becomes so extreme as to be transmogrified into something else?

Lovecraft bases his view on a somewhat complicated argument as to the effect of the weird upon our emotions. His canonical statement of the weird occurs early in "Supernatural Horror in Literature":

> The true weird tale has something more than secret murder, bloody bones, or a sheeted form clanking chains according to rule. A certain atmosphere of breathless and unexplainable dread of outer, unknown forces must be present; and there must be a hint, expressed with a seriousness and portentousness becoming its subject, of that most terrible conception of the human brain—a malign and particular suspension or defeat of those fixed laws of Nature which are our only safeguard against the assaults of chaos and the daemons of unplumbed space.

This view—specifically the notion of the violation of natural law—had been evolving for several years, and rested upon the critical formulation that the weird tale must depict phenomena that cannot be explained by science *as currently understood*. As early as 1921, in discussing "tales of a psycho-analytical, telepathic, and hypnotic order", he stated: "Telepathy, the only mythical member of this triad, may some time furnish me with a plot; but the other two are likely to become systematised by science in the course of the next few decades, hence will pass out of the realm of wonder into that of realism" (*IDOD* 21). He later used this formulation in his celebrated discussion of Faulkner's "A Rose for Emily". This story was included in Dashiell Hammett's *Creeps by Night* (1931), one of the most heterogeneous weird-suspense anthologies ever compiled, containing everything from the cosmic horror of Donald Wandrei's "The Red Brain" to John Collier's *conte cruel*, "Green Thoughts". The volume's appearance led to an illuminating debate between Lovecraft and August Derleth as to whether Faulkner's tale was weird, Derleth apparently averring that it was (we have lost his side of the correspondence) and Lovecraft emphatically affirming the contrary. Lovecraft first gives his opinion of the story itself:

> ... I'm far from denying the Faulkner yarn a high place as a realistic story. It is a fine piece of work—but is *not weird*. This sort of gruesomeness does *not* suggest anything beyond ordinary physical life & commonplace nature. Necrophily is horrible enough—but only *physically* so, like other repellent abnormalities. It excites loathing—but does not call up anything beyond Nature. We are horrified at Emily as at a cannibal—or as at some practitioner of nameless Sabbat-rites—but we do not feel the stark glimpse or monstrous doubt hinting at subversions of basic natural law.[31]

Derleth did not seem convinced by this, so Lovecraft continues in greater detail:

> Manifestly, this ["A Rose for Emily"] is a dark and horrible thing which *could happen*, whereas the crux of a *weird* tale is something which *could not possibly happen*. If any unexpected advance of physics, chemistry, or biology were to indicate the *possibility* of any phenomena related by the weird tale, that particular set of phenomena would cease to be *weird* in the ultimate sense because it would become surrounded by a different set of emotions. It would no longer represent imaginative liberation, because it would no longer indicate a suspension or violation of the natural laws against whose universal dominance our fancies rebel. (*SL* III.434)

Lovecraft's argument—fundamental to his view of weird fiction—is persuasive, but I believe it contains a few fallacies that may at least force us to qualify it. It is true enough that the horrible and the gruesome do not by themselves constitute weirdness; it is also true that necrophilia is horrible, but it is not merely "physically" so: the power of Faulkner's tale rests on our perception of the astonishing aberration of Emily's psyche that led her to kill her lover, keep the corpse in her bedroom, and lie next to it for decades, until her own death. I think Lovecraft's bias toward external, cosmic horror and his general lack of interest in human beings (I do not say this pejoratively, as I see nothing wrong with not being interested in human beings) caused him to underrate the degree to which the mysteries of the mind could be nearly as powerful and bizarre as the mysteries of the universe. One must grant, however, that there is no actual "subversion of basic natural laws" in Faulkner's tale—to say that it somehow subverts our norms of "human nature" is to say nothing in particular—and if in the end "A Rose for Emily" remains on the borderland of the weird, then it is closer to that realm than Lovecraft was willing to concede.

But in virtually outlawing the non-supernatural horror tale from the domain of weird fiction—in proclaiming, that is, that only those tales that convey some sense of the anomalous occurrence of that "which *could not possibly happen*"—is Lovecraft not contradicting his own later aesthetic of the weird? The critical passage, written in 1931, is this:

> The time has come when the normal revolt against time, space, and matter must assume a form not overtly incompatible with what is known of reality—when it must be gratified by images forming *supplements* rather than *contradictions* of the visible and mensurable universe. And what, if not a form of *non-supernatural cosmic art,* is to pacify this sense of revolt—as well as gratify the cognate sense of curiosity? (*SL* III.295-96)

It is possible that this remark applies more to the technique, rather than to the metaphysics, of weird fiction; in other words, Lovecraft is specifying a methodology of weird writing whereby a background of scientific realism, and an eschewing of scenarios and phenomena which contemporary science has proven demonstrably false (e.g., ghosts, werewolves, vampires, and the like), is maintained. As he wrote in "Notes on Writing Weird Fiction":

> Inconceivable events and conditions have a special handicap to overcome, and this can be accomplished only through the maintenance of a careful realism in every phase of the story *except* that touching on the one given marvel. This marvel must be treated very impressively and deliberately—with a careful emotional "build-up"—else it will seem flat and unconvincing. (*MW* 115)

Even if the utterance is interpreted metaphysically, it should not be understood as signaling Lovecraft's acceptance of the sort of non-supernatural phenomena—necrophilia, cannibalism, gruesome murders—that he had previously disallowed: these would not be representative of "non-supernatural *cosmic* art". Rather, what we find in Lovecraft's own later fiction is an instantiation of this conception by means of what Matthew H. Onderdonk termed the "supernormal": "scientifically conceived gods and associated lore to take the place in literature of the simon-pure supernaturalism and more strictly poetical gods of our past days".[32] What this means is that the various "supernatural" phenomena in Lovecraft's tales no longer defy natural law as such, but only our *conceptions* of natural law. This is made clear in a very carefully written passage in "Notes on Writing Weird Fiction":

I choose weird stories because they suit my inclinations best—one of my strongest and most persistent wishes being to achieve, momentarily, *the illusion* [my italics] of some strange suspension or violation of the galling limitations of time, space, and natural law which for ever imprison us and frustrate our curiosity about the infinite cosmic spaces beyond the radius of our sight and analysis. (*MW* 113)

Lovecraft's later fiction is a systematic working out of this idea.

We seem to have strayed far from "Supernatural Horror in Literature", but in fact Lovecraft's entire theory of weird fiction can be found encapsulated in that essay. It quite literally occupies a central place in his work: it was written at almost the midpoint of his career, a decade on either side of the commencement of his mature fiction-writing ("The Tomb", 1917) and his death in 1937. What is more, it not only allowed him to codify his views on the weird tale, but it seemed to galvanise him creatively: it is surely no accident that, shortly after the bulk of his work on the essay was finished in the summer of 1926, Lovecraft produced a torrent of fiction that included "The Call of Cthulhu" (1926), "Pickman's Model" (1926), "The Silver Key" (1926), *The Dream-Quest of Unknown Kadath* (1926–27), *The Case of Charles Dexter Ward* (1927), and "The Colour out of Space" (1927).

"Supernatural Horror in Literature" also provides important evidence as to literary influences upon Lovecraft's own work. A careful reading of both the well-known and obscure works cited in the essay can reveal much about the sources of Lovecraft's tales: Drake's *The Shadowy Thing* is a clear influence upon "The Thing on the Doorstep"; Gorman's *The Place Called Dagon* may have influenced "The Shadow over Innsmouth" and "The Dreams in the Witch House"; "The Haunter of the Dark" draws upon Hanns Heinz Ewers' "The Spider". Many other such influences could be traced upon further investigation. It hardly need be added that these purely literary influences do not compromise the fundamental originality of Lovecraft's work, for in his later work he transmuted what he borrowed and made it uniquely his own: his days of slavishly imitating Dunsany or Machen were long over.

Lovecraft, then, is certainly at liberty to dismiss his essay, with characteristically exaggerated humility, as "an exceedingly cursory touching of high spots—being based on a criminally desultory reading programme & containing some woefully regrettable omissions—& inclusions" (*SL* II.209); but students of his work will find it an inexhaustible mine of information about his life, work, and mind, and students of weird fiction can derive from it valuable insights on the theory and practice of weird fiction. Far from thinking that Lovecraft somehow wasted his time on the writing and revision of this work, we ought instead to be grateful for such a felicitous union of creative and analytical genius.

Supernatural Horror in Literature

I. Introduction

The oldest and strongest emotion of mankind is fear, and the oldest and strongest kind of fear is fear of the unknown. These facts few psychologists will dispute, and their admitted truth must establish for all time the genuineness and dignity of the weirdly horrible tale as a literary form. Against it are discharged all the shafts of a materialistic sophistication which clings to frequently felt emotions and external events, and of a naively insipid idealism which deprecates the aesthetic motive and calls for a didactic literature to uplift the reader toward a suitable degree of smirking optimism.[1] But in spite of all this opposition the weird tale has survived, developed, and attained remarkable heights of perfection; founded as it is on a profound and elementary principle whose appeal, if not always universal, must necessarily be poignant and permanent to minds of the requisite sensitiveness.[2]

The appeal of the spectrally macabre is generally narrow because it demands from the reader a certain degree of imagination and a capacity for detachment from every-day life. Relatively few are free enough from the spell of the daily routine to respond to rappings from outside, and tales of ordinary feelings and events, or of common sentimental distortions of such feelings and events, will always take first place in the taste of the majority; rightly, perhaps, since of course these ordinary matters make up the greater part of human experience. But the sensitive are always with us, and sometimes a curious streak of fancy invades an obscure corner of the very hardest head; so that no amount of rationalisation, reform, or Freudian analysis[3] can quite annul the thrill of the chimney-corner whisper or the lonely wood. There is here involved a psychological pattern or tradition as real and as deeply grounded in mental experience as any other pattern or tradition of mankind; coeval with the religious feeling and closely related to many aspects of it, and too much a part of our inmost biological heritage to lose keen potency over a very important, though not numerically great, minority of our species.

Man's first instincts and emotions formed his response to the environment in which he found himself.[4] Definite feelings based on pleasure and pain[5] grew up around the phenomena whose causes and effects he understood, whilst around those which he did not understand—and the universe teemed with them in the early days—were naturally woven such personifications, marvellous interpretations, and sensations of awe and fear as would be hit upon by a race having few and simple ideas and limited experience. The unknown, being likewise the unpredictable, became for our primitive forefathers a terrible and omnipotent source of boons and calamities visited upon mankind for cryptic and wholly extra-terrestrial reasons, and thus clearly belonging to spheres of existence whereof we know nothing and wherein we have no part. The phenomenon of dreaming likewise helped to build up the notion of an unreal or spiritual world; and in general, all the conditions of savage dawn-life so strongly conduced toward a feeling of the supernatural, that we need not wonder at the thoroughness with which man's very hereditary essence has become saturated with religion and superstition. That saturation must, as a matter of plain scientific fact, be regarded as virtually permanent so far as the subconscious mind and inner instincts are concerned; for though the area of the unknown has been steadily contracting for thousands of years, an infinite reservoir of mystery still engulfs most of the outer cosmos,[6] whilst a vast residuum of powerful inherited associations clings around all the objects and processes that were once mysterious, however well they may now be explained. And more than this, there is an actual physiological fixation of the old instincts in our nervous tissue, which would make them obscurely operative even were the conscious mind to be purged of all sources of wonder.

Because we remember pain and the menace of death more vividly than pleasure, and because our feelings toward the beneficent aspects of the unknown have from the first been captured and formalised by conventional religious rituals, it has fallen to the lot of the darker and more maleficent side of cosmic mystery to figure chiefly in our popular supernatural folklore. This tendency, too, is naturally enhanced by the fact that uncertainty and danger are always closely allied; thus making any kind of an unknown world a world of peril and evil possibilities. When to this sense of fear and evil the inevitable fascination of wonder and curiosity is superadded, there is born a composite body of keen emotion and imaginative provocation whose vitality must of necessity endure as long as the human race itself. Children will always be afraid of the dark, and men with minds sensitive to hereditary impulse will always tremble at the thought of the hidden and fathomless worlds of strange life which may pulsate in the gulfs beyond the stars, or press hideously upon our own globe in unholy dimensions which only the dead and the moonstruck can glimpse.

With this foundation, no one need wonder at the existence of a literature of cosmic fear. It has always existed, and always will exist; and no better evidence of its tenacious vigour can be cited than the impulse which now and then drives writers of totally opposite leanings to try their hands at it in isolated tales, as if to discharge from their minds certain phantasmal shapes which would otherwise haunt them. Thus Dickens wrote several eerie narratives; Browning, the hideous poem "Childe Roland"; Henry James, *The Turn of the Screw;* Dr. Holmes, the subtle novel *Elsie Venner;* F. Marion Crawford, "The Upper Berth" and a number of other examples; Mrs. Charlotte Perkins Gilman, social worker, "The Yellow Wall Paper"; whilst the humourist W. W. Jacobs produced that able melodramatic bit called "The Monkey's Paw".

This type of fear-literature must not be confounded with a type externally similar but psychologically widely different; the literature of mere physical fear and the mundanely gruesome.[7] Such writing, to be sure, has its place, as has the conventional or even whimsical or humorous ghost story where formalism or the author's knowing wink removes the true sense of the morbidly unnatural;[8] but these things are not the literature of cosmic fear in its purest sense. The true weird tale has something more than secret murder, bloody bones, or a sheeted form clanking chains according to rule. A certain atmosphere of breathless and unexplainable dread of outer, unknown forces must be present; and there must be a hint, expressed with a seriousness and portentousness becoming its subject, of that most terrible conception of the human brain—a malign and particular suspension or defeat of those fixed laws of Nature which are our only safeguard against the assaults of chaos and the daemons of unplumbed space.[9]

Naturally we cannot expect all weird tales to conform absolutely to any theoretical model. Creative minds are uneven, and the best of fabrics have their dull spots. Moreover, much of the choicest weird work is unconscious; appearing in memorable fragments scattered through material whose massed effect may be of a very different cast. Atmosphere is the all-important thing, for the final criterion of authenticity is not the dovetailing of a plot but the creation of a given sensation. We may say, as a general thing, that a weird story whose intent is to teach or produce a social effect,[10] or one in which the horrors are finally explained away by natural means,[11] is not a genuine tale of cosmic fear; but it remains a fact that such narratives often possess, in isolated sections, atmospheric touches which fulfil every condition of true supernatural horror-literature. Therefore we must judge a weird tale not by the author's intent, or by the mere mechanics of the plot; but by the emotional level which it attains at its least mundane point. If the proper sensations are excited, such a "high spot" must be admitted on its own merits as weird literature, no matter how prosaically it is later dragged down. The one test of the really weird is simply this—whether or not there be excited in the reader a profound sense of dread, and of contact with unknown spheres and powers; a subtle attitude of awed listening, as if for the beating of black wings or the scratching of outside shapes and entities on the known universe's utmost rim. And of course, the more completely and unifiedly a story conveys this atmosphere, the better it is as a work of art in the given medium.

II. The Dawn of the Horror-Tale

As may naturally be expected of a form so closely connected with primal emotion, the horror-tale is as old as human thought and speech themselves.

Cosmic terror appears as an ingredient of the earliest folklore of all races, and is crystallised in the most archaic ballads, chronicles, and sacred writings. It was, indeed, a prominent feature of the elaborate ceremonial magic, with its rituals for the evocation of daemons and spectres, which flourished from prehistoric times, and which reached its highest development in Egypt and the Semitic nations. Fragments like the Book of Enoch[1] and the Claviculae of Solomon[2] well illustrate the power of the weird over the ancient Eastern mind, and upon such things were based enduring systems and traditions whose echoes extend obscurely even to the present time. Touches of this transcendental fear are seen in classic literature, and there is evidence of its still greater emphasis in a ballad literature which paralleled the classic stream but vanished for lack of a written medium. The Middle Ages, steeped in fanciful darkness, gave it an enormous impulse toward expression; and East and West alike were busy preserving and amplifying the dark heritage, both of random folklore and of academically formulated magic and cabbalism,[3] which had descended to them. Witch, werewolf, vampire, and ghoul brooded ominously on the lips of bard and grandam,[4] and needed but little encouragement to take the final step across the boundary that divides the chanted tale or song from the formal literary composition. In the Orient, the weird tale tended to assume a gorgeous colouring and sprightliness which almost transmuted it into sheer phantasy. In the West, where the mystical Teuton had come down from his black Boreal forests and the Celt remembered strange sacrifices in Druidic groves, it assumed a terrible intensity and convincing seriousness of atmosphere which doubled the force of its half-told, half-hinted horrors.

Much of the power of Western horror-lore was undoubtedly due to the hidden but often suspected presence of a hideous cult of nocturnal worshippers whose strange customs—descended from pre-Aryan and pre-agricultural times when a squat race of Mongoloids roved over Europe with their flocks and herds—were rooted in the most revolting fertility-rites of immemorial antiquity.[5] This secret religion, stealthily handed down amongst peasants for thousands of years despite the outward reign of the Druidic, Graeco-Roman, and Christian faiths in the regions involved, was marked by wild "Witches' Sabbaths" in lonely woods and atop distant hills on Walpurgis-Night and Hallowe'en, the traditional breeding-seasons of the goats and sheep and cattle; and became the source of vast riches of sorcery-legend, besides provoking extensive witchcraft-prosecutions of which the Salem affair forms the chief American example.[6] Akin to it in essence, and perhaps connected with it in fact, was the frightful secret system of inverted theology or Satan-worship which produced such horrors as the famous "Black Mass"; whilst operating toward the same end we may note the activities of those whose aims were somewhat more scientific or philosophical—the astrologers, cabbalists, and alchemists of the Albertus Magnus[7] or Raymond Lully[8] type, with whom such rude ages invariably abound. The prevalence and depth of the mediaeval horror-spirit in Europe, intensified by the dark despair which waves of pestilence brought, may be fairly gauged by the grotesque carvings slyly introduced into much of the finest later Gothic ecclesiastical work of the time; the daemoniac gargoyles of Notre Dame and Mont St. Michel being among the most famous specimens.[9] And throughout the period, it must be remembered, there existed amongst educated and uneducated alike a most unquestioning faith in every form of the supernatural; from the gentlest of Christian doctrines to the most monstrous morbidities of witchcraft and black magic. It was from no empty background that the Renaissance magicians and alchemists—Nostradamus,[10] Trithemius,[11] Dr. John Dee,[12] Robert Fludd,[13] and the like—were born.

In this fertile soil were nourished types and characters of sombre myth and legend which persist in weird literature to this day, more or less disguised or altered by modern technique. Many of them were taken from the earliest oral sources, and form part of mankind's permanent heritage. The shade which appears and demands the burial of its bones, the daemon lover who comes to bear away his still living bride, the death-fiend or psychopomp[14] riding the night-wind,[15] the man-wolf, the sealed chamber, the deathless sorcerer[16]—all these may be found in that curious body of mediaeval lore which the late Mr. Baring-Gould so effectively assembled in book form.[17] Wherever the mystic Northern blood was strongest, the atmosphere of the popular tales became most intense; for in the Latin races there is a touch of basic rationality which denies to even their strangest superstitions many of the overtones of glamour so characteristic of our own forest-born and ice-fostered whisperings.

Just as all fiction first found extensive embodiment in poetry, so is it in poetry that we first encounter the permanent entry of the weird into standard literature. Most of the ancient instances, curiously enough, are in prose; as the werewolf incident in Petronius,[18] the gruesome passages in Apuleius,[19] the brief but celebrated letter of Pliny the Younger to Sura, and the odd compilation *On Wonderful Events* by the Emperor Hadrian's Greek freedman, Phlegon.[20] It is in Phlegon that we first find that hideous tale of the corpse-bride, "Philinnion and Machates",[21] later related by Proclus[22] and in modern times forming the inspiration of Goethe's "Bride of Corinth" and Washington Irving's "German Student". But by the time the old Northern myths take literary form, and in that later time when the weird appears as a steady element in the literature of the day, we find it mostly in metrical dress; as indeed we find the greater part of the strictly imaginative writing of the Middle Ages and Renaissance. The Scandinavian Eddas[23] and Sagas[24] thunder with cosmic horror, and shake with the stark fear of Ymir and his shapeless spawn;[25] whilst our own Anglo-Saxon *Beowulf* and the later Continental Nibelung tales[26] are full of eldritch weirdness. Dante is a pioneer in the classic capture of macabre atmosphere, and in Spenser's stately stanzas will be seen more than a few touches of fantastic terror in landscape, incident, and character. Prose literature gives us Malory's *Morte d'Arthur,* in which are presented many ghastly situations taken from early ballad sources—the theft of the sword and silk from the corpse in Chapel Perilous by Sir Launcelot, the ghost of Sir Gawaine, and the tomb-fiend seen by Sir Galahad[27]—whilst other and cruder specimens were doubtless set forth in the cheap and sensational "chapbooks" vulgarly hawked about and devoured by the ignorant. In Elizabethan drama, with its *Dr. Faustus,* the witches in *Macbeth,* the ghost in *Hamlet,* and the horrible gruesomeness of Webster, we may easily discern the strong hold of the daemoniac on the public mind; a hold intensified by the very real fear of living witchcraft, whose terrors, first wildest on the Continent, begin to echo loudly in English ears as the witch-hunting crusades of James the First gain headway.[28] To the lurking mystical prose of the ages is added a long line of treatises on witchcraft and daemonology which aid in exciting the imagination of the reading world.[29]

Through the seventeenth and into the eighteenth century we behold a growing mass of fugitive legendry and balladry of darksome cast; still, however, held down beneath the surface of polite and accepted literature. Chapbooks of horror and weirdness multiplied, and we glimpse the eager interest of the people through fragments like Defoe's "Apparition of Mrs. Veal", a homely tale of a dead woman's spectral visit to a distant friend, written to advertise covertly a badly selling theological disquisition on death.[30] The upper orders of society were now losing faith in the supernatural, and indulging in a period of classic rationalism. Then, beginning with the translations of Eastern tales in Queen Anne's reign[31] and taking definite form toward the middle of the century, comes the revival of romantic feeling—the era of new joy in Nature, and in the radiance of past times, strange scenes, bold deeds, and incredible marvels. We feel it first in the poets, whose utterances take on new qualities of wonder, strangeness, and shuddering.[32] And finally, after the timid appearance of a few weird scenes in the novels of the day—such as Smollett's *Adventures of Ferdinand, Count Fathom*[33]—the released instinct precipitates itself in the birth of a new school of writing; the "Gothic" school of horrible and fantastic prose fiction, long and short, whose literary posterity is destined to become so numerous, and in many cases so resplendent in artistic merit. It is, when one reflects upon it, genuinely remarkable that weird narration as a fixed and academically recognised literary form should have been so late of final birth. The impulse and atmosphere are as old as man, but the typical weird tale of standard literature is a child of the eighteenth century.

III. The Early Gothic Novel

The shadow-haunted landscapes of "Ossian",[1] the chaotic visions of William Blake, the grotesque witch-dances in Burns's "Tam O'Shanter", the sinister daemonism of Coleridge's "Christabel" and *Ancient Mariner,* the ghostly charm of James Hogg's *Kilmeny,*[2] and the more restrained approaches to cosmic horror in *Lamia* and many of Keats's other poems, are typical British illustrations of the advent of the weird to formal literature. Our Teutonic cousins of the Continent were equally receptive to the rising flood, and Bürger's *Wild Huntsman* and the even more famous daemon-bridegroom ballad of *Lenore*—both imitated in English by Scott, whose respect for the supernatural was always great—are only a taste of the eerie wealth which German song had commenced to provide. Thomas Moore adapted from such sources the legend of the ghoulish statue-bride (later used by Prosper Mérimée in "The Venus of Ille", and traceable back to great antiquity) which echoes so shiveringly in his ballad of "The Ring"; whilst Goethe's deathless masterpiece *Faust,* crossing from mere balladry into the classic, cosmic tragedy of the ages, may be held as the ultimate height to which this German poetic impulse arose.

But it remained for a very sprightly and worldly Englishman—none other than Horace Walpole himself—to give the growing impulse definite shape and become the actual founder of the literary horror-story as a permanent form. Fond of mediaeval romance and mystery as a dilettante's diversion, and with a quaintly imitated Gothic castle as his abode at Strawberry Hill, Walpole in 1764[3] published *The Castle of Otranto;* a tale of the supernatural which, though thoroughly unconvincing and mediocre in itself, was destined to exert an almost unparalleled influence on the literature of the weird. First venturing it only as a translation by one "William Marshal, Gent." from the Italian of a mythical "Onuphrio Muralto", the author later acknowledged his connexion with the book and took pleasure in its wide and instantaneous popularity—a popularity which extended to many editions,[4] early dramatisation,[5] and wholesale imitation both in England and in Germany.[6]

The story—tedious, artificial, and melodramatic—is further impaired by a brisk and prosaic style whose urbane sprightliness nowhere permits the creation of a truly weird atmosphere. It tells of Manfred, an unscrupulous and usurping prince determined to found a line, who after the mysterious sudden death of his only son Conrad on the latter's bridal morn, attempts to put away his wife Hippolita and wed the lady destined for the unfortunate youth—the lad, by the way, having been crushed by the preternatural fall of a gigantic helmet in the castle courtyard. Isabella, the widowed bride, flees from this design; and encounters in subterranean crypts beneath the castle a noble young preserver, Theodore, who seems to be a peasant yet strangely resembles the old lord Alfonso who ruled the domain before Manfred's time. Shortly thereafter supernatural phenomena assail the castle in divers ways; fragments of gigantic armour being discovered here and there, a portrait walking out of its frame, a thunderclap destroying the edifice, and a colossal armoured spectre of Alfonso rising out of the ruins to ascend through parting clouds to the bosom of St. Nicholas. Theodore, having wooed Manfred's daughter Matilda and lost her through death—for she is slain by her father by mistake—is discovered to be the son of Alfonso and rightful heir to the estate. He concludes the tale by wedding Isabella and preparing to live happily ever after, whilst Manfred—whose usurpation was the cause of his son's supernatural death and his own supernatural harassings—retires to a monastery for penitence; his saddened wife seeking asylum in a neighbouring convent.[7]

Such is the tale; flat, stilted, and altogether devoid of the true cosmic horror which makes weird literature.[8] Yet such was the thirst of the age for those touches of strangeness and spectral antiquity which it reflects, that it was seriously received by the soundest readers and raised in spite of its intrinsic ineptness to a pedestal of lofty importance in literary history. What it did above all else was to create a novel type of scene, puppet-characters, and incidents; which, handled to better advantage by writers more naturally adapted to weird creation, stimulated the growth of an imitative Gothic school which in turn inspired the real weavers of cosmic terror—the line of actual artists beginning with Poe. This novel dramatic paraphernalia consisted first of all of the Gothic castle,[9] with its awesome antiquity, vast distances and ramblings, deserted or ruined wings, damp corridors, unwholesome hidden catacombs, and galaxy of ghosts and appalling legends, as a nucleus of suspense and daemoniac fright. In addition, it included the tyrannical and malevolent nobleman as villain; the saintly, long-persecuted, and generally insipid heroine who undergoes the major terrors and serves as a point of view and focus for the reader's sympathies; the valorous and immaculate hero, always of high birth but often in humble disguise; the convention of high-sounding foreign names, mostly Italian, for the characters; and the infinite array of stage properties which includes strange lights, damp trap-doors,[10] extinguished lamps, mouldy hidden manuscripts,[11] creaking hinges, shaking arras,[12] and the like. All this paraphernalia reappears with amusing sameness, yet sometimes with tremendous effect, throughout the history of the Gothic novel; and is by no means extinct even today, though subtler technique now forces it to assume a less naive and obvious form. An harmonious milieu for a new school had been found, and the writing world was not slow to grasp the opportunity.

German romance at once responded to the Walpole influence, and soon became a byword for the weird and ghastly. In England one of the first imitators was the celebrated Mrs. Barbauld, then Miss Aikin, who in 1773 published an unfinished fragment called "Sir Bertrand", in which the strings of genuine terror were truly touched with no clumsy hand. A nobleman on a dark and lonely moor, attracted by a tolling bell and distant light, enters a strange and ancient turreted castle whose doors open and close and whose bluish will-o'-the-wisps lead up mysterious staircases toward dead hands and animated black statues. A coffin with a dead lady, whom Sir Bertrand kisses, is finally reached; and upon the kiss the scene dissolves to give place to a splendid apartment where the lady, restored to life, holds a banquet in honour of her rescuer. Walpole admired this tale, though he accorded less respect to an even more prominent offspring of his *Otranto—The Old English Baron,* by Clara Reeve, published in 1777.[13] Truly enough, this tale lacks the real vibration to the note of outer darkness and mystery which distinguishes Mrs. Barbauld's fragment; and though less crude than Walpole's novel, and more artistically economical of horror in its possession of only one spectral figure, it is nevertheless too definitely insipid for greatness. Here again we have the virtuous heir to the castle disguised as a peasant and restored to his heritage through the ghost of his father; and here again we have a case of wide popularity leading to many editions, dramatisation,[14] and ultimate translation into French.[15] Miss Reeve wrote another weird novel, unfortunately unpublished and lost.[16]

The Gothic novel was now settled as a literary form, and instances multiply bewilderingly as the eighteenth century draws toward its close. *The Recess,* written in 1785 by Mrs. Sophia Lee, has the historic element, revolving round the twin daughters of Mary, Queen of Scots; and though devoid of the supernatural, employs the Walpole scenery and mechanism with great dexterity. Five years later, and all existing lamps are paled by the rising of a fresh luminary of wholly superior order—Mrs. Ann Radcliffe (1764–1823), whose famous novels made terror and suspense a fashion, and who set new and higher standards in the domain of macabre and fear-inspiring atmosphere despite a provoking custom of destroying her own phantoms at the last through laboured mechanical explanations. To the familiar Gothic trappings of her predecessors Mrs. Radcliffe added a genuine sense of the unearthly in scene and incident which closely approached genius; every touch of setting and action contributing artistically to the impression of illimitable frightfulness which she wished to convey. A few sinister details like a track of blood on castle stairs, a groan from a distant vault, or a weird song in a nocturnal forest can with her conjure up the most powerful images of imminent horror; surpassing by far the extravagant and toilsome elaborations of others. Nor are these images in themselves any the less potent because they are explained away before the end of the novel. Mrs. Radcliffe's visual imagination was very strong, and appears as much in her delightful landscape touches—always in broad, glamorously pictorial outline, and never in close detail—as in her weird phantasies. Her prime weaknesses, aside from the habit of prosaic disillusionment, are a tendency toward erroneous geography and history and a fatal predilection for bestrewing her novels with insipid little poems, attributed to one or another of the characters.

Mrs. Radcliffe wrote six novels; *The Castles of Athlin and Dunbayne* (1789), *A Sicilian Romance* (1790), *The Romance of the Forest* (1791), *The Mysteries of Udolpho* (1794), *The Italian* (1797), and *Gaston de Blondeville*, composed in 1802 but first published posthumously in 1826. Of these *Udolpho* is by far the most famous, and may be taken as a type of the early Gothic tale at its best. It is the chronicle of Emily, a young Frenchwoman transplanted to an ancient and portentous castle in the Apennines through the death of her parents and the marriage of her aunt to the lord of the castle—the scheming nobleman Montoni. Mysterious sounds, opened doors, frightful legends, and a nameless horror in a niche behind a black veil all operate in quick succession to unnerve the heroine and her faithful attendant Annette; but finally, after the death of her aunt, she escapes with the aid of a fellow-prisoner whom she has discovered. On the way home she stops at a chateau filled with fresh horrors—the abandoned wing where the departed chatelaine dwelt, and the bed of death with the black pall—but is finally restored to security and happiness with her lover Valancourt, after the clearing-up of a secret which seemed for a time to involve her birth in mystery. Clearly, this is only the familiar material re-worked; but it is so well re-worked that *Udolpho* will always be a classic. Mrs. Radcliffe's characters are puppets, but they are less markedly so than those of her forerunners. And in atmospheric creation she stands preëminent among those of her time.

Of Mrs. Radcliffe's countless imitators, the American novelist Charles Brockden Brown stands the closest in spirit and method. Like her, he injured his creations by natural explanations; but also like her, he had an uncanny atmospheric power which gives his horrors a frightful vitality as long as they remain unexplained. He differed from her in contemptuously discarding the external Gothic paraphernalia and properties and choosing modern American scenes for his mysteries; but this repudiation did not extend to the Gothic spirit and type of incident. Brown's novels involve some memorably frightful scenes, and excel even Mrs.

Radcliffe's in describing the operations of the perturbed mind. *Edgar Huntly* starts with a sleep-walker digging a grave, but is later impaired by touches of Godwinian[17] didacticism. *Ormond* involves a member of a sinister secret brotherhood. That and *Arthur Mervyn*[18] both describe the plague of yellow fever, which the author had witnessed in Philadelphia and New York. But Brown's most famous book is *Wieland; or, The Transformation* (1798),[19] in which a Pennsylvania German, engulfed by a wave of religious fanaticism, hears voices and slays his wife and children as a sacrifice. His sister Clara, who tells the story, narrowly escapes. The scene, laid at the woodland estate of Mittingen on the Schuylkill's remote reaches, is drawn with extreme vividness; and the terrors of Clara, beset by spectral tones, gathering fears, and the sound of strange footsteps in the lonely house, are all shaped with truly artistic force. In the end a lame ventriloquial explanation is offered, but the atmosphere is genuine while it lasts. Carwin,[20] the malign ventriloquist, is a typical villain of the Manfred or Montoni type.[21]

IV. The Apex of Gothic Romance

Horror in literature attains a new malignity in the work of Matthew Gregory Lewis (1775–1818), whose novel *The Monk* (1796) achieved marvellous popularity and earned him the nickname of "Monk" Lewis. This young author, educated in Germany and saturated with a body of wild Teuton lore unknown to Mrs. Radcliffe, turned to terror in forms more violent than his gentle predecessor had ever dared to think of; and produced as a result a masterpiece of active nightmare whose general Gothic cast is spiced with added stores of ghoulishness. The story is one of a Spanish monk, Ambrosio, who from a state of overproud virtue is tempted to the very nadir of evil by a fiend in the guise of the maiden Matilda; and who is finally, when awaiting death at the Inquisition's hands, induced to purchase escape at the price of his soul from the Devil, because he deems both body and soul already lost. Forthwith the mocking Fiend snatches him to a lonely place, tells him he has sold his soul in vain since both pardon and a chance for salvation were approaching at the moment of his hideous bargain, and completes the sardonic betrayal by rebuking him for his unnatural crimes, and casting his body down a precipice whilst his soul is borne off for ever to perdition. The novel contains some appalling descriptions such as the incantation in the vaults beneath the convent cemetery, the burning of the convent, and the final end of the wretched abbot. In the sub-plot where the Marquis de las Cisternas meets the spectre of his erring ancestress, The Bleeding Nun, there are many enormously potent strokes; notably the visit of the animated corpse to the Marquis's bedside, and the cabbalistic ritual whereby the Wandering Jew helps him to fathom and banish his dead tormentor. Nevertheless *The Monk* drags sadly when read as a whole. It is too long and too diffuse, and much of its potency is marred by flippancy and by an awkwardly excessive reaction against those canons of decorum which Lewis at first despised as prudish. One great thing may be said of the author; that he never ruined his ghostly visions with a natural explanation. He succeeded in breaking up the Radcliffian tradition and expanding the field of the Gothic novel. Lewis wrote much more than *The Monk*. His drama, *The Castle Spectre*, was produced in 1798, and he later found time to pen other fictions in ballad form—*Tales of Terror* (1799), *Tales of Wonder* (1801), and a succession of translations from the German.[1]

Gothic romances, both English and German, now appeared in multitudinous and mediocre profusion.[2] Most of them were merely ridiculous in the light of mature taste, and Miss Austen's famous satire *Northanger Abbey* was by no means an unmerited rebuke to a school which had sunk far toward absurdity. This particular school was petering out, but before its final subordination there arose its last and greatest figure in the person of Charles Robert Maturin (1782–1824), an obscure and eccentric Irish clergyman. Out of an ample body of miscellaneous writing which includes one confused Radcliffian imitation called *Fatal Revenge; or, The Family of Montorio* (1807), Maturin at length evolved the vivid horror-masterpiece of *Melmoth the Wanderer* (1820), in which the Gothic tale climbed to altitudes of sheer spiritual fright which it had never known before.

Melmoth is the tale of an Irish gentleman who, in the seventeenth century, obtained a preternaturally extended life from the Devil at the price of his soul. If he can persuade another to take the bargain off his hands, and assume his existing state, he can be saved; but this he can never manage to effect, no matter how assiduously he haunts those whom despair has made reckless and frantic. The framework of the story is very clumsy; involving tedious length, digressive episodes, narratives within narratives, and laboured dovetailing and coincidences; but at various points in the endless rambling there is felt a pulse of power undiscoverable in any previous work of this kind—a kinship to the essential truth of human nature, an understanding of the profoundest sources of actual cosmic fear, and a white heat of sympathetic passion on the writer's part which makes the book a true document of aesthetic self-expression[3] rather than a mere clever compound of artifice. No unbiased reader can doubt that with *Melmoth* an enormous stride in the evolution of the horror-tale is represented. Fear is taken out of the realm of the conventional and exalted into a hideous cloud over mankind's very destiny. Maturin's shudders, the work of one capable of shuddering himself, are of the sort that convince. Mrs. Radcliffe and Lewis are fair game for the parodist, but it would be difficult to find a false note in the feverishly intensified action and high atmospheric tension of the Irishman whose less sophisticated emotions and strain of Celtic mysticism gave him the finest possible natural equipment for his task. Without a doubt Maturin is a man of authentic genius, and he was so recognised by Balzac, who grouped Melmoth with Molière's Don Juan, Goethe's Faust, and Byron's Manfred as the supreme allegorical figures of modern European literature,[4] and wrote a whimsical piece called "Melmoth Reconciled", in which the Wanderer succeeds in passing his infernal bargain on to a Parisian bank defaulter, who in turn hands it along a chain of victims until a revelling gambler dies with it in his possession, and by his damnation ends the curse. Scott,[5] Rossetti,[6] Thackeray,[7] and Baudelaire[8] are the other titans who gave Maturin their unqualified admiration, and there is much significance in the fact that Oscar Wilde, after his disgrace and exile, chose for his last days in Paris the assumed name of "Sebastian Melmoth".[9]

Melmoth contains scenes which even now have not lost their power to evoke dread. It begins with a deathbed—an old miser is dying of sheer fright because of something he has seen, coupled with a manuscript he has read and a family portrait which hangs in an obscure closet of his centuried home in County Wicklow. He sends to Trinity College, Dublin, for his nephew John; and the latter upon arriving notes many uncanny things. The eyes of the portrait in the closet glow horribly,[10] and twice a figure strangely resembling the portrait appears momentarily at the door. Dread hangs over that house of the Melmoths, one of whose ancestors, "J. Melmoth, 1646", the portrait represents. The dying miser declares that this man—at a date slightly before 1800—is alive. Finally the miser dies, and the nephew is told in the will to destroy both the portrait and a manuscript to be found in a certain drawer. Reading the manuscript, which was written late in the seventeenth century by an Englishman named Stanton, young John learns of a terrible incident in Spain in 1677, when the writer met a horrible fellow-countryman and was told of how he had stared to death a priest who tried to denounce him as one filled with fearsome evil. Later, after meeting the man again in London, Stanton is cast into a madhouse and visited by the stranger, whose approach is heralded by spectral music and whose eyes have a more than mortal glare. Melmoth the Wanderer—for such is the malign visitor—offers the captive freedom if he will take over his bargain with the Devil; but like all others whom Melmoth has approached, Stanton is proof against temptation. Melmoth's description of the horrors of a life in a madhouse, used to tempt Stanton, is one of the most potent passages of the book. Stanton is at length liberated, and spends the rest of his life tracking down Melmoth, whose family and ancestral abode he discovers. With the family he leaves the manuscript, which by young John's time is sadly ruinous and fragmentary. John destroys both portrait and manuscript, but in sleep is visited by his horrible ancestor, who leaves a black and blue mark on his wrist.[11]

Young John soon afterward receives as a visitor a shipwrecked Spaniard, Alonzo de Monçada, who has escaped from compulsory monasticism and from the perils of the Inquisition. He has suffered horribly—and the descriptions of his experiences under torment and in the vaults through which he once essays escape are classic—but had the strength to resist Melmoth the Wanderer when approached at his darkest hour in prison. At the house of a Jew who sheltered him after his escape he discovers a wealth of manuscript relating other exploits of Melmoth including his wooing of an Indian island maiden, Immalee, who later comes to her birthright in Spain and is known as Donna Isidora; and of his horrible marriage to her by the corpse of a dead anchorite at midnight in the ruined chapel of a shunned and abhorred monastery. Monçada's narrative to young John takes up the bulk of Maturin's four-volume book; this disproportion being considered one of the chief technical faults of the composition.[12]

At last the colloquies of John and Monçada are interrupted by the entrance of Melmoth the Wanderer himself, his piercing eyes now fading, and decrepitude swiftly overtaking him. The term of his bargain has approached its end, and he has come home after a century and a half to meet his fate. Warning all others from the room, no matter what sounds they may hear in the night, he awaits the end alone. Young John and Monçada hear frightful ululations, but do not intrude till silence comes toward morning. They then find the room empty. Clayey footprints lead out a rear door to a cliff overlooking the sea, and near the edge of the precipice is a track indicating the forcible dragging of some heavy body. The Wanderer's scarf is found on a crag some distance below the brink, but nothing further is ever seen or heard of him.

Such is the story, and none can fail to notice the difference between this modulated, suggestive, and artistically moulded horror and—to use the words of Professor George Saintsbury—"the artful but rather jejune rationalism of Mrs. Radcliffe, and the too often puerile extravagance, the bad taste, and the sometimes slipshod style of Lewis."[13] Maturin's style in itself deserves particular praise, for its forcible directness and vitality lift it altogether above the pompous artificialities of which his predecessors are guilty. Professor Edith Birkhead, in her history of the Gothic novel, justly observes that with all his faults Maturin was the greatest as well as the last of the Goths.[14] *Melmoth* was widely read and eventually dramatised,[15] but its late date in the evolution of the Gothic tale deprived it of the tumultuous popularity of *Udolpho* and *The Monk*.[16]

V. The Aftermath of Gothic Fiction

Meanwhile other hands had not been idle, so that above the dreary plethora of trash like Marquis von Grosse's *Horrid Mysteries* (1796),[1] Mrs. Roche's *Children of the Abbey* (1796),[2] Miss Dacre's *Zofloya; or, The Moor* (1806),[3] and the poet Shelley's schoolboy effusions *Zastrozzi* (1810) and *St. Irvyne* (1811) (both imitations of *Zofloya*) there arose many memorable weird works both in English and German. Classic in merit, and markedly different from its fellows because of its foundation in the Oriental tale rather than the Walpolesque Gothic novel, is the celebrated *History of the Caliph Vathek*[4] by the wealthy dilettante William Beckford, first written in the French language but published in an English translation before the appearance of the original. Eastern tales, introduced to European literature early in the eighteenth century through Galland's French translation of the inexhaustibly opulent *Arabian Nights*,[5] had become a reigning fashion; being used both for allegory[6] and for amusement. The sly humour which only the Eastern mind knows how to mix with weirdness had captivated a sophisticated generation, till Bagdad and Damascus[7] names became as freely strown through popular literature as dashing Italian and Spanish ones were soon to be. Beckford, well read in Eastern romance, caught the atmosphere with unusual receptivity; and in his fantastic volume reflected very potently the haughty luxury, sly disillusion, bland cruelty, urbane treachery, and shadowy spectral horror of the Saracen spirit. His seasoning of the ridiculous seldom mars the force of his sinister theme, and the tale marches onward with a phantasmagoric pomp in which the laughter is that of skeletons feasting under Arabesque[8] domes. *Vathek* is a tale of the grandson of the Caliph Haroun, who, tormented by that ambition for super-terrestrial power, pleasure, and learning which animates the average Gothic villain or Byronic hero (essentially cognate types), is lured by an evil genius to seek the subterranean throne of the mighty and fabulous pre-Adamite sultans in the fiery halls of Eblis, the Mahometan Devil. The descriptions of Vathek's palaces and diversions, of his scheming sorceress-mother Carathis and her witch-tower with the fifty one-eyed negresses, of his pilgrimage to the haunted ruins of Istakhar (Persepolis)[9] and of the impish bride Nouronihar whom he treacherously acquired on the way, of Istakhar's primordial towers and terraces in the burning moonlight of the waste, and of the terrible Cyclopean halls of Eblis, where, lured by glittering promises, each victim is compelled to wander in anguish for ever, his right hand upon his blazingly ignited and eternally burning heart, are triumphs of weird colouring which raise the book to a permanent place in English letters. No less notable are the three *Episodes of Vathek*, intended for insertion in the tale as narratives of Vathek's fellow-victims in Eblis' infernal halls, which remained unpublished throughout the author's lifetime and were discovered as recently as 1909 by the scholar Lewis Melville whilst collecting material for his *Life and Letters of William Beckford*.[10] Beckford, however, lacks the essential mysticism which marks the acutest form of the weird; so that his tales have a certain knowing Latin hardness and clearness preclusive of sheer panic fright.[11]

But Beckford remained alone in his devotion to the Orient. Other writers, closer to the Gothic tradition and to European life in general, were content to follow more faithfully in the lead of Walpole. Among the countless producers of terror-literature in these times may be mentioned the Utopian economic theorist William Godwin, who followed his famous but non-supernatural *Caleb Williams* (1794) with the intendedly weird *St. Leon* (1799), in which the theme of the elixir of life, as developed by the imaginary secret order of "Rosicrucians",[12] is handled with ingeniousness if not with atmospheric convincingness. This element of Rosicrucianism, fostered by a wave of popular magical interest exemplified in the vogue of the charlatan Cagliostro[13] and the publication of Francis Barrett's *The Magus* (1801), a curious and compendious treatise on occult principles and ceremonies, of which a reprint was made as lately as 1896,[14] figures in Bulwer-Lytton and in many late Gothic novels, especially that remote and enfeebled posterity which straggled far down into the nineteenth century and was represented by George W. M. Reynolds' *Faust and the Demon* and *Wagner, the Wehr-wolf*.[15] *Caleb Williams*, though non-supernatural, has many authentic touches of terror. It is the tale of a servant persecuted by a master whom he has found guilty of murder, and displays an invention and skill which have kept it alive in a fashion to this day. It was dramatised as *The Iron Chest*,[16] and in that form was almost equally celebrated. Godwin, however, was too much the conscious teacher and prosaic man of thought to create a genuine weird masterpiece.[17]

His daughter, the wife of Shelley, was much more successful; and her inimitable *Frankenstein; or, The Modern Prometheus* (1818) is one of the horror-classics of all time. Composed in competition with her husband, Lord Byron, and Dr. John William Polidori in an effort to prove supremacy in horror-making, Mrs. Shelley's *Frankenstein* was the only one of the rival narratives to be brought to an elaborate completion;[18] and criticism has failed to prove that the best parts are due to Shelley rather than to her. The novel, somewhat tinged but scarcely marred by moral didacticism, tells of the artificial human being moulded from charnel fragments by Victor Frankenstein, a young Swiss medical student.[19] Created by its designer "in the mad pride of intellectuality", the monster possesses full intelligence but owns a hideously loathsome form. It is rejected by mankind, becomes embittered, and at length begins the successive murder of all whom young Frankenstein loves best, friends and family. It demands that Frankenstein create a wife for it; and when the student finally refuses in horror lest the world be populated with such monsters, it departs with a hideous threat 'to be with him on his wedding night'. Upon that night the bride is strangled, and from that time on Frankenstein hunts down the monster, even into the wastes of the Arctic. In the end, whilst seeking shelter on the ship of the man who tells the story, Frankenstein himself is killed by the shocking object of his search and creation of his presumptuous pride. Some of the scenes in *Frankenstein* are unforgettable, as when the newly animated monster enters its creator's room, parts the curtains of his bed, and gazes at him in the yellow moonlight with watery eyes—"if eyes they may be called". Mrs. Shelley wrote other novels, including the fairly notable *Last Man;* but never duplicated the success of her first effort.[20] It has the true touch of cosmic fear, no matter how much the movement may lag in places. Dr. Polidori developed his competing idea as a long short story, "The Vampyre"; in which we behold a suave villain of the true Gothic or Byronic type, and encounter some excellent passages of stark fright, including a terrible nocturnal experience in a shunned Grecian wood.

In this same period Sir Walter Scott frequently concerned himself with the weird, weaving it into many of his novels and poems, and sometimes producing such independent bits of narration as "The Tapestried Chamber" or "Wandering Willie's Tale" in *Redgauntlet,* in the latter of which the force of the spectral and the diabolic is enhanced by a grotesque homeliness of speech and atmosphere. In 1830 Scott published his *Letters on Demonology and Witchcraft,* which still forms one of our best compendia of European witch-lore. Washington Irving is another famous figure not unconnected with the weird; for though most of his ghosts are too whimsical and humorous to form genuinely spectral literature, a distinct inclination in this direction is to be noted in many of his productions. "The German Student" in *Tales of a Traveller* (1824) is a slyly concise and effective presentation of the old legend of the dead bride, whilst woven into the comic tissue of "The

Money-Diggers" in the same volume is more than one hint of piratical apparitions in the realms which Captain Kidd once roamed. Thomas Moore also joined the ranks of the macabre artists in the poem *Alciphron,* which he later elaborated into the prose novel of *The Epicurean* (1827).[21] Though merely relating the adventures of a young Athenian duped by the artifice of cunning Egyptian priests, Moore manages to infuse much genuine horror into his account of subterranean frights and wonders beneath the primordial temples of Memphis. De Quincey more than once revels in grotesque and arabesque terrors, though with a desultoriness and learned pomp which deny him the rank of specialist.[22]

This era likewise saw the rise of William Harrison Ainsworth, whose romantic novels teem with the eerie and the gruesome.[23] Capt. Marryat, besides writing such short tales as "The Werewolf", made a memorable contribution in *The Phantom Ship* (1839),[24] founded on the legend of the Flying Dutchman, whose spectral and accursed vessel sails for ever near the Cape of Good Hope.[25] Dickens now rises with occasional weird bits like "The Signalman", a tale of ghostly warning conforming to a very common pattern and touched with a verisimilitude which allies it as much with the coming psychological school as with the dying Gothic school.[26] At this time a wave of interest in spiritualistic charlatanry, mediumism, Hindoo theosophy, and such matters, much like that of the present day,[27] was flourishing; so that the number of weird tales with a "psychic" or pseudo-scientific basis became very considerable. For a number of these the prolific and popular Lord Edward Bulwer-Lytton was responsible; and despite the large doses of turgid rhetoric and empty romanticism in his products, his success in the weaving of a certain kind of bizarre charm cannot be denied.

"The House and the Brain", which hints of Rosicrucianism and at a malign and deathless figure perhaps suggested by Louis XV's mysterious courtier St. Germain,[28] yet survives as one of the best short haunted-house tales ever written. The novel *Zanoni* (1842) contains similar elements more elaborately handled, and introduces a vast unknown sphere of being pressing on our own world and guarded by a horrible "Dweller of the Threshold"[29] who haunts those who try to enter and fail. Here we have a benign brotherhood kept alive from age to age till finally reduced to a single member, and as a hero an ancient Chaldaean[30] sorcerer surviving in the pristine bloom of youth to perish on the guillotine of the French Revolution. Though full of the conventional spirit of romance, marred by a ponderous network of symbolic and didactic meanings, and left unconvincing through lack of perfect atmospheric realisation of the situations hinging on the spectral world, *Zanoni* is really an excellent performance as a romantic novel; and can be read with genuine interest today by the not too sophisticated reader. It is amusing to note that in describing an attempted initiation into the ancient brotherhood the author cannot escape using the stock Gothic castle of Walpolian lineage.

In *A Strange Story* (1862) Bulwer-Lytton shews a marked improvement in the creation of weird images and moods. The novel, despite enormous length, a highly artificial plot bolstered up by opportune coincidences, and an atmosphere of homiletic pseudo-science designed to please the matter-of-fact and purposeful Victorian reader, is exceedingly effective as a narrative; evoking instantaneous and unflagging interest, and furnishing many potent—if somewhat melodramatic—tableaux and climaxes. Again we have the mysterious user of life's elixir in the person of the soulless magician Margrave, whose dark exploits stand out with dramatic vividness against the modern background of a quiet English town and of the Australian bush;[31] and again we have shadowy intimations of a vast spectral world of the unknown in the very air about us—this time handled with much greater power and vitality than in *Zanoni*. One of the two great incantation passages, where the hero is driven by a luminous evil spirit to rise at night in his sleep, take a strange Egyptian wand, and evoke nameless presences in the haunted and mausoleum-facing pavilion of a famous Renaissance alchemist, truly stands among the major terror scenes of literature. Just enough is suggested, and just little enough is told. Unknown words are twice dictated to the sleep-walker, and as he repeats them the ground trembles, and all the dogs of the countryside begin to bay at half-seen amorphous shadows that stalk athwart the moonlight.[32] When a third set of unknown words is prompted, the sleep-walker's spirit suddenly rebels at uttering them, as if the soul could recognise ultimate abysmal horrors concealed from the mind; and at last an apparition of an absent sweetheart and good angel breaks the malign spell. This fragment well illustrates how far Lord Lytton was capable of progressing beyond his usual pomp and stock romance toward that crystalline essence of artistic fear which belongs to the domain of poetry. In describing certain details of incantations, Lytton was greatly indebted to his amusingly serious occult studies, in the course of which he came in touch with that odd French scholar and cabbalist Alphonse-Louis Constant ("Eliphas Lévi"),[33] who claimed to possess the secrets of ancient magic, and to have evoked the spectre of the old Grecian wizard Apollonius of Tyana, who lived in Nero's time.[34]

The romantic, semi-Gothic, quasi-moral tradition here represented was carried far down the nineteenth century by such authors as Joseph Sheridan LeFanu,[35] Thomas Preskett Prest with his famous *Varney, the Vampyre* (1847),[36] Wilkie Collins,[37] the late Sir H. Rider Haggard (whose *She* is really remarkably good),[38] Sir A. Conan Doyle, H. G. Wells, and Robert Louis Stevenson—the latter of whom, despite an atrocious tendency toward jaunty mannerisms, created permanent classics in "Markheim", "The Body-Snatcher", and *Dr. Jekyll and Mr. Hyde*. Indeed, we may say that this school still survives; for to it clearly belong such of our contemporary horror-tales as specialise in events rather than atmospheric details, address the intellect rather than the impressionistic imagination, cultivate a luminous glamour rather than a malign tensity or psychological verisimilitude, and take a definite stand in sympathy with mankind and its welfare. It has its undeniable strength, and because of its "human element" commands a wider audience than does the sheer artistic nightmare. If not quite so potent as the latter, it is because a diluted product can never achieve the intensity of a concentrated essence.

Quite alone both as a novel and as a piece of terror-literature stands the famous *Wuthering Heights* (1847) by Emily Brontë, with its mad vista of bleak, windswept Yorkshire moors and the violent, distorted lives they foster. Though primarily a tale of life, and of human passions in agony and conflict, its epically cosmic setting affords room for horror of the most spiritual sort. Heathcliff, the modified Byronic villain-hero, is a strange dark waif found in the streets as a small child and speaking only a strange gibberish till adopted by the family he ultimately ruins. That he is in truth a diabolic spirit rather than a human being is more than once suggested, and the unreal is further approached in the experience of the visitor who encounters a plaintive child-ghost at a bough-brushed upper window. Between Heathcliff and Catherine Earnshaw is a tie deeper and more terrible than human love. After her death he twice disturbs her grave, and is haunted by an impalpable presence which can be nothing less than her spirit. The spirit enters his life more and more, and at last he becomes confident of some imminent mystical reunion. He says he feels a strange change approaching, and ceases to take nourishment. At night he either walks abroad or opens the casement by his bed. When he dies the casement is still swinging open to the pouring rain, and a queer smile pervades the stiffened face. They bury him in a grave beside the mound he has haunted for eighteen years, and small shepherd boys say that he yet walks with his Catherine in the churchyard and on the moor when it rains. Their faces, too, are sometimes seen on rainy nights behind that upper casement at Wuthering Heights. Miss Brontë's eerie terror is no mere Gothic echo, but a tense expression of man's shuddering reaction to the unknown. In this respect, *Wuthering Heights* becomes the symbol of a literary transition, and marks the growth of a new and sounder school.

VI. Spectral Literature on the Continent

On the Continent literary horror fared well. The celebrated short tales and novels of Ernst Theodor Wilhelm Hoffmann (1776–1822)[1] are a byword for mellowness of background and maturity of form, though they incline to levity and extravagance, and lack the exalted moments of stark, breathless terror which a less sophisticated writer might have achieved. Generally they convey the grotesque rather than the terrible.[2] Most artistic of all the Continental weird tales is the German classic *Undine* (1811), by Friedrich Heinrich Karl, Baron de la Motte Fouqué. In this story of a water-spirit who married a mortal and gained a human soul there is a delicate fineness of craftsmanship which makes it notable in any department of literature, and an easy naturalness which places it close to the genuine folk-myth. It is, in fact, derived from a tale told by the Renaissance physician and alchemist Paracelsus in his *Treatise on Elemental Sprites*.[3]

Undine, daughter of a powerful water-prince, was exchanged by her father as a small child for a fisherman's daughter, in order that she might acquire a soul by wedding a human being. Meeting the noble youth Huldbrand at the cottage of her foster-father by the sea at the edge of a haunted wood, she soon marries him, and accompanies him to his ancestral castle of Ringstetten. Huldbrand, however, eventually wearies of his wife's supernatural affiliations, and especially of the appearances of her uncle, the malicious woodland waterfall-spirit Kühleborn;[4] a weariness increased by his growing affection for Bertalda, who turns out to be the fisherman's child for whom Undine was exchanged. At length, on a voyage down the Danube, he is provoked by some innocent act of his devoted wife to utter the angry words which consign her back to her supernatural element; from which she can, by the laws of her species, return only once—to kill him, whether she will or no, if ever he prove unfaithful to her memory. Later, when Huldbrand is about to be married to Bertalda, Undine returns for her sad duty, and bears his life away in tears. When he is buried among his fathers in the village churchyard a veiled, snow-white female figure appears among the mourners, but after the prayer is seen no more. In her place is seen a little silver spring, which murmurs its way almost completely around the new grave, and empties into a neighbouring lake. The villagers shew it to this day, and say that Undine and her Huldbrand are thus united in death. Many passages and atmospheric touches in this tale reveal Fouqué as an accomplished artist in the field of the macabre; especially the descriptions of the haunted wood with its gigantic snow-white man and various unnamed terrors, which occur early in the narrative.

Not so well known as *Undine*, but remarkable for its convincing realism and freedom from Gothic stock devices, is the *Amber Witch* of Wilhelm Meinhold, another product of the German fantastic genius of the earlier nineteenth century.[5] This tale, which is laid in the time of the Thirty Years' War, purports to be a clergyman's manuscript found in an old church at Coserow, and centres round the writer's daughter, Maria Schweidler, who is wrongly accused of witchcraft. She has found a deposit of amber which she keeps secret for various reasons, and the unexplained wealth obtained from this lends colour to the accusation; an accusation instigated by the malice of the wolf-hunting nobleman Wittich Appelmann, who has vainly pursued her with ignoble designs. The deeds of a real witch, who afterward comes to a horrible supernatural end in prison, are glibly imputed to the hapless Maria; and after a typical witchcraft trial with forced confessions under torture she is about to be burned at the stake when saved just in time by her lover, a noble youth from a neighbouring district. Meinhold's great strength is in his air of casual and realistic verisimilitude, which intensifies our suspense and sense of the unseen by half persuading us that the menacing events must somehow be either the truth or very close to the truth. Indeed, so thorough is this realism that a popular magazine once published the main points of *The Amber Witch* as an actual occurrence of the seventeenth century![6]

[In the present generation German horror-fiction is most notably represented by Hanns Heinz Ewers, who brings to bear on his dark conceptions an effective knowledge of modern psychology. Novels like *The Sorcerer's Apprentice* and *Alraune*, and short stories like "The Spider",[7] contain distinctive qualities which raise them to a classic level.[8]]

But France as well as Germany has been active in the realm of weirdness. Victor Hugo, in such tales as *Hans of Iceland,* and Balzac, in *The Wild Ass's Skin, Séraphîta,* and *Louis Lambert,*[9] both employ supernaturalism to a greater or less extent; though generally only as a means to some more human end, and without the sincere and daemonic intensity which characterises the born artist in shadows. It is in Théophile Gautier that we first seem to find an authentic French sense of the unreal world, and here there appears a spectral mastery which, though not continuously used, is recognisable at once as something alike genuine and profound. Short tales like "Avatar", "The Foot of the Mummy", and "Clarimonde" display glimpses of forbidden visits that allure, tantalise, and sometimes horrify; whilst the Egyptian visions evoked in "One of Cleopatra's Nights" are of the keenest and most expressive potency. Gautier captured the inmost soul of aeon-weighted Egypt, with its cryptic life and Cyclopean architecture, and uttered once and for all the eternal horror of its nether world of catacombs, where to the end of time millions of stiff, spiced corpses will stare up in the blackness with glassy eyes, awaiting some awesome and unrelatable summons.[10] Gustave Flaubert ably continued the tradition of Gautier in orgies of poetic phantasy like *The Temptation of St. Anthony,* and but for a strong realistic bias might have been an arch-weaver of tapestried terrors.[11] Later on we see the stream divide, producing strange poets and fantaisistes of the Symbolist and Decadent schools whose dark interests really centre more in abnormalities of human thought and instinct than in the actual supernatural, and subtle story-tellers whose thrills are quite directly derived from the night-black wells of cosmic unreality. Of the former class of "artists in sin" the illustrious poet Baudelaire,[12] influenced vastly by Poe, is the supreme type; whilst the psychological novelist Joris-Karl Huysmans,[13] a true child of the eighteen-nineties, is at once the summation and finale. The latter and purely narrative class is continued by Prosper Mérimée, whose "Venus of Ille" presents in terse and convincing prose the same ancient statue-bride theme which Thomas Moore cast in ballad form in "The Ring".

The horror-tales of the powerful and cynical Guy de Maupassant, written as his final madness gradually overtook him, present individualities of their own; being rather the morbid outpourings of a realistic mind in a pathological state than the healthy imaginative products of a vision naturally disposed toward phantasy and sensitive to the normal illusions of the unseen. Nevertheless they are of the keenest interest and poignancy; suggesting with marvellous force the imminence of nameless terrors, and the relentless dogging of an ill-starred individual by hideous and menacing representatives of the outer blackness. Of these stories "The Horla" is generally regarded as the masterpiece. Relating the advent to France of an invisible being who lives on water and milk, sways the minds of others, and seems to be the vanguard of a horde of extra-terrestrial organisms arrived on earth to subjugate and overwhelm mankind,[14] this tense narrative is perhaps without a peer in its particular department; notwithstanding its indebtedness to a tale by the American Fitz-James O'Brien[15] for details in describing the actual presence of the unseen monster. Other potently dark creations of de Maupassant are "Who Knows?", "The Spectre",

"He?", "The Diary of a Madman", "The White Wolf", "On the River", and the grisly verses entitled "Horror".

The collaborators Erckmann-Chatrian enriched French literature with many spectral fancies like *The Man-Wolf,* in which a transmitted curse works toward its end in a traditional Gothic-castle setting.[16] Their power of creating a shuddering midnight atmosphere was tremendous despite a tendency toward natural explanations and scientific wonders; and few short tales contain greater horror than "The Invisible Eye", where a malignant old hag weaves nocturnal hypnotic spells which induce the successive occupants of a certain inn chamber to hang themselves on a cross-beam. "The Owl's Ear" and "The Waters of Death" are full of engulfing darkness and mystery, the latter embodying the familiar overgrown-spider theme so frequently employed by weird fictionists. Villiers de l'Isle-Adam[17] likewise followed the macabre school; his "Torture by Hope", the tale of a stake-condemned prisoner permitted to escape in order to feel the pangs of recapture, being held by some to constitute the most harrowing short story in literature. This type, however, is less a part of the weird tradition than a class peculiar to itself—the so-called *conte cruel,* in which the wrenching of the emotions is accomplished through dramatic tantalisations, frustrations, and gruesome physical horrors. Almost wholly devoted to this form is the living writer Maurice Level,[18] whose very brief episodes have lent themselves so readily to theatrical adaptation in the "thrillers" of the Grand Guignol.[19] As a matter of fact, the French genius is more naturally suited to this dark realism than to the suggestion of the unseen; since the latter process requires, for its best and most sympathetic development on a large scale, the inherent mysticism of the Northern mind.

A very flourishing, though till recently quite hidden, branch of weird literature is that of the Jews, kept alive and nourished in obscurity by the sombre heritage of early Eastern magic, apocalyptic literature, and cabbalism. The Semitic mind, like the Celtic and Teutonic, seems to possess marked mystical inclinations; and the wealth of underground horror-lore surviving in ghettoes and synagogues must be much more considerable than is generally imagined. Cabbalism itself, so prominent during the Middle Ages, is a system of philosophy explaining the universe as emanations of the Deity, and involving the existence of strange spiritual realms and beings apart from the visible world, of which dark glimpses may be obtained through certain secret incantations. Its ritual is bound up with mystical interpretations of the Old Testament, and attributes an esoteric significance to each letter of the Hebrew alphabet—a circumstance which has imparted to Hebrew letters a sort of spectral glamour and potency in the popular literature of magic.[20] Jewish folklore has preserved much of the terror and mystery of the past, and when more thoroughly studied is likely to exert considerable influence on weird fiction. The best examples of its literary use so far are the German novel *The Golem,* by Gustav Meyrink,[21] and the drama *The Dybbuk,* by the Jewish writer using the pseudonym "Ansky".[22] [The former, with its haunting shadowy suggestions of marvels and horrors just beyond reach, is laid in Prague, and describes with singular mastery that city's ancient ghetto with its spectral, peaked gables. The name is derived from a fabulous artificial giant supposed to be made and animated by mediaeval rabbis according to a certain cryptic formula.[23]] *The Dybbuk,* translated and produced in America in 1925,[24] and more recently produced as an opera,[25] describes with singular power the possession of a living body by the evil soul of a dead man. Both golems and dybbuks are fixed types, and serve as frequent ingredients of later Jewish tradition.

VII. Edgar Allan Poe

In the eighteen-thirties occurred a literary dawn directly affecting not only the history of the weird tale, but that of short fiction as a whole; and indirectly moulding the trends and fortunes of a great European aesthetic school.[1] It is our good fortune as Americans to be able to claim that dawn as our own, for it came in the person of our illustrious and unfortunate fellow-countryman Edgar Allan Poe.[2] Poe's fame has been subject to curious undulations, and it is now a fashion amongst the "advanced intelligentsia" to minimise his importance both as an artist and as an influence;[3] but it would be hard for any mature and reflective critic to deny the tremendous value of his work and the pervasive potency of his mind as an opener of artistic vistas. True, his type of outlook may have been anticipated;[4] but it was he who first realised its possibilities and gave it supreme form and systematic expression. True also, that subsequent writers may have produced greater single tales than his;[5] but again we must comprehend that it was only he who taught them by example and precept the art which they, having the way cleared for them and given an explicit guide, were perhaps able to carry to greater lengths. Whatever his limitations, Poe did that which no one else ever did or could have done; and to him we owe the modern horror-story in its final and perfected state.

Before Poe the bulk of weird writers had worked largely in the dark; without an understanding of the psychological basis of the horror appeal, and hampered by more or less of conformity to certain empty literary conventions such as the happy ending, virtue rewarded, and in general a hollow moral didacticism, acceptance of popular standards and values, and striving of the author to obtrude his own emotions into the story and take sides with the partisans of the majority's artificial ideas. Poe, on the other hand, perceived the essential impersonality of the real artist; and knew that the function of creative fiction is merely to express and interpret events and sensations as they are, regardless of how they tend or what they prove—good or evil, attractive or repulsive, stimulating or depressing—with the author always acting as a vivid and detached chronicler rather than as a teacher, sympathiser, or vendor of opinion. He saw clearly that all phases of life and thought are equally eligible as subject-matter for the artist, and being inclined by temperament to strangeness and gloom, decided to be the interpreter of those powerful feeling, and frequent happenings which attend pain rather than pleasure, decay rather than growth, terror rather than tranquillity, and which are fundamentally either adverse or indifferent to the tastes and traditional outward sentiments of mankind, and to the health, sanity, and normal expansive welfare of the species.

Poe's spectres thus acquired a convincing malignity possessed by none of their predecessors, and established a new standard of realism in the annals of literary horror. The impersonal and artistic intent, moreover, was aided by a scientific attitude not often found before; whereby Poe studied the human mind rather than the usages of Gothic fiction, and worked with an analytical knowledge of terror's true sources which doubled the force of his narratives and emancipated him from all the absurdities inherent in merely conventional shudder-coining. This example having been set, later authors were naturally forced to conform to it in order to compete at all; so that in this way a definite change began to affect the main stream of macabre writing. Poe, too, set a fashion in consummate craftsmanship; and although today some of his own work seems slightly melodramatic and unsophisticated, we can constantly trace his influence in such things as the maintenance of a single mood and achievement of a single impression in a tale, and the rigorous paring down of incidents to such as have a direct bearing on the plot and will figure prominently in the climax. Truly may it be said that Poe invented the short story in its present form. His elevation of disease, perversity, and decay to the level of artistically expressible themes was likewise infinitely far-reaching in effect; for avidly seized, sponsored, and intensified by his eminent French admirer Charles Pierre Baudelaire,[6] it became the nucleus of the principal aesthetic movements in France, thus making Poe in a sense the father of the Decadents and the Symbolists.[7]

Poet and critic by nature and supreme attainment, logician and philosopher by taste and mannerism, Poe was by no means immune from defects and affectations. His pretence to profound and obscure scholarship,[8] his blundering ventures in stilted and laboured pseudo-humour,[9] and his often vitriolic outbursts of critical prejudice[10] must all be recognised and forgiven. Beyond and above them, and dwarfing them to insignificance, was a master's vision of the terror that stalks about and within us, and the worm that writhes and slavers in the hideously close abyss. Penetrating to every festering horror in the gaily painted mockery called existence, and in the solemn masquerade called human thought and feelings that vision had power to project itself in blackly magical crystallisations and transmutations; till there bloomed in the sterile America of the 'thirties and 'forties such a moon-nourished garden of gorgeous poison fungi as not even the nether slope of Saturn might boast. Verses and tales alike sustain the burthen[11] of cosmic panic. The raven whose noisome beak pierces the heart,[12] the ghouls that toll iron bells in pestilential steeples,[13] the vault of Ulalume in the black October night,[14] the shocking spires and domes under the sea,[15] the "wild, weird clime that lieth, sublime, out of Space—out of Time"[16]—all these things and more leer at us amidst maniacal rattlings in the seething nightmare of the poetry. And in the prose there yawn open for us the very jaws of the pit—inconceivable abnormalities slyly hinted into a horrible half-knowledge by words whose innocence we scarcely doubt till the cracked tension of the speaker's hollow voice bids us fear their nameless implications; daemoniac patterns and presences slumbering noxiously till waked for one phobic instant into a shrieking revelation that cackles itself to sudden madness or explodes in memorable and cataclysmic echoes. A Witches' Sabbath of horror flinging off decorous robes is flashed before us—a sight the more monstrous because of the scientific skill with which every particular is marshalled and brought into an easy apparent relation to the known gruesomeness of material life.

Poe's tales, of course, fall into several classes; some of which contain a purer essence of spiritual horror than others. The tales of logic and ratiocination,[17] forerunners of the modern detective story, are not to be included at all in weird literature; whilst certain others, probably influenced considerably by Hoffmann,[18] possess an extravagance which relegates them to the borderline of the grotesque. Still a third group deal with abnormal psychology and monomania in such a way as to express terror but not weirdness.[19] A substantial residuum, however, represent the literature of supernatural horror in its acutest form; and give their author a permanent and unassailable place as deity and fountain-head of all modern diabolic fiction. Who can forget the terrible swollen ship poised on the billow-chasm's edge in "MS. Found in a Bottle"—the dark intimations of her unhallowed age and monstrous growth, her sinister crew of unseeing greybeards, and her frightful southward rush under full sail through the ice of the Antarctic night, sucked onward by some resistless devil-current toward a vortex of eldritch enlightenment which must end in destruction? Then there is the unutterable "M. Valdemar",[20] kept together by hypnotism for seven months after his death, and uttering frantic sounds but a moment before the breaking of the spell leaves him "a nearly liquid mass of loathsome—of detestable putrescence".[21] In the *Narrative of A. Gordon Pym* the voyagers reach first a strange south polar land of murderous savages where nothing is white and where vast rocky ravines have the form of titanic Egyptian letters spelling terrible primal arcana of earth; and thereafter a still more mysterious realm where everything is white, and where shrouded giants and snowy-plumed birds guard a cryptic cataract of mist which empties from immeasurable celestial heights into a torrid milky sea.[22] "Metzengerstein" horrifies with its malign hints of a monstrous metempsychosis—the mad nobleman who burns the stable of his hereditary foe; the colossal unknown horse that issues from the blazing building after the owner has perished therein; the vanishing bit of ancient tapestry where was shewn the giant horse of the victim's ancestor in the Crusades;[23] the madman's wild and constant riding on the great horse, and his fear and hatred of the steed; the meaningless prophecies that brood obscurely over the warring houses; and finally, the burning of the madman's palace and the death therein of the owner, borne helpless into the flames and up the vast staircases astride the beast he has ridden so strangely. Afterward the rising smoke of the ruins takes the form of a gigantic horse. "The Man of the Crowd", telling of one who roams day and night to mingle with streams of people as if afraid to be alone, has quieter effects, but implies nothing less of cosmic fear. Poe's mind was never far from terror and decay, and we see in every tale, poem, and philosophical dialogue a tense eagerness to fathom unplumbed wells of night,[24] to pierce the veil of death, and to reign in fancy as lord of the frightful mysteries of time and space.

Certain of Poe's tales possess an almost absolute perfection of artistic form which makes them veritable beacon-lights in the province of the short story. Poe could, when he wished, give to his prose a richly poetic cast; employing that archaic and Orientalised style with jewelled phrase, quasi-Biblical repetition, and recurrent burthen so successfully used by later writers like Oscar Wilde[25] and Lord Dunsany;[26] and in the cases where he has done this we have an effect of lyrical phantasy almost narcotic in essence—an opium pageant of dream in the language of dream, with every unnatural colour and grotesque image bodied forth in a symphony of corresponding sound. "The Masque of the Red Death", "Silence—A Fable", and "Shadow—A Parable" are assuredly poems in every sense of the word save the metrical one, and owe as much of their power to aural cadence as to visual imagery.[27] But it is in two of the less openly poetic tales, "Ligeia" and "The Fall of the House of Usher"—especially the latter—that one finds those very summits of artistry whereby Poe takes his place at the head of fictional miniaturists. Simple and straightforward in plot, both of these tales owe their supreme magic to the cunning development which appears in the selection and collocation of every least incident. "Ligeia" tells of a first wife of lofty and mysterious origin, who after death returns through a preternatural force of will to take possession of the body of a second wife; imposing even her physical appearance on the temporary reanimated corpse of her victim at the last moment.[28] Despite a suspicion of prolixity and topheaviness, the narrative reaches its terrific climax with relentless power. "Usher", whose superiority in detail and proportion is very marked, hints shudderingly of obscure life in inorganic things, and displays an abnormally linked trinity of entities at the end of a long and isolated family history—a brother, his twin sister, and their incredibly ancient house all sharing a single soul and meeting one common dissolution at the same moment.[29]

These bizarre conceptions, so awkward in unskilful hands, become under Poe's spell living and convincing terrors to haunt our nights; and all because the author understood so perfectly the very mechanics and physiology of fear[30] and strangeness—the essential details to emphasise, the precise incongruities and conceits to select as preliminaries or concomitants to horror, the exact incidents and allusions to throw out innocently in advance as symbols or prefigurings of each major step toward the hideous denouement to come, the nice adjustments of cumulative force and the unerring accuracy in linkage of parts which make for faultless unity throughout and thunderous effectiveness at the climactic moment, the delicate nuances of scenic and landscape value to select in establishing and sustaining the desired mood and vitalising the desired illusion—principles of this kind, and dozens of obscurer ones too elusive to be described or even fully comprehended by any ordinary commentator. Melodrama and unsophistication there may be—we are told of one fastidious Frenchman who could not bear to read Poe except in Baudelaire's urbane and Gallically modulated translation[31]—but all traces of such things are wholly overshadowed by a potent and inborn sense of the spectral, the morbid, and the horrible which gushed forth from every cell of the artist's creative mentality and stamped his macabre work with the ineffaceable mark of supreme genius. Poe's weird tales are *alive* in a manner that few others can ever hope to be.

Like most fantaisistes, Poe excels in incidents and broad narrative effects rather than in character drawing. His typical protagonist is generally a dark, handsome, proud, melancholy, intellectual, highly sensitive, capricious, introspective, isolated, and sometimes slightly mad gentleman of ancient family and opulent circumstances; usually deeply learned in strange lore, and darkly ambitious of penetrating to forbidden secrets of the universe.[32] Aside from a high-sounding name, this character obviously derives little from the early Gothic novel; for he is clearly neither the wooden hero nor the diabolical villain of Radcliffian or Ludovician[33] romance. Indirectly, however, he does possess a sort of genealogical connexion; since his gloomy, ambitious, and anti-social qualities savour strongly of the typical Byronic hero, who in turn is definitely an offspring of the Gothic Manfreds, Montonis, and Ambrosios. More particular qualities appear to be derived from the psychology of Poe himself, who certainly possessed much of the depression, sensitiveness, mad aspiration, loneliness, and extravagant freakishness which he attributes to his haughty and solitary victims of Fate.

VIII. The Weird Tradition in America

The public for whom Poe wrote, though grossly unappreciative of his art, was by no means unaccustomed to the horrors with which he dealt. America, besides inheriting the usual dark folklore of Europe, had an additional fund of weird associations to draw upon; so that spectral legends had already been recognised as fruitful subject-matter for literature. Charles Brockden Brown had achieved phenomenal fame with his Radcliffian romances, and Washington Irving's lighter treatment of eerie themes had quickly become classic. This additional fund proceeded, as Paul Elmer More has pointed out,[1] from the keen spiritual and theological interests of the first colonists, plus the strange and forbidding nature of the scene into which they were plunged. The vast and gloomy virgin forests in whose perpetual twilight all terrors might well lurk; the hordes of coppery Indians whose strange, saturnine visages and violent customs hinted strongly at traces of infernal origin; the free rein given under the influence of Puritan theocracy to all manner of notions respecting man's relation to the stern and vengeful God of the Calvinists, and to the sulphureous Adversary of that God, about whom so much was thundered in the pulpits each Sunday; and the morbid introspection developed by an isolated backwoods life devoid of normal amusements and of the recreational mood, harassed by commands for theological self-examination, keyed to unnatural emotional repression, and forming above all a mere grim struggle for survival—all these things conspired to produce an environment in which the black whisperings of sinister grandams[2] were heard far beyond the chimney corner, and in which tales of witchcraft and unbelievable secret monstrosities lingered long after the dread days of the Salem nightmare.[3]

Poe represents the newer, more disillusioned, and more technically finished of the weird schools that rose out of this propitious milieu. Another school—the tradition of moral values, gentle restraint, and mild, leisurely phantasy tinged more or less with the whimsical—was represented by another famous, misunderstood, and lonely figure in American letters—the shy and sensitive Nathaniel Hawthorne,[4] scion of antique Salem and great-grandson of one of the bloodiest of the old witchcraft judges.[5] In Hawthorne we have none of the violence, the daring, the high colouring, the intense dramatic sense, the cosmic malignity, and the undivided and impersonal artistry of Poe. Here, instead, is a gentle soul cramped by the Puritanism of early New England; shadowed and wistful, and grieved at an unmoral universe which everywhere transcends the conventional patterns thought by our forefathers to represent divine and immutable law. Evil, a very real force to Hawthorne, appears on every hand as a lurking and conquering adversary; and the visible world becomes in his fancy a theatre of infinite tragedy and woe, with unseen half-existent influences hovering over it and through it, battling for supremacy and moulding the destinies of the hapless mortals who form its vain and self-deluded population. The heritage of American weirdness was his to a most intense degree, and he saw a dismal throng of vague spectres behind the common phenomena of life; but he was not disinterested enough to value impressions, sensations, and beauties of narration for their own sake. He must needs weave his phantasy into some quietly melancholy fabric of didactic[6] or allegorical cast, in which his meekly resigned cynicism may display with naive moral appraisal the perfidy of a human race which he cannot cease to cherish and mourn despite his insight into its hypocrisy. Supernatural horror, then, is never a primary object with Hawthorne; though its impulses were so deeply woven into his personality that he cannot help suggesting it with the force of genius when he calls upon the unreal world to illustrate the pensive sermon he wishes to preach.

Hawthorne's intimations of the weird, always gentle, elusive, and restrained, may be traced throughout his work. The mood that produced them found one delightful vent in the Teutonised retelling of classic myths for children contained in *A Wonder Book* and *Tanglewood Tales*,[7] and at other times exercised itself in casting a certain strangeness and intangible witchery or malevolence over events not meant to be actually supernatural; as in the macabre posthumous novel *Dr. Grimshawe's Secret*, which invests with a peculiar sort of repulsion a house existing to this day in Salem, and abutting on the ancient Charter Street Burying Ground.[8] In *The Marble Faun*,[9] whose design was sketched out in an Italian villa reputed to be haunted, a tremendous background of genuine phantasy and mystery palpitates just beyond the common reader's sight; and glimpses of fabulous blood in mortal veins[10] are hinted at during the course of a romance which cannot help being interesting despite the persistent incubus of moral allegory, anti-Popery propaganda, and a Puritan prudery which has caused the late D. H. Lawrence to express a longing to treat the author in a highly undignified manner.[11] *Septimius Felton*, a posthumous novel whose idea was to have been elaborated and incorporated into the unfinished *Dolliver Romance*, touches on the Elixir of Life in a more or less capable fashion; whilst the notes for a never-written tale to be called "The Ancestral Footstep" shew what Hawthorne would have done with an intensive treatment of an old English superstition—that of an ancient and accursed line whose members left footprints of blood as they walked—which appears incidentally in both *Septimius Felton* and *Dr. Grimshawe's Secret*.

Many of Hawthorne's shorter tales exhibit weirdness, either of atmosphere or of incident, to a remarkable degree. "Edward Randolph's Portrait", in *Legends of the Province House*, has its diabolic moments.[12] "The Minister's Black Veil" (founded on an actual incident) and "The Ambitious Guest" imply much more than they state, whilst "Ethan Brand"—a fragment of a longer work never completed—rises to genuine heights of cosmic fear with its vignette of the wild hill country and the blazing, desolate lime-kilns, and its delineation of the Byronic "unpardonable sinner",[13] whose troubled life ends with a peal of fearful laughter in the night as he seeks rest amidst the flames of the furnace. Some of Hawthorne's notes tell of weird tales he would have written had he lived longer—an especially vivid plot being that concerning a baffling stranger who appeared now and then in public assemblies, and who was at last followed and found to come and go from a very ancient grave.[14]

But foremost as a finished, artistic unit among all our author's weird material is the famous and exquisitely wrought novel, *The House of the Seven Gables*,[15] in which the relentless working out of an ancestral curse is developed with astonishing power against the sinister background of a very ancient Salem house—one of those peaked Gothic affairs which formed the first regular building-up of our New England coast towns, but which gave way after the seventeenth century to the more familiar gambrel-roofed or classic Georgian types now known as "Colonial". Of these old gabled Gothic houses scarcely a dozen are to be seen today in their original condition throughout the United States, but one well known to Hawthorne still stands in Turner Street, Salem, and is pointed out with doubtful authority as the scene and inspiration of the romance. Such an edifice, with its spectral peaks, its clustered chimneys, its overhanging second story, its grotesque corner-brackets, and its diamond-paned lattice windows, is indeed an object well calculated to evoke sombre reflections; typifying as it does the dark Puritan age of concealed horror and witch-whispers which preceded the beauty, rationality, and spaciousness of the eighteenth century.[16] Hawthorne saw many in his youth, and knew the black tales connected with some of them. He heard, too, many rumours of a curse upon his own line as the result of his great-grandfather's severity as a witchcraft judge in 1692.

From this setting came the immortal tale—New England's greatest contribution to weird literature—and we can feel in an instant the authenticity of the atmosphere presented to us. Stealthy horror and disease lurk within the weather-blackened, moss-crusted, and elm-shadowed walls of the archaic dwelling so vividly displayed, and we grasp the brooding malignity of the place when we read that its builder—old Colonel Pyncheon—snatched the land with peculiar ruthlessness from its original settler, Matthew Maule, whom he condemned to the gallows as a wizard in the year of the panic. Maule died cursing old Pyncheon—"God will give him blood to drink"[17]—and the waters of the old well on the seized land turned bitter. Maule's carpenter son consented to build the great gabled house for his father's triumphant enemy, but the old Colonel died strangely on the day of its dedication. Then followed generations of odd vicissitudes, with queer whispers about the dark powers of the Maules, and peculiar and sometimes terrible ends befalling the Pyncheons.

The overshadowing malevolence of the ancient house—almost as alive as Poe's House of Usher, though in a subtler way—pervades the tale as a recurrent motif pervades an operatic tragedy;[18] and when the main story is reached, we behold the modern Pyncheons in a pitiable state of decay. Poor old Hepzibah, the eccentric reduced gentlewoman; child-like, unfortunate Clifford, just released from undeserved imprisonment; sly and treacherous Judge Pyncheon, who is the old Colonel all over again—all these figures are tremendous symbols, and are well matched by the stunted vegetation and anaemic fowls in the garden. It was almost a pity to supply a fairly happy ending, with a union of sprightly Phoebe, cousin and last scion of the Pyncheons, to the prepossessing young man who turns out to be the last of the Maules. This union, presumably, ends the curse. Hawthorne avoids all violence of diction or movement, and keeps his implications of terror well in the background; but occasional glimpses amply serve to sustain the mood and redeem the work from pure allegorical aridity. Incidents like the bewitching of Alice Pyncheon in the early eighteenth century, and the spectral music of her harpsichord which precedes a death in the family—the latter a variant of an immemorial type of Aryan myth—link the action directly with the supernatural; whilst the dead nocturnal vigil of old Judge Pyncheon in the ancient parlour, with his frightfully ticking watch, is stark horror of the most poignant and genuine sort. The way in which the Judge's death is first adumbrated by the motions and sniffing of a strange cat outside the window, long before the fact is suspected either by the reader or by any of the characters, is a stroke of genius which Poe could not have surpassed. Later the strange cat watches intently outside that same window in the night and on the next day, for—something. It is clearly the psychopomp of primeval myth, fitted and adapted with infinite deftness to its latter-day setting.[19]

But Hawthorne left no well-defined literary posterity. His mood and attitude belonged to the age which closed with him, and it is the spirit of Poe—who so clearly and realistically understood the natural basis of the horror-appeal and the correct mechanics of its achievement—which survived and blossomed. Among the earliest of Poe's disciples may be reckoned the brilliant young Irishman Fitz-James O'Brien (1828–1862), who became naturalised as an American and perished honourably in the Civil War. It is he who gave us "What Was It?", the first well-shaped short story of a tangible but invisible being, and the prototype of de Maupassant's "Horla"; he also who created the inimitable "Diamond Lens", in which a young microscopist falls in love with a maiden of an infinitesimal world which he has discovered in a drop of water.[20] O'Brien's early death undoubtedly deprived us of some masterful tales of strangeness and terror, though his genius was not, properly speaking, of the same titan quality which characterised Poe and Hawthorne.

Closer to real greatness was the eccentric and saturnine journalist Ambrose Bierce,[21] born in 1842; who likewise entered the Civil War, but survived to write some immortal tales and to disappear in 1913 in as great a cloud of mystery as any he ever evoked from his nightmare fancy.[22] Bierce was a satirist and pamphleteer of note, but the bulk of his artistic reputation must rest upon his grim and savage short stories; a large number of which deal with the Civil War and form the most vivid and realistic expression which that conflict has yet received in fiction. Virtually all of Bierce's tales are tales of horror; and whilst many of them treat only of the physical and psychological horrors within Nature, a substantial proportion admit the malignly supernatural and form a leading element in America's fund of weird literature. Mr. Samuel Loveman, a living poet and critic who was personally acquainted with Bierce,[23] thus sums up the genius of the great shadow-maker in the preface to some of his letters:

"In Bierce, the evocation of horror becomes for the first time, not so much the prescription or perversion of Poe and Maupassant, but an atmosphere definite and uncannily precise. Words, so simple that one would be prone to ascribe them to the limitations of a literary hack, take on an unholy horror, a new and unguessed transformation. In Poe one finds it a *tour de force,* in Maupassant a nervous engagement of the flagellated climax. To Bierce, simply and sincerely, diabolism held in its tormented depth, a legitimate and reliant means to the end. Yet a tacit confirmation with Nature is in every instance insisted upon.

"In 'The Death of Halpin Frayser', flowers, verdure, and the boughs and leaves of trees are magnificently placed as an opposing foil to unnatural malignity. Not the accustomed golden world, but a world pervaded with the mystery of blue and the breathless recalcitrance of dreams, is Bierce's. Yet, curiously, inhumanity is not altogether absent."[24]

The "inhumanity" mentioned by Mr. Loveman finds vent in a rare strain of sardonic comedy and graveyard humour, and a kind of delight in images of cruelty and tantalising disappointment.[25] The former quality is well illustrated by some of the subtitles in the darker narratives; such as "One does not always eat what is on the table", describing a body laid out for a coroner's inquest, and "A man though naked may be in rags", referring to a frightfully mangled corpse.[26]

Bierce's work is in general somewhat uneven. Many of the stories are obviously mechanical, and marred by a jaunty and commonplacely artificial style derived from journalistic models; but the grim malevolence stalking through all of them is unmistakable, and several stand out as permanent mountain-peaks of American weird writing. "The Death of Halpin Frayser",[27] called by Frederic Taber Cooper the most fiendishly ghastly tale in the literature of the Anglo-Saxon race,[28] tells of a body skulking by night without a soul in a weird and horribly ensanguined wood, and of a man beset by ancestral memories who met death at the claws of that which had been his fervently loved mother. "The Damned Thing", frequently copied in popular anthologies, chronicles the hideous devastations of an invisible entity that waddles and flounders on the hills and in the wheatfields by night and day. "The Suitable Surroundings"[29] evokes with singular subtlety yet apparent simplicity a piercing sense of the terror which may reside in the written word.[30] In the story the weird author Colston says to his friend Marsh, "You are brave enough to read me in a street-car, but—in a deserted house—alone—in the forest—at night! Bah! I have a manuscript in my pocket that would kill you!" Marsh reads the manuscript in "the suitable surroundings"—and it does kill him. "The Middle Toe of the Right Foot"[31] is clumsily developed, but has a powerful climax. A man named Manton[32] has horribly killed his two children and his wife, the latter of whom lacked the middle toe of the right foot. Ten years later he returns much altered to the neighbourhood; and, being secretly recognised, is provoked into a bowie-knife duel in the dark, to be held in the now abandoned house where his crime was committed. When the moment of the duel arrives a trick is played upon him; and he is left without an antagonist, shut in a night-black ground floor room of the reputedly haunted edifice, with the thick dust of a decade on every hand. No knife is drawn against him, for only a thorough scare is intended; but on the next day he is found crouched in a corner with distorted face, dead of sheer fright at something he has seen. The only clue visible to the discoverers is one having terrible implications: "In the dust of years that lay thick upon the floor—leading from the door by which they had entered, straight across the room to within a yard of Manton's crouching corpse—were three parallel lines of footprints—light but definite impressions of bare feet, the outer ones those of small children, the inner a woman's. From the point at which they ended they did not return; they pointed all one way." And, of course, the woman's prints shewed a lack of the middle toe of the right foot. "The Spook House",[33] told with a severely homely air of journalistic verisimilitude, conveys terrible hints of shocking mystery. In 1858 an entire family of seven persons disappears suddenly and unaccountably from a plantation house in eastern Kentucky, leaving all its possessions untouched—furniture, clothing, food supplies, horses, cattle, and slaves. About a year later two men of high standing are forced by a storm to take shelter in the deserted dwelling, and in so doing stumble into a strange subterranean room lit by an unaccountable greenish light and having an iron door which cannot be opened from within. In this room lie the decayed corpses of all the missing family; and as one of the discoverers rushes forward to embrace a body he seems to recognise, the other is so overpowered by a strange foetor that he accidentally shuts his companion in the vault and loses consciousness. Recovering his senses six weeks later, the survivor is unable to find the hidden room; and the house is burned during the Civil War. The imprisoned discoverer is never seen or heard of again.

Bierce seldom realises the atmospheric possibilities of his themes as vividly as Poe; and much of his work contains a certain touch of naiveté, prosaic angularity, or early-American provincialism which contrasts somewhat with the efforts of later horror-masters. Nevertheless the genuineness and artistry of his dark intimations are always unmistakable, so that his greatness is in no danger of eclipse. As arranged in his definitively collected works, Bierce's weird tales occur mainly in two volumes, *Can Such Things Be?* and *In the Midst of Life*.[34] The former, indeed, is almost wholly given over to the supernatural.[35]

Much of the best in American horror-literature has come from pens not mainly devoted to that medium. Oliver Wendell Holmes's[36] historic *Elsie Venner*[37] suggests with admirable restraint an unnatural ophidian element in a young woman pre-natally influenced, and sustains the atmosphere with finely discriminating landscape touches. In *The Turn of the Screw* Henry James triumphs over his inevitable pomposity and prolixity[38] sufficiently well to create a truly potent air of sinister menace; depicting the hideous influence of two dead and evil servants, Peter Quint and the governess Miss Jessel, over a small boy and girl who had been under their care. James is perhaps too diffuse, too unctuously urbane, and too much addicted to subtleties of speech to realise fully all the wild and devastating horror in his situations; but for all that there is a rare and mounting tide of fright, culminating in the death of the little boy, which gives the novelette a permanent place in its special class.[39]

F. Marion Crawford produced several weird tales of varying quality, now collected in a volume entitled *Wandering Ghosts*.[40] "For the Blood Is the Life" touches powerfully on a case of moon-cursed vampirism near an ancient tower on the rocks of the lonely South Italian sea-coast. "The Dead Smile" treats of family horrors in an old house and an ancestral vault in Ireland, and introduces the banshee with considerable force. "The Upper Berth", however, is Crawford's weird masterpiece; and is one of the most tremendous horror-stories in all literature. In this tale of a suicide-haunted stateroom such things as the spectral salt-water dampness, the strangely open porthole, and the nightmare struggle with the nameless object are handled with incomparable dexterity.[41]

Very genuine, though not without the typical mannered extravagance of the eighteen-nineties, is the strain of horror in the early work of Robert W. Chambers, since renowned for products of a very different quality.[42] *The King in Yellow,* a series of vaguely connected short stories having as a background a monstrous and suppressed book whose perusal brings fright, madness, and spectral tragedy,[43] really achieves notable heights of cosmic fear in spite of uneven interest and a somewhat trivial and affected cultivation of the Gallic studio atmosphere made popular by Du Maurier's *Trilby*. The most powerful of its tales, perhaps, is "The Yellow Sign", in which is introduced a silent and terrible churchyard watchman with a face like a puffy grave-worm's. A boy, describing a tussle he has had with this creature, shivers and sickens as he relates a certain detail. "Well, sir, it's Gawd's truth that when I 'it 'im 'e grabbed me wrists, sir, and when I twisted 'is soft, mushy fist one of 'is fingers come off in me 'and." An artist, who after seeing him has shared with another a strange dream of a nocturnal hearse, is shocked by the voice with which the watchman accosts him. The fellow emits a muttering sound that fills the head like thick oily smoke from a fat-rendering vat or an odour of noisome decay. What he mumbles is merely this: "Have you found the Yellow Sign?"

A weirdly hieroglyphed onyx talisman, picked up in the street by the sharer of his dream, is shortly given the artist; and after stumbling queerly upon the hellish and forbidden book of horrors the two learn, among other hideous things which no sane mortal should know, that this talisman is indeed the nameless Yellow Sign handed down from the accursed cult of Hastur[44]—from primordial Carcosa,[45] whereof the volume treats, and some nightmare memory of which seems to lurk latent and ominous at the back of all men's minds. Soon they hear the rumbling of the black-plumed hearse driven by the flabby and corpse-faced watchman. He enters the night-shrouded house in quest of the Yellow Sign, all bolts and bars rotting at his touch. And when the people rush in, drawn by a scream that no human throat could utter, they find three forms on the floor—two dead and one dying. One of the dead shapes is far gone in decay. It is the churchyard watchman, and the doctor exclaims, "That man must have been dead for months." It is worth observing that the author derives most of the names and allusions connected with his eldritch land of primal memory from the tales of Ambrose Bierce. Other early works of Mr. Chambers displaying the outré and macabre element are *The Maker of Moons* and *In Search of the Unknown.* One cannot help regretting that he did not further develop a vein in which he could so easily have become a recognised master.[46]

Horror material of authentic force may be found in the work of the New England realist Mary E. Wilkins; whose volume of short tales, *The Wind in the Rose-Bush,* contains a number of noteworthy achievements. In "The Shadows on the Wall" we are shewn with consummate skill the response of a staid New England household to uncanny tragedy; and the sourceless shadow of the poisoned brother well prepares us for the climactic moment when the shadow of the secret murderer, who has killed himself in a neighbouring city, suddenly appears beside it. Charlotte Perkins Gilman, in "The Yellow Wall Paper", rises to a classic level in subtly delineating the madness which crawls over a woman dwelling in the hideously papered room where a madwoman was once confined.

[In "The Dead Valley" the eminent architect and mediaevalist Ralph Adams Cram achieves a memorably potent degree of vague regional horror through subtleties of atmosphere and description.[47]]

Still further carrying on our spectral tradition is the gifted and versatile humourist Irvin S. Cobb, whose work both early and recent contains some finely weird specimens. "Fishhead",[48] an early achievement, is banefully effective in its portrayal of unnatural affinities between a hybrid idiot and the strange fish of an isolated lake, which at the last avenge their biped kinsman's murder. Later work of Mr. Cobb introduces an element of possible science, as in the tale of hereditary memory where a modern man with a negroid strain utters words in African jungle speech when run down by a train under visual and aural circumstances recalling the maiming of his black ancestor by a rhinoceros a century before.[49]

[Extremely high in artistic stature is the novel *The Dark Chamber* (1927), by the late Leonard Cline.[50] This is the tale of a man who—with the characteristic ambition of the Gothic or Byronic hero-villain—seeks to defy Nature and recapture every moment of his past life through the abnormal stimulation of memory. To this end he employs endless notes, records, mnemonic objects, and pictures—and finally odours, music, and exotic drugs. At last his ambition goes beyond his personal life and reaches toward the black abysses of *hereditary* memory—even back to pre-human days amidst the steaming swamps of the Carboniferous age, and to still more unimaginable deeps of primal time and entity. He calls for madder music and takes stronger drugs, and finally his great dog grows oddly afraid of him. A noxious animal stench encompasses him, and he grows vacant-faced and sub-human. In the end he takes to the woods, howling at night beneath windows. He is finally found in a thicket, mangled to death. Beside him is the mangled corpse of his dog. They have killed each other. The atmosphere of this novel is malevolently potent, much attention being paid to the central figure's sinister home and household.[51]

A less subtle and well-balanced but nevertheless highly effective creation is Herbert S. Gorman's novel, *The Place Called Dagon*, which relates the dark history of a western Massachusetts backwater where the descendants of refugees from the Salem witchcraft still keep alive the morbid and degenerate horrors of the Black Sabbat.[52]

Sinister House, by Leland Hall, has touches of magnificent atmosphere but is marred by a somewhat mediocre romanticism.

Very notable in their way are some of the weird conceptions of the novelist and short-story writer Edward Lucas White, most of whose themes arise from actual dreams.[53] "The Song of the Sirens"[54] has a very pervasive strangeness, while such things as "Lukundoo" and "The Snout"[55] rouse darker apprehensions. Mr. White imparts a very peculiar quality to his tales—an oblique sort of glamour which has its own distinctive type of convincingness.]

Of younger Americans, none strikes the note of cosmic terror so well as the California poet, artist, and fictionist Clark Ashton Smith, whose bizarre writings, drawings, paintings, and stories are the delight of a sensitive few.[56] Mr. Smith has for his background a universe of remote and paralysing fright—jungles of poisonous and iridescent blossoms on the moons of Saturn, evil and grotesque temples in Atlantis, Lemuria, and forgotten elder worlds, and dank morasses of spotted death-fungi in spectral countries beyond earth's rim. His longest and most ambitious poem, *The Hashish-Eater*,[57] is in pentameter blank verse; and opens up chaotic and incredible vistas of kaleidoscopic nightmare in the spaces between the stars. In sheer daemonic strangeness and fertility of conception, Mr. Smith is perhaps unexcelled by any other writer dead or living. Who else has seen such gorgeous, luxuriant, and feverishly distorted visions of infinite spheres and multiple dimensions and lived to tell the tale? [His short stories deal powerfully with other galaxies, worlds, and dimensions, as well as with strange regions and aeons on the earth. He tells of primal Hyperborea and its black amorphous god Tsathoggua;[58] of the lost continent Zothique, and of the fabulous, vampire-curst land of Averoigne in mediaeval France. Some of Mr. Smith's best work can be found in the brochure entitled *The Double Shadow and Other Fantasies* (1933).[59]]

IX. The Weird Tradition in the British Isles

Recent British literature, besides including the three or four greatest fantaisistes of the present age, has been gratifyingly fertile in the element of the weird. Rudyard Kipling has often approached it; and has, despite the omnipresent mannerisms, handled it with indubitable mastery in such tales as "The Phantom 'Rickshaw", "'The Finest Story in the World'", "The Recrudescence of Imray", and "The Mark of the Beast".[1] This latter is of particular poignancy; the pictures of the naked leper-priest who mewed like an otter, of the spots which appeared on the chest of the man that priest cursed, of the growing carnivorousness of the victim and of the fear which horses began to display toward him, and of the eventually half-accomplished transformation of that victim into a leopard, being things which no reader is ever likely to forget.[2] The final defeat of the malignant sorcery does not impair the force of the tale or the validity of its mystery.

Lafcadio Hearn, strange, wandering, and exotic, departs still farther from the realm of the real; and with the supreme artistry of a sensitive poet weaves phantasies impossible to an author of the solid roast-beef type. His *Fantastics,* written in America, contains some of the most impressive ghoulishness in all literature; whilst his *Kwaidan,* written in Japan, crystallises with matchless skill and delicacy the eerie lore and whispered legends of that richly colourful nation. Still more of Hearn's weird wizardry of language is shewn in some of his translations from the French, especially from Gautier and Flaubert.[3] His version of the latter's *Temptation of St. Anthony* is a classic of fevered and riotous imagery clad in the magic of singing words.

Oscar Wilde may likewise be given a place amongst weird writers, both for certain of his exquisite fairy tales,[4] and for his vivid *Picture of Dorian Gray,*[5] in which a marvellous portrait for years assumes the duty of ageing and coarsening instead of its original, who meanwhile plunges into every excess of vice and crime without the outward loss of youth, beauty, and freshness. There is a sudden and potent climax when Dorian Gray, at last become a murderer, seeks to destroy the painting whose changes testify to his moral degeneracy. He stabs it with a knife, and a hideous cry and crash are heard; but when the servants enter they find it in all its pristine loveliness. "Lying on the floor was a dead man, in evening dress, with a knife in his heart. He was withered, wrinkled, and loathsome of visage. It was not till they had examined the rings that they recognised who it was."[6]

Matthew Phipps Shiel, author of many weird, grotesque, and adventurous novels and tales, occasionally attains a high level of horrific magic. "Xélucha" is a noxiously hideous fragment,[7] but is excelled by Mr. Shiel's undoubted masterpiece, "The House of Sounds",[8] floridly written in the "yellow 'nineties", and re-cast with more artistic restraint in the early twentieth century.[9] This story, in final form, deserves a place among the foremost things of its kind. It tells of a creeping horror and menace trickling down the centuries on a sub-arctic island off the coast of Norway; where, amidst the sweep of daemon winds and the ceaseless din of hellish waves and cataracts, a vengeful dead man built a brazen tower of terror. It is vaguely like, yet infinitely unlike, Poe's "Fall of the House of Usher".[10] [In the novel *The Purple Cloud* Mr. Shiel describes with tremendous power a curse which came out of the arctic[11] to destroy mankind, and which for a time appears to have left but a single inhabitant on our planet.[12] The sensations of this lone survivor as he realises his position, and roams through the corpse-littered and treasure-strown cities of the world as their absolute master, are delivered with a skill and artistry falling little short of actual majesty. Unfortunately the second half of the book, with its conventionally romantic element, involves a distinct "letdown".[13]]

Better known than Shiel is the ingenious Bram Stoker, who created many starkly horrific conceptions in a series of novels whose poor technique sadly impairs their net effect. *The Lair of the White Worm*, dealing with a gigantic primitive entity that lurks in a vault beneath an ancient castle, utterly ruins a magnificent idea by a development almost infantile.[14] *The Jewel of Seven Stars*, touching on a strange Egyptian resurrection, is less crudely written. But best of all is the famous *Dracula*, which has become almost the standard modern exploitation of the frightful vampire myth.[15] Count Dracula, a vampire, dwells in a horrible castle in the Carpathians; but finally migrates to England with the design of populating the country with fellow vampires. How an Englishman fares within Dracula's stronghold of terrors, and how the dead fiend's plot for domination is at last defeated, are elements which unite to form a tale now justly assigned a permanent place in English letters.[16] *Dracula* evoked many similar novels of supernatural horror, among which the best are perhaps *The Beetle*, by Richard Marsh,[17] *Brood of the Witch-Queen*, by "Sax Rohmer" (Arthur Sarsfield Ward),[18] and *The Door of the Unreal*, by Gerald Biss.[19] The latter handles quite dexterously the standard werewolf superstition. Much subtler and more artistic, and told with singular skill through the juxtaposed narratives of the several characters, is the novel *Cold Harbour*, by Francis Brett Young, in which an ancient house of strange malignancy is powerfully delineated. The mocking and well-nigh omnipotent fiend Humphrey Furnival holds echoes of the Manfred-Montoni type of early Gothic "villain", but is redeemed from triteness by many clever individualities. Only the slight diffuseness of explanation at the close, and the somewhat too free use of divination as a plot factor, keep this tale from approaching absolute perfection.[20]

[In the novel *Witch Wood* John Buchan depicts with tremendous force a survival of the evil Sabbat in a lonely district of Scotland. The description of the black forest with the evil stone, and of the terrible cosmic adumbrations when the horror is finally extirpated, will repay one for wading through the very gradual action and plethora of Scottish dialect. Some of Mr. Buchan's short stories[21] are also extremely vivid in their spectral intimations; "The Green Wildebeest", a tale of African witchcraft, "The Wind in the Portico", with its awakening of dead Britanno-Roman horrors, and "Skule Skerry", with its touches of sub-arctic fright, being especially remarkable.[22]]

Clemence Housman, in the brief novelette "The Were-wolf", attains a high degree of gruesome tension and achieves to some extent the atmosphere of authentic folklore.[23] [In *The Elixir of Life* Arthur Ransome attains some darkly excellent effects despite a general naiveté of plot,[24] while H. B. Drake's *The Shadowy Thing* summons up strange and terrible vistas.[25] George Macdonald's *Lilith* has a compelling bizarrerie all its own; the first and simpler of the two versions being perhaps the more effective.[26]]

Deserving of distinguished notice as a forceful craftsman to whom an unseen mystic world is ever a close and vital reality is the poet Walter de la Mare,[27] whose haunting verse and exquisite prose alike bear consistent traces of a strange vision reaching deeply into veiled spheres of beauty and terrible and forbidden dimensions of being. In the novel *The Return* we see the soul of a dead man reach out of its grave of two centuries and fasten itself upon the flesh of the living, so that even the face of the victim becomes that which had long ago returned to dust.[28] Of the shorter tales, of which several volumes exist, many are unforgettable for their command of fear's and sorcery's darkest ramifications; notably "Seaton's Aunt", in which there lowers a noxious background of malignant vampirism; "The Tree", which tells of a frightful vegetable growth in the yard of a starving artist; "Out of the Deep", wherein we are given leave to imagine what thing answered the summons of a dying wastrel in a dark lonely house when he pulled a long-feared bell-cord in the attic chamber of his dread-haunted boyhood; ["A Recluse", which hints at what sent a chance guest flying from a house in the night;] "Mr. Kempe", which shews us a mad clerical hermit in quest of the human soul, dwelling in a frightful sea-cliff region beside an archaic abandoned chapel; and "All-Hallows", a glimpse of daemoniac forces besieging a lonely mediaeval church and miraculously restoring the rotting masonry. De la Mare does not make fear the sole or even the dominant element of most of his tales, being apparently more interested in the subtleties of character involved. Occasionally he sinks to sheer whimsical phantasy of the Barrie order. Still, he is among the very few to whom unreality is a vivid, living presence; and as such he is able to put into his occasional fear-studies a keen potency which only a rare master can achieve. His poem "The Listeners" restores the Gothic shudder to modern verse.[29]

The weird short story has fared well of late, an important contributor being the versatile E. F. Benson, whose "The Man Who Went Too Far"[30] breathes whisperingly of a house at the edge of a dark wood, and of Pan's hoof-mark on the breast of a dead man. Mr. Benson's volume, *Visible and Invisible,* contains several stories of singular power; notably *"Negotium Perambulans",* whose unfolding reveals an abnormal monster from an ancient ecclesiastical panel which performs an act of miraculous vengeance in a lonely village on the Cornish coast, and "The Horror-Horn", through which lopes a terrible half-human survival dwelling on unvisited Alpine peaks. ["The Face", in another collection,[31] is lethally potent in its relentless aura of doom. H. R. Wakefield, in his collections *They Return at Evening* and *Others Who Return,* manages now and then to achieve great heights of horror despite a vitiating air of sophistication. The most notable stories are The Red Lodge with its slimy aqueous evil, "'He Cometh and He Passeth By'", "'And He Shall Sing . . .'", "The Cairn", "'Look Up There!'", "Blind Man's Buff", and that bit of lurking millennial horror, "The Seventeenth Hole at Duncaster".[32] Mention has been made of the weird work of H. G. Wells and A. Conan Doyle. The former, in "The Ghost of Fear",[33] reaches a very high level; while all the items in *Thirty Strange Stories* have strong fantastic implications.[34] Doyle now and then struck a powerfully spectral note, as in "The Captain of the 'Pole-Star'", a tale of arctic ghostliness, and "Lot No. 249", wherein the reanimated mummy theme is used with more than ordinary skill.[35] Hugh Walpole, of the same family as the founder of Gothic fiction, has sometimes approached the bizarre with much success; his short story "Mrs. Lunt" carrying a very poignant shudder.[36]] John Metcalfe, in the collection published as *The Smoking Leg,* attains now and then a rare pitch of potency; the tale entitled "The Bad Lands" containing graduations of horror that strongly savour of genius.[37] More whimsical and inclined toward the amiable and innocuous phantasy of Sir J. M. Barrie[38] are the short tales of E. M. Forster, grouped under the title of *The Celestial Omnibus.* Of these only one, dealing with a glimpse of Pan and his aura of fright,[39] may be said to hold the true element of cosmic horror.[40] [Mrs. H. D. Everett, though adhering to very old and conventional models, occasionally reaches singular heights of spiritual terror in her collection of short stories.[41] L. P. Hartley is notable for his incisive and extremely ghastly tale, "A Visitor from Down Under".[42]] May Sinclair's *Uncanny Stories* contain more of traditional occultism than of that creative treatment of fear which marks mastery in this field, and are inclined to lay more stress on human emotions and psychological delving than upon the stark phenomena of a cosmos utterly unreal.[43] It may be well to remark here that occult believers are probably less effective than materialists in delineating the spectral and the fantastic, since to them the phantom world is so commonplace a reality that they tend to refer to it with less awe, remoteness, and impressiveness than do those who see in it an absolute and stupendous violation of the natural order.

[Of rather uneven stylistic quality, but vast occasional power in its suggestion of lurking worlds and beings behind the ordinary surface of life, is the work of William Hope Hodgson, known today far less than it deserves to be.[44] Despite a tendency toward conventionally sentimental conceptions of the universe, and of man's relation to it and to his fellows, Mr. Hodgson is perhaps second only to Algernon Blackwood in his serious treatment of unreality. Few can equal him in adumbrating the nearness of nameless forces and monstrous besieging entities through casual hints and insignificant details, or in conveying feelings of the spectral and the abnormal in connexion with regions or buildings.

In *The Boats of the "Glen Carrig"* (1907) we are shewn a variety of malign marvels and accursed unknown lands as encountered by the survivors of a sunken ship. The brooding menace in the earlier parts of the book is impossible to surpass, though a letdown in the direction of ordinary romance and adventure occurs toward the end. An inaccurate and pseudo-romantic attempt to reproduce eighteenth-century prose detracts from the general effect, but the really profound nautical erudition everywhere displayed is a compensating factor.

The House on the Borderland (1908)—perhaps the greatest of all Mr. Hodgson's works—tells of a lonely and evilly regarded house in Ireland which forms a focus for hideous other-world forces and sustains a siege by blasphemous hybrid anomalies from a hidden abyss below. The wanderings of the narrator's spirit through limitless light-years of cosmic space and kalpas[45] of eternity, and its witnessing of the solar system's final destruction, constitute something almost unique in standard literature.[46] And everywhere there is manifest the author's power to suggest vague, ambushed horrors in natural scenery. But for a few touches of commonplace sentimentality this book would be a classic of the first water.

The Ghost Pirates (1909), regarded by Mr. Hodgson as rounding out a trilogy with the two previously mentioned works, is a powerful account of a doomed and haunted ship on its last voyage, and of the terrible sea-devils (of quasi-human aspect, and perhaps the spirits of bygone buccaneers) that besiege it and finally drag it down to an unknown fate. With its command of maritime knowledge, and its clever selection of hints and incidents suggestive of latent horrors in Nature, this book at times reaches enviable peaks of power.

The Night Land (1912) is a long-extended (583 pp.) tale of the earth's infinitely remote future—billions of billions of years ahead, after the death of the sun. It is told in a rather clumsy fashion, as the dreams of a man in the seventeenth century, whose mind merges with its own future incarnation; and is seriously marred by painful verboseness, repetitiousness, artificial and nauseously sticky romantic sentimentality, and an attempt at archaic language even more grotesque and absurd than that in *"Glen Carrig"*.

Allowing for all its faults, it is yet one of the most potent pieces of macabre imagination ever written. The picture of a night-black, dead planet, with the remains of the human race concentrated in a stupendously vast metal pyramid and besieged by monstrous, hybrid, and altogether unknown forces of the darkness, is something that no reader can ever forget. Shapes and entities of an altogether non-human and inconceivable sort—the prowlers of the black, man-forsaken, and unexplored world outside the pyramid—are *suggested* and *partly* described with ineffable potency; while the night-bound landscape with its chasms and slopes and dying volcanism takes on an almost sentient terror beneath the author's touch.

Midway in the book the central figure ventures outside the pyramid on a quest through death-haunted realms untrod by man for millions of years—and in his slow, minutely described, day-by-day progress over unthinkable leagues of immemorial blackness there is a sense of cosmic alienage, breathless mystery, and terrified expectancy unrivalled in the whole range of literature. The last quarter of the book drags woefully, but fails to spoil the tremendous power of the whole.

Mr. Hodgson's later volume, *Carnacki, the Ghost-Finder,* consists of several longish short stories published many years before in magazines. In quality it falls conspicuously below the level of the other books. We here find a more or less conventional stock figure of the "infallible detective" type—the progeny of M. Dupin and Sherlock Holmes, and the close kin of Algernon Blackwood's John Silence—moving through scenes and events badly marred by an atmosphere of professional "occultism". A few of the episodes, however, are of undeniable power; and afford glimpses of the peculiar genius characteristic of the author.[47]]

Naturally it is impossible in a brief sketch to trace out all the classic modern uses of the terror element. The ingredient must of necessity enter into all work both prose and verse treating broadly of life; and we are therefore not surprised to find a share in such writers as the poet Browning, whose "'Childe Roland to the Dark Tower Came'" is instinct with hideous menace, or the novelist Joseph Conrad, who often wrote of the dark secrets within the sea, and of the daemoniac driving power of Fate as influencing the lives of lonely and maniacally resolute men.[48] Its trail is one of infinite ramifications; but we must here confine ourselves to its appearance in a relatively unmixed state, where it determines and dominates the work of art containing it.

Somewhat separate from the main British stream is that current of weirdness in Irish literature which came to the fore in the Celtic Renaissance of the later nineteenth and early twentieth centuries. Ghost and fairy lore have always been of great prominence in Ireland, and for over an hundred years have been recorded by a line of such faithful transcribers and translators as William Carleton,[49] T. Crofton Croker,[50] Lady Wilde[51]—mother of Oscar Wilde—Douglas Hyde,[52] and W. B. Yeats.[53] Brought to notice by the modern movement, this body of myth has been carefully collected and studied; and its salient features reproduced in the work of later figures like Yeats, J. M. Synge, "A. E.",[54] Lady Gregory, Padraic Colum, James Stephens, and their colleagues.[55]

Whilst on the whole more whimsically fantastic than terrible, such folklore and its consciously artistic counterparts contain much that falls truly within the domain of cosmic horror. Tales of burials in sunken churches beneath haunted lakes, accounts of death-heralding banshees and sinister changelings, ballads of spectres and "the unholy creatures of the raths"—all these have their poignant and definite shivers, and mark a strong and distinctive element in weird literature. Despite homely grotesqueness and absolute naivet,, there is genuine nightmare in the class of narrative represented by the yarn of Teig O'Kane, who in punishment for his wild life was ridden all night by a hideous corpse that demanded burial and drove him from churchyard to churchyard as the dead rose up loathsomely in each one and refused to accommodate the newcomer with a berth. Yeats, undoubtedly the greatest figure of the Irish revival if not the greatest of all living poets, has accomplished notable things both in original work and in the codification of old legends.

X. The Modern Masters

The best horror-tales of today, profiting by the long evolution of the type, possess a naturalness, convincingness, artistic smoothness, and skilful intensity of appeal quite beyond comparison with anything in the Gothic work of a century or more ago. Technique, craftsmanship, experience, and psychological knowledge have advanced tremendously with the passing years, so that much of the older work seems naive and artificial; redeemed, when redeemed at all, only by a genius which conquers heavy limitations. The tone of jaunty and inflated romance, full of false motivation and investing every conceivable event with a counterfeit significance and carelessly inclusive glamour, is now confined to lighter and more whimsical phases of supernatural writing. Serious weird stories are either made realistically intense by close consistency and perfect fidelity to Nature except in the one supernatural direction which the author allows himself,[1] or else cast altogether in the realm of phantasy,[2] with atmosphere cunningly adapted to the visualisation of a delicately exotic world of unreality beyond space and time, in which almost anything may happen if it but happen in true accord with certain types of imagination and illusion normal to the sensitive human brain. This, at least, is the dominant tendency; though of course many great contemporary writers slip occasionally into some of the flashy postures of immature romanticism, or into bits of the equally empty and absurd jargon of pseudo-scientific "occultism",[3] now at one of its periodic high tides.

Of living creators of cosmic fear raised to its most artistic pitch, few if any can hope to equal the versatile Arthur Machen;[4] author of some dozen tales long and short, in which the elements of hidden horror and brooding fright attain an almost incomparable substance and realistic acuteness. Mr. Machen, a general man of letters and master of an exquisitely lyrical and expressive prose style, has perhaps put more conscious effort into his picaresque *Chronicle of Clemendy*, his refreshing essays,[5] his vivid autobiographical volumes,[6] his fresh and spirited translations,[7] and above all his memorable epic of the sensitive aesthetic mind, *The Hill of Dreams*, in which the youthful hero responds to the magic of that ancient Welsh environment which is the author's own, and lives a dream-life in the Roman city of Isca Silurum, now shrunk to the relic-strown village of Caerleon-on-Usk.[8] But the fact remains that his powerful horror-material of the 'nineties and earlier nineteen-hundreds stands alone in its class, and marks a distinct epoch in the history of this literary form.

Mr. Machen, with an impressionable Celtic heritage linked to keen youthful memories of the wild domed hills, archaic forests, and cryptical Roman ruins of the Gwent countryside, has developed an imaginative life of rare beauty, intensity, and historic background. He has absorbed the mediaeval mystery of dark woods and ancient customs, and is a champion of the Middle Ages in all things—including the Catholic faith. He has yielded, likewise, to the spell of the Britanno-Roman life which once surged over his native region; and finds strange magic in the fortified camps, tessellated pavements, fragments of statues, and kindred things which tell of the day when classicism reigned and Latin was the language of the country. A young American poet, Frank Belknap Long, Jun., has well summarised this dreamer's rich endowments and wizardry of expression in the sonnet "On Reading Arthur Machen":

> "There is a glory in the autumn wood;
> The ancient lanes of England wind and climb
> Past wizard oaks and gorse and tangled thyme
> To where a fort of mighty empire stood:
> There is a glamour in the autumn sky;
> The reddened clouds are writhing in the glow
> Of some great fire, and there are glints below
> Of tawny yellow where the embers die.
>
> I wait, for he will show me, clear and cold,
> High-rais'd in splendour, sharp against the North,
> The Roman eagles, and thro' mists of gold
> The marching legions as they issue forth:
> I wait, for I would share with him again
> The ancient wisdom, and the ancient pain."[9]

Of Mr. Machen's horror-tales the most famous is perhaps "The Great God Pan" (1894), which tells of a singular and terrible experiment and its consequences. A young woman, through surgery of the brain-cells, is made to see the vast and monstrous deity of Nature, and becomes an idiot in consequence, dying less than a year later. Years afterward a strange, ominous, and foreign-looking child named Helen Vaughan is placed to board with a family in rural Wales, and haunts the woods in unaccountable fashion. A little boy is thrown out of his mind at sight of someone or something he spies with her, and a young girl comes to a terrible end in similar fashion. All this mystery is strangely interwoven with the Roman rural deities of the place, as sculptured in antique fragments. After another lapse of years, a woman of strangely exotic beauty appears in society, drives her husband to horror and death, causes an artist to paint unthinkable paintings of Witches' Sabbaths, creates an epidemic of suicide among the men of her acquaintance,[10] and is finally discovered to be a frequenter of the lowest dens of vice in London, where even the most callous degenerates are shocked at her enormities. Through the clever comparing of notes on the part of those who have had word of her at various stages of her career, this woman is discovered to be the girl Helen Vaughan; who is the child—by no mortal father—of the young woman on whom the brain experiment was made.[11] She is a daughter of hideous Pan himself, and at the last is put to death amidst horrible transmutations of form involving changes of sex and a descent to the most primal manifestations of the life-principle.

But the charm of the tale is in the telling. No one could begin to describe the cumulative suspense and ultimate horror with which every paragraph abounds without following fully the precise order in which Mr. Machen unfolds his gradual hints and revelations. Melodrama is undeniably present, and coincidence is stretched to a length which appears absurd upon analysis; but in the malign witchery of the tale as a whole these trifles are forgotten, and the sensitive reader reaches the end with only an appreciative shudder and a tendency to repeat the words of one of the characters: "It is too incredible, too monstrous; such things can never be in this quiet world. . . . Why, man, if such a case were possible, our earth would be a nightmare."[12]

Less famous and less complex in plot than "The Great God Pan", but definitely finer in atmosphere and general artistic value, is the curious and dimly disquieting chronicle called "The White People", whose central portion purports to be the diary or notes[13] of a little girl whose nurse has introduced her to some of the forbidden magic and soul-blasting traditions of the noxious witch-cult[14]—the cult whose whispered lore was handed down long lines of peasantry throughout Western Europe, and whose members sometimes stole forth at night, one by one, to meet in black woods and lonely places for the revolting orgies of the Witches' Sabbath. Mr. Machen's narrative, a triumph of skilful selectiveness and restraint, accumulates enormous power as it flows on in a stream of innocent childish prattle; introducing allusions to strange "nymphs", "Dôls",[15] "voolas", "White, Green, and Scarlet Ceremonies", "Aklo letters",[16] "Chian language", "Mao games", and the like. The rites learned by the nurse from her witch grandmother are taught to the child by the time she is three years old, and her artless accounts of the dangerous secret revelations possess a lurking terror generously mixed with pathos. Evil charms well known to anthropologists are described with juvenile naiveté, and finally there comes a winter afternoon journey into the old Welsh hills, performed under an imaginative spell which lends to the wild scenery an added weirdness, strangeness, and suggestion of grotesque sentience. The details of this journey are given with marvellous vividness, and form to the keen critic a masterpiece of fantastic writing, with almost unlimited power in the intimation of potent hideousness and cosmic aberration. At length the child—whose age is then thirteen—comes upon a cryptic and banefully beautiful thing in the midst of a dark and inaccessible wood. She flees in awe, but is permanently altered and repeatedly revisits the wood. In the end horror overtakes her in a manner deftly prefigured by an anecdote in the prologue, but she poisons herself in time. Like the mother of Helen Vaughan in The Great God Pan, she has seen that frightful deity. She is discovered dead in the dark wood beside the cryptic thing she found; and that thing—a whitely luminous statue of Roman workmanship about which dire mediaeval rumours had clustered—is affrightedly hammered into dust by the searchers.

In the episodic novel of *The Three Impostors,* a work whose merit as a whole is somewhat marred by an imitation of the jaunty Stevenson manner,[17] occur certain tales which perhaps represent the high-water mark of Machen's skill as a terror-weaver. Here we find in its most artistic form a favourite weird conception of the author's; the notion that beneath the mounds and rocks of the wild Welsh hills dwell subterraneously that squat primitive race whose vestiges gave rise to our common folk legends of fairies, elves, and the "little people",[18] and whose acts are even now responsible for certain unexplained disappearances, and occasional substitutions of strange dark "changelings" for normal infants.[19] This theme receives its finest treatment in the episode entitled "The Novel of the Black Seal"; where a professor, having discovered a singular identity between certain characters scrawled on Welsh limestone rocks and those existing in a prehistoric black seal[20] from Babylon, sets out on a course of discovery which leads him to unknown and terrible things. A queer passage in the ancient geographer Solinus,[21] a series of mysterious disappearances in the lonely reaches of Wales, a strange idiot son born to a rural mother after a fright in which her inmost faculties were shaken; all these things suggest to the professor a hideous connexion and a condition revolting to any friend and respecter of the human race. He hires the idiot boy, who jabbers strangely at times in a repulsive hissing voice, and is subject to odd epileptic seizures. Once, after such a seizure in the professor's study by night, disquieting odours and evidences of unnatural presences are found; and soon after that the professor leaves a bulky document and goes into the weird hills with feverish expectancy and strange terror in his heart. He never returns, but beside a fantastic stone in the wild country are found his watch, money, and ring, done up with catgut in a parchment bearing the same terrible characters as those on the black Babylonish seal and the rock in the Welsh mountains.

The bulky document explains enough to bring up the most hideous vistas. Professor Gregg, from the massed evidence presented by the Welsh disappearances, the rock inscription, the accounts of ancient geographers, and the black seal, has decided that a frightful race of dark primal beings of immemorial antiquity and wide former diffusion still dwells beneath the hills of unfrequented Wales. Further research has unriddled the message of the black seal, and proved that the idiot boy, a son of some father more terrible than mankind, is the heir of monstrous memories and possibilities. That strange night in the study the professor invoked 'the awful transmutation of the hills' by the aid of the black seal, and aroused in the hybrid idiot the horrors of his shocking paternity. He "saw his body swell and become distended as a bladder, while the face blackened. . . ." And then the supreme effects of the invocation appeared, and Professor Gregg knew the stark frenzy of cosmic panic in its darkest form. He knew the abysmal gulfs of abnormality that he had opened, and went forth into the wild hills prepared and resigned. He would meet the unthinkable 'Little People'—and his document ends with a rational observation: "If I unhappily do not return from my journey, there is no need to conjure up here a picture of the awfulness of my fate."

Also in *The Three Impostors* is the "Novel of the White Powder", which approaches the absolute culmination of loathsome fright. Francis Leicester, a young law student nervously worn out by seclusion and overwork, has a prescription filled by an old apothecary none too careful about the state of his drugs. The substance, it later turns out, is an unusual salt which time and varying temperature have accidentally changed to something very strange and terrible; nothing less, in short, than the mediaeval *Vinum Sabbati,* whose consumption at the horrible orgies of the Witches' Sabbath gave rise to shocking transformations and—if injudiciously used—to unutterable consequences. Innocently enough, the youth regularly imbibes the powder in a glass of water after meals; and at first seems substantially benefited. Gradually, however, his improved spirits take the form of dissipation; he is absent from home a great deal, and appears to have undergone a repellent psychological change. One day an odd livid spot appears on his right hand, and he afterward returns to his seclusion; finally keeping himself shut within his room and admitting none of the household. The doctor calls for an interview, and departs in a palsy of horror, saying that he can do no more in that house. Two weeks later the patient's sister, walking outside, sees a monstrous thing at the sickroom window;[22] and servants report that food left at the locked door is no longer touched. Summons at the door bring only a sound of shuffling and a demand in a thick gurgling voice to be let alone. At last an awful happening is reported by a shuddering housemaid. The ceiling of the room below Leicester's is stained with a hideous black fluid, and a pool of viscid abomination has dripped to the bed beneath. Dr. Haberden, now persuaded to return to the house, breaks down the young man's door and strikes again and again with an iron bar at the blasphemous semi-living thing he finds there. It is "a dark and putrid mass, seething with corruption and hideous rottenness, neither liquid nor solid, but melting and changing". Burning points like eyes shine out of its midst, and before it is despatched it tries to lift what might have been an arm. Soon afterward the physician, unable to endure the memory of what he has beheld, dies at sea while bound for a new life in America.[23]

Mr. Machen returns to the daemoniac "Little People" in "The Red Hand" and "The Shining Pyramid";[24] and in *The Terror,* a wartime story, he treats with very potent mystery the effect of man's modern repudiation of spirituality on the beasts of the world, which are thus led to question his supremacy and to unite for his extermination.[25] Of utmost delicacy, and passing from mere horror into true mysticism, is *The Great Return,* a story of the Graal, also a product of the war period. Too well known to need description here is the tale of "The Bowmen"; which, taken for authentic narration, gave rise to the widespread legend of the "Angels of

Mons"—ghosts of the old English archers of Crécy and Agincourt who fought in 1914 beside the hard-pressed ranks of England's glorious "Old Contemptibles".[26]

Less intense than Mr. Machen in delineating the extremes of stark fear, yet infinitely more closely wedded to the idea of an unreal world constantly pressing upon ours, is the inspired and prolific Algernon Blackwood, amidst whose voluminous and uneven work may be found some of the finest spectral literature of this or any age.[27] Of the quality of Mr. Blackwood's genius there can be no dispute; for no one has even approached the skill, seriousness, and minute fidelity with which he records the overtones of strangeness in ordinary things and experiences, or the preternatural insight with which he builds up detail by detail the complete sensations and perceptions leading from reality into supernormal life or vision. Without notable command of the poetic witchery of mere words, he is the one absolute and unquestioned master of weird atmosphere; and can evoke what amounts almost to a story from a simple fragment of humourless psychological description. Above all others he understands how fully some sensitive minds dwell forever on the borderland of dream, and how relatively slight is the distinction betwixt those images formed from actual objects and those excited by the play of the imagination.

Mr. Blackwood's lesser work is marred by several defects such as ethical didacticism, occasional insipid whimsicality, the flatness of benignant supernaturalism, and a too free use of the trade jargon of modern "occultism". A fault of his more serious efforts is that diffuseness and long-windedness which results from an excessively elaborate attempt, under the handicap of a somewhat bald and journalistic style devoid of intrinsic magic, colour, and vitality, to visualise precise sensations and nuances of uncanny suggestion. But in spite of all this, the major products of Mr. Blackwood attain a genuinely classic level, and evoke as does nothing else in literature an awed and convinced sense of the immanence of strange spiritual spheres or entities.

The well-nigh endless array of Mr. Blackwood's fiction includes both novels and shorter tales, the latter sometimes independent and sometimes arrayed in series. Foremost of all must be reckoned "The Willows", in which the nameless presences on a desolate Danube island are horribly felt and recognised by a pair of idle voyagers. Here art and restraint in narrative reach their very highest development, and an impression of lasting poignancy is produced without a single strained passage or a single false note. Another amazingly potent though less artistically finished tale is "The Wendigo", where we are confronted by horrible evidences of a vast forest daemon about which North Woods lumbermen whisper at evening. The manner in which certain footprints tell certain unbelievable things is really a marked triumph in craftsmanship.[28] In "An Episode in a Lodging House"[29] we behold frightful presences summoned out of black space by a sorcerer, and "The Listener" tells of the awful psychic residuum creeping about an old house where a leper died. In the volume titled *Incredible Adventures*[30] occur some of the finest tales which the author has yet produced, leading the fancy to wild rites on nocturnal hills,[31] to secret and terrible aspects lurking behind stolid scenes,[32] and to unimaginable vaults of mystery below the sands and pyramids of Egypt;[33] all with a serious finesse and delicacy that convince where a cruder or lighter treatment would merely amuse. Some of these accounts are hardly stories at all, but rather studies in elusive impressions and half-remembered snatches of dream. Plot is everywhere negligible, and atmosphere reigns untrammelled.

John Silence—Physician Extraordinary is a book of five related tales, through which a single character runs his triumphant course. Marred only by traces of the popular and conventional detective-story atmosphere—for Dr. Silence is one of those benevolent geniuses who employ their remarkable powers to aid worthy fellow-men in difficulty—these narratives contain some of the author's best work, and produce an illusion at once emphatic and lasting. The opening tale, "A Psychical Invasion", relates what befell a sensitive author in a house once the scene of dark deeds, and how a legion of fiends was exorcised. "Ancient Sorceries", perhaps the finest tale in the book, gives an almost hypnotically vivid account of an old French town where once the unholy Sabbath was kept by all the people in the form of cats.[34] In "The Nemesis of Fire" a hideous elemental is evoked by new-spilt blood, whilst "Secret Worship" tells of a German school where Satanism held sway, and where long afterward an evil aura remained. "The Camp of the Dog" is a werewolf tale, but is weakened by moralisation and professional "occultism".

Too subtle, perhaps, for definite classification as horror-tales, yet possibly more truly artistic in an absolute sense, are such delicate phantasies as *Jimbo* or *The Centaur*. Mr. Blackwood achieves in these novels a close and palpitant approach to the inmost substance of dream, and works enormous havock with the conventional barriers between reality and imagination.

Unexcelled in the sorcery of crystalline singing prose, and supreme in the creation of a gorgeous and languorous world of iridescently exotic vision, is Edward John Moreton Drax Plunkett, Eighteenth Baron Dunsany, whose tales and short plays form an almost unique element in our literature.[35] Inventor of a new mythology and weaver of surprising folklore, Lord Dunsany stands dedicated to a strange world of fantastic beauty, and pledged to eternal warfare against the coarseness and ugliness of diurnal reality. His point of view is the most truly cosmic of any held in the literature of any period. As sensitive as Poe to dramatic values and the significance of isolated words and details, and far better equipped rhetorically through a simple lyric style based on the prose of the King James Bible, this author draws with tremendous effectiveness on nearly every body of myth and legend within the circle of European culture; producing a composite or eclectic cycle of phantasy in which Eastern colour, Hellenic form, Teutonic sombreness, and Celtic wistfulness are so superbly blended that each sustains and supplements the rest without sacrifice of perfect congruity and homogeneity. In most cases Dunsany's lands are fabulous—"beyond the East", or "at the edge of the world". His system of original personal and place names, with roots drawn from classical, Oriental, and other sources, is a marvel of versatile inventiveness and poetic discrimination; as one may see from such specimens as "Argimenes", "Bethmoora", "Poltarnees", "Camorak", "Illuriel", or "Sardathrion".[36]

Beauty rather than terror is the keynote of Dunsany's work. He loves the vivid green of jade and of copper domes, and the delicate flush of sunset on the ivory minarets of impossible dream-cities. Humour and irony, too, are often present to impart a gentle cynicism and modify what might otherwise possess a naive intensity. Nevertheless, as is inevitable in a master of triumphant unreality, there are occasional touches of cosmic fright which come well within the authentic tradition. Dunsany loves to hint slyly and adroitly of monstrous things and incredible dooms, as one hints in a fairy tale. In *The Book of Wonder* we read of Hlo-hlo, the gigantic spider-idol which does not always stay at home;[37] of what the Sphinx feared in the forest;[38] of Slith, the thief who jumps over the edge of the world after seeing a certain light lit and knowing *who* lit it;[39] of the anthropophagous Gibbelins, who inhabit an evil tower and guard a treasure;[40] of the Gnoles, who live in the forest and from whom it is not well to steal;[41] of the City of Never, and the eyes that watch in the Under Pits;[42] and of kindred things of darkness. *A Dreamer's Tales* tells of the mystery that sent forth all men from Bethmoora in the desert;[43] of the vast gate of Perdóndaris, that was carved from a *single piece* of ivory;[44] and of the voyage of poor old Bill, whose captain cursed the crew and paid calls on nasty-looking isles new-risen from the sea, with low thatched cottages having evil, obscure windows.[45]

Many of Dunsany's short plays are replete with spectral fear. In *The Gods of the Mountain* seven beggars impersonate the seven green idols on a distant hill, and enjoy ease and honour in a city of worshippers until they hear that *the real idols are missing from their wonted seats*. A very ungainly sight in the dusk is reported to them—"rock should not walk in the evening"[46]—and at last, as they sit awaiting the arrival of a troop of dancers, they note that the approaching footsteps are heavier than those of good dancers ought to be. Then things ensue, and in the end the presumptuous blasphemers are turned to green jade statues by the very walking statues whose sanctity they outraged. But mere plot is the very least merit of this marvellously effective play. The incidents and developments are those of a supreme master, so that the whole forms one of the most important contributions of the present age not only to drama, but to literature in general. *A Night at an Inn* tells of four thieves who have stolen the emerald eye of Klesh, a monstrous Hindoo god. They lure to their room and succeed in slaying the three priestly avengers who are on their track, but in the night Klesh comes gropingly for his eye; and having gained it and departed, calls each of the despoilers out into the darkness for an unnamed punishment. In *The Laughter of the Gods* there is a doomed city at the jungle's edge, and a ghostly lutanist heard only by those about to die (cf. Alice's spectral harpsichord in Hawthorne's *House of the Seven Gables*); whilst *The Queen's Enemies*[47] retells the anecdote of Herodotus[48] in which a vengeful princess[49] invites her foes to a subterranean banquet and lets in the Nile to drown them.

But no amount of mere description can convey more than a fraction of Lord Dunsany's pervasive charm. His prismatic cities and unheard-of rites are touched with a sureness which only mastery can engender, and we thrill with a sense of actual participation in his secret mysteries. To the truly imaginative he is a talisman and a key unlocking rich storehouses of dream and fragmentary memory; so that we may think of him not only as a poet, but as one who makes each reader a poet as well.

At the opposite pole of genius from Lord Dunsany, and gifted with an almost diabolic power of calling horror by gentle steps from the midst of prosaic daily life, is the scholarly Montague Rhodes James, Provost of Eton College, antiquary of note, and recognised authority on mediaeval manuscripts and cathedral history.[50] Dr. James, long fond of telling spectral tales at Christmastide, has become by slow degrees a literary weird fictionist of the very first rank; and has developed a distinctive style and method likely to serve as models for an enduring line of disciples.[51]

The art of Dr. James is by no means haphazard, and in the preface to one of his collections[52] he has formulated three very sound rules for macabre composition. A ghost story, he believes, should have a familiar setting in the modern period, in order to approach closely the reader's sphere of experience. Its spectral phenomena, moreover, should be malevolent rather than beneficent; since *fear* is the emotion primarily to be excited. And finally, the technical patois of "occultism" or pseudo-science ought carefully to be avoided; lest the charm of casual verisimilitude be smothered in unconvincing pedantry.[53]

Dr. James, practicing what he preaches, approaches his themes in a light and often conversational way. Creating the illusion of every-day events, he introduces his abnormal phenomena cautiously and gradually; relieved at every turn by touches of homely and prosaic detail, and sometimes spiced with a snatch or two of antiquarian scholarship. Conscious of the close relation between present weirdness and accumulated tradition, he generally provides remote historical antecedents for his incidents; thus being able to utilise very aptly his exhaustive knowledge of the past, and his ready and convincing command of archaic diction and colouring. A favourite scene for a James tale is some centuried cathedral, which the author can describe with all the familiar minuteness of a specialist in that field.

Sly humorous vignettes and bits of life-like genre portraiture and characterisation are often to be found in Dr. James's narratives, and serve in his skilled hands to augment the general effect rather than to spoil it, as the same qualities would tend to do with a lesser craftsman. In inventing a new type of ghost, he has departed considerably from the conventional Gothic tradition; for where the older stock ghosts were pale and stately, and apprehended chiefly through the sense of sight, the average James ghost is lean, dwarfish, and hairy—a sluggish, hellish night-abomination midway betwixt beast and man[54]—and usually *touched* before it is *seen*.[55] Sometimes the spectre is of still more eccentric composition; a roll of flannel with spidery eyes,[56] or an invisible entity which moulds itself in bedding and shews *a face of crumpled linen.*[57] Dr. James has, it is clear, an intelligent and scientific knowledge of human nerves and feelings; and knows just how to apportion statement, imagery, and subtle suggestions in order to secure the best results with his readers. He is an artist in incident and arrangement rather than in atmosphere, and reaches the emotions more often through the intellect than directly. This method, of course, with its occasional absences of sharp climax, has its drawbacks as well as its advantages; and many will miss the thorough atmospheric tension which writers like Machen are careful to build up with words and scenes. But only a few of the tales are open to the charge of tameness. Generally the laconic unfolding of abnormal events in adroit order is amply sufficient to produce the desired effect of cumulative horror.

The short stories of Dr. James are contained in four small collections, entitled respectively *Ghost-Stories of an Antiquary, More Ghost Stories of an Antiquary, A Thin Ghost and Others,* and *A Warning to the Curious.* There is also a delightful juvenile phantasy, *The Five Jars,* which has its spectral adumbrations. Amidst this wealth of material it is hard to select a favourite or especially typical tale, though each reader will no doubt have such preferences as his temperament may determine.

"Count Magnus"[58] is assuredly one of the best, forming as it does a veritable Golconda of suspense and suggestion. Mr. Wraxall is an English traveller of the middle nineteenth century, sojourning in Sweden to secure material for a book. Becoming interested in the ancient family of De la Gardie, near the village of Råbäck, he studies its records; and finds particular fascination in the builder of the existing manor-house, one Count Magnus, of whom strange and terrible things are whispered. The Count, who flourished early in the seventeenth century, was a stern landlord, and famous for his severity toward poachers and delinquent tenants. His cruel punishments were bywords, and there were dark rumours of influences which even survived his interment in the great mausoleum he built near the church—as in the case of the two peasants who hunted on his preserves one night a century after his death. There were hideous screams in the woods, and near the tomb of Count Magnus an unnatural laugh and the clang of a great door. Next morning the priest found the two men; one a maniac, and the other dead, with the flesh of his face sucked from the bones.

Mr. Wraxall hears all these tales, and stumbles on more guarded references to a *Black Pilgrimage* once taken by the Count; a pilgrimage to Chorazin[59] in Palestine, one of the cities denounced by Our Lord in the Scriptures, and in which old priests say that Antichrist is to be born. No one dares to hint just what that Black Pilgrimage was, or what strange being or thing the Count brought back as a companion. Meanwhile Mr. Wraxall is increasingly anxious to explore the mausoleum of Count Magnus, and finally secures permission to do so, in the company of a deacon. He finds several monuments and three copper sarcophagi, one of which is the Count's. Round the edge of this latter are several bands of engraved scenes, including a singular and hideous delineation of a pursuit—the pursuit of a frantic man through a forest by a squat muffled figure with a devil-fish's tentacle, directed by a tall cloaked man on a neighbouring hillock. The sarcophagus has three massive steel padlocks, one of which is lying open on the floor, reminding the traveller of a metallic clash he heard the day before when passing the mausoleum and wishing idly that he might see Count Magnus.

His fascination augmented, and the key being accessible, Mr. Wraxall pays the mausoleum a second and solitary visit and finds another padlock unfastened. The next day, his last in Råbäck, he again goes alone to bid the long-dead Count farewell. Once more queerly impelled to utter a whimsical wish for a meeting with the buried nobleman, he now sees to his disquiet that only one of the padlocks remains on the great sarcophagus. Even as he looks, that last lock drops noisily to the floor, and there comes a sound as of creaking hinges. Then the monstrous lid appears very slowly to rise, and Mr. Wraxall flees in panic fear without refastening the door of the mausoleum.

During his return to England the traveller feels a curious uneasiness about his fellow-passengers on the canal-boat which he employs for the earlier stages. Cloaked figures make him nervous, and he has a sense of being watched and followed. Of twenty-eight persons whom he counts, only twenty-six appear at meals; and the missing two are always a tall cloaked man and a shorter muffled figure. Completing his water travel at Harwich, Mr. Wraxall takes frankly to flight in a closed carriage, but sees two cloaked figures at a crossroad. Finally he lodges at a small house in a village and spends the time making frantic notes. On the second morning he is found dead, and during the inquest seven jurors faint at sight of the body. The house where he stayed is never again inhabited, and upon its demolition half a century later his manuscript is discovered in a forgotten cupboard.[60]

In "The Treasure of Abbot Thomas"[61] a British antiquary unriddles a cipher on some Renaissance painted windows, and thereby discovers a centuried hoard of gold in a niche half way down a well in the courtyard of a German abbey. But the crafty depositor had set a guardian over that treasure, and something in the black well twines its arms around the searcher's neck in such a manner that the quest is abandoned, and a clergyman sent for. Each night after that the discoverer feels a stealthy presence and detects a horrible odour of mould outside the door of his hotel room, till finally the clergyman makes a daylight replacement of the stone at the mouth of the treasure-vault in the well—out of which something had come in the dark to avenge the disturbing of old Abbot Thomas's gold. As he completes his work the cleric observes a curious toad-like carving on the ancient well-head, with the Latin motto *"Depositum custodi*—keep that which is committed to thee."

Other notable James tales are "The Stalls of Barchester Cathedral",[62] in which a grotesque carving comes curiously to life to avenge the secret and subtle murder of an old Dean by his ambitious successor; "'Oh, Whistle, and I'll Come to You, My Lad'",[63] which tells of the horror summoned by a strange metal whistle found in a mediaeval church ruin; and "An Episode of Cathedral History",[64] where the dismantling of a pulpit uncovers an archaic tomb whose lurking daemon spreads panic and pestilence. Dr. James, for all his light touch, evokes fright and hideousness in their most shocking forms; and will certainly stand as one of the few really creative masters in his darksome province.

For those who relish speculation regarding the future, the tale of supernatural horror provides an interesting field. Combated by a mounting wave of plodding realism, cynical flippancy, and sophisticated disillusionment, it is yet encouraged by a parallel tide of growing mysticism, as developed both through the fatigued reaction of "occultists" and religious fundamentalists against materialistic discovery and through the stimulation of wonder and fancy by such enlarged vistas and broken barriers as modern science has given us with its intra-atomic chemistry, advancing astrophysics, doctrines of relativity, and probings into biology and human thought. At the present moment the favouring forces would appear to have somewhat of an advantage; since there is unquestionably more cordiality shewn toward weird writings than when, thirty years ago, the best of Arthur Machen's work fell on the stony ground of the smart and cocksure 'nineties. Ambrose Bierce, almost unknown in his own time, has now reached something like general recognition.[65]

Startling mutations, however, are not to be looked for in either direction. In any case an approximate balance of tendencies will continue to exist; and while we may justly expect a further subtilisation of technique, we have no reason to think that the general position of the spectral in literature will be altered. It is a narrow though essential branch of human expression, and will chiefly appeal as always to a limited audience with keen special sensibilities. Whatever universal masterpiece of tomorrow may be wrought from phantasm or terror will owe its acceptance rather to a supreme workmanship than to a sympathetic theme. Yet who shall declare the dark theme a positive handicap? Radiant with beauty, the Cup of the Ptolemies was carven of onyx.[66]

Appendix

The Favourite Weird Stories of H. P. Lovecraft[1]

Algernon Blackwood: "The Willows"
Arthur Machen: "The Novel of the White Powder"
Arthur Machen: "The Novel of the Black Seal"
Arthur Machen: "The White People"
Edgar Allan Poe: "The Fall of the House of Usher"
M. P. Shiel: "The House of Sounds"
Robert W. Chambers: "The Yellow Sign"[2]
M. R. James: "Count Magnus"
Ambrose Bierce: "The Death of Halpin Frayser"[3]
A. Merritt: "The Moon Pool"[4]

---

[1] The list was prepared by H. C. Koenig and published in the *Fantasy Fan* 2, No. 2 (October 1934): 22.

[2] In a list of best horror stories sent to B. K. Hart, author of the column "The Sideshow" in the *Providence Journal*, HPL listed the above seven stories as "the best" (a list which Hart labelled "a little masterpiece of comparative criticism"—*Providence Journal*, 23 November 1929, p. 2).

[3] In the *Providence Journal* list (see n. 2 above), these two tales, along with Bierce's "The Suitable Surroundings" and de la Mare's "Seaton's Aunt", are listed "as a group of second choices".

[4] HPL refers to the original novelette version (*All-Story*, 22 June 1918), not the later novelisation.

Notes

Introduction

[1] HPL to Lillian D. Clark, 11–14 Nov. 1925 (ms., JHL).

[2] Ibid.

[3] HPL to Lillian D. Clark, 13 Dec. 1925 (ms., JHL).

[4] HPL to Lillian D. Clark, 29–30 Sept. 1924 (ms., JHL).

[5] For Dunsany see *SL* I.91f. For Bierce see *SL* II.222.

[6] See *SL* II.36 (5 January 1926).

[7] HPL to Lillian D. Clark, 5 March 1926 and 6 March 1926 (mss., JHL).

[8] HPL to Lillian D. Clark, 12–13 April 1926 (ms., JHL).

[9] *SL* II.60. This letter is dated July 1926 in *SL*, but this must be an error for July 1927, since the letter mentions the two novels, *The Dream-Quest of Unknown Kadath* and *The Case of Charles Dexter Ward*, written in late 1926 and early 1927, as already complete.

[10] Printed in David E. Schultz's edition of the *Commonplace Book* (West Warwick, RI: Necronomicon Press, 1987), I.14–15.

[11] Cf. *LAL* 86, 97. Cf. also this remark in a letter to J. V. Shea, 8–22 Nov. 1933 (ms., JHL): "[*Etidorhpa* by John Uri Lloyd] just missed inclusion in my article", indicating that the entire revision (or at least the revision of Chapter VIII, where a note on this work would presumably have been included) had already been completed. It is not likely that HPL's remark implies a literary judgment on *Etidorhpa*, i.e. that the novel somehow did not merit inclusion in his article.

[12] "I've prepared a note [about Hodgson] to insert in my article at the proper point (near the end of Ch. IX) & sent it to Hornig." HPL to R. H. Barlow, [22 Aug. 1934] (ms., JHL). This clearly suggests that an entirely revised text had already been sent to Hornig.

[13] "Meanwhile I have already prepared a brief article on the tales of William Hope Hodgson at [Herman C.] Koenig's request—which he will send you in connexion with a biographical article of his own." HPL to Wilson Shepherd, 29 May 1936 (ms., JHL).

[14] This condensation, first published in *Weird Tales* 47, No. 2 (Fall 1973): 52–56, was issued separately by Conover as *Supernatural Horror in Literature as Revised in 1936* (Arlington, VA: Carrollton-Clark, 1974), and was also included in *LAL* 147–53.

[15] Review of *Supernatural Horror in Literature* (Ben Abramson, 1945), *American Literature* 18 (1946): 175.

[16] Cf. *The Supernatural in Fiction* (1952); portions reprinted in *FDOC* 63f. (but cf. my note ad loc.).

[17] Cf. *Elegant Nightmares: The English Ghost Story from LeFanu to Blackwood* (Athens: Ohio University Press, 1978), p. 32.

[18] Letter to the editor, *Times Literary Supplement,* 17 July 1981, p. 814. This letter was in response to S. S. Prawer's praise of "Supernatural Horror in Literature" in his review of *FDOC* in *Times Literary Supplement,* 19 June 1981, p. 687.

[19] HPL's citation of Pliny the Younger's letter to Sura (*D* 371) derives from Joseph Lewis French's *Masterpieces of Mystery* (1920), where the item was included. HPL's mention of Phlegon's "Philinnion and Machates" (*D* 371) probably derives from Lacy Collison-Morley's *Greek and Roman Ghost Stories* (1912; rpt. Chicago: Argonaut, 1968); see n. 21 to Chapter 2.

[20] *Odyssey,* Book XI (Odysseus).

[21] *Georgics,* Book IV (Orpheus); *Aeneid,* Book VI (Aeneas).

[22] *Metamorphoses,* Book X (Orpheus)—a probable parody of Vergil.

[23] "The horrible death of Glauce and Creon is described exhaustively in the terrible style of which Euripides was such a master. It is sheer Grand Guignol." H. D. F. Kitto, *Greek Tragedy* (1939), ch. 8.

[24] Lucian's work was probably an influence upon *The Dream-Quest of Unknown Kadath,* for both works contain an almost identical scene where a galley suddenly leaps into space. For Catullus cf. "The Rats in the Walls" (1923): "The reference to Atys made me shiver, for I had read Catullus and knew something of the hideous rites of the Eastern god, whose worship was so mixed with that of Cybele" (*DH* 37).

[25] T. O. Mabbott, in his review of *The Outsider and Others* in *American Literature* 12 (1940): 136, remarks that HPL "tends to underrate Stevenson", while both he and Edmund Wilson ("Tales of the Marvellous and the Ridiculous" [1945]; rpt. in *FDOC* 46f.) feel that HPL's praise for Dunsany is excessive (Wilson also feels that HPL rated Machen too highly). None of these judgments has been supported by subsequent criticism.

[26] "Introduction to the Dover Edition" of *Supernatural Horror in Literature* (New York: Dover, 1973), p. viii.

[27] *Elegant Nightmares,* p. 5.

[28] "Introduction" to *Supernatural Horror in Literature* (New York: Ben Abramson, 1945), p. 10.

[29] HPL did not, incidentally, read Dorothy Scarborough's *The Supernatural in Modern English Fiction* (1917) until March 1932; cf. HPL to August Derleth, 31 Mar. 1932 (envelope; ms., SHSW). He charitably says that it is "Rather good as far as it goes." He read Eino Railo's *The Haunted Castle: A Study of the Elements of English Romanticism* (1927) only after writing his essay (cf. *SL* II.186).

[30] Cf. S. T. Joshi, *Lovecraft's Library: A Catalogue,* rev. ed. (www.necropress), no. 942. HPL read the biographies of Hervey Allen and Joseph Wood Krutch after writing his essay.

[31] HPL to August Derleth, 6 November 1931 (ms., SHSW).

[32]"The Lord of R'lyeh" (1945), rpt. *Lovecraft Studies* No. 7 (Fall 1982): 12.

Supernatural Horror in Literature
I. Introduction

[1]Cf. "The Defence Reopens!" (1921): "It is not his [the fantaisiste's] business to fashion a pretty trifle to please the children, to point a useful moral, to concoct superficial 'uplift' stuff for the mid-Victorian hold-over, or to rehash insolvable human problems didactically" (*IDOD* 11).

[2]Cf. "The Defence Reopens!": "[The fantaisiste] is the poet of twilight visions and childhood memories, but sings only for the sensitive" (*IDOD* 12).

[3]HPL always maintained a certain scorn for the psychological theories of Sigmund Freud, although recognising their revolutionary import upon culture: note the passing reference, "Freud to the contrary with his puerile symbolism" (*D* 23), in the first paragraph of the revised version of "Beyond the Wall of Sleep".

[4]The following anthropological analysis is probably derived from HPL's reading of such important scholarly volumes as E. B. Tylor's *Primitive Culture* (1871), John Fiske's *Myths and Myth-Makers* (1872), and Sir James George Frazer's *The Golden Bough* (1890–1915).

[5]A reflection of HPL's adherence to the central tenet of Epicureanism, where the goal of life is the maximisation of pleasure through the minimisation of pain and the resultant attainment of tranquillity (*ataraxia*). Cf. *SL* I.87, 135; "Life for Humanity's Sake" (*MW* 145–46).

[6]HPL was to make this conception the basis for many of his finest tales, particularly such "cosmic" works as *At the Mountains of Madness* (1931) ands "The Shadow out of Time" (1934–35).

[7]I.e. the *conte cruel*. See below (p. 41).

[8]"I don't care for humour as an ingredient of the weird tale—in fact, I think it is a definitely diluting element" (*SL* IV.83). HPL was probably thinking of such works as Wilde's "The Canterville Ghost" and H. G. Wells' "The Inexperienced Ghost". That HPL was not above including very subtle humour in his own work, and that this practice was consonant with the theory here expressed, is indicated by Donald R. Burleson, "Humour beneath Horror", *Lovecraft Studies* No. 2 (Spring 1980): 5f.

[9]Cf. "Notes on Writing Weird Fiction" (1933): "I choose weird stories because they suit my inclination best—one of my strongest and most persistent wishes being to achieve, momentarily, the illusion of some strange suspension or violation of the galling limitations of time, space, and natural law which forever imprison us and frustrate our curiosity about the infinite cosmic spaces beyond the radius of our sight and analysis"

(*MW* 113). On the philosophical significance of this idea see S. T. Joshi, "'Reality' and Knowledge", *Lovecraft Studies* No. 3 (Fall 1980): 17f.

[10] Cf. HPL's similar strictures in regard to science fiction: "Social and political satire is always undesirable, since such intellectual and ulterior objects detract from the story's power as a crystallisation of a mood." "Some Notes on Interplanetary Fiction" (*MW* 120). HPL's hostility to didacticism in literature was of long standing.

[11] A clear reference to Ann Radcliffe and her followers; see below (pp. 9–10).

II. The Dawn of the Horror-Tale

[1] The reference is presumably to the first Book of Enoch; there are two others. Enoch was the seventh patriarch from Adam (Genesis 5:18), around whose name many works and legends clustered. The Book of Enoch (part of the Pseudepigrapha of the Old Testament) is a composite work dating roughly to the second and first centuries B.C. and relates Enoch's voyages through the heavens; one section contains a prophetic account of the dissolution of the universe. For a translation see R. H. Charles, *The Apocrypha and Pseudepigrapha of the Old Testament* (Oxford, 1913; rpt. 1963), Vol. II.

[2] The Clavicula (singular) or Key of Solomon is a book of Jewish magic of unknown date; it claims to date to great antiquity, but has been known only since the sixteenth century. Its two books (the Greater Key and the Lesser Key) discuss such things as magic spells, rituals, talismans, and evocations of spirits. The first English translation was *The Key of Solomon the King,* tr. S. Liddell MacGregor Mathers (London: Redway, 1889).

[3] For cabbalism see below (p. 41).

[4] Syncopated form of "grand dame"; cf. "The Nameless City" (1921): "There is no legend so old as to give it a name, or to recall that it was ever alive; but it is told of in whispers around campfires and muttered about by grandams in the tents of sheiks" (*D* 98).

[5] This idea was derived by HPL from Margaret A. Murray's *The Witch-Cult in Western Europe* (Oxford: Clarendon Press, 1921); cf. *SL* III.181. It is no longer accepted by anthropologists.

[6] For HPL's connexion of Murray's witch-cult theory with the Salem witch trials see *SL* III.178f.

[7] Albertus Magnus (1193?–1280), French Aristotelian and tutor of St. Thomas Aquinas, was said to have communed with the devil and practised magic. Twenty-one volumes of alchemy are attributed to him; few are probably authentic. His *Opera Omnia* have been edited by Bernhard Geyer (Westfalen: Aschendorff, 1951f.). See Paola Zambelli, *The* Speculum Astronomiae *and Its Enigma: Astrology, Theology, and Science in Albertus Magnus and His Contemporaries* (1992).

[8] Raymond Lully (c. 1235–1316), or Ramon Lull, Spanish Platonist, wrote a number of alchemical works and was renowned throughout Europe. His works have been edited in Catalan by M. Obrador et al. (1905–32; 21 vols.). See also J. N. Hillgarth, *Ramon Hill and Lullism in Fourteenth-Century France* (1971); E. A. Peers, *Ramon Lull: A Biography* (1929); A. E. Waite, *Raymond Lully, Illuminated Doctor, Alchemist and Christian Mystic* (1922).

[9] For the gargoyle theme in HPL see George T. Wetzel, "The Cthulhu Mythos: A Study" (*FDOC* 88f.). Wetzel traces the mentions of gargoyles in HPL's *Commonplace Book* to George Macdonald's *Phantastes* (not mentioned in SHL).

[10] Nostradamus (Michel de Notredame, 1503–1566) wrote a series of prophecies that were ultimately published as the *Centuries* and placed on the *Index Expurgatorius*. For texts see *The Complete Prophecies of Nostradamus*, tr. Henry C. Roberts (1947); *The Prophecies of Nostradamus*, tr. Erika Cheetham (1974). See also Charles A. Ward, *Oracles of Nostradamus* (1892), Roger Frontenac, *Le Clef secrète de Nostradamus* (1950), and James Randi, *The Mask of Nostradamus* (1993).

[11] Johannes Trithemius (1462–1516), German abbot and mystic, wrote several curious religious and philosophical works, including *Steganographia* (1500; publ. 1606) and *De Lapide Philosophorum* (1619), the latter cited (inaccurately) by HPL in *The Case of Charles Dexter Ward* (*MM* 121). See Noel L. Brann, *The Abbot Trithemius (1462–1516): The Renaissance of Monastic Humanism* (1981) and Wayne Shumaker, *Renaissance Curiosa* (1982).

[12] John Dee (1527–1608) was the celebrated English statesman, mathematician, and royal astrologer for Queen Elizabeth. Frank Belknap Long in "The Space-Eaters" (1927) made him the first English translator of HPL's *Necronomicon*, and HPL follows Long (see "History of the *Necronomicon*" [1927; *MW* 53]). George Hay's hoax, *The Necronomicon* (1978), purports to be an edition of the surviving fragments of Dee's translation. For Dee see Daivd McCormick, *John Dee, Scientist, Geographer, Astrologer and Secret Agent to Elizabeth I* (1968), Francis A. Yates, *Theatre of the World* (1969), Peter J. French, *John Dee: The World of an Elizabethan Magus* (London: Routledge & Kegan Paul, 1972), and Nicholas H. Clulee, *John Dee's Natural Philosophy* (1988).

[13] Robert Fludd (1574–1637), English physician and Rosicrucian, influenced strongly by Paracelsus, wrote a number of astrological and alchemical works, including *Clavis Philosophiae et Alchymiae* (1633) and *Philosophia Moysaica* (1638). See J. B. Craven, *Doctor Robert Fludd* (1902), Serge Hutin, *Robert Fludd* (Paris, 1971), Allen G. Debus, *Chemistry, Alchemy and the New Philosophy 1550–1700* (1987), and William H. Huffman, *Robert Fludd and the End of the Renaissance* (1988). Fludd is also mentioned by HPL in *The Case of Charles Dexter Ward* (*MM* 121).

[14] From the Greek *psychopompos* or "conveyer of the dead" (attribute of Hermes). Used by HPL in the poem "Psychopompos" (1917–18) and in "The Dunwich Horror"

(1928), where whippoorwills are the psychopomps. See also below on Hawthorne's *House of the Seven Gables* (p. 30).

[15] Cf. "Psychopompos": "I am He who howls in the night; . . . My breath is the north wind's breath" (ll. 1, 7).

[16] An important device in HPL, connecting with his use of the *hybris* or Faust theme. Cf. such of his characters as Joseph Curwen (*The Case of Charles Dexter Ward*) and Ephraim/Asenath Waite ("The Thing on the Doorstep").

[17] Sabine Baring-Gould (1834–1924), *Curious Myths of the Middle Ages* (1866; *LL* 66). For the influence of this volume on HPL's "The Rats in the Walls" see Steven J. Mariconda, "Baring-Gould and the Ghouls", *Crypt of Cthulhu* No. 14 (St John's Eve 1983): 3–7, 27. A modern reprint of this work (London: Jupiter Books, 1977) is greatly abridged.

[18] I.e. chapters 61–62 of the *Satyricon*. The work as we have it is a small fraction of the original.

[19] Presumably the novel, the *Metamorphoses* or *Golden Ass;* other of Apuleius' works are philosophical.

[20] Almost nothing is known about Phlegon of Tralles, freedman of the Emperor Hadrian (r. A.D. 117–38). Aside from the work mentioned here, he wrote a treatise on long-lived individuals and on the Olympiads.

[21] Since Phlegon's work has never been fully translated into English, HPL probably derived his information on it from Lacy Collison-Morley's *Greek and Roman Ghost Stories* (1912), where the story of Philinnion and Machates is translated on pp. 67–71.

[22] Proclus, a fifth-century Platonist, apparently retold the tale of Phlegon in a work called "How One Ought to Believe the Soul Enters and Leaves the Body" (*Pos dei noein eisienai kai exienai psychen apo somatos*); see Lacy Collison-Morley, *Greek and Roman Ghost Stories*, pp. 65f.

[23] The Eddas are two works of Old Icelandic literature (the *Elder Edda*, in verse, and the *Younger Edda*, in prose) dealing with Norse mythology; the first dates from the 8th to the 12th centuries C.E., and the second from the 13th century.

[24] The Sagas are a variety of Icelandic works composed in the 12th and 13th centuries C.E. relating Norse myth, history, and other accounts. Contrary to what HPL suggests, they are in prose.

[25] Ymir was, in Norse myth, a giant born from icy chaos who gave birth to a daughter, Bestla, and two sons, Mimir and the six-headed child sprung from his feet. He and his horde were slain by Odin.

[26] The *Nibelungenlied* (Song of the Nibelungs) is a narrative poem written in Middle High German in 1204 relating myths of ancient Germany. Richard Wagner used them as well as the Norse sagas as the basis for his opera-cycle, *The Ring of the Nibelungs*.

[27] These episodes come, respectively, from Book V, Chapter 15; Book XXI, Chapter 3; and Book XIII, Chapter 12.

[28] James I of England (r. 1603–25) himself wrote a treatise on witchcraft, *Daemonologie* (1597).

[29] For which see George L. Barr, "The Literature of Witchcraft", *Papers of the American Historical Association* 4 (1890): 237–66.

[30] Viz., Charles Drelincourt's *Christian's Defence against the Fears of Death* (1675). This account of the genesis and purpose of Defoe's tract has now been discredited; see R. M. Baine, *Daniel Defoe and the Supernatural* (1968), pp. 105f.

[31] *The Arabian Nights' Entertainments* were translated into French by Antoine Galland (1704–12), and his rendition was then translated into English (1706f.). German translations of Galland's version followed in 1759f.

[32] For which see Patricia Meyer Spacks, *The Insistence of Horror: Aspects of the Supernatural in Eighteenth-Century Poetry* (Cambridge, MA: Harvard University Press, 1962).

[33] See esp. ch. 47 ("The Art of Borrowing further explained, and an Account of a Strange Phenomenon") and ch. 62 ("His [Fathom's] Return to England and Midnight-Pilgrimage to Monimia's Tomb").

III. The Early Gothic Novel

[1] "Ossian" is an invention of the Scottish poet James Macpherson, who attempted to pass off some poetry he had written as translations of the fragments of the ancient Scottish poet Ossian. The chief works he produced were *Fingal* (1762) and *Temora* (1763). The hoax was exploded in the early nineteenth century.

[2] Hogg also wrote a weird novel, *The Private Memoirs and Confessions of a Justified Sinner* (1824), and a variety of weird short stories.

[3] The date on the first edition is 1765, but it was published on Christmas Day of 1764.

[4] For which see A. T. Hazen, *A Bibliography of Horace Walpole* (New Haven: Yale University Press, 1948), pp. 52f.

[5] Of which the earliest was Robert Jephson's *The Count of Narbonne: A Tragedy* (1781).

[6] See K. K. Mehrotra, *Horace Walpole and the English Novel* (1934).

[7] Other works of fantasy by Walpole are the play *The Mysterious Mother* (1768) and *Hieroglyphic Tales* (1785).

[8] "Have you read *The Castle of Otranto* itself? If not, *don't!* Let the summary [in Birkhead's *The Tale of Terror*] continue to give you a 'kick', for the original certainly won't! Walpole was too steeped in the classical tradition of the early 18th century to

catch the Gothic spirit of the latter half. His choice of words and rhythm is the brisk, cheerful Addisonian one; and his nonchalant and atmosphereless way of describing the most prodigious horrors is enough to empty them of all their potency" (*SL* II.231).

[9] Used by HPL himself in varying degrees in "The Alchemist" (1908), "The Tomb" (1917), "The Picture in the House" (1920), "The Outsider" (1921), "The Hound" (1922), "The Lurking Fear" (1922), "The Rats in the Walls" (1923), "The Shunned House" (1924), "The Strange High House in the Mist" (1926), *The Case of Charles Dexter Ward* (1927), and "The Dreams in the Witch House" (1932).

[10] Used in *The Case of Charles Dexter Ward*.

[11] Perhaps one of the sources for HPL's creation of such mythical books as the *Necronomicon*.

[12] Used in a masterly fashion in "The Rats in the Walls" (although there it may have been borrowed from Poe's "Metzengerstein" and other tales).

[13] For Walpole's remarks on "Sir Bertrand" see Walpole to William Mason, 8 April 1778 (*Correspondence,* Yale Ed., 28.382) and Walpole to Robert Jephson, 27 January 1780 (*Correspondence,* Yale Ed., 41.410). Walpole discusses *The Old English Baron* in the above two letters as well as in letters to William Cole, 17 August 1778 and 22 August 1778 (*Correspondence,* Yale Ed., II.107–10). In the letter to Jephson he remarks: "I cannot compliment the author of *The Old English Baron,* professedly written in imitation, but as a corrective of *The Castle of Otranto.* It was totally void of imagination and interest; had scarce any incidents; and though it condemned the marvellous, admitted a ghost—I suppose the author thought a tame ghost might come within the laws of probability."

[14] As *Edmond, Orphan of the Castle* (1799) by John Broster; published anonymously.

[15] *Le Vieux Baron anglais, ou les revenants vengés,* tr. M. d[e] l[a] P[lace] (Paris: Didot, 1787). There was also a German translation, *Der alte Englische,* tr. F. S———t (Nurnberg, 1789).

[16] This was *Castle Connor, an Irish Story.* Another (extant) Gothic novel by Reeve is *The Exiles; or, Memoirs of the Count de Cronstadt* (1788).

[17] A reference to William Godwin; see below (p. 34).

[18] For the possibility that the title inspired HPL's similar title "Arthur Jermyn" (i.e. "Facts concerning the Late Arthur Jermyn and His Family") see Barton L. St Armand, "Facts in the Case of H. P. Lovecraft" (*FDOC* 184n.17). Jermyn, however, is a British noble family of long standing.

[19] HPL later confessed (HPL to R. H. Barlow, 1 December 1934; ms., JHL) that he never read the entirety of *Wieland* but only the excerpt printed in Vol. 9 of Julian Hawthorne's *The Lock and Key Library* (1909), which he acquired in New York in 1922.

[20]Cf. HPL's villain Joseph Curwen in *The Case of Charles Dexter Ward*. HPL remarks on the variant spellings of the name: ". . . the Curwens or Corwins of Salem needed no introduction in New England" (*MM* 120).

[21]Other weird works by Brown are *Jane Talbot* (1801), *Clara Howard* (1801), and some short stories.

IV. The Apex of Gothic Romance

[1]Actually, *Tales of Wonder* is an anthology of ballads edited by Lewis and containing the work of Southey, Sir Walter Scott, Lewis himself, and others. *Tales of Terror* (1801, not 1799) is a parody of *Tales of Wonder,* and was probably not written or edited by Lewis at all.

[2]For a chronological list see Mehrotra (note 6 to chapter 3), pp. 173f.; see also Frederick S. Frank in *Horror Literature,* ed. Marshall Tymn (New York: Bowker, 1981), pp. 34–175.

[3]For the importance of "self-expression" in HPL's aesthetic theory, see "The Defence Remains Open!" (1921): "There are probably seven persons, in all, who really like my work; and they are enough. I should write even if I were the only patient reader, for my aim is merely self-expression" (*IDOD* 21).

[4]See Balzac's prefatory note to the first appearance of "Melmoth Reconcilié", in *Le Livre des conteurs* (1835): "Ce roman [i.e. Melmoth] est pris dans l'idée mère à laquelle nous devions déjà le drame de Faust, et dans laquelle Lord Byron nous a taillé depuis Manfred" (rpt. *Oeuvres Complètes* [Paris; Guy le Prat, 1961], Vol. 18).

[5]Scott corresponded with Maturin between 1812 and 1824 (see *The Correspondence of Sir Walter Scott and Charles Robert Maturin* [Austin: University of Texas Press, 1937]), and also reviewed Maturin's *Fatal Revenge* (*Quarterly Review* 3 [1810]: 339f.) and his *Women* (*Edinburgh Review* 30 [1818]: 234f.).

[6]Henry Dunn, friend and associate of Dante Gabriel Rossetti, records: "According to his brother, any writing about devils, spectres, or the supernatural generally, whether in poetry or prose, had a fascination for him; at one time—say 1844—his supreme delight was the blood-curdling romance of Maturin, *Melmoth the Wanderer*" (Gale Pedrick, *Life with Rossetti* [London: Macdonald, 1964], p. 96). In *Dante Gabriel Rossetti as Designer and Writer* (London: Cassell, 1889) William Michael Rossetti records that in 1843, when Rossetti was fifteen, he began a "thriller" entitled *Sorrentino* (non-extant), inspired by a wide reading of Gothic romance, among which *Melmoth* is cited (pp. 123–25).

[7]In recounting to George Henry Lewes his meeting with Goethe in 1830, Thackeray says the following: "His [Goethe's] eyes [were] extraordinarily dark, piercing and brilliant. I felt quite afraid before them, and recollect comparing them to the eyes of the hero of a certain romance called *Melmoth the Wanderer,* which used to alarm us boys

thirty years ago; eyes of an individual who had made a bargain with a Certain Person, and at an extreme old age retained these eyes in all their awful splendour." Letter to George Henry Lewes, 28 April 1855; quoted in Lewes' *The Life and Works of Goethe* (Boston: Ticknor & Fields, 1856), II.450–51.

[8] In his essay "De l'essence du rire et géneralement du comique dans les arts plastiques" [On the Essence of Laughter and, in General, the Comic in the Plastic Arts] Baudelaire speaks of Melmoth, "La grande création satanique du reverend Maturin" [the great Satanic creation of the reverend Maturin], and goes on to say: "Quoi du plus grand, quoi de plus puissant relativement à la pauvre humanité que ce pâle et ennuyé Melmoth?" [What could be greater, what could be more powerful in relation to feeble humanity than this pale and weary Melmoth?] *Curiosités esthétiques*, ed. F.-F. Gautier (Paris: Editions de la Nouvelle Revue Française, 1925), p. 342.

[9] From Reading Gaol, Wilde wrote: "Mr Melmoth is my name: so let it be that." (Letter to Reginald Turner, [17 May 1897].) In the year of his death he wrote: "You asked me about 'Melmoth': of course I have not changed my name. . . . But to prevent postmen having fits I sometimes have my letters inscribed with the name of a curious novel by my grand-uncle, Maturin: a novel that was part of the romantic revival of the early century, and though imperfect, a pioneer: it is still read in France and Germany. . . . I laugh at it, but it thrilled Europe, and is played as a play in modern Spain." (Letter to Louis Wilkinson, [4 January 1900].) *Letters of Oscar Wilde*, ed. Rupert Hart-Davis (London: Hart-Davis, 1962), pp. 555, 813. In a note Hart-Davis writes: "Robert Ross and More Adley had collaborated in an anonymous biographical introduction to a new edition of the novel in 1892, and Ross suggested this alias to Wilde. The Christian name Sebastian was probably in memory of the martyred saint" (p. 555).

[10] Cf. a similar idea in HPL's *The Case of Charles Dexter Ward*, where the portrait of Joseph Curwen is said to follow young Charles about the room with its eyes (*MM* 162).

[11] Note the similar mark ("a very peculiar mole or blackish spot" [*MM* 108]) which distinguishes Joseph Curwen from Ward in *The Case of Charles Dexter Ward*.

[12] HPL is forced into this hesitant circumlocution because he never read the whole of Melmoth but only two large excerpts of it, in Julian Hawthorne's *Lock and Key Library* (1909) and George Saintsbury's *Tales of Mystery* (see n. 13 below). Late in life W. Paul Cook gave him a three-volume edition of the novel (London: Richard Bentley & Son, 1892); see *SL* V.92.

[13] George Saintsbury, "Introduction" to *Tales of Mystery: Mrs. Radcliffe, Lewis, Maturin* (New York: Macmillan, 1891), p. xxviii.

[14] Edith Birkhead, *The Tale of Terror* (New York: E. P. Dutton, 1921), p. 93.

[15] As *Melmoth the Wanderer: A Melo-dramatic Romance, in Three Acts* (Baltimore: J. Robinson, 1831). The adapter is unknown.

[16] Among Maturin's voluminous writings the tragedy *Bertram* (1816) can classify as weird.

V. The Aftermath of Gothic Fiction

[1] Among von Grosse's other works is *Der Dolch* (translated as *The Dagger*).

[2] For a list of Mrs Roche's voluminous writings see Montague Summers, *A Gothic Bibliography* (London: Fortune Press, 1940), p. 163.

[3] Other Gothic novels by Charlotte Dacre are *Confessions of the Nun of St. Omer* (1805), *The Libertine* (1807), and *The Passions* (1811).

[4] For Beckford's influence on HPL see Peter Cannon, "The Influence of *Vathek* on H. P. Lovecraft's *The Dream-Quest of Unknown Kadath*" (*FDOC* 153–57). HPL also remarks that his unfinished work "Azathoth" (1922) was to have been a "weird Vathek-like novel" (*SL* 1.185). HPL first read *Vathek* around July 1921 (HPL to Rheinhart Kleiner, 30 July 1921; AHT).

[5] See n. 31 to chapter 2.

[6] A reference, perhaps, to Samuel Johnson's short novel *Rasselas, Prince of Abissinia* (1759).

[7] Residence of Abdul Alhazred when he wrote the *Necronomicon* ("History of the *Necronomicon*" [*MW* 52]).

[8] "Arabesque" with the capital A means "Arabian"; so used frequently by HPL.

[9] Persepolis, one of the major centres of the Persian empire, was destroyed by Alexander the Great and his companions, according to tradition, in 331 B.C.E. during a drunken bout (cf. Curtius, *Histories* 5.7f.). Istakhar, or Istakhr, was a later Muslim fortress built near the ruins of Persepolis.

[10] London: William Heinemann, 1910. Lewis Melville was the pseudonym of Benjamin S. Lewis. HPL later lent his copy of *The Episodes of Vathek* to Clark Ashton Smith and urged him to complete the unfinished third episode, which Smith did.

[11] Another work of fantasy by Beckford is *The Vision* (first published 1930). His *Travel-Diaries* (first published 1928) also contain some weird passages.

[12] A band of mystics arising in the late sixteenth century and believing in alchemy, astrology, and the occult in general. The term is probably derived from the Latin *rosa* (rose) and *crux* (cross); the symbol of the order was a rose crucified in the centre of a cross. A. E. Waite's *The Real History of the Rosicrucians* (1887) brought the order into publicity. See now Hargrave Jennings, *The Rosicrucians: Their Rites and Mysteries* (1907), Waite, *The Brotherhood of the Rosy Cross* (1924), Paul Arnold, *Histoire des rose-croix et les origines de la franc-maçonnerie* (1955), Francis A. Yates, *The Rosicrucian Enlightenment* (1972), and J. Gordon Melton, ed., *Rosucricianism in America* (1990).

[13] Alessandro, Conte di Cagliostro [Giuseppe Balsamo] (1743–1795), Sicilian charlatan who held séances throughout France and Italy. Banished from France by Louis XVI in 1786, he was later condemned as a heretic by his wife and spent his last years impris-

oned in the fortress of San Leo. See W. R. H. Trowbridge, *Cagliostro: The Splendour and Misery of a Master of Magic* (1910), Marc Haven [*pseud.*], *Le Maitre inconnu, Cagliostro* (1912; rev. ed. 1932), Grete de Francesco, *The Power of the Charlatan* (1939), and Philippe Brunet, *Cagliostro: Biographie* (1992). Alexandre Dumas *père* wrote two historical romances, *Les Mémoires d'un médicin* (1846; *The Memoirs of a Physician*) and *Le Collier de la reine* (1849; *The Queen's Necklace*) involving Cagliostro.

[14] As *The Book of the Magi* (Boston: W. W. Harmon, 1896).

[15] For a list of the stupendously prolific output of George W. M. Reynolds, see Summers, *A Gothic Bibliography*, pp. 146f.

[16] George Colman, *The Iron Chest: A Play in Three Acts* (Dublin, 1796), with music to the songs by Stephen Storace. Henry Irving staged the play in 1879.

[17] Godwin, of course, is best known for such political and historical works as *An Enquiry concerning Political Justice* (1793), *Of Population* (1820), and *History of the Commonwealth of England* (1824–28). He also wrote a memoir of his wife, the celebrated feminist Mary Wollstonecraft, *A Memoir of the Author of* A Vindication of the Rights of Woman (1798), and the curious *Lives of the Necromancers* (1834). Godwin also wrote several other novels, including *Mandeville* (1817), *Imogen* (1784), and *Fleetwood* (1804).

[18] Byron conceived the idea for a ghost story but only wrote a few pages (see Leslie A. Marchand, *Byron: A Biography* [New York: Knopf, 1947], II.628f.). These are reprinted in E. F. Bleiler, ed., *The Castle of Otranto* [et al.] (New York: Dover, 1966). Byron was also said to have provided the plot for Polidori's "The Vampyre". P. B. Shelley apparently never began a work.

[19] One hardly need remark on the similarity to HPL's "Herbert West—Reanimator" (1921–22), although West reanimates entire corpses and does not assemble disparate fragments of them.

[20] Mary Shelley also wrote the novels *Valperga* (1823), *Lodore* (1835), *Falkner* (1837), and *Mathilda* (ed. Elizabeth Nichie; Chapel Hill, NC: University of North Carolina Press, 1959). Her *Collected Tales and Stories* was edited by Charles E. Robinson (Baltimore: Johns Hopkins University Press, 1976).

[21] Moore's verses are quoted in both "The Nameless City" (1921) and "Under the Pyramids" (1924).

[22] Some of De Quincey's works which border upon the weird are the celebrated *Confessions of an English Opium-Eater* (1821f., rev. 1856), "On Murder Considered as One of the Fine Arts" (1827), "Suspiria de Profundis" (1845), "The English Mail Coach" (1849), and "The Vision of Sudden Death" (1849).

[23] "As for me—my current diversion is still the writing of that . . . article on the weird tale, and the reading and re-reading appertaining thereto. I want to know, to a slight extent, what I'm talking about—though I shall doubtless mention scores of things I

never even glanced at. I wonder if William Harrison Ainsworth is worth reading?" (*SL* II.37–38). Apparently HPL never read him. Among his novels most clearly related to the weird are *The Tower of London* (1840), *Guy Fawkes* (1841), *Windsor Castle* (1843), *The Lancashire Witches* (1849), and *Auriol; or, The Elixir of Life* (1865).

[24] Actually, "The Werewolf" is only a chapter from *The Phantom Ship*.

[25] Another work of weird fiction by Marryat is *Snarleyyow; or, The Dog Fiend* (1837).

[26] Other works of fantasy by Dickens (mostly whimsical) are *A Christmas Carol* (1843), *The Chimes* (1844), *The Cricket on the Hearth* (1845), *The Haunted Man and the Ghost's Bargain* (1848), and several short stories now collected as *The Supernatural Short Stories of Charles Dickens*, ed. Michael Hayes (London: J. Calder; Dallas: Riverrun Press, 1978). Many of these short tales were insertions in his novels.

[27] On the rise of spiritualism in HPL's day see his essay, "Merlinus Redivivus" (1918); rpt. *The Conservative* (West Warwick, RI: Necronomicon Press, 1990), pp. 29–30.

[28] The Comte de Saint-Germain (d. 1784?), whose real name is not known, practised feats of magic at the court of Louis XV from 1748 to about 1755. According to Cagliostro he later went to Germany and became the founder of freemasonry.

[29] Certainly an evocatively Lovecraftian title, perhaps leading to his own title "The Thing on the Doorstep" (1933). See also Robert Hichens' weird novel *The Dweller on the Threshold* (1911).

[30] The Chaldaeans, inhabiting the area now represented by southern Iraq, were known to the ancients as adepts in astronomy and astrology: cf. Herodotus 1.182f., Diodorus Siculus 2.29f., Lucretius 5.727f., Tacitus, *Annales* 6.20, 12.52 et al., Juvenal 6.553f. See Franz Cumont, *Astrology and Religion among the Greeks and Romans* (1912), and Hans Lewy, *Chaldaean Oracles and Theurgy* (1956).

[31] Note the Australian setting employed by HPL in "The Shadow out of Time" (1934–35).

[32] Note the similar baying of dogs when Dr Willett utters the spell destroying Joseph Curwen in *The Case of Charles Dexter Ward* (*MM* 233).

[33] (1810–1875). See such of Constant's writings as *The History of Magic* (1913) and *Transcendental Magic* (1896), both tr. A. E. Waite; also Paul Chacornac, *Eliphas Lévi, le rénovateur de l'occultisme en France* (1925) and Alain Mercier, *Eliphas Levi et la pensée magique au XIXe siècle* (1974). Lévi is cited in *The Case of Charles Dexter Ward* (*MM* 170, 216).

[34] For Apollonius of Tyana (fl. 1st c. C.E.), the wandering Pythagorean philosopher and mystic, see Philostratus' rather fanciful biography (ed. and tr. F. C. Conybeare [London & New York, 1912]; tr. J. S. Phillimore [Oxford, 1912]; tr. Charles P. Eells [Stanford, 1923]); also G. R. S. Mead, *Apollonius of Tyana* (1901), F. W. Groves Campbell, *Apollonius of Tyana* (1908), and Jaap-Jan Flinterman, *Power, Paideia and Pythagoreanism* (1995).

[35]Of the voluminous work of LeFanu (1814–1873), which included fifteen novels and many short stories, the most notable are these: *The House by the Churchyard* (1863; rpt. New York: AMS Press, 1975), *Wylder's Hand* (1864; rpt. New York: Dover, 1978), *Uncle Silas* (1864; rpt. New York: Dover, 1966), *All in the Dark* (1866), and *The Wyvern Mystery* (1869) among the novels; of short story collections, the celebrated *In a Glass Darkly* (1872), *The Purcell Papers* (1880; rpt. with different contents by Arkham House, 1975), and *Madam Crowl's Ghost and Other Tales of Mystery*, ed. M. R. James (1923). His best short work has been reprinted in two volumes from Dover, *Best Ghost Stories* (1964) and *Ghost Stories and Mysteries* (1975), both ed. E. F. Bleiler. See also S. M. Ellis, *Wilkie Collins, Le Fanu and Others* (1931; with bibliographies); Nelson Browne, *Sheridan Le Fanu* (1951); W. J. McCormack, *Sheridan Le Fanu and Victorian England* (Oxford, 1980); and the chapters on LeFanu in Jack Sullivan's *Elegant Nightmares* (1978).

The slight notice accorded to LeFanu—now recognised as a major weird writer of the nineteenth century—is perhaps HPL's greatest critical misjudgment in this essay. He had been prejudiced against LeFanu after reading the rather tedious *House by the Churchyard*, but even when, in 1932, he read "Green Tea" (in Dorothy L. Sayers' *Omnibus of Crime*), he did not change his opinion significantly: "It is certainly better than anything else of LeFanu's that I have ever seen, though I'd hardly put it in the Poe-Blackwood-Machen class" (HPL to Clark Ashton Smith, 16 January 1932 [ms., JHL]).

[36]There is now doubt as to whether Prest is the author of *Varney the Vampire*. Some scholars believe the author was James Malcolm Rymer (1814–1881).

[37]Of Wilkie Collins' (1824–1889) prolific output the following approach the domain of the weird: *The Dead Secret* (1857), *The Woman in White* (1860), *No Name* (1862), *The Moonstone* (1868), *The Haunted Hotel* (1870), and the short story collections *After Dark* (1856), *The Queen of Hearts* (1859), and *Little Novels* (1887). See also his *Tales of Suspense* (1954), ed. Robert Ashley and Herbert Van Thal. See Dorothy L. Sayers, *Wilkie Collins: A Critical and Biographical Study*, ed. E. R. Gregory (Toledo: University of Toledo Libraires, 1977). Audrey Peterson, *Victorian Masters of Mystery* (1984), William M. Clarke, *The Secret Life of Wilkie Collins* (1988), Nicholas Rauce, *Wilkie Collins and Other Sensation Novelists* (1991), and Tamar Heller, *Dead Secrets: Wilkie Collins and the Female Gothic* (1992).

[38]HPL did not read *She* until late 1926: "I've recently begun reading the work of Sir H. Rider Haggard *for the first time*. 'She' is very good, & if the others are at all commensurate, I have quite a treat ahead" (HPL to August Derleth, 31 October 1926; ms., SHSW).

Other fantastic works by Haggard include *King Solomon's Mines* (1885), *Allan Quatermain* (1887), *The World's Desire* (1890; with Andrew Lang), *Montezuma's Daughter* (1893), *The People of the Mist* (1894), *Ayesha: The Return of She* (1905), *Wisdom's Daughter* (1923), and many others.

VI. Spectral Literature on the Continent

[1] HPL spent three days reading Hoffmann's stories at the New York Public Library in February 1926 (HPL to Lillian D. Clark, 4 March 1926; ms., JHL).

[2] In the first publication of SHL appears a sentence at this point—"Adalbert von Chamisso, in his famous *Peter Schlemihl*, (1814) tells of a man who lost his own shadow as the consequence of a misdeed, and of the strange developments that resulted"—that HPL removed in later versions.

[3] Paracelsus (1493–1541) wrote many other works aside from the *Liber de Nymphis, Sylvis, Pygmaeis, et Salamandris, et de Caeteris Spiritibus* (ed. Robert Blaser [Bern: Francke Verlag, 1960]; ed. Will-Erich Peuckert, in Paracelsus' *Werke* [Basel/Stuttgart: Schwabe & Co., 1967], Vol. 2) referred to here by HPL. See Anna M. Stoddard, *The Life of Paracelsus* (London, 1911), Walter Pagel, *Paracelsus: An Introduction to Philosophical Medicine in the Era of the Renaissance* (1958, rev. 1982), Allen G. Debus, *The Chemical Philosophy: Paracelsian Science and Medicine in the Sixteenth and Seventeenth Centuries* (1976), and Charles Webster, *From Paracelsus to Newton: Magic and the Making of Modern Science* (1980).

[4] J. Vernon Shea's belief (*FDOC* 121) of a resemblance in sound between Külheborn and HPL's Cthulhu is probably unfounded; Shea, does, however, remark astutely that "This sexual traffic with water-creatures brings to mind the characters of 'The Shadow over Innsmouth.'"

[5] Another work of weird fiction by Meinhold is *Sidonia von Bork, die Klosterhexe* (1847), tr. as *Sidonia the Sorceress* (tr. Lady Wilde [Kelmscott Press, 1893; London: Ernest Benn, 1926]).

[6] A précis of the novel appeared under the title "The Convent Witch" in *Fraser's Magazine* 38 (October 1848): 363–78. The editor-translator is unknown.

[7] The tale bears a clear resemblance to HPL's "The Haunter of the Dark" (1935) and must have influenced it. In both tales the narrator keeps a diary, constantly looks out the window of his room, and at the last Ewers' narrator cries out, "My name—Richard Bracquemont . . ."—reminiscent of HPL's "My name is Blake—Robert Harrison Blake . . ." (*DH* 115). "The Spider" was included in Hammett's *Creeps by Night* (1931; see Bibliography), which also included HPL's "The Music of Erich Zann".

[8] Other weird works by Ewers include *Vampir* (1921), tr. by Fritz Sallagar as *Vampire* (New York: John Day, 1934; London: Jarrolds, 1937); *Reiter in deutscher Nacht* (1932), tr. by George Halasz as *Rider of the Night* (New York: John Day, 1932); and several collections of short stories: *Das Grauen* (1908), *Grotesken* (1910), and *Die Besessenen* (1916). Ewers also wrote a brief study of Edgar Allan Poe (1905), tr. by Adele Lewisohn as *Edgar Allan Poe* (New York: Huebsch, 1917).

[9] HPL, in a letter to *Weird Tales* (published in the September 1923 issue), also mentions Balzac's short story "Le Chef-d'oeuvre inconnu" [The Unknown Masterpiece] (*MW* 507). See also his earlier discussion of "Melmoth Reconcilié" (p. 31).

[10] The tale was probably an influence upon HPL's "Under the Pyramids" (but see also n. 21 to chapter 5).

[11] Flaubert's *Salammbô* (1862), an historical novel about Carthage, also borders upon the weird.

[12] From the middle 1920s onward HPL was reading manuscript copies of Clark Ashton Smith's translations of Baudelaire's prose-poems and poems from *Les Fleurs du mal*. HPL also owned a volume, *Baudelaire: His Prose and Poetry* (1919), from which he derived the epigraph for his tale, "Hypnos" (1922).

[13] The most celebrated weird tales of Huysmans are *A Rebours* (1884) and *Là-Bas* (1891). For the influence of the former on HPL's "The Hound" see Steven J. Mariconda, "The Hound—A Dead Dog?" (1986), in Mariconda's *On the Emergence of Cthulhu and Other Observations* (West Warwick, RI: Necronomicon Press, 1995), pp. 45–49.

[14] This description makes it clear that "The Horla" was a dominant influence upon the conception and development of HPL's "The Call of Cthulhu" (1926). The mention of the "invisible being" perhaps suggests an influence also on "The Dunwich Horror" (1928), although the attributes of the creature in that tale are perhaps more directly derived from Blackwood's "The Wendigo".

[15] "What Was It?" See below (p. 50).

[16] The four works by Erckmann-Chatrian cited here are all included in Vol. 5 of Julian Hawthorne's *The Lock and Key Library* (1909), which HPL purchased in New York in 1922; so that he must have read these tales sometime between then and the writing of SHL.

[17] Villiers de l'Isle-Adam wrote several collections of tales that border on the weird, including *Contes cruels* (1883), *Nouveaux contes cruels* (1888), and *Histoires insolites* (1888). English translations include *Sardonic Tales,* tr. Hamish Miles (New York & London: Knopf, 1927), and *Cruel Tales,* tr. Robert Baldick (Oxford: Oxford University Press, 1963).

[18] Level (1875–1926) published many novels and tales of horror. Novels include *L'Epouvante* (1908), tr. as *The Grip of Fear* (1911); *Les Portes d'enfer* (1910); *L'Ile sans nom* (1922); *L'Ombre* (1921), tr. by B. Drillien as *Those Who Return* (New York: McBride, 1923; *LL* 530); and *Le Marchand des secrets* (1929). English collections of his tales include *Tales of Mystery and Horror,* tr. Alys Eyre Macklin (New York: McBride, 1920; *LL* 529); *Crises: Tales of Mystery and Horror,* tr. Alys Eyre Macklin (London, 1921); and *Grand Guignol Stories,* tr. Alys Eyre Macklin (London, 1922). Several of his tales appeared in *Weird Tales*.

[19] The Théâtre du Grand Guignol was founded in 1897 and featured plays emphasising pain, torture, rape, murder, fantasy, and the like. It closed in 1962.

[20] For cabbalism see Adolphe Franck, *Le Kabbale* (1843; Eng. tr. 1926), A. E. Waite, *The Doctrine and Literature of the Kabalah* (1902), Joshua Abelson, *Jewish Mysticism* (1913), G. A. V. Encausse, *Le Cabbale, tradition secrète de l'occident* (4th ed. 1937), Moses Luzzatto, *General Principles of the Kabbalah* (1970), and Gershom Scholem, *Kaballah* (1974).

[21] Other weird works by Meyrink include the novels *Das grüne Gesicht* (1916) and *Walpurgisnacht* (1917), and the short story collections *Orchideen* (1904) and *Der violette Tod und andere Novellen* (1913). For a more complete bibliography see the one in the special issue of *L'Herne* on Meyrink (see Bibliography). Aside from *The Golem* almost none of his work has been translated into English.

[22] Real name: Solomon Rappoport.

[23] In the first publication of SHL the above passage read: "The former, widely popular through the cinema a few years ago, treats of a legendary artificial giant animated by a mediaeval rabbin of Prague according to a certain cryptic formula." HPL comments on this change in January 1937: "To explain that Golem business I must confess that when I wrote the treatise I hadn't read the novel. I had seen the cinema version, and thought it was faithful to the original—but when I came to read the book only a year ago [actually in April 1935; cf. *SL* V.138] . . . Holy Yuggoth! The film had nothing of the novel save the mere title and the Prague ghetto setting—indeed, in the book the Golem-monster never appeared at all, but merely lurked in the background as a shadowy symbol. That was one on the old man!" (*SL* V.389). The novel had been lent to him by R. H. Barlow. HPL saw the film version of *The Golem* in 1921.

[24] HPL saw it in New York on December 17, 1925 (HPL to Lillian D. Clark, 22 December 1925; ms., JHL).

[25] The opera, in Italian, was entitled *Il dibuk* (1934), and was composed by Lodovico Rocca. The first production was at the Teatro alla Scala in Milan, 24 March 1934.

VII. Edgar Allan Poe

[1] I.e. the Decadents and Symbolists; see below (p. 43).

[2] HPL read Poe as early as the age of eight. "Then I struck *Edgar Allan Poe!!* It was my downfall, and at the age of eight I saw the blue firmament of Argos and Sicily darkened by the miasmal exhalations of the tomb!" (*SL* II.109).

[3] Cf., e.g., such hostile studies as William Dean Howells' "Edgar Allan Poe" (*Harper's Weekly*, 16 January 1900), John Macy's "The Fame of Poe" (*Atlantic Monthly*, December 1908), Van Wyck Brooks' *America's Coming of Age* (1915), John Robertson's *Edgar Allan Poe: A Study* (1921), H. L. Mencken's "The Mystery of Poe" (*Nation*, 17 March 1926), and V. L. Parrington's *Romantic Revolution in America* (1927). Bernard Shaw, Edward J. O'Brien, William Carlos Williams, and Edmond

Gosse (see his *Edgar Allan Poe and His Detractors,* 1928) were among those who came to Poe's defence in the 1910s and 1920s.

[4]HPL presumably refers to Poe's extensive borrowing of aesthetic theories from Coleridge and such German theoreticians as A. W. Schlegel. See Floyd Stovall, "Poe's Debt to Coleridge", *University of Texas Studies in English* 10 (July 1930): 70–127; G. R. Thompson, *Poe's Fiction* (1973).

[5]Here HPL may be referring to Blackwood's "The Willows" and Machen's "The White People", which he regarded as the two finest tales in the history of weird fiction.

[6]For Poe and Baudelaire see Léon Lemonnier, "Baudelaire, Edgar Poe et la romantisme", *Mercure de France* (1 August 1923); Léon Saisset, *Les Histoires extroardinaires d'Edgar Poe* (1939); Don Max Anderson, "Edgar Allan Poe's Influence upon Baudelaire's Style", Ph.D. diss.: University of Iowa, 1955; and Peter M. Wetherill, *Charles Baudelaire et le poésie d'Edgar Allan Poe* (1962). See also the volume *Baudelaire on Poe,* ed. Lois and Francis E. Hyslop (1952), giving a bibliography of Baudelaire's translations of Poe; also Baudelaire's *Edgar Allan Poe: Sa Vie et ses oeuvres* [1852], ed. W. T. Bandy (Toronto: University of Toronto Press, 1973).

[7]For which see Louis Seylaz, *Edgar Poe et les premiers symbolistes français* (1923); Celestin P. Cambiaire, *The Influence of Edgar Allan Poe in France* (1927); Léon Lemonnier, *Edgar Poe et les poètes français* (1932); E. Noulet, *Etudes littéraires* (1944); Léon Lemonnier, *Edgar Poe et les conteurs français* (1947); Patrick Quinn, *The French Face of Edgar Allan Poe* (1957); Lucienne Cain, *Trois Essais sur Valéry* (5th ed. 1958; incl. "Edgar Poe et Valéry"); W. T. Bandy, *The Influence and Reputation of Edgar Allan Poe in Europe* (1962); Joseph Chiari, *Symbolisme from Poe to Mallarmé* (1970); Jean Avon Alexander, ed., *Affidavits of Genius: Edgar Allan Poe and the French Critics 1847–1924* (1971).

[8]See especially his strange scientific postulates in *Eureka* and his pretence of knowledge of Greek and Hebrew.

[9]Cf. "The Defence Remains Open!" (1921), discussing why HPL avoids humour in weird fiction: "I have the sanction of the best models—Poe's intense tales are wholly humourless" (*IDOD* 22n). But cf. Thompson (*Poe's Fiction*) for the strong element of Romantic irony inherent not merely in such farces as "Some Words with a Mummy" but even in such tales as "Metzengerstein" and "The Fall of the House of Usher".

[10]Notably his attacks upon Longfellow (see his reviews of Longfellow's *Hyperion, Voices of the Night,* and *Ballades*). For Poe as critic see Margaret Alterton, *Origins of Poe's Critical Theory* (1963); Edd W. Parks, *Edgar Allan Poe as Literary Critic* (1964); Robert D. Jacobs, *Poe: Journalist and Critic* (1969).

[11]"Import" or "message"; also spelled "burden". Cf. HPL's poem "The Cats" (1925): "Yelling the burden of Pluto's red rune." *The Fantastic Poetry,* 2nd ed. (West Warwick, RI: Necronomicon Press, 1993), p. 51.

[12]"The Raven."

[13] "The Bells."

[14] "Ulalume."

[15] "The City in the Sea."

[16] "Dream-Land."

[17] Namely, "The Murders in the Rue Morgue", "The Mystery of Marie Rogêt", "The Purloined Letter", "The Gold Bug", and some minor tales. Poe's interest in cryptography may have influence HPL's own fascination with cryptograms, as is evidenced in "The Dunwich Horror" (1928), where many volumes of cryptography are cited, and other tales.

[18] For which see G. Gruener, "Notes on the Influence of E. T. A. Hoffmann upon Edgar Allan Poe", *PMLA* 19 (1904): 1–25; Palmer Cobb, "The Influence of E. T. A. Hoffmann on the Tales of Edgar Allan Poe", *Studies in Philology* 3 (1908): 1–104.

[19] It is curious, then, that HPL below cites "The Man of the Crowd", which surely falls into this third category.

[20] This tale's influence upon HPL's "Cool Air" would seem to be self-evident; but HPL himself believed his tale to have been more directly influenced by Machen's "Novel of the White Powder" (HPL to Henry Kuttner, 29 July 1936; *Letters to Henry Kuttner* [West Warwick, RI: Necronomicon Press, 1990], p. 21)—a conclusion at which J. Vernon Shea (*FDOC* 134) had independently arrived.

[21] The final word in the most authoritative version of Poe's text—a copy made by Sarah Helen Whitman of the text in the *Broadway Journal* (Dec. 20, 1845) with manuscript revisions—is "putridity"; many other texts, including many collected editions of Poe, read "putrescence". Late in life HPL came upon the revised reading and found it unsatisfying: "The loss in power—as connected with prose *rhythm*—is obvious. It is curious—almost incredible—how deaf & callous the moderns are to one of the most important factors in prose writing—i.e., cadence or rhythm. Much of the magic of Poe resides in his masterful employment of this element—hence his work is gravely impaired if any part of the text be tampered with" (HPL to R. H. Barlow, [10 February 1935; ms., JHL).

[22] *Pym* has frequently been said to have influenced HPL's *At the Mountains of Madness* (1931), but any connexions between the two tales aside from the Antarctic setting are hard to distinguish. HPL may have intended the novel partially as a tongue-in-cheek continuation of *Pym* (it is mentioned twice in the novel), as Jules Verne did more consciously in his *Sphinx of the Ice-Fields* (1897); but the conceptions and themes of the two tales differ so much that any strong influence may well be discounted.

[23] Cf. the arras used in HPL's "The Rats in the Walls" (1923).

[24] Cf. "The Horror at Red Hook" (1925): "The world and Nature were helpless against such assaults from unsealed wells of night" (*D* 260).

[25] Especially in his fairy tales; see below (p. 55) and note 4 to chapter 9.

[26] For Poe's influence on Dunsany see Dunsany's autobiography *Patches of Sunlight* (London: Heinemann, 1938), in which he records reading Poe as a boy: "One day at Cheam I was introduced to Poe's Tales, from the school library, and I read them all; and the ahunted desolation and weird gloom of the misty mid-region of Weir remained for many years something that seemed to me more eerie than anything earth had, something that it required the brain of a poet like Poe to invent" (p. 32).

[27] That Poe's prose-poems influenced HPL's four prose-poems, and may also have led to HPL's anticipation of the "Dunsanian" style in "Polaris" (1918), written a full year before he encountered Dunsany, is now established: Poe's "Silence—a Fable" and HPL's "Memory" (1919) both use a "Demon" for a character, while HPL's attempts at hypnotic prose in these works also recall Poe's tales. The similarity of conception in "The Masque of the Red Death" and HPL's "The Outsider" (1921)—which "represents my literal though unconscious imitation of Poe at its very height" (*SL* III.379)—is too obvious for comment.

[28] The character of Ligeia may have had some role in influencing the character of Asenath Waite in "The Thing on the Doorstep" (1933), although for the most part Asenath is a compound of HPL's mother and ex-wife.

[29] See Mabbott ("Lovecraft as a Student of Poe", *Fresco* 8, No. 3 [Spring 1958]: 37–39) for a discussion of this interpretation of "Usher", representing HPL's greatest contribution to Poe studies (see also Mabbott's edition of Poe's *Tales and Sketches* [1978], I.393). Wetzel (*FDOC* 92) has examined the passage in "The Haunter of the Dark" (1936) where the narrator's diary note—"Roderick Usher—am mad or going mad . . . I am it and it is I" (*DH* 115)—is indicative of the narrator's sharing a soul with the avatar of Nyarlathotep.

[30] Cf. HPL's "Pickman's Model" (1926): ". . . only a real artist knows the actual anatomy of the terrible or the physiology of fear" (*DH* 13).

[31] I have not been able to ascertain the source for HPL's knowledge of this anecdote.

[32] This description could apply to many of HPL's own characters, especially among his early "macabre" stories; see especially Jervas Dudley in "The Tomb" (1917), the two protagonists of "The Hound" (1922), and others.

[33] A Latinised adjectival form of "Lewis", referring to M. G. Lewis.

VIII. The Weird Tradition in America

[1] See Paul Elmer More (1864–1937), "The Origins of Hawthorne and Poe", in *Shelburne Essays: First Series* (New York: Putnam's, 1904): "The unearthly visions of Poe and Hawthorne are in no wise the result of literary whim or of unbridled individualism, but are deep-rooted in American history" (p. 53). Cf. *SL* II.140: "It is easy to see how the critic Paul Elmer More traces the horror-element in American literature to the remote New England countryside with its solitude-warped religious fanaticism."

Notes

²See n. 4 to chapter 2.

³Cf. "The Picture in the House" (1920): "In such houses [i.e. those of the New England backwoods] have dwelt generations of strange people, whose like the world has never seen. Seized with a gloomy and fanatical belief which exiled them from their kind, their ancestors sought the wilderness for freedom. There the scions of a conquering race indeed flourished free from the restrictions of their fellows, but cowered in an appalling slavery to the dismal phantasms of their own minds. Divorced from the enlightenment of civilisation, the strength of these Puritans turned into singular channels; and in their isolation, morbid self-repression, and struggle for life with relentless Nature, there came to them dark furtive traits from the prehistoric depths of their cold Northern heritage. By necessity practical and by philosophy stern, these folk were not beautiful in their sins. Erring as all mortals must, they were forced by their rigid code to seek concealment above all else; so that they came to use less and less taste in waht they concealed" (*DH* 117). For HPL's fictional use of the Salem witchcraft incident, see "The Dreams in the Witch House" (1932).

⁴For Hawthorne's influence on HPL see Donald R. Burleson, "H. P. Lovecraft: The Hawthorne Influence", *Extrapolation* 22 (Fall 1981): 262–69.

⁵Viz., Judge John Hathorne (1641–1717), son of William Hathorne, earliest American settler of the Hathorne family, who came to Massachusetts in 1630. See Vernon Loggins, *The Hawthornes* (New York: Columbia University Press, 1951).

⁶For HPL's hostility to didacticism in literature see p. 21 above and note 1 to chapter 1.

⁷These two volumes, read by HPL at the age of seven, were the ultimate sources for his abiding interest in classical antiquity (see *SL* I.7).

⁸Judge Hathorne (see n. 5 above) is buried in this cemetery. George T. Wetzel believed that entry 112 of HPL's *Commonplace Book* ("Man lives near graveyard—how does he live? Eats no food") was inspired by *Dr. Grimshawe's Secret*.

⁹Entry 129 of the *Commonplace Book* ("strange & prehistoric Italian city of stone") is explicitly derived from this novel.

¹⁰An idea broached in HPL's *The Dream-Quest of Unknown Kadath* (1926–27), although it is unlikely that he derived it from Hawthorne, as it was a widely expressed conception in classical literature.

¹¹Presumably a reference to two chapters on Hawthorne in *Studies in Classic American Literature* (1923) by D. H. Lawrence (1885–1930); but I have not been able to identify the remark to which HPL here alludes.

¹²There may be some connexion between this tale and HPL's *The Case of Charles Dexter Ward*, where a portrait of Joseph Curwen plays a role; although a similar device is found in *Melmoth the Wanderer* (see n. 10 to chapter 4) and *The Picture of Dorian Gray* (see below, p. 55). See also entry 210 of the *Commonplace Book*.

[13]"Ethan Brand" was first published under the title "The Unpardonable Sinner" (see Bibliography).

[14]See HPL's *Commonplace Book* (entry 46): "Hawthorne—unwritten plot[:] Visitor from tomb—stranger at some publick concourse followed at midnight to graveyard where he descends into the earth." On the passage see Wetzel (*FDOC* 87). The Hawthorne note is in his *American Notebooks* for 6 December 1837.

[15]Entry 83 of the *Commonplace Book* is a quotation from this novel ("... a defunct nightmare, which had perished in the midst of its wickedness, & left its flabby corpse on the breast of the tormented one, to be gotten rid of as it might").

[16]This sentence perhaps most succinctly expresses HPL's adherence to the ideals of the Augustan Age.

[17]Cf. a somewhat analogous prophecy uttered by Old Whateley—*"some day yew folks'll hear a child o' Lavinny's a-callin' its father's name on the top o' Sentinel Hill!"* (*DH* 160)—in "The Dunwich Horror" (1928), although of course the prophecy does not eventuate exactly as Whateley intended.

[18]This analogy may point to HPL's absorption of the Wagnerian operatic form, with its employment of the *leitmotiv;* for the average opera does not employ a recurring motif or theme. (For HPL's enjoyment of Wagner see *SL* III.342.)

[19]See n. 14 to chapter 2.

[20]HPL, too, had had an early fascination with chemistry, producing such juvenile works as *The Scientific Gazette* (1899f.) and a six-volume "textbook", *Chemistry* (1899?). This may account for HPL's fondness for O'Brien's tale.

[21]HPL first read Bierce in 1919, at the suggestion of Samuel Loveman (*SL* II.222).

[22]Much has been written on the disappearance of Ambrose Bierce. Aside from the standard biographies, see: Edward H. Smith, *Mysteries of the Missing* (1927); Adolphe de Castro, *A Portrait of Ambrose Bierce* (1929), a work HPL saw in ms.; Harold Tom Wilkins, *Strange Mysteries of Time and Space* (1958); the very curious volume *Ambrose Bierce, F. A. Mitchell-Hedges, and the Crystal Skull* by Sibley S. Morrill (1972); and Joe Nickell, *Ambrose Bierce Is Missing and Other Historical Mysteries* (1992).

[23]He was, of course, known to HPL as well; see Loveman's memoir, "Howard Phillips Lovecraft", in *Something about Cats and Other Pieces* (1949), pp. 229–33.

[24]From the preface to *Twenty-one Letters of Ambrose Bierce* (Cleveland: George Kirk, 1922), p. 4.

[25]HPL may have been influenced by this "strain of sardonic comedy and graveyard humour" in such of his tales as "The Terrible Old Man" (1920), "The Hound" (1922), "The Unnamable" (1923), "In the Vault" (1925), and some others.

[26]These are the subtitles, respectively, for the first and third chapters of "The Damned Thing", in *Can Such Things Be?*

[27] In *Can Such Things Be?* J. Vernon Shea (*FDOC* 125) sees an autobiographical connexion in regard to HPL's appreciation of this tale.

[28] "In all imaginative literature it would be difficult to find a parallel for this story in sheer, unadulterated hideousness." Frederic Taber Cooper, "Ambrose Bierce", in *Some American Story Tellers* (1911), p. 352.

[29] In *In the Midst of Life*. See also Appendix 1.

[30] Cf. HPL to August Derleth, n.d. [1927]: "One of my favourites [among Bierce's tales] is 'The Suitable Surroundings'. This is a horror-story *about a horror-story*" (ms., SHSW). See also entry 56 of the *Commonplace Book* ("Book or MS. too horrible to read—warned against reading it—someone reads & is found dead. . . ."), which appears to summarise the Bierce story and also suggests an inspiration for HPL's invention of the *Necronomicon* and other books of occult lore.

[31] In *Can Such Things Be?*

[32] A character named Joel Manton is featured in HPL's "The Unnamable" (1923). See S. T. Joshi, "Autobiography in Lovecraft", *Lovecraft Studies* No. 1 (Fall 1979): 13n.

[33] Included in the section "Some Haunted Houses" appended to *Can Such Things Be?* in the third volume of Bierce's *Collected Works*.

[34] Volumes III and II, respectively, of Bierce's *Collected Works*.

[35] Bierce's *Collected Works* contains much other fantastic or quasi-fantastic writing; see especially several Swiftian satires in Volume I ("Ashes of the Beacon", "The Land Beyond the Blow", "For the Ahkoond" [rpt. Necronomicon Press, 1980]); *The Monk and the Hangman's Daughter,* a novel by Richard Voss co-translated by Bierce and Adolphe Danziger, and *Fantastic Fables* (Volume VI); "Negligible Tales" and "The Parenticide Club" (Volume VIII); and others. For a selection of Bierce's fantastic and satiric poetry (collected in Volumes IV and V of the *Collected Works*) see *A Vision of Doom,* ed. Donald Sidney-Fryer (West Kingston, RI: Donald M. Grant, 1980).

[36] HPL was, of course, slightly acquainted with Holmes; the latter was said to have dandled the two-year-old HPL on his knee during one of his visits to the home of the poet Louise Imogen Guiney in Auburndale (*SL* I.296). HPL also enjoyed Holmes' poetry (*SL* I.73).

[37] "About 'Elsie Venner'—it has a subtly haunting power, though I'm not sure whether the horror element is concentrated enough to make it a major weird classic. Some, of course, might consider it all the greater on that account. It certainly has atmosphere. I haven't read it in years, but can still recall the malign aura that hangs over the great hill against which the town is built. Possibly that suggested my Yuggothian fungus 'Zaman's Hill' [*Fungi from Yuggoth* VII]" (HPL to R. H. Barlow, [26 October 1934]; ms., JHL).

[38] "As you know, James had three distinct literary periods—which some wit has called those of James the First, James the Second, and the Old Pretender" (*SL* IV.342).

[39] A number of James' short stories contain elements of fantasy and terror; they have been collected in *The Ghostly Tales of Henry James*, ed. Leon Edel (1948).

[40] "It may interest you to know that in an XIth hour codicil I amplified my F. Marion Crawford paragraph . . .; this enlarged horizon resulting from the perusal of a collection called *Wandering Ghosts*, lent me by my newest prodigy great-grandchild, Donald Wandrei of St. Paul, Minn." (*SL* II.123).

[41] Other tales in *Wandering Ghosts* are "The Screaming Skull", "Man Overboard!", "By the Waters of Paradise", and "The Doll's Ghost". Several of Crawford's novels contain elements of weirdness in varying degrees, notably *Zoroaster* (1885), *Khaled: A Tale of Arabia* (1891), and *The Witch of Prague* (1891).

[42] "I made some eleventh-hour inserts in the proofs [of SHL] which you won't find in the carbon—mainly regarding the forgotten early work of *Robert W. Chambers* (can you believe it?) who turned out some powerful bizarre stuff between 1895 and 1904" (*SL* II.127). HPL alludes to the drearily endless array of best-selling shopgirl romances produced by Chambers after his early fantasy period. "Chambers is like Rupert Hughes and a few other fallen Titans—equipped with the right brains and education, but wholly out of the habit of using them" (*SL* II.148).

[43] The resemblance here to HPL's mythical tome, the *Necronomicon*, is obvious; but since HPL had invented his book five years before he read Chambers (in "The Hound" [1922]), any literary influence from *The King in Yellow* can be discounted. Indeed, HPL ironically hints in "History of the *Necronomicon*" that Chambers was inspired by the *Necronomicon* to create *The King in Yellow!*

[44] The Yellow Sign and Hastur are both mentioned in passing in "The Whisperer in Darkness" (*DH* 223). There is no intimation at all in HPL that Hastur is even an entity (Bierce, in "Haïta the Shepherd", made Hastur a god of the shepherds, but Chambers in various stories refers to Hastur either as a constellation or as a person), hence no justification for the inclusion of Hastur among the pantheon of gods in HPL's "Cthulhu Mythos", as has been done by many writers in the "Lovecraft tradition".

[45] Invented by Bierce in "The Inhabitant of Carcosa" (*Can Such Things Be?*).

[46] HPL (see *SL* III.187) was especially fond of "The Harbor-Master" (originally a short story but later rewritten as the first five chapters of *In Search of the Unknown*), a tale that may have influenced "The Shadow over Innsmouth" in its depiction of a hybrid fish-man. Other volumes by Chambers that are either exclusively or partly weird are the story collections *The Mystery of Choice* (1897), *The Tracer of Lost Persons* (1906), *The Tree of Heaven* (1907), *Police!!!* (1915), and the novel *The Slayer of Souls* (1920). HPL read the last-named: "a vast disappointment—he can't get back to the *King in Yellow* mood after a quarter-century of best-sellerism!" (*SL* II.174).

[47] Included in Cram's rare collection of weird tales, *Black Spirits and White* (see Bibliography); although HPL read it in Joseph Lewis French's anthology *Ghosts Grim and*

Gentle (1926); see HPL's *Commonplace Book,* ed. David E. Schultz (West Warwick, RI: Necronomicon Press, 1987), I.14.

[48] HPL read this tale in its original appearance in the *Argosy,* 11 January 1913; in the 8 February 1913 issue was published a letter of comment on the tale by HPL: "It is the belief of the writer that very few short stories of equal merit have been published anywhere during recent years. It is easy to imagine with what genuine regret the editors to whom it was submitted declined to print it." The tale was clearly an influence upon "The Shadow over Innsmouth".

[49] "The Unbroken Chain", in *On an Island That Cost $24.00* (1926). HPL read the story in its first appearance (*Cosmpolitan,* September 1923), and it clearly influenced "The Rats in the Walls". See S. T. Joshi, *H. P. Lovecraft: A Life* (West Warwick, RI: Necronomicon Press, 1996), pp. 301–2.

[50] August Derleth, discovering a plot description of this novel among HPL's notes and believing it to be a story idea by HPL himself, performed an unwitting plagiarism by writing up the plot in his "posthumous collaboration", "The Ancestor" (in *The Survivor and Others* [1957] and *The Watchers out of Time* [1974]).

[51] Other works by Cline that border upon the weird are the novels *God Head* (1925) and *Listen, Moon!* (1926).

[52] The novel is a probable influence upon HPL's "The Shadow over Innsmouth" and "The Dreams in the Witch House". See my afterword to the reprint of the novel by Hippocampus Press (2003).

[53] See the "Afterword" to *Lukundoo and Other Stories;* now rpt. in *Studies in Weird Fiction* No. 11 (Spring 1992): 22–24.

[54] In *the Song of the Sirens and Other Stories.* Cf. "Final Words" (September 1921): ". . . it may not be amiss to mention an excellent collection of tales to which my attention has just been drawn—*The Song of the Sirens, and Other Stories,* by Edward Lucas White (Dutton, 1919)—which possesses considerable charm, artistry, and scholarship" (*IDOD* 35).

[55] Both stories are in *Lukundoo and Other Stories.*

[56] HPL came into contact with Smith in 1922. They corresponded voluminously for the next fifteen years, but they never met.

[57] In *Ebony and Crystal* (1922) and *Selected Poems* (1971). See also *SL* I.195, 213f.

[58] Invented by Smith in the story "The Tale of Satampra Zeiros" and cited by HPL in "The Mound" (1929–30) and "The Whisperer in Darkness" (1930).

[59] See Bibliography for modern editions of Smith's poetry and prose. See also *Planets and Dimensions: Collected Essays* (Baltimore: Mirage Press, 1973).

IX. The Weird Tradition in the British Isles

[1]Kipling wrote a number of other horror, fantasy, and science fiction tales, including "The Strange Ride of Morrowbie Jukes", "My Own True Ghost Story", "'They'", and several others. The fantasy tales have been collected in *Kipling's Fantasy* (1992); the science fiction tales in *Kipling's Science Fiction* (1992). "The Phantom 'Rickshaw" (*Quartette*, 1885), "The Strange Ride . . ." (*Quartette*, 1885), and "My Own True Ghost Story" (*Week's News*, February 25, 1888) were first collected in *The Phantom 'Rickshaw and Other Tales* (1888); "'The Finest Story in the World'" (*Contemporary Review*, July 1891) in *Many Inventions* (1891); "The Recrudescence of Imray" (later titled "The Return of Imray") in *Mine Own People* (1891); "The Mark of the Beast" (*Pioneer*, July 12 and 14, 1890) in *Life's Handicap* (1891).

[2]The man-to-beast theme, of course, is very common in HPL's work, although it is usually the product of inbreeding or miscegenation; see such tales as "The Lurking Fear" (1922) and "The Shadow over Innsmouth" (1931).

[3]Hearn translated Gautier's *One of Cleopatra's Nights and Other Fantastic Romances* (1882), Maupassant's *Saint Anthony and Other Stories* (1924) and *The Adventures of Walter Schnaffs* (1931), and Anatole France's *the Crime of Sylvestre Bonnard* (1890). His translation of Flaubert's *Temptation of St. Anthony* was first published in 1910.

[4]Collected in *The Happy Prince* (1888) and *A House of Pomegranates* (1891). Colin Wilson (*The Strength to Dream* [Boston: Houghton Mifflin, 1962], p. 8) suggested that Wilde's "Birthday of the Infanta" may have been an influence upon HPL's "The Outsider". See also HPL's poem "With a Copy of Wilde's Fairy Tales" (*Saturnalia and Other Poems* [1984], p. 25), written in July 1920.

[5]As Peter Cannon (*H. P. Lovecraft* [New York: Twayne, 1989], p. 72) points out, Wilde's novel had a strong influence upon HPL's *The Case of Charles Dexter Ward*, where a portrait is used in a roughly similar manner (but see n. 10 to chapter 4).

[6]Wilde also wrote the humorous short story "The Canterville Ghost", while the play *Salomé* has touches of fantastic exoticism. Some of his poems and poems in prose are also filled with bizarrerie.

[7]A revised version of this tale appeared in *Dark Mind, Dark Heart* (1962), ed. August Derleth; later printed in Shiel's *Xélucha and Others* (1975).

[8]First read by HPL in 1923 in the collection *The Pale Ape and Other Pulses* (1911), lent to him by W. Paul Cook (*SL* I.255). See also HPL's letter to the editor of *Weird Tales* for January 1924 (*Uncollected Letters* [1986], p. 7), where he speaks of the story in virtually the same terms as he does here. Entries 115 and 116 of the *Commonplace Book* appear to derive from HPL's reading of the work.

[9]"The House of Sounds" originally appeared as "Vaila" in *Shapes in the Fire* (1896); revised and retitled, it appeared in *The Pale Ape*.

[10] HPL refers to the fact that in both tales a house and its inhabitants appear to share a common soul (on Poe see above, p. 45), so that both the house and its occupants experience a common dissolution.

[11] The early parts of Shiel's novel bear affinities with the early parts of HPL's *At the Mountains of Madness* (1931), especially in the descriptions of the outfitting and manning of the respective polar expeditions.

[12] The similarity to Mary Shelley's *The Last Man* is obvious; see p. 35. See also on Hodgson's *The Night Land* (p. 59 below).

[13] Other fantastic works by Shiel include *Prince Zaleski* (1895), *The Lord of the Sea* (1901), *The Weird o' It* (1902), *The Isle of Lies* (1908), *The Invisible Voices* (1935), and others.

[14] "[W. Paul] Cook . . . hath lent me . . . Stoker's last production, *The Lair of the White Worm*. The plot idea is colossal, but the development is so childish that I cannot imagine how the thing ever got into print—unless on the reputation of *Dracula*. The rambling and unmotivated narration, the puerile and stagey characterisation, the irrational propensity of everyone to do the most stupid possible thing at precisely the wrong moment and for no cause at all, and the involved development of a personality afterward relegated to utter insignificance—all this proves to me either that *Dracula* . . . and *The Jewel of Seven Stars* were touched up Bushwork-fashion by a superior hand which arranged *all* the details, or that by the end of his life . . . he trickled out in a pitiful and inept senility" (*SL* I.255). Entry 79 of the *Commonplace Book* ("Shapeless living *thing* forming nucleus of ancient building") may derive from HPL's reading of this novel.

[15] HPL frequently asserted that his associate Edith Miniter was offered a chance to revise and edit the text of *Dracula* but turned it down because of the slovenly condition of the ms.; see HPL's "Mrs. Miniter—Recollections and Estimates" (*MW* 472) and *SL* I.255. No independent confirmation of this anecdote has emerged, however. For HPL's own imaginative treatment of the vampire myth see "The Shunned House" (1924).

[16] Other weird works by Stoker are the story collection *Dracula's Guest* (1914), containing such tales as "The Judge's House" and "The Squaw", and the novels *The Mystery of the Sea* (1902) and *The Lady of the Shroud* (1909).

[17] As both *Dracula* and *The Beetle* were published in 1897, there may be some question as to whether the former directly influenced the latter. Marsh wrote a few other weird tales, scattered in his collections *Curios* (1898) and *The Seen and the Unseen* (1900).

[18] Rohmer of course wrote many novels and tales about the detective Fu Manchu and other heroes.

[19] Other works by Biss include *The Dupe* (1909) and *The White Rose Mystery* (1909).

[20] Little of Francis Brett Young's other voluminous work—largely novels and poems—is fantastic.

[21] All three stories cited are in *The Runagates Club* (1928). HPL read the volume in the late summer of 1928 (HPL to August Derleth, 12 August and 5 October 1928; mss., SHSW). Entry 222 of the *Commonplace Book* quotes the epigraph to another story in the collection, "Sing a Song of Sixpence".

[22] Buchan wrote an enormous amount of adventure and historical fiction, including *Prester John* (1910), *The 39 Steps* (1915), and *Greenmantle* (1916). There are a few weird tales in the collection *The Watcher by the Threshold and Other Tales* (1902), while *The Gap in the Curtain* (1932) is a weird novel.

[23] Aside from "The Werewolf", Clemence Housman (sister of A. E. Housman) wrote an historical novel, *The Life of Sir Aglovale de Galis* (1905), based on Malory's *Morte d'Arthur,* and a fantastic novel, *The Unknown Sea* (1898).

[24] Ransome, better known as a critic (see his volumes, *Edgar Allan Poe: A Critical Study* [1910], *Oscar Wilde: A Critical Study* [1912], and *Portraits and Speculations* [1913]) and as the author of fairy tales, also did much work in Russian literature and civilisation. *The Stone Lady* (1905) has some weird tales.

[25] *The Shadowy Thing* was first published in England under the title *The Remedy* (1925). Other weird novels by Drake are *The Children Reap* (1929) and *Hush-a-by Baby* (1952; *Children of the Wind* in the U.S.).

[26] But the earlier version of the novel has yet to be published, and HPL knew of it only in a paraphrase by Greville Macdonald in an introduction to a later edition (London: George Allen & Unwin, 1924). William Raeper, in *George Macdonald* (1987), remarks of the earlier version that it "is much less threatening than the published version, as it is rational, coherent and ordered" (p. 422). No doubt this is why HPL would have preferred it. The copy of *Lilith* he owned is, of course, the later version.

Among the prolific output of George Macdonald the most notable fantasies (aside from *Lilith* and *Phantastes*) are *Dealings with the Fairies* (1867), *The Princess and the Goblin* (1872), *Sir Gibbie* (1879), and *The Princess and Curdie* (1883).

[27] HPL came upon de la Mare's weird work only in the summer of 1926 (*SL* II.53, 57).

[28] The resemblance in plot to HPL's *The Case of Charles Dexter Ward* is obvious (see Wetzel in *FDOC* 90 and my note ad loc.). See also entry 194 of the *Commonplace Book,* which appears to summarise the opening of de la Mare's novel.

[29] Much of de la Mare's other poetry has fantastic touches; see his *Complete Poems* (1969; superseding the incomplete *Collected Poems* of 1941).

[30] In *The Room in the Tower* (1912). This collection also contains "Caterpillars".

[31] *Spook Stories* (1928). HPL explains in a letter why he did not cite the volume by name: "No—I don't like the title '*Spook* Stories'. It has a suggestion of triviality" (HPL to August Derleth, 21 August [1932]; ms., SHSW).

Benson also wrote *More Spook Stories* (1934), while there are other weird tales in *The Countess of Lowndes Square and Other Stories* (1920). *The Collected Ghost Sto-*

ries of E. F. Benson (1992) collects the contents of Benson's four major weird collections; Jack Adrian has assembled further tales in *The Flint Knife* (1988). Several of Benson's many novels contain weird elements.

Benson's brothers A. C. and R. H. Benson also wrote weird tales.

[32] The first three stories mentioned and the last are in *They Return at Evening;* the other three are in *Others Who Returned.* Other collections of weird tales by Wakefield are *Imagine a Man in a Box* (1931), *The Clock Strikes Twelve* (1940), and *Strayers from Sheol* (1961).

[33] "The Ghost of Fear" is nothing more than the early story "The Red Room" (in *The Plattner Story and Others* and *Thirty Strange Stories* [both 1897]), apparently retitled by Joseph Lewis French for his anthology, *Ghosts, Grim and Gentle* (1926). HPL had read *Thirty Strange Stories* in 1924 (*SL* I.287), but evidently the story did not make an impression upon him at that time.

[34] While the majority of Wells' work falls into the realms of science fiction or mainstream fiction, mention may be made of his novels, *The Time Machine* (1895; read by HPL in late 1924 [HPL to Lillian D. Clark, 29 November 1924; ms., JHL], *The Island of Dr. Moreau* (1896), and *The Invisible Man* (1897), and such macabre short tales as the cosmic "The Star" (in *Tales of Space and Time* [1899]), "The Story of the Late Mr. Elvesham" (in *The Plattner Story and Others* [1897]), "Empire of the Ants" and "The Country of the Blind" (in *The Time Machine and Other Stories* [1895]), "Æpyornis Island" (in *Thirty Strange Stories*), and "The Valley of Spiders" and "A Dream of Armageddon" (in *Twelve Stories and a Dream* [1903]).

[35] Doyle wrote a notable series of science fiction/fantasy/mystery tales, the Professor Challenger stories (collected in 1952), including *The Lost World* (1912), *The Poison Belt* (1913), *The Land of Mist* (1926), and the short stories "The Disintegration Machine" and "When the World Screamed" (both in *The Maracot Deep and Other Stories* [1929]). The short novel *The Maracot Deep* is a fascinating tale of an underwater civilisation; HPL read it upon its appearance (*SL* III.39). Other collections containing weird tales include *My Friend the Murderer* (1893), *Last Gallery* (1911), *Tales of Long Ago* (1922), *Tales of Twilight and the Unseen* (1922), and *The Black Doctor* (1925).

[36] See also the novel *Portrait of a Man with Red Hair* (1925) and the collections *The Silver-Thorn* (1928) and *All Souls' Night* (1933). Walpole also edited the notable anthology *A Century of Creepy Stories* (1937).

[37] Other fantastic works by Metcalfe include the short novel *The Feasting Dead* (1954) and the collection *Judas and Other Stories* (1931).

[38] Aside from the celebrated play *Peter Pan* (1904), Barrie's grim drama *Shall We Join the Ladies?* (1921) can be classified as weird.

[39] "The Story of a Panic."

[40] Another collection of horror tales is *The Eternal Moment and Other Stories* (1928).

[41] The collection is entitled *The Death Mask.* See also her novel *Iras: A Mystery* (1896), published under the pseudonym "Theo. Douglas".

[42] Originally published in Cynthia Asquith, ed., *The Ghost Book* (1927), where HPL read it; later included in *The Travelling Grave and Other Stories* (1948). Many of Hartley's short tales contain elements of fantasy and horror; see *Night Fears and Other Stories* (1924), *The Killing Bottle* (1932), *The White Wand and Other Stories* (1954), and *Two for the River* (1961). *The Complete Short Stories of L. P. Hartley* was published in 1973. The futuristic novel *Facial Justice* appeared in 1960.

[43] Another collection of weird tales by Sinclair is *The Intercessor and Other Stories* (1931).

[44] Hodgson was brought to HPL's attention only in 1934 by H. C. Koenig (*SL* V.26, 41). The essay "The Weird Work of William Hope Hodgson" (*Phantagraph*, February 1937), written prior to the passage on Hodgson in SHL, contains the following introductory paragraph:

"Mr. H. C. Koenig has conferred a great service on American 'fandom' by calling attention to the remarkable work of an author relatively unknown in this country, yet actually forming one of the few who have captured the illusive inmost essence of the weird. Among connoisseurs of phantasy fiction William Hope Hodgson deserves a high and prominent rank; for triumphing over a sadly uneven stylistic quality, he now and then equals the best masters in his vague suggestions of lurking worlds and beings behind the ordinary surface of life."

The rest of the essay appears without substantial alteration in SHL, although HPL has here added a discussion of *The Ghost Pirates,* which does not appear in the essay.

The championing of Hodgson by Koenig and HPL is largely responsible for the continued availability of his work today.

[45] *kalpa:* An immense span of time, in Hindu mythology. Cf. *The Dream-Quest of Unknown Kadath:* ". . . all things became as they were unreckoned kalpas before" (*MM* 406).

[46] These "wanderings" could not have influenced the conclusion of *The Dream-Quest of Unknown Kadath* (where Randolph Carter undertakes a similar experience), as that novel was written nearly a decade before HPL read Hodgson; but they could have influenced the wanderings through space of George Campbell, narrator of the round-robin tale "The Challenge from Beyond" (1935).

[47] Other collections of short tales by Hodgson are *Men of the Deep Waters* (1914), *The Luck of the Strong* (1916), *Deep Waters* (1967), *Out of the Storm* (1975), and several other recent compilations.

[48] It is not wholly clear which works by Conrad were read by HPL, nor is it certain that he read the celebrated *Heart of Darkness,* which some have classed as a weird tale. Consider this discussion of *Lord Jim,* in which he remarks that he had "previously read only the shorter and minor productions of Conrad": "Conrad is at heart supremely a

poet, and though his narration is often very heavy and involved, he displays an infinitely potent command of the soul of men and things, reflecting the tides of affairs in an unrivalled procession of graphic pictures which burn their imagery indelibly upon the mind. . . . No artist I have yet encountered has so keen an appreciation of the essential *solitude* of the high-grade personality . . ." (HPL to Lillian D. Clark, 25 May 1925; ms., JHL).

[49] Most of the work of William Carleton (1794–1869) is rooted in Irish legend; see especially *Traits and Stories of the Irish Peasantry* (1830). Carleton's *Stories* (1880) contains an introduction by W. B. Yeats.

[50] The major work of Thomas Crofton Croker (1798–1854) was the *Fairy Legends and Traditions of the South of Ireland* (1825–28; 3 vols.).

[51] See the *Ancient Legends, Mystic Charms, and Superstitions of Ireland* (1887), by Lady Jane Francesca Wilde (1826–1896), written under the pseudonym "Speranza".

[52] Douglas Hyde (1860–1949), President of the Irish Free State (1938–45), did much work in the preservation of Irish culture and language; see *Legends of Saints and Sinners* (1915) and *The Love Songs of Connacht* (1896), both translated from the Irish.

[53] See such works by Yeats (1865–1939) as *The Celtic Twilight* (1893), *In the Seven Woods* (1903), *Stories of Red Hanrahan* (1905; with Lady Gregory), *Plays for an Irish Theatre* (1911), and *Mythologies* (1962). Among books edited by Yeats are *Fairy and Folk Tales of the Irish Peasantry* (1888), *Irish Fairy Tales* (1892), and *A Book of Irish Verse* (1895). HPL considered Yeats the finest poet of his day.

[54] Pseudonym of George William Russell.

[55] For the "Irish renaissance" in general see *Ideals in Ireland* (1901), ed. Lady Gregory, with contributions by "A.E.", Douglas Hyde, Yeats, and others; Ernest Boyd, *Ireland's Literary Renaissance* (1916); Richard Fallis, *The Irish Renaissance* (1977); and John Wilson Foster, *Fictions of the Irish Literary Revival: A Changeling Art* (1987).

X. The Modern Masters

[1] Cf. "Notes on Writing Weird Fiction" (1933): "Inconceivable events and conditions have a special handicap to overcome, and this can be accomplished only through the maintenance of a careful realism in every phase of the story *except* that touching on the one given marvel" (*MW* 115).

[2] Presumably a reference to the work of Lord Dunsany and/or Clark Ashton Smith.

[3] A reference to Algernon Blackwood; see below (p. 66).

[4] First read by HPL, at Frank Belknap Long's suggestion, in the summer of 1923 (*SL* I.228, 233–34).

[5] Including *The Anatomy of Tobacco* (1884), *Hieroglyphics: A Note upon Ecstasy in Literature* (1902), *War and the Christian Faith* (1918), *Dog and Duck* (1924), *Notes*

and Queries (1926), and others. Machen did much journalistic writing for the *Academy*, the *Daily Mail*, the *Evening News*, the *Independent, Literature*, the *London Graphic*, *Walford's Antiquarian*, and other British periodicals.

[6]*Far-Off Things* (1922), *Things Near and Far* (1923), and *The London Adventure; or, The Art of Wandering* (1924). The first two have been reprinted as *The Autobiography of Arthur Machen* (1951).

[7]Machen translated the complete *Memoirs* of Casanova (1894) as well as the *Heptameron* of Marguerite of Navarre (1886) and random works by Cervantes, Beroalde de Verville, and others.

[8]"And I have read *The Hill of Dreams!!* Surely a masterpiece—though I hope it isn't quite as autobiographical as some reviewers claim. I'd hate to think of Machen himself as that young neurotic with his sloppy sentimentalities, his couch of thorns, his urban eccentricities, and all that! But Pegāna, what an imagination! Cut out the emotional hysteria, and you have a marvellously appealing character—how vivid is that exquisite Roman day-dreaming! . . . even if the *spirit* is sadly un-Roman. Machen is a Titan—perhaps the greatest living author—and I must read everything of his" (*SL* II.233–34). See also *SL* IV.373–74.

[9]Originally published in *The Man from Genoa and Other Poems* (Athol, MA: W. Paul Cook, 1926), p. 28; rpt. in *In Mayan Splendor* (Sauk City, WI: Arkham House, 1977), p. 14. Long was, of course, a close associate of HPL.

[10]The description is somewhat reminiscent of a similar catalogue of bizarre events caused by the emergence of Cthulhu in "The Call of Cthulhu" (1926): "Here was a nocturnal suicide in London. . . . Here likewise a rambling letter to the editor of a paper in South America. . . . A fantastic painter named Ardois-Bonnot hangs a blasphemous 'Dream Landscape' in the Paris spring salon of 1926" (*DH* 132).

[11]The root conception of this story was clearly borrowed by HPL in "The Dunwich Horror" (1928), where Wilbur Whateley and his twin are also the offspring of a human woman and a non-human father, Yog-Sothoth.

[12]For the controversy raised by the publication of the tale see Machen's *Things Near and Far,* ch. 7. He reprints some of the hostile reviews of the work in *Precious Balms* (1924).

[13]Cf. the similar diary kept by Wilbur Whateley in "The Dunwich Horror"; where, indeed, such terms from "The White People" as "Aklo" and "Voorish sign" occur (see n. 16 below).

[14]See above (p. 24) and n. 5 there.

[15]HPL mentions creatures named "Doels" in "The Whisperer in Darkness" (*DH* 256), evidently a borrowing from Machen, although HPL's direct source appears to have been Frank Belknap Long's "The Hounds of Tindalos", where "Doels" are also mentioned. Creatures named "dholes" were formerly thought to be cited in *The Dream-Quest of Unknown Kadath,* but this proves to have been a textual error for "bholes".

[16] Cf. Wilbur Whateley's diary in "The Dunwich Horror": "Today learned the Aklo for the Sabaoth" (*DH* 184).

[17] Cf. Machen's introduction to the Knopf (1923) edition of *The Hill of Dreams*: "I was told [by reviewers of *The Three Impostors*] that I was merely a second-rate imitator of Stevenson. This was not quite all the truth, but there was a great deal of truth to it, and I am glad to say that I took my correction in a proper spirit."

[18] Cf. Wilmarth's remark in "The Whisperer in Darkness": "Most of my foes, however, were merely romanticists who insisted on trying to transfer to real life the fantastic lore of lurking 'little people' made popular by the magnificent horror-fiction of Arthur Machen" (*DH* 214).

[19] For the "ghoul-changeling" theme in HPL see George T. Wetzel, "The Cthulhu Mythos: A Study" (*FDOC* 85f.).

[20] Cf. the similar black stone with strange hieroglyphs discovered by Akeley in "The Whisperer in Darkness".

[21] C. Lucius Solinus, Latin writer of the third century C.E., author of the *Collectanea Rerum Memorabilium* or the *Polyhistor* (as it is more commonly known), a compendium of natural history and geography largely derived from the *Natural History* of Pliny the Elder. There was an early English translation by Arthur Golding (1587). The Latin text has been edited by Theodor Mommsen (Berlin, 1895; rev. 1958).

[22] Cf. a similar figure at a window in HPL's "The Thing on the Doorstep" (1933).

[23] For the influence of this tale on "Cool Air" see above (n. 20 to chapter 7). See also entry 191 of the *Commonplace Book*.

[24] Read in May 1925. HPL found it "fair though not Machen's best" (*SL* II.12).

[25] "And your Grandpa hath read *The Terror!* Child, 'tis monstrous well done, with an horror that gathers each moment to the imminence of catastrophic evil. . . . This tale I conceive to be inferior to *The Three Impostors*, not only because of the excessive looseness of the author's later style, but because of the laborious explanation at the end" (*SL* I.304).

[26] Machen discusses this matter in his introduction to *The Angels of Mons: The Bowmen and and Other Legends of the War* (1915).

[27] HPL's first exposure to Blackwood occurred in early 1920, and it was not favourable: "At the recommendation of James F. Morton, Jr., I am perusing the works of a modern imaginative author named Algernon Blackwood . . . I can't say that I am very much enraptured, for somehow Blackwood lacks the power to create a really haunting atmosphere. He is too diffuse, for one thing; and for another thing, his horrors and weirdness are too obviously symbolical—symbolical rather than convincingly outré. And his symbolism is not of that luxuriant kind which makes Dunsany so phenomenal a fabulist. Just to see what he's like, youse fellers might read 'Incredible Adventures', a collective of five very long 'short' stories. It ain't half bad, and if the first one tires you

out, you are not compelled to swallow the remainder" (HPL to the Gallomo, [January? 1920]; AHT). But HPL later read "The Willows" in an anthology in late 1924 (see introduction) and became a Blackwood devotee for life.

[28] A similar device (as well as an invisible monster) is used in HPL's "The Dunwich Horror".

[29] More properly "Smith: An Episode in a Lodging House".

[30] "A weird story, to be a serious aesthetic effort, must form primarily a *picture of a mood*—and such a picture certainly does not call for any clever jack-in-the-box fillip. There *are* weird stories which more or less conform to this description . . . especially in Blackwood's *Incredible Adventures*" (*SL* V.160).

[31] "The Regeneration of Lord Ernie."

[32] "The Damned."

[33] "A Descent into Egypt."

[34] Perhaps an influence on HPL's "The Shadow over Innsmouth".

[35] First read by HPL in the fall of 1919 (*SL* I.91f.), whereupon HPL immediately commenced a series of pastiches of Dunsany's work (e.g., "The White Ship", "The Doom That Came to Sarnath", etc.).

[36] These names are, respectively, from *King Argimēnēs and the Unknown Warrior* (in *Five Plays*), "Bethmoora" (in *A Dreamer's Tales*), "Poltarnees, Beholder of Ocean" (in *A Dreamer's Tales*), "Carcassonne" (in *A Dreamer's Tales*), *King Argimenes and the Unknown Warrior,* and "Time and the Gods" (in *Time and the Gods*).

[37] "Distressing Tale of Thangobrind the Jeweller."

[38] "The House of the Sphinx."

[39] "Probable Adventure of the Three Literary Men"; perhaps an influence on HPL's "The Terrible Old Man" (1920).

[40] "The Hoard of the Gibbelins."

[41] "How Nuth Would Have Practised His Art upon the Gnoles."

[42] "How One Came, as Was Foretold, to the City of Never." Cf. HPL's "The Defence Reopens!" (1921): "[The sincere artist] is not practical, poor fellow, and sometimes dies in poverty; for his friends all live in the City of Never above the sunset" (*IDOD* 12).

[43] "Bethmoora."

[44] "Idle Days on the Yann." HPL borrowed the detail in "The Doom That Came to Sarnath" (1919): "And [the throne] was wrought of one piece of ivory, though no man lives who knows whence so vast a piece could have come" (*D* 46).

[45] "Poor Old Bill."

[46]Cf. "The Defence Reopens!": "The thought of a *rock walking* is not necessarily repulsive, but in Dunsany's *Gods of the Mountain* a man says with a great deal of terror and repulsion, 'Rock should not walk in the evening!'" (*IDOD* 12).

[47]HPL heard Dunsany read this play in Boston in 1919 (*SL* 1.91–93).

[48]See Herodotus, *Histories* 2.100; also my discussion in *Lord Dunsany: Master of the Anglo-Irish Imagination* (1995), pp. 67–68.

[49]I.e. Nitokris. Cf. "The Outsider" (1921): "I know . . . no gaiety save the unnamed feasts of Nitokris beneath the Great Pyramid" (*DH* 52). Also "Under the Pyramids" (1924): "Even the smallest of [the pyramids] held a hint of the ghastly—for was it not in this that they had buried Queen Nitokris alive in the Sixth Dynasty; subtle Queen Nitokris, who once invited all her enemies to a feast in a temple below the Nile, and drowned them by opening the water-gates? I recalled that the Arabs whispered things about Nitokris, and shun the Third Pyramid at certain phases of the moon" (*D* 226–27).

[50]Among James' important works of scholarship in these fields are *On the Abbey of S. Edmund at Bury* (1895), "The Christian Renaissance" (in *The Cambridge Modern History*, I [1902]), *The Ancient Libraries of Canterbury and Dover* (1903), *The Wanderings and Homes of Manuscripts* (1919), *Abbeys* (1925), *Suffolk and Norfolk* (1930), and many others.

[51]Among James' disciples can be numbered E. G. Swain, R. H. Malden, A. N. L. Munby, and others. See Jack Sullivan's chapter "Ghost Stories of Other Antiquaries" in *Elegant Nightmares* (1978).

[52]"Preface" to *More Ghost Stories of an Antiquary*.

[53]It will be noticed how well HPL himself adopted these principles in his later fiction.

[54]See n. 2 to chapter 9.

[55]Cf. "The Lurking Fear", where the narrator feels the "heavy arm" of the monster before seeing it in the flash of lightning that follows (*D* 184).

[56]"The Ash-Tree."

[57]" 'Oh, Whistle, and I'll Come to You, My Lad.' " The words are an almost exact quotation from the story: ". . . it is a horrible, an intensely horrible, face *of crumpled linen.*"

[58]In *Ghost-Stories of an Antiquary*.

[59]Cf. HPL's facetious reference to his pseudonym L. Theobald, Jun.'s position as "Professor of Satanism and Applied Irreverence in Philistine University, Chorazin, Nebraska" ("Some Causes of Self-Immolation" [1931]; *MW* 179).

[60]For the influence of this story upon HPL, see Richard Ward, "In Search of the Dread Ancestor: M. R. James' 'Count Magnus' and Lovecraft's *The Case of Charles Dexter Ward*", *Lovecraft Studies* No. 36 (Spring 1997): 14–17.

[61]In *Ghost-Stories of an Antiquary*.

[62] In *More Ghost Stories of an Antiquary.*

[63] In *Ghost-Stories of an Antiquary.*

[64] In *A Thin Ghost and Others.*

[65] But only six years previous HPL had written: "And nine persons out of ten *never heard of* Ambrose Bierce, the greatest story writer except Poe whom America ever produced" ("The Defence Reopens!" [1921]; *IDOD* 11). In 1929, however, four biographical works on Bierce appeared simultaneously.

[66] "The cup of the Ptolemies, formerly known as the cup of St Denis, is preserved in the Cabinet des Médailles of the Bibliothèque Nationale in Paris. It is a cup 4 3/4 in. high and 5 1/8 in. in diameter, and richly decorated with Dionysiac emblems and attributes in relief." Alexander Murray Stuart and Arthur Hamilton Smith, "Gem", *Encyclopaedia Britannica,* 11th ed. (1910–11), 11:567. Sardonyx is a variety of onyx having layers of sard (a kind of chalcedony).

Bibliography of Authors and Works

APULEUIS, LUCIUS (C. a.d. 123–?)

Metamorphoses (or *Golden Ass*)

Text: Leipzig: Teubner, 1902 (2nd ed. 1913; 3rd ed. 1931) (ed. R. Helm). Cambridge, MA/London: Harvard/Heinemann (Loeb Classical Library), 1915 (ed. S. Gaselee; with Adlington's Eng. tr.).

Translation: William Adlington (1566; often rpt.). H. E. Butler (Oxford, 1910). Jack Lindsay (Bloomington: Indiana University Press, 1960).

Criticism: Paul Monceaux, *Apulée: Roman et magie* (Paris, n.d.). Carl C. Schlam, *The Metamorphoses of Apuleius: On Making an Ass of Oneself* (Chapel Hill: University of North Carolina Press, 1992). James Tatum, *Apuleius and* The Golden Ass (Ithaca, NY: Cornell University Press, 1979). P. G. Walsh, *The Roman Novel: The* Satyricon *of Petronius and the* Metamorphoses *of Apuleius* (Cambridge: Cambridge University Press, 1970).

AUSTEN, JANE (1775–1817)

Northanger Abbey (written 1803)

Text: London: John Murray, 1818 (with *Persuasion;* 4 vols.). Oxford, 1923 (ed. R. W. Chapman). London & New York: Dent/Dutton (Everyman's Library), 1966 (ed. Mary Lascelles). Harmondsworth: Penguin, 1972 (ed. Anne Henry Ehrenpreis).

Criticism: Frank W. Bradbrook, *Jane Austen and Her Predecessors* (Cambridge: Cambridge University Press, 1966). W. A. Craik, *Jane Austen: The Six Novels* (New York: Barnes & Noble, 1965), ch. 1. Susan Payne, *The Strange within the Real: The Function of Fantasy in Austen, Brontë, and Eliot* (Rome: Bulzoni, 1992). Michael Sadleir, *The Northanger Novels: A Footnote* (Oxford, 1927). Judith Wilt, *Ghosts of the Gothic: Austen, Eliot and Lawrence* (Princeton: Princeton University Press, 1980).

BALZAC, HONORÉ DE (1799–1850)

Histoire intellectuelle de Louis Lambert

Text: Paris: C. Gosselin, 1832. In Balzac's *Oeuvres Complètes,* ed. Société des Etudes Balzaciennes (Paris: Guy le Prat, 1961), Vol. 20. Paris: Livre de Poche, 1968.

Translation: Katherine Prescott Wormeley (Boston: Roberts Brothers, 1889).

Criticism: Henri Evans, *Louis Lambert et la philosophie de Balzac* (Paris: Corti, 1951).

"Melmoth Réconcilié" ("Melmoth Reconciled") (*LL* 400)

Text: Le Livre des conteurs 6 (1835). In Balzac's *Oeuvres Complètes,* ed. Société des Etudes Balzaciennes (Paris: Guy le Prat, 1961).

Translation: In *The Complete Novelettes of Honoré de Balzac* (New York: Collier, 1926). In Balzac's *Christ in Flanders and Other Stories,* tr. Ellen Marriage (London & New York: Dent/Dutton [Everyman's Library], 1908).

Le Peau de chagrin (*The Wild Ass's Skin*)

Text: Paris: C. Gosselin, 1831 (2 vols.). Paris: Garnier Frères, 1960. Paris: Gallimard, 1974. In Balzac's *Oeuvres Complètes* (Paris: Société d'Editions Litteraires et Artistiques, 1900), Vol. 37.

Translation: George Frederic Parsons (Boston: Roberts Brothers, 1888; as *The Magic Skin*). Ellen Marriage (Philadelphia: Gebbie, 1897; London & New York: Dent/Dutton [Everyman's Library], 1906; as *The Wild Ass's Skin*). Cedar Paul (London: Hamish Hamilton, 1942; New York: Pantheon, 1949; as *The Fatal Skin*). Herbert J. Hunt (Harmondsworth: Penguin, 1977; as *The Wild Ass's Skin*).

Criticism: Pierre Bayard, *Balzac et le troc de l'imaginaire* (Paris: Les Lettres Modernes, 1978). Claude Duchet, ed., *Balzac et* Le Peau de chagrin (Paris: Société d'enseignement superieur, 1979). Maximilian Rudwin, "Balzac and the Fantastic", *Sewanee Review* 33 (1925): 2–24. Samuel Weber, *Unwrapping Balzac: A Reading of* Le Peau de chagrin (Toronto: University of Toronto Press, 1979).

Séraphita

Text: Paris: Werdet, 1836. Paris: P. J. Oswald, 1973. In Balzac's *Oeuvres Complètes,* ed. Société des Etudes Balzaciennes (Paris: Guy le Prat, 1961), Vol. 21.

Translation: Katherine Prescott Wormeley (Boston: Roberts Brothers, 1889; rpt. Freeport, NY: Books for Libraries Press, 1970). Anon. (Blauvelt, NY: Steinerbooks, 1976).

Criticism: Jacques Borel, Séraphita *et le mysticisme balzacien* (Paris: Corti, 1967).

BALBAULD, MRS ANNA LETITIA (MISS AIKIN) (1743–1825)

"Sir Bertrand"

Text: In "On the Pleasure Derived from Objects of Terror", in John and Letitia Aikin, *Miscellaneous Pieces in Prose* (London: J. Johnson, 1773). In Peter Haining, ed., *Gothic Tales of Terror* (New York: Taplinger, 1972).

Criticism (General): Grace A. Oliver, *The Story of the Life of Anna Laetitia Barbauld; with Many of Her Letters* (Boston: Cupples, Upham, 1886).

BAUDELAIRE, CHARLES PIERRE (1821–1867)

[*Works*] (*LL* 69)

Text: Les Fleurs du mal (Paris: Poulet-Malassis et de Broise, 1857). *Oeuvres,* ed. Jacques Crepet (Paris: Louis Conrad, 1923–65; 19 vols.).

Translation: The Flowers of Evil, tr. George Dillon and Edna St Vincent Millay (London & New York: Harper & Brothers, 1936; often rpt.). *Poems in Prose*, tr. Arthur Symons (London, 1905; often rpt.). Arthur F. Kraetzer (New York: R. R. Smith, 1950). Richard Howard (Boston: David R. Godine, 1982). James McGowan (Oxford: Oxford University Press [World's Classics], 1993).

Criticism: Georges Blis, *Le Sadisme de Baudelaire* (Paris: Corti, 1948). Pierre Emanuel, *Baudelaire: The Paradox of Redemptive Satanism*, tr. Robert T. Cargo (University: University of Alabama Press, 1970). Théophile Gautier, *Baudelaire* (Paris: Klincksieck, 1986). Suzanne Guerlac, *The Impersonal Sublime: Hugo, Baudelaire, Lautréamont* (Stanford: Stanford University Press, 1990). D. J. Mossop, *Baudelaire's Tragic Hero: A Study of the Architecture of* Les Fleurs du mal (London: Oxford University Press, 1961). Yvonne Bargues Rollins, *Baudelaire et le grotesque* (Washington, DC: University Press of America, 1978). Marcel A. Ruff, *L'Esprit de mal et l'esthetique baudelairienne* (Paris: Armand Colin, 1955). Jean Paul Sartre, *Baudelaire*, tr. Martin Turnell (Norfolk, CT: New Directions, 1950). Arthur Symons, *Charles Baudelaire: A Study* (New York: E. P. Dutton, 1920). G. Turquet-Milnes, *The Influence of Baudelaire in France and England* (London: Constable, 1913). Peter Michael Wetherill, *Charles Baudelaire et la poésie d'Edgar Allan Poe* (Paris: A. G. Nizet, 1962).

BECKFORD, WILLIAM (1760–1844)

The Episodes of Vathek (*LL* 73)

Text: See *The Episodes of Vathek*, tr. Frank T. Marzials (below). In *Vathek et les episodes* (Lausanne: Société Cooperative/Editions Rencontre, 1962).

Translation: Frank T. Marzials; introduction by Louis Melville (London: Stephen Swift, 1912 [with French text]; Boston: Small, Maynard, 1922; Cambridge: Cambridge University Press, 1929 [with *Vathek*]; Rutherford, NJ: Fairleigh Dickinson University Press, 1975).

Criticism: Lewis Melville, *The Life and Letters of William Beckford* (London: Heinemann, 1910).

The History of the Caliph Vathek (*LL* 74, 75)

Text: Vathek, conte arabe (Paris: Poincot, 1787; Lausanne: Hignou, 1787; Paris: Corti, 1946).

Translation: Samuel Henley (London: J. Johnson, 1786; London: Chapman & Dodd, 1932; Delmar, NY: Scholars' Facsimiles and Reprints, 1972 [with French text]; New York: Dover, 1966 [with *The Castle of Otranto* et al.]; in Peter Fairclough, ed., *Three Gothic Novels* [Harmondsworth: Penguin, 1968]). In *Four Gothic Novels* (Oxford: Oxford University Press, 1994).

Criticism: Jorge Luis Borges, "About William Beckford's *Vathek*", in Borges' *Other Inquisitions*, tr. Ruth L. C. Simms (Austin: University of Texas Press, 1964).

Kenneth W. Graham, ed., Vathek *and the Escape from Time: Bicentenary Revaluations* (New York: AMS Press, 1990). Marcel May, *La Jeunesse de William Beckford et la genèse de son* Vathek (Paris: Presses Universitaires de France, 1928).

Criticism (General): Alexander Boyd, *England's Wealthiest Son: A Study of William Beckford* (London: Centaur Press, 1962). Robert P. Gemmett, *William Beckford* (Boston: Twayne, 1977). Didier Girard, *Willaim Beckford: Terroriste au palais de la Raison* (Paris: Corti, 1993). Lafcadio Hearn, "William Beckford", in Hearn's *Some Strange Literary Figures of the Eighteenth and Nineteenth Centuries,* ed. R. Tanabe (Tokyo: Hokuseido Press, 1927). Fatma Mousa Mahmoud, ed., *William Beckford of Fonthill 1760–1844: Bicentenary Essays* (Port Washington, NY: Kennikat Press, 1972). André Parreaux, *William Beckford, auteur de Vathek* (Paris: A. G. Nizet, 1960).

BENSON, E[DWARD] F[REDERIC] (1867–1940)

The Room in the Tower and Other Stories

> *Text:* London: Mill & Boon, 1912. New York: Alfred A. Knopf, 1929. In *The Collected Ghost Stories of E. F. Benson,* ed. Richard Dalby (New York: Carroll & Graf, 1992).

Spook Stories

> *Text:* London: Hutchinson, 1928. New York: Arno Press, 1976. In *The Collected Ghost Stories of E. F. Benson* (q.v.).

Visible and Invisible (*LL*79)

> *Text:* London: Hutchinson, 1923. New York: George H. Doran, 1924. In *The Collected Ghost Stories of E. F. Benson* (q.v.).

Criticism (General): E. F. Benson, *As We Are* (London & New York: Longmans, Green, 1932). E. F. Benson, *As We Were: A Victorian Peep Show* (London & New York: Longmans, Green, 1930).

BIERCE, AMBROSE (1842–1914?)

Can Such Things Be? (*LL* 87)

> *Text:* New York: Cassell, 1893. Washington, DC: Neale Publishing Co., 1903, 1909 (in *Collected Works,* Vol. 3). New York: Boni & Liveright, 1918. London: Jonathan Cape, 1927. Secaucus, NY: Citadel Press, 1946, 1974. London: White Lion, 1972.

In the Midst of Life: Tales of Soldiers and Civilians (*LL* 88)

> *Text:* San Francisco: E. L. G. Steele, 1891 (as *Tales of Soldiers and Civilians*). London: Chatto & Windus, 1892. New York: G. P. Putnam's Sons, 1898. Washington, DC: Neale Publishing Co., 1909 (in *Collected Works,* Vol. 2). New York: Boni & Liveright, 1918. New York: Modern Library, [1927]. Harmondsworth:

Penguin, 1939. New York: Limited Editions Club, 1943. New York: New American Library, 1961.

Criticism (General): Cathy N. Davidson, *The Experimental Fictions of Ambrose Bierce* (Lincoln: University of Nebraska Press, 1984). Paul Fatout, *Ambrose Bierce: The Devil's Lexicographer* (Norman: University of Oklahoma Press, 1951). Paul Fatout, *Ambrose Bierce and the Black Hills* (Norman: University of Oklahoma Press, 1956). M. E. Grenander, *Ambrose Bierce* (New York: Twayne, 1971). Carroll D. Hall, *Bierce and the Poe Hoax* (San Francisco: Book Club of California, 1943). S. T. Joshi, "Ambrose Bierce: Horror as Satire", in Joshi's *The Weird Tale* (Austin: University of Texas Press, 1990). Carey McWilliams, *Ambrose Bierce: A Biography* (New York: A. & C. Boni, 1929; Hamden, CT: Archon, 1967). Roy Morris, Jr, *Ambrose Bierce: Alone in Bad Company* (New York: Crown, 1995). Edmund Wilson, "Ambrose Bierce on the Owl Creek Bridge", in Wilson's *Patriotic Gore: Studies in the Literature of the American Civil War* (New York: Oxford University Press, 1962). Stuart C. Woodruff, *The Short Stories of Ambrose Bierce* (Pittsburgh: University of Pittsburgh Press, 1964).

BISS, GERALD

The Door of the Unreal

Text: London: Eveleigh Nash, 1919. New York: G. P. Putnam's Sons, 1920. London: Eveleigh Nash & Grayson, 1928.

Criticism: Review, *New York Times Book Review*, 19 September 1920, p. 23.

BLACKWOOD, ALGERNON (1869–1951)

The Centaur

Text: London: Macmillan, 1911. Harmondsworth: Penguin, 1938. New York: Arno Press, 1976.

Incredible Adventures

Text: London: Macmillan, 1914.

Jimbo: A Fantasy (*LL* 95)

Text: London: Macmillan, 1909.

John Silence—Physician Extraordinary (*LL* 96, 97)

Text: London: Eveleigh Nash, 1908. Boston: John W. Luce, 1909. London: Macmillan, 1912. New York: Alfred A. Knopf, 1917. New York: E. P. Dutton, 1920. London: Unwin, 1928. London: Richards Press, 1942.

"The Listener"

Text: In Blackwood's *The Listener and Other Stories* (London: Eveleigh Nash, 1907, 1914; New York: Alfred A. Knopf, 1917; Freeport, NY: Books for Libraries Press, 1971). In *The Best Ghost Stories of Algernon Blackwood* (New York: Dover, 1973). In Blackwood's *Tales of Terror and the Unknown* (New York: E. P. Dutton, 1965).

"Smith: An Episode in a Lodging House"

Text: In Blackwood's *The Empty House and Other Ghost Stories* (London: Eveleigh Nash, 1906, 1915; London: Richards Press, 1947).

"The Wendigo"

Text: In Blackwood's *The Lost Valley and Other Stories* (London: Eveleigh Nash, 1910; New York: Alfred A. Knopf, 1917; London: Grayson, 1936; Freeport, NY: Books for Libraries Press, 1971). In *The Best Ghost Stories of Algernon Blackwood* (q.v.). In *Tales of Terror and the Unknown* (q.v.).

"The Willows" (*LL* 558)

Text: In *The Listener and Other Stories* (q.v.). In *The Best Ghost Stories of Algernon Blackwood* (q.v.). In *Tales of Terror and the Unknown* (q.v.).

Additional Works:

The Bright Messenger. London: Cassell, 1921. New York: E. P. Dutton, 1922.

The Dance of Death and Other Tales. New York: Dial Press, 1928.

Day and Night Stories. London: Cassell, 1917. New York: E. P. Dutton, 1917.

The Garden of Survival. London: Macmillan, 1918. New York: E. P. Dutton, 1918.

Julius Le Vallon: An Episode. London: Cassell, 1916. New York: E. P. Dutton, 1916. (*LL* 98)

Pan's Garden: A Volume of Nature Stories. London: Macmillan, 1912. Freeport, NY: Books for Libraries Press, 1971.

Shocks. London: Grayson & Grayson, 1935. New York: E. P. Dutton, 1936. (*LL* 100)

The Tales of Algernon Blackwood. London: Secker, 1938. New York: E. P. Dutton, 1939.

Ten Minute Stories. London: John Murray, 1914. New York: E. P. Dutton, 1914. Freeport, NY: Books for Libraries Press, 1969.

Tongues of Fire and Other Sketches. London: H. Jenkins, 1924. New York: E. P. Dutton, 1925.

The Wave: An Egyptian Aftermath. London: Macmillan, 1916. New York: E. P. Dutton, 1916.

Tales of the Mysterious and the Macabre. London: Spring Books, 1967.

Tales of the Uncanny and Supernatural. London: Spring Books, 1962.

Criticism (General): Mike Ashley, *Algernon Blackwood: A Bio-Bibliography* (Westport, CT: Greenwood Press, 1987). Algernon Blackwood, *Episodes Before Thirty* (London & New York: Cassell, 1923; New York: E. P. Dutton, 1924; London: Peter Nevill, 1950). Stuart Gilbert, "Algernon Blackwood: Novelist and Mystic", *Transition*

23 (1935): 89–96. S. T. Joshi, "Algernon Blackwood: The Expansion of Consciousness", in Joshi's *The Weird Tale* (Austin: University of Texas Press, 1990). Peter Penzoldt, "Algernon Blackwood", in Penzoldt's *The Supernatural in Fiction* (London: Peter Nevill, 1952; Atlantic Highlands, NJ: Humanities Press, 1965). Jack Sullivan, *Elegant Nightmares: The English Ghost Story from Le Fanu to Blackwood* (Athens: Ohio University Press, 1978).

BRONTË, EMILY (1818–1848)

Wuthering Heights (*LL* 611)

Text: London: Thomas Cautley Newby, 1847 (2 vols.; as by "Ellis Bell"). New York: Harper, 1903 (rpt. New York: AMS Press, 1973). Oxford: Shakespeare Head Press, 1931 (ed. Thomas J. Wise and J. A. Symington). Oxford: Clarendon Press, 1976 (ed. Hilda Marsden and Ian Jack).

Criticism: Miriam Allott, ed., *Emily Brontë's* Wuthering Heights: *A Casebook* (London: Macmillan, 1970). Florence Dry, *The Sources of* Wuthering Heights (Cambridge: W. Heffer & Sons, 1937). Stevie Davies, *Emily Brontë* (London: Women's Press, 1994). Alastair Everett, ed., Wuthering Heights: *An Anthology of Criticism* (London: Cass, 1967). David Holbrook, Wuthering Heights: *A Drama of Being* (Sheffield, UK: Sheffield Academic Press, 1997). Carol Jacobs, *Uncontainable Romanticism: Shelley, Brontë, Kleist* (Baltimore: Johns Hopkins University Press, 1989). Meg Harris Williams, *A Strange Way of Killing: The Poetic Structure of* Wuthering Heights (Strathtay, UK: Clunie Press, 1987).

BROWN, CHARLES BROCKDEN (1771–1810).

Arthur Mervyn; or, Memoirs of the Year 1793

Text: Philadelphia: H. Maxwell; New York: George F. Hopkins, 1799–1800 (2 vols.). New York: David McKay, 1887 (rpt. Port Washington, NY: Kennikat Press, 1963). New York: Holt, Rinehart & Winston, 1962 (ed. Warner Berthoff). Kent, OH: Kent State University Press, 1980 (ed. Sydney J. Krause et al.).

Edgar Huntly; or, Memoirs of a Sleep-Walker

Text: Philadelphia: H. Maxwell, 1799. New York: David McKay, 1887 (rpt. Port Washington, NY: Kennikat Press, 1963). New York: Macmillan, 1923 (ed. David Lee Clark). New Haven, CT: College and University Press, 1973 (ed. David Stinebeck). Kent, OH: Kent State University Press, 1984 (ed. Sydney J. Krause et al.).

Ormond; or, The Secret Witness

Text: New York: G. Forman for H. Caritat, 1799. New York: David McKay, 1887 (rpt. Port Washington, NY: Kennikat Press, 1963). New York: American Book, Co., 1937 (rpt. New York: Hafner, 1962) (ed. Ernest Marchand). Kent, OH: Kent State University Press, 1982 (ed. Sydney J. Krause et al.).

Wieland; or, The Transformation

Text: New York: T. & J. Swords for H. Caritat, 1798. New York: David McKay, 1887 (rpt. Port Washington, NY: Kennikat Press, 1963). New York: Harcourt, Brace, 1926 (rpt. New York: Hafner, 1958) (ed. Fred Lewis Pattee). Kent, OH: Kent State University Press, 1977 (ed. Sydney S. Krause et al.).

Criticism (General): Alan Axelrod, *Charles Brockden Brown: An American Tale* (Austin: University of Texas Press, 1983). Leslie A. Fiedler, "Charles Brockden Brown and the Invention of the American Gothic", in Fiedler's *Love and Death in the American Novel* (1960; rev. ed. New York: Stein & Day, 1966). Frederick S. Frank, "Perverse Pilgrimage: The Role of the Gothic in the Works of Charles Brockden Brown, Edgar Allan Poe, and Nathaniel Hawthorne", Ph.D. diss.: Rutgers, 1968. Arthur Kimball, *Rational Fiction: A Study of Charles Brockden Brown* (McMinnville, OR: Linfield Research Inst., 1968). Donald A. Ringe, *Charles Brockden Brown* (New York: Twayne, 1966). Bernard Rosenthal, ed., *Critical Essays on Charles Brockden Brown* (Boston: G. K. Hall, 1981). Harry R. Warfel, *Charles Brockden Brown: American Gothic Novelist* (Gainesville: University of Florida Press, 1949). Lulu Ramsey Wiley, *The Sources and Influence of the Novels of Charles Brockden Brown* (New York: Vantage Press, 1950).

BROWNING, ROBERT (1812–1889)

"Childe Roland to the Dark Tower Came" (*LL* 124)

Text: In Browning's *Men and Women* (London: Chapman & Hall, 1885 [2 vols.]; London: J. M. Dent, 1896; Oxford: Clarendon Press, 1911 [ed. G. E. Hadoco]). In *The Complete Poetical Works of Browning* (Boston: Houghton Mifflin, 1887). In *The Brownings: Letters and Poetry,* ed. Christopher Ricks (Garden City, NY: Doubleday, 1970). In *Robert Browning: The Poems,* ed. John Pettigrew (New Haven: Yale University Press, 1981), Vol. 1.

Criticism: David V. Erdman, "Browning's Industrial Nightmare", *Philological Quarterly* 36 (1957): 417–35. Barbara Melchiovi, "The Tapestry House: 'Childe Roland' and 'Metzengerstein' ", *English Miscellany* 14 (1963): 185–93. Joyce B. Meyers, " 'Childe Roland to the Dark Tower Came': A Nightmare Confrontation with Death", *Victorian Poetry* 8 (1970): 335–39.

BUCHAN, JOHN (1875–1940)

The Runagates Club (*LL* 129)

Text: London: Hodder & Stoughton, 1928. Boston & New York: Houghton Mifflin, 1928. London & New York: Thomas Nelson, 1950.

Witch Wood

Text: Boston & New York: Houghton Mifflin, 1927. London & New York: Thomas Nelson, 1929. Edinburgh: Canongate Press, 1988. Oxford: Oxford University Press [World's Classics], 1993) (ed. James C. G. Greig).

Criticism (General): Andrew Lownie, *John Buchan: The Presbyterian Cavalier* (London: Constable, 1995). M. R. Ridley, "A Misrated Author?", in Ridley's *Second Thoughts* (London: J. M. Dent, 1965). Janet Adam Smith, *John Buchan: A Biography* (London: R. Hart-Davis, 1965). Janet Adam Smith, *John Buchan and His World* (New York: Scribner's, 1979).

BÜRGER, GOTTFRIED AUGUST (1747–1794)

Lenore

Text: In *Göttinger Musenalmanach,* 1773. In Bürger's *Sammtliche Schriften,* ed. Karl Reinhard (Göttingen, 1796; rpt. Hildesheim: Georg Olms Verlag, 1970), Vol. 1. In Bürger's *Werke,* ed. Eduard Grifebach (Berlin, 1881). In Bürger's *Sämtliche Werke,* ed. Günter and Hilfred Häntzschel (Munich: Carl Hanser Verlag, 1987).

Translation: Henry James Pye (London: Sampson, Low, 1796). Dante Gabriel Rossetti (London: Ellis & Elvey, 1900).

Der wilde Jäger (The Wild Huntsman)

Text: In *Sammtliche Schriften* (q.v.), Vol. II. In *Werke* (q.v.).

Translation: The Chase, and William and Helen, tr. Sir Walter Scott (Edinburgh: Mundell & Son, 1796) [tr. of *Der wilde Jäger* and *Lenore*]. [Henry James Pye] (London: Sampson, Low, 1798). Charles J. Lukens (Philadelphia: Collins, 1870).

Criticism (General): William A. Little, *Gottfried August Bürger* (New York: Twayne, 1974). G. Bonet Maury, *G. A. Bürger et les origines de la ballade littéraire en Allemagne* (Paris, 1889).

BURNS, ROBERT (1759–1796)

"Tam O'Shanter" (*LL* 137)

Text: Edinburgh Herald, 18 March 1791. In *The Complete Poetical Works of Robert Burns* (Boston: Houghton Mifflin, 1897). In *The Poems and Songs of Robert Burns,* ed. James Kinsey (Oxford: Clarendon Press, 1968), Vol. 2.

Criticism: Thomas Crawford, *Burns: A Study of the Poems and Songs* (Edinburgh: Oliver & Boyd, 1960). David Daiches, *Robert Burns* (New York: Macmillan, 1966).

CHAMBERS, ROBERT W[ILLIAM] (1865–1933)

In Search of the Unknown (*LL* 166)

Text: New York: Harper, 1904. Westport, CT: Hyperion, 1974.

The King in Yellow (*LL* 167)

Text: Chicago: F. Tennyson Neely, 1895. New York: Harper, 1902. New York: D. Appleton, 1938 (foreword by Rupert Hughes). New York: Ace, 1965. New York: Dover, 1970 (with other tales). New York: Arno Press, 1977.

The Maker of Moons

Text: New York: G. P. Putnam's Sons, 1896. New York: Arno Press, 1977.

Criticism (General): Frederic Taber Cooper, *Some American* Story *Tellers* (New York: Henry Holt, 1911; rpt. Freeport, NY: Books for Libraries Press, 1968). S. T. Joshi, "Robert W. Chambers", *Crypt of Cthulhu* 22 (Roodmas 1984): 26–33, 17. Lee Weinstein, "Chambers and *The King in Yellow*", *Romantist* 3 (1979): 51–57.

CLINE, LEONARD (1893–1929)

The Dark Chamber (*LL* 183)

Text: New York: Viking Press, 1927. New York: Popular Library, n.d. New York: Pinnacle, 1982.

Criticism: Donald Douglas, Review, *New York Herald Tribune Books,* 4 September 1927, p. 4. Allan Nevins, Review, *Saturday Review of Literature,* 10 September 1927, p. 101.

COBB, IRVIN S. (1876–1944)

"Fishhead" (*LL* 397)

Text: Argosy, 11 January 1913. In Cobb's *The Escape of Mr. Trimm and Other Plights* (New York: George H. Doran, 1913; New York: Review of Reviews, 1918, 1923). In T. Everett Harré, ed., *Beware After Dark!* (New York: Macaulay, 1929; New York: Emerson Books, 1942). In Alfred Hitchcock, ed., *Stories That Scared Even Me* (New York: Random House, 1967).

Criticism (General): Wayne Chatterton, *Irvin S. Cobb* (Boston: Twayne, 1986). Elizabeth Chapman Cobb, *My Wayward Parent* (Indianapolis: Bobbs-Merrill, 1945). Irvin S. Cobb, *Exit Laughing* (Indianapolis: Bobbs-Merrill, 1941). Anita Lawson, *Irvin S. Cobb* (Bowling Green, OH: Bowling Green State University Popular Press, 1984).

COLERIDGE, SAMUEL TAYLOR (1772–1834)

[*Poetical Works*] (*LL* 188)

Text: London: William Pickering, 1834 (3 vols.). London: Macmillan, 1903 (ed. James Dykes Campbell). Oxford: Clarendon Press, 1912 (ed. Ernest Hartley Coleridge).

Criticism (General): James D. Boulger, ed., *Twentieth Century Interpretations of* The Rime of the Ancient Mariner (Englewood Cliffs, NJ: Prentice-Hall, 1969). R. L. Brett, *Reason and Imagination* (London, 1960). John Livingston Lowes, *The Road to Xanadu* (Boston: Houghton Mifflin, 1927). Susan M. Luther, *"Christabel" as Dream-Reverie* (Salzburg, 1976). Bernard Martin, The Ancient Mariner *and the Authentic Narrative* (London: William Heinemann, 1949; rpt. Folcroft, PA: Folcroft Press, 1970). Arthur H. Nethercot, *The Road to Tryermaine: A Study of the History, Background, and Purposes of Coleridge's "Christabel"* (Chicago: University of Chicago Press, 1939). I. A. Richards, *Coleridge on Imagination* (Bloomington: Indiana University Press, 1960). Elizabeth Schneider, *Coleridge, Opium, and "Kubla Khan"* (Chicago: University of Chicago Press, 1953). Marshall Suther, *Visions of Xanadu* (New York: Columbia University Press, 1965).

CRAM, RALPH ADAMS (1863–1942)

"The Dead Valley"

Text: In Cram's *Black Spirits and White* (Chicago: Stone & Kimball, 1895; London: Chatto & Windus, 1896; West Warwick, RI: Necronomicon Press, 1993). In Joseph Lewis French, ed., *Ghosts, Grim and Gentle* (New York: Dodd, Mead, 1926).

Criticism (General): Robert Muccigrosso, *American Gothic: The Mind and Art of Ralph Adams Cram* (Washington, DC: University Press of America, 1980).

CRAWFORD, F[RANCIS] MARION (1854–1909)

Wandering Ghosts

Text: New York: Macmillan, 1911. London: Unwin, 1911 (as *Uncanny Tales*).

Criticism (General): S. T. Joshi, "The Weird Work of F. Marion Crawford", *Studies in Weird Fiction* No. 22 (Winter 1998): 20–29. John C. Moran, *Seeking Refuge in Torre San Nicola* (Nashville: F. Marion Crawford Society, 1980). John C. Moran, *An F. Marion Crawford Companion* (Westport, CT: Greenwood Press, 1981). John Pilkington, *Francis Marion Crawford* (New York: Twayne, 1964). Hugh Walpole, "The Stories of Francis Marion Crawford", *Yale Review* 12 (1923): 673–91.

DACRE, CHARLOTTE (1782–1842?)

Zofloya; or, The Moor

Text: London: Longman, Hurst, Rees, & Orme, 1806 (3 vols.). London: Fortune Press, 1928 (intro. by Montague Summers). New York: Arno Press, 1974 (3 vols.).

Criticism (General): Montague Summers, "Byron's Lovely Rosa", in his *Essays in Petto* (London: Fortune Press, 1928; rpt. Freeport, NY: Books for Libraries Press, 1967).

DANTE ALIGHIERI (1265–1321)

La commedia divina (*The Divine Comedy*) (*LL* 218, 219)

Text: Milan: Mondadori, 1966–67 (4 vols.; ed. Giorgio Petrocchi). Oxford, 1946 (3 vols.; ed. John Sinclair; with Eng. tr. & notes). Princeton: Princeton University Press, 1970–75 (6 vols.; ed. Charles S. Singleton; with Eng. tr. & commentary).

Translation: Henry Francis Cary (1805f.; often rpt.). Henry Wadsworth Longfellow (1867; with English notes). Dorothy L. Sayers (Harmondsworth: Penguin, 1955–62; 3 vols.).

Criticism: René Guenon, *L'Esoterisme de Dante* (Paris: Bosse, 1925; Italian tr. 1971). Fortunato Laurenzi, *Ermetica ed ermeneutica dantesca* (Milan: Castello, 1931). Gerard Lucinai, *Les monstres dans* La Divine Comedie (Paris: Les Lettres Modernes, 1975). Giovanni Pischedda, *L'orrido e l'ineffabile nella tematica dantesca* (L'Aquila: La Bodoniana Tipografica, 1958). Ricardo J. Quinones, *Dante Alighieri* (Boston: Twayne, 1979). Luigi Tonelli, *Dante e la poesia dell'ineffabile* (Florence: G. Barbeva, 1934).

DEFOE, DANIEL (1661?–1731)

A True Relation of the Apparition of one Mrs. Veal, the Next Day after Her Death, to one Mrs. Bargrave at Canterbury, the 8th of Sept., 1705

Text: London: B. Bragg, 1706. In *The Works of Daniel Defoe,* ed. G. H. Maynadier (1903f.), Vol. 15. In Defoe's *Colonel Jack* (Oxford: Clarendon Press, 1940), pp. 337–56.

Criticism: Rodney M. Baine, *Daniel Defoe and the Supernatural* (Athens: University of Georgia Press, 1968).

DE LA MARE, WALTER (1873–1956)

"All-Hallows" (*LL* 228)

Text: In de la Mare's *The Connoisseur and Other Stories* (London: William Collins, 1926; New York: Alfred A. Knopf, 1926). In de la Mare's *Collected Tales,* ed. Edward Wagenknecht (New York: Alfred A. Knopf, 1950). In Colin de la Mare, ed., *They Walk Again* (New York: Dutton, 1931).

"The Listeners"

Text: In de la Mare's *The Listener and Other Poems* (London: Constable, 1912; London: Faber & Faber, 1942). In *The Complete Poems of Walter de la Mare* (London: Faber & Faber, 1969).

"Mr. Kempe" (*LL* 228)

Text: In *The Connoisseur and Other Stories* (q.v.).

"Out of the Deep" (*LL* 229)

Text: In de la Mare's *The Riddle and Other Stories* (London: Selwyn & Blount, 1923; New York: Alfred A. Knopf, 1923; London: Faber & Faber, 1928). In Herbert A. Wise and Phyllis Fraser, eds., *Great Tales of Terror and the Supernatural* (New York: Random House, 1944).

"A Recluse"

Text: In Cynthia Asquith, ed., *The Ghost Book* (New York: Scribner's, 1927; London: Pan Books, 1970). In de la Mare's *On the Edge* (London: Faber & Faber, 1930, 1947; New York: Alfred A. Knopf, 1931).

The Return

Text: London: Edward Arnold, 1910. New York: Alfred A. Knopf, 1922 (rev.). London: Faber & Faber, 1945. New York: Arno Press, 1976 (rpt. of 1910 ed.). Mineola, NY: Dover, 1997.

"Seaton's Aunt"

Text: In *The Riddle and Other Stories* (q.v.). In *Collected Tales* (q.v.). In August Derleth, ed., *The Night Side* (New York: Rinehart, 1947). In Clifton Fadiman, ed., *Fifty Years* (New York: Alfred A. Knopf, 1965).

"The Tree" (*LL* 229)

Text: In *The Riddle and Other Stories* (q.v.). In *Collected Tales* (q.v.). In Dorothy L. Sayers, ed., *The Second Omnibus of Crime* (New York: Coward-McCann, 1932).

Criticism (General): Sir Walter Russell Brain, *Tea with Walter de la Mare* (London: Faber & Faber, 1957). Kenneth Hopkins, *Walter de la Mare* (London: Longmans, Green, 1953). Diana Ross McCrosson, *Walter de la Mare* (New York: Twayne, 1966). Forrest Reid, *Walter de la Mare: A Critical Study* (London: Faber & Faber, 1929). Theresa Whistler, *Imagination of the Heart: The Life of Walter de la Mare* (London: Duckworth, 1993).

DICKENS, CHARLES (1812–1870)

"No. 1 Branch Line: The Signal-Man"

Text: All the Year Round, Christmas 1866. In Edward Gorey, ed., *The Haunted Looking Glass* (New York: Random House, 1959). In Herbert Van Thal, ed., *Great Ghost Stories* (New York: Hill & Wang, 1960).

Criticism: Robert Newsom, *Dickens on the Romantic Side of Familiar Things* (New York: Columbia University Press, 1977). Harry Stone, *Dickens and the Invisible World* (New York: Macmillan, 1980).

DOYLE, SIR ARTHUR CONAN (1859–1930)

"The Captain of the Pole-Star"

Text: In Doyle's *The Captain of the Pole-Star and Other Tales* (London: Longmans, Green, 1890). In Doyle's *The Great Keinplatz Experiment and Other Stories* (Chicago: Rand McNally, 1894; not in Doran ed. [see below]).

"Lot No. 249"

Text: In Doyle's *Round the Red Lamp* (London: Methuen, 1894; New York: D. Appleton, 1894). In Doyle's *The Great Keinplatz Experiment and Other Tales of Twilight and the Unseen* (New York: George H. Doran, 1919; Garden City, NY: Garden City Publishing Co., 1937). In John Keir Cross, ed., *Best Horror Stories* (London: Faber & Faber, 1957). In Henry Mazzeo, ed., *Hauntings* (Garden City, N.Y.: Doubleday, 1968).

Criticism (General): John Dickson Carr, *The Life of Sir Arthur Conan Doyle* (New York: Harper, 1949). Pierre Norden, *Conan Doyle: A Biography,* tr. Francis Partridge (New York: Holt, Rinehart & Winston, 1967). Hesketh Pearson, *Conan Doyle: His Life and Art* (London: Methuen, 1943).

DRAKE, H[ENRY] B[URGESS]
The Shadowy Thing

Text: London: John Long, 1925 (as *The Remedy*). New York: Macy-Masius, 1928.

Criticism: Will Cuppy, Review, *New York Herald Tribune Books,* 14 October 1928, p. 20. Review, *New York Times Book Review,* 4 November 1928, p. 6. Review, *Saturday Review of Literature,* 1 December 1928, p. 440.

DUNSANY, EDWARD JOHN MORETON DRAX PLUNKETT, 18TH BARON (1878–1957)
The Book of Wonder (*LL* 271)

Text: London: William Heinemann, 1912. Boston: John W. Luce, 1913. New York: Boni & Liveright, 1918 (with *Time and the Gods*). London: Elkin Mathews, 1919. Freeport, NY: Books for Libraries Press, 1972.

A Dreamer's Tales (*LL* 273)

Text: London: George Allen & Sons, 1910. Boston: John W. Luce, 1916. New York: Boni & Liveright, 1919 (with *The Sword of Welleran*). Freeport, NY: Books for Libraries Press, 1969.

The Gods of the Mountain (*LL* 275)

Text: Irish Review No. 10 (December 1911): 486–504. In Dunsany's *Five Plays* (London: Grant Richards, 1914; New York: Mitchell Kennerley, 1914; Boston: Little, Brown, 1916).

Criticism: Edward Hale Bierstadt, *Dunsany the Dramatist* (Boston: Little, Brown, 1917; rev. 1919) (*LL* 91).

The Laughter of the Gods (*LL* 279)

Text: In Dunsany's *Plays of Gods and Men* (Dublin: Talbot Press, 1917; Boston: John W. Luce, 1917; London: Unwin, 1917; New York & London: G. P. Putnam's Sons, 1917; Great Neck, NY: Core Collection Books, 1977).

A Night at an Inn (*LL* 279)

Text: New York: The Sunwise Turn, 1916. New York: G. P. Putnam's Sons, 1922. In *Plays of Gods and Men* (q.v.).

The Queen's Enemies (*LL* 279)

Text: *In Plays of Gods and Men* (q.v.).

Additional Works:

Alexander and Three Small Plays. London & New York: G. P. Putnam's Sons, 1925.

The Blessing of Pan. London & New York: G. P. Putnam's Sons, 1927. (*LL* 270)

The Charwoman's Shadow. London & New York: G. P. Putnam's Sons, 1926. New York: Ballantine Books, 1973.

The Chronicles of Rodriguez. London & New York: G. P. Putnam's Sons, 1922. New York & London: G. P. Putnam's Sons, 1922 (as *Don Rodriguez: Chronicles of Shadow Valley*). London: Pan/Ballantine, 1972. (*LL* 272)

The Curse of the Wise Woman. London: William Heinemann, 1933. New York & Toronto: Longmans, Green, 1933. London: Collins, 1972.

Fifty-one Tales. London: Elkin Mathews, 1915. New York: Mitchell Kennerley, 1915. Boston: Little, Brown, 1917. Hollywood, CA: Newcastle, 1974 (as *The Food of Death*). (*LL* 274)

Fifty Poems. London & New York: G. P. Putnam's Sons, 1929.

The Fourth Book of Jorkens. London: Jarrolds, [1947]. Sauk City, WI: Arkham House, 1948.

The Gods of Pegāna. London: Elkin Mathews, 1905. Boston: John W. Luce, 1916. (*LL* 276)

If. London & New York: G. P. Putnam's Sons, 1922.

Jorkens Borrows Another Whiskey. London: Michael Joseph, 1954.

Jorkens Has a Large Whiskey. London: G. P. Putnam's Sons, 1940.

Jorkens Remembers Africa. London: William Heinemann, 1934. New York & Toronto: Longmans, Green, 1934. Freeport, NY: Books for Libraries Press, 1972.

The King of Elfland's Daughter. London & New York: G. P. Putnam's Sons, 1924. New York: Ballantine, 1969. London: Unwin Paperbacks, 1982. (*LL* 277)

The Last Book of Wonder. London: Elkin Mathews, 1916 (as *Tales of Wonder*). Boston: John W. Luce, 1916. Freeport, NY: Books for Libraries Press, 1969. (*LL* 278)

Mirage Water [poems]. London: Putnam's, 1938.

Patches of Sunlight [autobiography]. London: William Heinemann, 1938. New York: Reynal & Hitchcock, 1938.

Plays for Earth and Air. London: William Heinemann, 1937.

Plays of Near and Far. London & New York: G. P. Putnam's Sons, 1922. (*LL* 280)

Rory and Bran. London & New York: G. P. Putnam's Sons, 1936.

The Sword of Welleran and Other Stories. London: George Allen & Sons, 1908. Boston: John W. Luce, 1916. (See also *A Dreamer's Tales.*) (*LL* 273)

Tales of Three Hemispheres. Boston: John W. Luce, 1919. London: Unwin, 1920. Philadelphia: Owlswick, 1976. (*LL* 281)

Time and the Gods. London: William Heinemann, 1906. Boston: John W. Luce, n.d. London & New York: G. P. Putnam's Sons, 1922. Freeport, NY: Books for Libraries Press, 1970. (See also *The Book of Wonder.*)

The Travel Tales of Mr. Joseph Jorkens. London & New York: G. P. Putnam's Sons, 1931. (*LL* 282)

Unhappy Far-Off Things [autobiography]. London: Elkin Mathews, 1919. Boston: Little, Brown, 1919. (*LL* 283)

Criticism (General): Mark Amory, *Lord Dunsany: A Biography* (London: Collins, 1972). Ernest Boyd, "Lord Dunsany: Fantaisiste", in Boyd's *Appreciations and Depreciations* (Dublin, 1917; New York: John Lane, 1918). S. T. Joshi, *Lord Dunsany: Master of the Anglo-Irish Imagination* (Westport, CT: Greenwood Press, 1995). S. T. Joshi and Darrell Schweitzer, *Lord Dunsany: A Bibliography* (Metuchen, NJ: Scarecrow Press, 1993). Hazel Littlefield, *Lord Dunsany: King of Dreams: A Personal Portrait* (New York: Exposition Press, 1959). Darrell Schweitzer, *Pathways to Elfland: The Writings of Lord Dunsany* (Philadelphia: Owlswick Press, 1989).

ERCKMANN, EMILE (1822–1899) AND CHATRIAN, ALEXANDRE (1826–1890)

Hughes-le-Loup (*The Man-Wolf*) (*LL* 400)

>*Text:* In Erckmann-Chatrian's *Le Cabaliste Hans Weinland et autres contes* (Paris: Editions de l'Erable, 1969). In Erckmann-Chatrian's *Hughes-le-Loup et autres contes fantastiques* (Verviers: Gerard, 1966). In Erckmann-Chatrian's *Contes et romans nationaux et populaires* (Paris: J.-J. Pauvert, 1962), Vol. 3.

>*Translation:* In Julian Hawthorne, ed., *The Lock and Key Library* (New York: Review of Reviews, 1909), Vol. 5. In Erckmann-Chatrian's *The Man-Wolf and Other Tales* (London: Ward, Lock, 1876; rpt. New York: Arno Press, 1976).

"L'oeil invisible" ("The Invisible Eye") (*LL* 400)

>*Text:* In *Le Cabaliste Hans Weinland* (q.v.). In *Contes et romans nationaux et populaires* (q.v.), Vol. 7 (1963).

>*Translation:* In *The Lock and Key Library* (q.v.), Vol. 5.

"L'Oreille de la chouette" ("The Owl's Ear") (*LL* 400)

>*Text:* In *Contes fantastiques* (Paris: Hachette, 1860). In Erckmann-Chatrian's *L'Oreille de la chouette et autres recits fantastiques* (Verviers: Gerard, 1969).

>*Translation:* In *The Lock and Key Library* (q.v.), Vol. 5.

"Llaraignée crabe" ("The Waters of Death") (*LL* 400)

>*Text:* In *Contes et romans nationaux et populaires* (q.v.), Vol. 7 (1963).

Translation: In *The Lock and Key Library* (q.v.), Vol. 5.

Criticism: Georges P. L. Benoit-Guyod, *La Vie et l'oeuvre d'Ertkmann-Chatrian* (Paris: J.-J. Pauvert, 1963). Jean-Pierre Rioux, *Erckmann et Chatrian; ou, Le Trait d'union* (Paris: Gallimard, 1989).

EVERETT, MRS H. D.

The Death Mask and Other Ghosts

Text: London: Philip Allan, 1920.

EWERS, HANNS HEINZ (1871–1943)

Alraune: Die Geschichte eines lebenden Wesens

Text: Munich: Georg Müller, 1911. Munich: Herbig, 1973.

Translation: S. Guy Endore (New York: John Day, 1929; New York: Arno Press, 1976).

"Die Spinne" ("The Spider") (*LL* 394. 395)

Text: In Ewers' *Die Spinne* (Munich: Georg Müller, 1913; Vienna: K. Desch, 1964). In Ewers' *Die Besessenen: Seltsame Geschichten* (Munich: Georg Müller, 1916). In Ewers' *Mein Begräbnis und andere seltsame Geschichten* (Munich: Georg Müller, 1917).

Translation: In *Creeps by Night,* ed. Dashiell Hammett (New York: John Day, 1931). In Leonard Wolf, ed., *Wolf's Complete Book of Terror* (New York: Clarkson N. Potter, 1979).

Der Zauberlehrling, oder Die Teufelsjäger (*The Sorcerer's Apprentice*)

Text: Munich: Georg Müller, 1910.

Translation: Ludwig Lewisohn (New York: John Day, 1927).

Criticism (General): Michael Sennewald, *Hanns Heinz Ewers: Phantastik und Jugendstil* (Meisenheim am Glan: A. Hain, 1973). Hans Kruger-Welf, *Hanns Heinz Ewers: Die Geschichte seiner Entwicklung* (Leipzig: R. Wunderlich, 1922).

FLAUBERT, GUSTAVE (1831–1880)

La Tentation de Saint Antoine (*The Temptation of St Anthony*) (*LL* 321)

Text: Paris: Charpentier & Co., 1872 (definitive ed.). Paris: Société des Belles Lettres, 1940 (ed. René Dumesnil). In *Les Oeuvres de Gustave Flaubert* (Lausanne: Editions Rencontre, 1964f.), Vol. 15.

Translation: In *The Complete Works of Gustave Flaubert,* Brunetiere Ed. (Akron: St Dustan Society, 1904), Vol. 7. Lafcadio Hearn (New York: Alice Harriman Co., 1910; often rpt.). G. F. Monkshood (London: Greening, 1910). Kitty Mrosovsky (Harmondsworth: Penguin, 1980).

Criticism: Stratton Buck, *Gustave Flaubert* (New York: Twayne, 1966), esp. ch. 4. Alfred Lombard, *Flaubert et Saint Antoine* (Paris: Editions Victor Attinger, 1934). Jean Seznec, *Nouvelles Etudes sur* La Tentation de Saint Antoine (London: The Warburg Institute/University of London, 1949).

FORSTER, E[DWARD] M[ORGAN] (1897–1970)

The Celestial Omnibus and Other Stories

Text: London: Sidgwick & Jackson, 1911. New York: Alfred A. Knopf, 1923. In *Collected Short Stories of E. M. Forster* (London: Sidgwick & Jackson, 1947; Harmondsworth: Penguin, 1954; New York: Alfred A. Knopf, 1947 [as *Collected Tales*...]).

Criticism: J. B. Beer, *The Achievement of E. M. Forster* (London: Chatto & Windus, 1968). John Colmer, *E. M. Forster: The Personal Voice* (London: Routledge & Kegan Paul, 1975), ch. 2. David Shusterman, *The Quest for Certitude in E. M. Forster's Fiction* (Bloomington: Indiana University Press, 1963), ch. 3.

FREEMAN, MARY ELEANOR WILKINS (1852–1930)

The Wind in the Rose-bush and Other Stories of the Supernatural (LL 333)

Text: New York: Doubleday, Page, 1903. New York: A. Wessels, 1907. New York: Garnett Press, 1969. Chicago: Academy Chicago, 1986. In Freeman's *Collected Ghost Stories* (Sauk City, WI: Arkham House, 1974).

Criticism (General): Edward Foster, *Mary E. Wilkins Freeman* (New York: Hendricks House, 1956). Abigail Ann Hamblen, *The New England Art of Mary E. Wilkins Freeman* (Amherst, MA: Green Knight Press, 1966). Mary R. Reichardt, *A Web of Relationship: Women in the Short Stories of Mary Wilkins Freeman* (Jackson: University of Mississippi Press, 1992). Perry D. Westbrook, *Mary Wilkins Freeman* (New York: Twayne, 1967).

GAUTIER, THÉOPHILE (1811–1872)

"Avatar" (*LL* 347)

Text: Moniteur Universal, 29 February–3 April 1856. In Gautier's *Romans et contes* (Paris: Charpentier, 1863; often rpt.).

Translation: In *Tales Before Supper,* tr. Myndart Verelst [pseud. of Edgar Saltus] (New York: Brentano's, 1887); New York: AMS Press, 1970). In *The Works of Gautier,* tr. F. C. de Sumichrast (Boston: C. T. Brainard, 1900–03), Vol. 8.

Criticism: Maximilian Rudwin, "Satanism and Spiritism in Gautier", *Open Court* (Chicago) 37 (1923): 385–95.

"La Morte amoureuse" ("Clarimonde")

Text: In Gautier's *Nouvelles* (Paris: Charpentier, 1845; often rpt.).

Translation: In Gautier's *One of Cleopatra's Nights,* tr. Lafcadio Hearn (New York: Worthington, 1882; often rpt.). In *The Works of Gautier* (q.v.), Vol. 6. In Elinore Blaisdell, ed., *Tales of the Undead* (New York: Crowell, 1947).

"Une Nuit de Cléopatre" ("One of Cleopatra's Nights") (*LL* 346)

Text: In *Nouvelles* (q.v.). Paris: A. Ferroud, 1894 (preface by Anatole France).

Translation: In *One of Cleopatra's Nights* (q.v.). In *The Works of Gautier,* tr. F. C. de Sumichrast (q.v.), Vol. 4.

"Le Pied de momie" ("The Foot of the Mummy") (*LL* 346)

Text: In *Romans et contes* (q.v.). In Edward Marielle, ed., *The Penguin Book of French Short Stories* (Harmondsworth: Penguin, 1968).

Translation: In *One of Cleopatra's Nights* (q.v.). In *The Works of Gautier,* tr. F. C. de Sumichrast (q.v.), Vol. 6. In Joseph Lewis French, ed., *Masterpieces of Mystery* (q.v.), Vol. 3.

Criticism (General): Adolphe Boschot, *Théophile Gautier* (Paris: Desclée, de Brouwer, 1933). Richard P. Grant, *Théophile Gautier* (New York: Twayne, 1975). Bernhard Payr, *Théophile Gautier und E. T. A. Hoffmann* (Berlin: E. Ebering, 1932). Joanna Richardson, *Théophile Gautier: His Life and Times* (London: Reinhardt, 1958). Albert B. Smith, *Théophile Gautier and the Fantastic* (University, MS: Romance Monographs, 1977). P. E. Tennant, *Théophile Gautier* (London: Athlone Press, 1975).

GILMAN, CHARLOTTE PERKINS (1860–1935)

"The Yellow Wall Paper"

Text: New England Magazine, January 1892. Boston: Small, Maynard, 1899. In William Dean Howells, ed., *Great Modern American Short Stories* (New York: Boni & Liveright, 1920). In Philip Van Doren Stern, ed., *The Midnight Reader* (New York: Holt, Rinehart, 1942). In Seon Manley and Gogo Lewis, eds., *Ladies of Horror* (New York: Lothrop, Lee & Shepard, 1971).

Criticism: Catherine Golden, ed., *The Captive Imagination: A Casebook on "The Yellow Wallpaper"* (New York: Feminist Press/City University of New York, 1992).

Criticism (General): Mary A. Hill, *Charlotte Perkins Gilman: The Making of a Radical Feminist, 1860–1896* (Philadelphia: Temple University Press, 1980). Carol Farley Kessler, *Charlotte Perkins Gilman: Her Progress toward Utopia, with Selected Writings* (Syracuse: Syracuse University Press, 1995). Ann J. Lane, *To Herland and Beyond: The Life and Work of Charlotte Perkins Gilman* (New York: Pantheon, 1990). Sheryl L. Meyering, ed., *Charlotte Perkins Gilman: The Woman and Her Work* (Ann Arbor, MI: UMI Research Press, 1989). Gary Scharnhorst, *Charlotte Perkins Gilman* (Boston: Twayne, 1985).

GODWIN, WILLIAM (1756–1836)

St. Leon: A Tale of the Sixteenth Century

Text: London: Printed for G. G. & J. Robinson ... [by] R. Noble, 1799 (4 vols.). London: Bentley, 1850. New York: Arno Press, 1972. New York: Garland, 1974 (4 vols.). New York: AMS Press, 1975 (rpt. of 1831 ed.). London: Pickering, 1992. Oxford: Oxford University Press, 1994 (ed. Pamela Clemit).

Criticism: Marie Roberts, *Gothic Immortals: The Fiction of the Brotherhood of the Rosy Cross* (London: Routledge, 1990).

Things as They Are; or, The History of Caleb Williams

Text: London: B. Crosby, 1794 (3 vols.). London: Routledge, 1903. New York: Greenberg, 1926. London: Oxford University Press, 1970; New York: W. W. Norton, 1977 (ed. David McCracken). Harmondsworth: Penguin, 1987 (ed. Maurice Hindle).

Criticism: Kenneth W. Graham, *The Politics of Narrative: Ideology and Social Change in William Godwin's* Caleb Williams (New York: AMS Press, 1990).

Criticism (General): H. N. Brailsford, *Shelley, Godwin, and Their Circle* (New York: Henry Holt, 1913). Pamela Clemit, *The Godwinian Novel* (Oxford: Clarendon Press, 1993). Jane T. Flanders, "Charles Brockden Brown and William Godwin", Ph.D. diss.: University of Wisconsin, 1965. George McCelvey, *William Godwin's Novels: Theme and Craft* (Durham, NC: Duke University Press, 1964). Peter H. Marshall, *William Godwin* (New Haven: Yale University Press, 1984). George Woodcock, *William Godwin* (London: Porcupine Press, 1946).

GOETHE, JOHANN WOLFGANG VON (1749–1832)

"Die Braut von Korinth" ("The Bride of Corinth") (*LL* 361)

Text: In *Musen Almanach,* 1798. In Goethe's *Gedichte,* ed. Erich Trunz (Frankfurt am Main: Fischer Bücherei, 1964), Vol. 1. In Goethe's *Poetische Werke,* Berliner Ausgabe (Berlin: Aufbau-Verlag, 1965), Vol. 1 (ed. Regine Otto).

Translation: In *The Poems of Goethe,* tr. Edgar Alfred Bowling (1853; often rpt.).

Faust (*LL* 359, 360)

Text: Heidelberg, 1832. Boston: D. C. Heath, 1954–55; Madison: University of Wisconsin Press, 1975 (2 vols.) (ed. R.-M. S. Heffner et al.).

Translation: Anna Swanwick (London: G. Bell, 1879; often rpt.). Bayard Taylor (Boston: Fields, Osgood, 1871; often rpt.). Walter Kaufmann (Garden City, NY: Doubleday, 1961; abridged; with German text).

Criticism (General): Eliza M. Butler, *Byron and Goethe* (London: Bowes & Bowes, 1956). Werner Danckert, *Goethe: Der mythische Urgrund seiner Weltschau* (Berlin: W. de Gruyter, 1951). L. Dieckmann, *Johann Wolfgang Goethe* (New York: Twayne, 1974).

GORMAN, HERBERT S[HERMAN] (1893–1954)

The Place Called Dagon

Text: New York; George H. Doran, 1927.

Criticism: Clifton P. Fadiman, Review, *Nation*, 30 November 1927, p. 608. Ford Madox Ford, Review, *New York Herald Tribune Books*, 30 October 1927, p. 5. S. T. Joshi, "Where Is the Place Called Dagon?", *Necrofile* No. 14 (Fall 1994): 19–21.

GROSSE, KARL FRIEDRICH AUGUST, MARQUIS VON (1768–1847)

Der Genius (*Horrid Mysteries*)

Text: Halle: J. C. Hendel, 1791–94.

Translation: Peter Will (London: William Lane, 1976; 4 vols.). London: R. Holden, 1927 (2 vols.). London: Folio Press, 1968 (4 vols. in 1).

Criticism: Robert Ignatius Le Tellier, *Kindred Spirits* (Salzburg, Austria: Institut für Anglistik und Amerikanistik, 1982).

HAGGARD, SIR H[ENRY] RIDER (1856–1925)

She: A History of Adventure (*LL* 385)

Text: New York: Harper & Brothers, 1886. London: Longmans, Green, 1887. London: Macdonald, 1948. New York: Ballantine, 1978. *The Annotated She*, ed. Norman Etherington (Bloomington: Indiana University Press, 1991).

Criticism: Morton N. Cohen, *Rider Haggard* (London: Hutchinson, 1960; New York: Walker & Co., 1961). Peter Berresford Ellis, *H. Rider Haggard: A Voice from the Infinite* (London: Routledge & Kegan Paul, 1978). D. S. Higgins, *Rider Haggard, the Great Storyteller* (London: Cassell, 1981). Wendy R. Katz, *Rider Haggard and the Fiction of Empire* (Cambridge: Cambridge University Press, 1987). Alan Sandison, "Rider Haggard: 'Some Call It Evolution . . .' ", in Sandison's *The Wheel of Empire* (London: Macmillan, 1967).

HALL, LELAND (1883–1957)

Sinister House

Text: Boston & New York: Houghton Mifflin, 1919. New York: Bookfinger, n.d.

Criticism: Review, *Boston Transcript*, 26 February 1919, p. 6. H. W. Boynton, Review, *Bookman* (New York), May 1919, p. 322. Review, *Dial*, 22 March 1919, p. 314.

HARTLEY, L[ESLIE] P[OLES] (1895–1972)

"A Visitor from Down Under"

Text: In Cynthia Asquith, ed., *The Ghost Book* (London: Hutchinson, 1927; New York: Scribner's, 1927). In Hartley's *The Travelling Grave and Other Stories*

(Sauk City, WI: Arkham House, 1948; London: J. Barrie, 1951; London: Hamish Hamilton, 1957). In *The Collected Short Stories of L. P. Hartley* (London: Hamish Hamilton, 1968). In Edward Gorey, ed., *The Haunted Looking Glass* (New York: Random House, 1959).

Criticism: Peter Bien, *L. P. Hartley* (University Park: Pennsylvania State University Press, 1963). Paul Bloomfield, *L. P. Hartley* (London: Longmans, 2nd ed. 1970). Edward T. Jones, *L. P. Hartley* (Boston: Twayne, 1978). S. T. Joshi, "The Weird Work of L. P. Hartley", *Niekas* No. 45 (1998): 27–32.

HAWTHORNE, NATHANIEL (1804–1864)

"The Ambitious Guest" (*LL* 408)

Text: New England Magazine 8 (June 1835): 425–31. In Hawthorne's *Twice-Told Tales*, 2nd ed. (Boston: James Munroe, 1842 [2 vols.]; Boston: Houghton Mifflin, 1883; Columbus: Ohio State University Press, 1974). In *The Complete Short Stories of Nathaniel Hawthorne* (Garden City, NY: Doubleday, 1959). In *Tales by Nathaniel Hawthorne*, ed. Carl Van Doren (London: Oxford University Press, 1921).

Criticism: K. W. Cameron, *Genesis of Hawthorne's "The Ambitious Guest"* (Hartford: Thistle Press, 1955). C. Hobart Edgren, "Hawthorne's 'The Ambitious Guest': An Interpretation", *Nineteenth-Century Fiction* 10 (1955): 151–56.

"The Ancestral Footstep"

Text: Atlantic Monthly, Dec. 1882–Feb. 1883. In Hawthorne's *The Dolliver Romance, Fanshawe, and Septimius Felton* (Boston: Houghton Mifflin, 1883).

Criticism: Edward H. Davidson, *Hawthorne's Last Phase* (New Haven: Yale University Press, 1949).

"Dr. Grimshawe's Secret"

Text: Boston: J. R. Osgood, 1883. Boston: Houghton Mifflin, 1889. Cambridge, MA: Harvard University Press, 1954.

Criticism: John A. Kouwenhoven, "Hawthorne's Notebooks and *Dr. Grimshawe's Secret*", *American Literature* 5 (1934): 349–58.

"Edward Randolph's Portrait" (*LL* 403, 408)

Text: United States Magazine and Democratic Review 2 (July 1838): 360–69. In *Twice-Told Tales*, 2nd ed. (q.v.). In Hawthorne's *Legends of the Province House* (Boston: J. R. Osgood, 1877). In *Tales by Nathaniel Hawthorne* (q.v.). In *The Complete Short Stories* (q.v.).

"Ethan Brand"

Text: Boston Weekly Museum, 5 January 1850 (as "The Unpardonable Sin"). In Hawthorne's *The Snow-Image and Other Twice-Told Tales* (Boston: Ticknor, Reed & Fields, 1852; Columbus: Ohio State University Press, 1974). In

Hawthorne's *The House of the Seven Gables and The Snow-Image* (Boston: Houghton Mifflin, 1883). In *Tales by Nathaniel Hawthorne* (q.v.). In *The Complete Short Stories* (q.v.).

Criticism: R. H. Fogle, "The Problem of Allegory in Hawthorne's 'Ethan Brand' ", *University of Toronto Quarterly* 17 (1948): 190–203. Alfred J. Levy, " 'Ethan Brand' and the Unpardonable Sin", *Boston University Studies in English* 5 (1961): 185–90. John McElroy, "The Brand Metaphor in 'Ethan Brand' ", *American Literature* 43 (1972): 633–37.

The House of the Seven Gables (*LL* 402)

Text: Boston: Ticknor, Reed & Fields, 1861. Boston: Houghton Mifflin, 1883. Columbus: Ohio State University Press, 1965. In *The Complete Novels and Selected Tales of Nathaniel Hawthorne,* ed. Norman Holmes Pearson (New York: Modern Library, 1937).

Criticism: Roger Asselineau, ed., *Studies in* The House of the Seven Gables (Columbus, OH: Charles E. Merrill, 1970). Donald Junkins, "Hawthorne's *House of the Seven Gables*", *Literature and Psychology* 17 (1967) 193–210. J. F. Klinkowitz, "The Significance of the Ending to *The House of the Seven Gables*", Ph.D. diss.: University of Wisconsin, 1970. Leo B. Levy, "Picturesque Style in *The House of the Seven Gables*", *New England Quarterly* 39 (1966): 147–60. Alfred H. Marks, "Who Killed Judge Pyncheon?", *PMLA* 71 (1956): 355–69.

The Marble Faun; or, the Romance of Monte Beni (*LL* 404)

Text: Boston: Ticknor & Fields, 1860. Boston: Houghton Mifflin, 1883. Columbus: Ohio State University Press, 1968. In *The Complete Novels and Selected Tales of Nathaniel Hawthorne* (q.v.).

Criticism: Patrick Brancaccio, "The Ramble and the Pilgrimage: A Critical Reading of Hawthorne's *Marble Faun*", Ph.D. diss.: Rutgers University, 1968. R. H. Fogle, "Simplicity and Complexity in *The Marble Faun*", *Tulane Studies in English* 2 (1950): 103–20. Harry Levin, "Statues from Italy: *The Marble Faun*", in *Hawthorne Centenary Essays* (Columbus: Ohio State University Press, 1964). S. W. Liebman, "The Design of *The Marble Faun*", *New England Quarterly* 40 (1967): 67–78. H. R. S. Mahan, "Hawthorne's *Marble Faun*", Ph.D. diss.: University of Rochester, 1966.

"The Minister's Black Veil" (*LL* 400, 408)

Text: In S. G. Goodrich, ed., *The Token and Atlantic Souvenir* (Boston: Charles Bowen, 1836), pp. 302–20. In Hawthorne's *Twice-Told Tales* (Boston: American Stationers Co., 1837; for later eds. see above).

Criticism: M. L. Allen, "The Black Veil: Three Versions of a Symbol", *English Studies* 47 (1966): 286–89. Robert D. Grie, "The Minister's Black Veil", *Literature and Psychology* 17 (1967): 211–17. W. Stein, "The Parable of the Antichrist in 'The Minister's Black Veil' ", *American Literature* 27 (1955): 386–92.

Septimius Felton

Text: Atlantic Monthly, Jan.–Aug. 1872. Boston: J. R. Osgood, 1872. Boston: Houghton Mifflin, 1883 (as *The Dolliver Romance, Fanshawe, and Septimius Felton*).

Criticism: Darrell Abel, "Immortality vs. Mortality in *Septimius Felton*", *American Literature* 27 (1956): 566–70.

Tanglewood Tales (*LL* 408)

Text: Boston: Ticknor & Fields, 1853. Boston: Houghton Mifflin, 1883 (with *A Wonder Book* and *Grandfather's Chair*). Columbus: Ohio State University Press, 1972 (with *A Wonder Book*).

Criticism: M. A. D. Howe, "The Tale of Tanglewood", *Yale Review* 32 (1942): 323–36.

A Wonder-Book for Girls and Boys (*LL* 409)

Text: Boston: Ticknor, Reed & Fields, 1852. Boston: Houghton Mifflin, 1883 (with *Tanglewood Tales* and *Grandfather's Chair*). Columbus: Ohio State University Press, 1972 (with *Tanglewood Tales*).

Criticism: Andrew Lang, "Nathaniel Hawthorne's Tales of Old Greece", *Independent* 62 (1904): 792–94. Hugo A. McPherson, "Hawthorne and the Greek Myths", Ph.D. diss.: University of Toronto, 1956.

Criticism (General): Richard M. Chisholm, "The Use of Gothic Materials in Hawthorne's Mature Romances", Ph.D. diss.: Columbia University, 1970. Ronald T. Curran, "Hawthorne as Gothicist", Ph.D. diss.: University of Pennsylvania, 1970. P. H. Frye, "Hawthorne's Supernaturalism", in his *Reviews and Criticisms* (New York: G. P. Putnam's Sons, 1908). David G. Halliburton, "The Grotesque in American Literature: Poe, Hawthorne, and Melville", Ph.D. diss.: University of California, 1967. E. C. Johnson, "Hawthorne and the Supernatural", Ph.D. diss.: Stanford University, 1938. Harry Levin, *The Power of Blackness: Hawthorne, Poe and Melville* (New York: Alfred A. Knopf, 1958). Terence Martin, *Nathaniel Hawthorne* (New York: Twayne, 1965). Edward Wagenknecht, *Nathaniel Hawthorne: Man and Writer* (New York: Oxford University Press, 1961). Hyatt Waggoner, *Hawthorne: A Critical Study* (Cambridge, MA: Harvard University Press, 1955; 2nd ed. 1963).

HEARN, LAFCADIO (1850–1904)

Fantastics and Other Fancies

Text: Boston & New York: Houghton Mifflin, 1914. New York: Arno Press, 1976.

Kwaidan: Stories and Studies of Strange Things (*LL* 412)

Text: London, Boston, & New York: Houghton Mifflin, 1904. London: Kegan Paul, 1904. New York: Limited Editions Club, 1932. New York: Dover, 1968.

Criticism (General): Yu Beongcheon, *An Ape of Gods: The Art and Thought of Laf-*

cadio Hearn (Detroit: Wayne State University Press, 1964). Jonathan Cott, *Wandering Ghost: The Odyssey of Lafcadio Hearn* (New York: Knopf, 1991). Carl Dawson, *Lafcadio Hearn and the Vision of Japan* (Baltimore: Johns Hopkins University Press, 1992). George M. Gould, *Concerning Lafcadio Hearn* (Philadelphia: Jacobs, 1908). Arthur E. Kunst, *Lafcadio Hearn* (New York: Twayne, 1969). Vera McWilliams, *Lafcadio Hearn* (Boston: Houghton Mifflin, 1946). Paul Murray, *A Fantastic Journey: The Life and Literature of Lafcadio Hearn* (Sandgate, UK: Japan Library, 1993). Elizabeth Stevenson, *Lafcadio Hearn* (New York: Macmillan, 1961).

HODGSON, WILLIAM HOPE (1877–1918)

The Boats of the "Glen Carrig"

Text: London: Chapman & Hall, 1907. London: Holden & Hardingham, 1920. Sauk City, WI: Arkham House (in *The House on the Borderland and Other Novels*). New York: Ballantine, 1971. Westport, CT: Hyperion, 1974.

Carnacki, the Ghost-Finder

Text: London: Eveleigh Nash, 1913. Sauk City, WI: Mycroft & Moran, 1947. London: Sphere, 1974.

The Ghost Pirates

Text: London: S. Paul, 1909. Sauk City, WI: Arkham House (in *The House on the Borderland and Other Novels*). Westport, CT: Hyperion, 1976.

The House on the Borderland

Text: London: Chapman & Hall, 1908. London: Holden & Hardingham, 1921. Sauk City, WI: Arkham House, 1946 (with other three novels). Westport, CT: Hyperion, 1976.

The Night Land

Text: London: Eveleigh Nash, 1912. Sauk City, WI: Arkham House (in *The House on the Borderland and Other Novels*). New York: Ballantine, 1972 (2 vols.; abridged). Westport, CT: Hyperion, 1976.

Criticism (General): Ian Bell, ed., *William Hope Hodgson: Voyages and Visions* (Oxford: I. Bell & Sons, 1987). R. Alain Everts, "William Hope Hodgson: Master of Fantasy", *Shadow*, April–October 1973; Madison, WI: The Strange Co., 1974. Sam Gafford et al., *William Hope Hodgson: A Bibliography* (West Warwick, RI: Necronomicon Press, forthcoming). Sam Moskowitz, ed., *Out of the Storm* (West Kingston, RI: Donald M. Grant, 1975).

HOFFMANN, E[RNST] T[HEODOR] A[MADEUS] (1776–1822)

[*Tales*]

Text: *Poetische Werke,* ed. K. Kanzog (Berlin: Walter de Gruyter, 1957–62; 12 vols.).

Translation: The Best Tales of Hoffmann, ed. E. F. Bleiler (New York: Dover, 1967). *The Tales of Hoffmann,* tr. Michael Bullock (New York: Frederick Ungar, 1963). *Tales of Hoffmann,* ed. Christopher Lazare (New York: A. A. Wyn, 1946).

Criticism (General): Palmer Cobb, *The Influence of E. T. A. Hoffmann on the Tales of E. A. Poe* (Chapel Hill: University of North Carolina Press, 1908; rpt. New York: Johnson Reprint, 1963). Thomas Cramer, *Das Groteske bei E. T. A. Hoffmann* (Munich: Wilhelm Fink Verlag, 1966). Horst S. Daemmrich, *The Shattered Self: E. T. A. Hoffmann's Tragic Vision* (Detroit: Wayne State University Press, 1973). Jean Mistler, *Hoffmann le fantastique* (Paris: Michel, 1950).

HOGG, JAMES (1770–1835)

"Kilmeny"

Text: In Hogg's *The Queen's Wake: A Legendary Poem* (Edinburgh: Andrew Balfour, 1813; London & Edinburgh, 1872). In *The Poems of James Hogg,* ed. William Wallace (London, 1903).

Criticism (General): Edith C. Batho, *The Ettrick Shepherd* (Cambridge: Cambridge University Press, 1927; rpt. Westport, CT: Greenwood Press, 1969). Douglas Gifford, *James Hogg* (Edinburgh: Ramsay Head Press, 1976). David Groves, *James Hogg: The Growth of a Writer* (Edinburgh: Scottish Academic Press, 1988). Louis Simpson, *James Hogg: A Critical Study* (New York: St Martin's Press, 1962). Nelson C. Smith, *James Hogg* (Boston: Twayne, 1980).

HOLMES, OLIVER WENDELL (1809–1894)

Elsie Venner: A Romance of Destiny

Text: Atlantic Monthly, January 1860–April 1861 (as *The Professor's Story*). Boston: Ticknor & Fields, 1861 (2 vols.). Boston: Houghton Mifflin, 1880. New York: A. L. Burt, 1903. New York: Signet, 1961. New York: Arno Press, 1976.

Criticism (General): John T. Morse, *Life and Letters of Oliver Wendell Holmes* (Boston: Houghton Mifflin, 1896; 2 vols.). Miriam Rossiter Small, *Oliver Wendell Holmes* (New York: Twayne, 1962).

HOUSMAN, CLEMENCE

"The Werewolf"

Text: London: John Lane/The Bodley Head; Chicago: Way & Williams, 1896. New York: Arno Press, 1976. In Seon Manley and Gogo Lewis, ed., *Ladies of Horror* (New York: Lothrop, Lee & Shepard, 1971). In Bill Pronzini, ed., *Werewolf!* (New York: Arbor House, 1979).

HUGO, VICTOR MARIE (1802–1885)

Han d'Islande (*Hans of Iceland*)

Text: Paris: Duriez, 1823. Paris: Chez Persan, 1823. In Hugo's *Oeuvres Complètes*

(Givors: A. Martel, 1948), Vol. 1. In Hugo's *Oeuvres Complètes* (Lausanne: Editions Rencontre, 1967), Vol. 6.

Translation: Anon. (New York: Street & Smith, 1891). George B. Ives (Boston: Little, Brown, 1894).

Criticism (General): Pierre Albouy, *La Création mythologique chez Victor Hugo* (Paris: Corti, 1963). Jean Bertrand Barrere, *La Fantasie de Victor Hugo* (Paris: Klinksieck, 1949–60; 2 vols.). Leon Lellier, *Baudelaire et Hugo* (Paris: Corti, 1970).

HUYSMANS, JORIS-KARL (1848–1907)

[*Works*]

Text: Oeuvres Complètes (Paris: Les Editions G. Cres, 1928), 17 vols.

Translation: Against the Grain [*A Rebours*], tr. John Howard [pseud. of Jacob Howard Lewis] (New York: Lieber & Lewis, 1922; New York: Albert & Charles Boni, 1930; New York: Dover, 1972) (*LL* 454). *Against Nature*, tr. Robert Baldick (Harmondsworth: Penguin, 1959). *Down There* [*Là-Bas*], tr. Keene Wallis (New York: A. & C. Boni, 1924; New York: Dover, 1972). *Là-Bas/Lower Depths*, tr. anon. (Sawtry, UK: Dedalus, 1986).

Criticism (General): Robert Baldick, *The Life of J.-K. Huysmans* (Oxford: Clarendon Press, 1955). Brian R. Banks, *The Image of Huysmans* (New York: AMS Press, 1990). François Livi, *J.-K. Huysmans: A Rebours et l'esprit decadent* (Paris: A. G. Nizet, 1972). Christopher Lloyd, *J.-K. Huysmans and the Fin-de-Siècle Novel* (Edinburgh: Edinburgh University Press/University of Durham, 1990).

IRVING, WASHINGTON (1783–1859)

Tales of a Traveller (*LL* 464)

Text: Philadelphia: H. C. Carey & I. Lea, 1824. New York: G. P. Putnam, 1849. Philadelphia: J. B. Lippincott, 1913. New York: AMS Press, 1973.

Criticism (General): John Clendenning, "Irving and the Gothic Tradition", *Bucknell Review* 12 (May 1964): 90–98. Jill Wilson Cohn, "The Short Fiction of Washington Irving", Ph.D. diss.: Michigan State University, 1971. Walter A. Reichart, *Washington Irving and Germany* (Ann Arbor: University of Michigan Press, 1957).

JACOBS, W[ILLIAM] W[YMARK] (1863–1943)

"The Monkey's Paw" (*LL* 761)

Text: In Jacobs' *The Lady of the Barge* (New York: Dodd, Mead, 1902). In Dorothy L. Sayers, ed., *The Omnibus of Crime* (New York: Payson & Clark, 1929). In Colin de la Mare, ed., *They Walk Again* (New York: E. P. Dutton, 1931). In Bennett Cerf, ed., *Famous Ghost Stories* (New York: Modern Library, 1944). In Herbert A. Wise and Phyllis Fraser, eds., *Great Tales of Terror and the Supernatural* (New York: Random House, 1944). In Edward Gorey, ed., *The Haunted*

Looking Glass (New York: Random House, 1959). In Jacobs' *The Monkey's Paw and Other Mysterious Tales* (Chicago: Academy, 1997).

Criticism (General): John D. Cloy, *Pensive Jester: The Literary Career of W. W. Jacobs* (Lanham, MD: University Press of America, 1996).

JAMES, HENRY (1843–1916)

The Turn of the Screw (*LL* 467)

Text: In James' *The Two Magics* (New York: Macmillan, 1898). New York: Albert & Charles Boni, 1924. London: J. M. Dent, 1935 (Everyman's Library; with *The Aspern Papers*). Los Angeles: Limited Editions Club, 1949. New York: W. W. Norton, 1966 (ed. Robert Kimbrough). Harmondsworth: Penguin, 1969.

Criticism: Martha Banta, *Henry James and the Occult* (Bloomington: Indiana University Press, 1972). Thomas M. Granfill and Robert L. Clark, *An Anatomy of "The Turn of the Screw"* (Austin: University of Texas Press, 1965). John Lydenberg, "The Governess Turns the Screws", *Nineteenth-Century Fiction* 12 (June 1957): 37–58. E. A. Sheppard, *Henry James and* The Turn of the Screw (Auckland, NZ: Auckland University Press, 1974). Jane P. Tompkins, ed., *Twentieth Century Interpretations of "The Turn of the Screw"* (Englewood Cliffs, NJ: Prentice-Hall, 1970). Gerald Willen, ed., *A Casebook on Henry James' "The Turn of the Screw"* (New York: Crowell, 1960; 2nd ed. 1969).

JAMES, M[ONTAGUE] R[HODES] (1862–1936)

The Five Jars

Text: London: Edward Arnold, 1922. New York: Arno Press, 1976.

Ghost-Stories of an Antiquary (*LL* 468)

Text: London: Edward Arnold, 1904. Harmondsworth: Penguin, 1937. Freeport, NY: Books for Libraries Press, 1969. New York: Dover, 1971. In *The Collected Ghost Stories of M. R. James* (London: Edward Arnold, 1931, 1974).

More Ghost Stories of an Antiquary (*LL* 469)

Text: London: Edward Arnold, 1911. Freeport, NY: Books for Libraries Press, 1971. In *The Collected Ghost Stories* (q.v.).

A Thin Ghost and Others (*LL* 470)

Text: London: Edward Arnold; New York: Longmans, Green, 1919. Freeport, NY: Books for Libraries Press, 1971. In *The Collected Ghost Stories* (q.v.).

A Warning to the Curious (*LL* 471)

Text: London: Edward Arnold, 1925. In *The Collected Ghost Stories* (q.v.).

Criticism (General): Julia Briggs, "No Mere Antiquarian: M. R. James", in Briggs' *Night Visitors: The Rise and Fall of the English Ghost Story* (London: Faber & Faber, 1977). Michael Andrew Cox, *M. R. James: An Informal Portrait* (Oxford: Oxford

University Press, 1983). Jack P. Frazetti, "A Study of the Preternatural Fiction of Sheridan Le Fanu and Its Impact upon the Tales of Montague Rhodes James" (Ph.D. diss.: St John's University, 1956). S. G. Lubbock, *A Memoir of Montague Rhodes James* (Cambridge: Cambridge University Press, 1939). Richard William Pfaff, *Montague Rhodes James (London: Scolar Press, 1980)*. Jack Sullivan, *Elegant Nightmares: The English Ghost Story from Le Fanu to Blackwood* (Athens: Ohio University Press, 1978).

KEATS, JOHN (1795–1821)

[*Poetical Works*] (*LL* 188)

Text: *The Poetical Works of Coleridge, Shelley and Keats* (Paris: A. & W. Galignani, 1829). *The Poetical Works of John Keats.* New York: G. P. Putnam, 1848; London: Macmillan, 1884 (ed. Francis T. Palgrave); London: Henry Frowde, 1903; London: Methuen, 1905 (ed. E. de Selincourt); New York: Modern Library, 1932 (with Shelley); Oxford: Clarendon Press, 1939 (ed. H. W. Garrod); Harmondsworth: Penguin, 1973, 2nd ed. 1977 (ed. John Barnard).

Criticism (General): John Middleton Murry, *Studies in Keats* (London: Oxford University Press, 1930). E. T. Norris, "Hermes and the Nymph in *Lamia*", *ELH* 2 (1935): 322–26. W. E. Peck, "Keats, Shelley, and Mrs Radcliffe", *Modern Language Notes* 39 (1924): 251–52. J. H. Roberts, "The Significance of *Lamia*", *PMLA* 50 (1935): 550–61. Martha H. Shackford, *"The Eve of St Agnes* and *The Mysteries of Udolpho*", *PMLA* 36 (1921): 104–18.

KIPLING, RUDYARD (1865–1936)

The Phantom 'Rickshaw and Other Tales (*LL* 502)

Text: Allahabad: A. H. Wheeler & Co., 1888. London: Sampson, Lowe, Marston, Searle, & Rivington, 1890. New York: John W. Lovell, 1890 (with *Wee Willie Winkie* &c.). New York: J. H. Sears, [1925?].

Criticism (General): Helen Pike Bauer, *Rudyard Kipling: A Study of the Short Fiction* (New York: Twayne, 1994). Charles Carrington, *Rudyard Kipling: His Life and Work* (London: Macmillan, 1978). Bonamy Dobrée, *Rudyard Kipling: Realist and Fabulist* (London: Oxford University Press, 1967). Elliot L. Gilbert, *The Good Kipling: Studies in the Short Story* (Athens: Ohio University Press, 1971). Sukeshi Kamara, *Kipling's Vision: A Study in His Short Stories* (New Delhi: Prestige Books, 1989). J. M. S. Tompkins, *The Art of Rudyard Kipling* (London: Methuen, 1959). Angus Wilson, *The Strange Ride of Rudyard Kipling* (London: Secker & Warburg, 1977; New York: Viking Press, 1978).

LA MOTTE FOUQUÉ, FRIEDRICH HEINRICH KARL, BARON DE (1777–1843)

Undine (*LL* 513)

Text: Die Jahreszeiten, 1811. New York: Holt, 1889 (ed. Hans C. G. Jagemann; with comm.). Wiesbaden: Kesselring, 1947 (ed. Max Preitz). London: Nelson, 1945 (ed. W. Walker Chambers).

Translation: Thomas Tracy (London, 1835; often rpt.). Edmund Gosse (London, 1896; often rpt.). W. L. Courtenay (London & New York, 1909; often rpt.).

Criticism: Wilhelm Pfeiffer, Über *Fouqués Undine* (Heidelberg, 1903).

LEE, SOPHIA (1750–1824)

The Recess; or, A Tale of Other Times

Text: London: Thomas Cadell, 1783–85 (3 vols.). London: S. Fisher, 1824. New York: Arno Press, 1972 (3 vols.).

LEWIS, MATTHEW GREGORY (1775–1818)

The Castle Spectre: A Dramatic Romance

Text: London: J. Bell, 1798. Dublin: G. Folingsby, 1798. London: J. Dicks, 188-. In Henry Willis Wells, ed., *Three Centuries of Drama* (New York: Readex Microprint, 1953f.).

The Monk (*LL* 531)

Text: London: J. Bell, 1796 (3 vols.). New York: Grove Press, 1952 (ed. Louis F. Peck). London: New English Library, 1973. London: Oxford University Press, 1973 (ed. Howard Anderson).

Criticism: Peter Brooks, "Virtue and Terror: *The Monk*", *ELH* 40 (1973): 249–63. Samuel Taylor Coleridge, "*The Monk, A Romance* by M. G. Lewis, Esq., M.P." (1797), in *Coleridge's Miscellaneous Criticism,* ed. Thomas Middleton Raysor (London: Constable, 1936). André Parreaux, *The Publication of* The Monk: *A Literary Event, 1796–1798* (Paris: M. Didier, 1960).

Tales of Terror

Text: London: Printed by W. Bulmer and sold by J. Bell, 1801.

Tales of Wonder

Text: Dublin: Printed by Nicholas Kelly, 1801 (2 vols.).

Criticism (General): Syndy M. Conger, *Matthew G. Lewis, Charles Robert Maturin and the Germans* (Salzburg, 1977). Joseph James Irwin, *M. G. "Monk" Lewis* (Boston: Twayne, 1976). Louis F. Peck, *A Life of Matthew G. Lewis* (Cambridge, MA: Harvard University Press, 1961).

LYTTON, EDWARD BULWER-LYTTON, LORD (1803–1873)

"The Haunted and the Haunters; or, The House and the Brain" (*LL* 133, 313, 400)

Text: *Blackwood's Magazine,* August 1859. In Bulwer-Lytton's *A Strange Story* (London: Routledge, 188-). In Dorothy L. Sayers, ed., *The Second Omnibus of Crime* (New York: Coward-McCann, 1932). In Bennett Cerf, ed., *Famous Ghost Stories* (New York: Modern Library, 1944). In Dorothy Tomlinson, ed., *Walk in Dread* (New York: Taplinger, 1972).

Criticism: Richard Kelly, "The Haunted House of Bulwer-Lytton", *Studies in Short Fiction* 8 (1971): 581–87.

A Strange Story (*LL* 133)

Text: *All the Year Round,* 1861–62. London: S. Low, 1862. Boston: Little, Brown, 1893. Berkeley: Shambala, 1973.

Zanoni (*LL* 133)

Text: *Monthly Chronicle,* 1841. London: Saunders & Otley, 1842. New York: Harper, 1842. Boston: Little, Brown, 1927. Blauvelt, NY: Rudolph Steiner, 1971.

Criticism (General): E. G. Bell, *Introduction to the Prose Romances, Plays and Comedies of Edward Bulwer, Lord Lytton* (Chicago: W. M. Hill, 1914). James L. Campbell, Sr., *Edward Bulwer-Lytton* (Boston: Twayne, 1986). Allan C. Christensen, *Edward Bulwer-Lytton* (Athens: University of Georgia Press, 1976). Joseph I. Fradin, "The Novels of Edward Bulwer-Lytton", Ph.D. diss.: Columbia University, 1956. Richard E. Lautz, "Bulwer-Lytton as Novelist", Ph.D. diss.: University of Pennsylvania, 1967. S. B. Liljegren, *Bulwer-Lytton's Novels and Isis Unveiled* (Cambridge, MA: Harvard University Press, 1957). Marie Roberts, *Gothic Immortals: The Fiction of the Brotherhood of the Rosy Cross* (London: Routledge, 1990). C. Nelson Stewart, *Bulwer-Lytton as Occultist* (London: Theosophical Publishing House, 1927). Richard A. Zipser, *Edward Bulwer-Lytton and Germany* (Berne: Herbert Lang, 1974).

MACDONALD, GEORGE (1824–1905)

Lilith (*LL* 567)

Text: London: Chatto & Windus, 1895. New York: Dodd, Mead, 1895. London: George Allen & Unwin, 1924. New York: E. P. Dutton, 1925. New York: Ballantine, 1969. In *Visionary Novels* (New York: Noonday Press, 1954; with *Phantastes*).

Criticism (General): Rolland Hein, *George Macdonald: Victorian Mythmaker* (Nashville, TN: Star Song Publishing Co., 1993). Joseph Johnson, *George Macdonald: A Biographical Critical Appreciation* (London: Sir L. Pitman, 1905). William Raeper, ed., *The Gold Thread: Essays on George Macdonald* (Edinburgh: Edinburgh University Press, 1990). Robert Lee Wolff, *The Golden Key: A Study of the Fiction of George Macdonald* (New Haven: Yale University Press, 1961).

MACHEN, ARTHUR (1863–1947)

"The Bowmen"

Text: Evening News (London), 29 September 1914. In Machen's *The Angels of Mons, the Bowmen, and Other Legends of the War* (London: Simpkin, Marshall, Hamilton, Kent, 1915; New York: G. P. Putnam's, 1915; London: Secker, 1923; Freeport, NY: Books for Libraries Press, 1972). In Machen's *Tales of Horror and the Supernatural* (New York: Knopf, 1948; London: Baker, 1964; New York: Pinnacle, 1971 [2 vols.]; St Albans: Panther, 1975 [2 vols.]).

The Chronicle of Clemendy

Text: London: Carbonnek, 1888. New York: Society of Pantagruelists, 1923. London: Secker, 1925. New York: Knopf, 1926.

"The Great God Pan" (*LL* 573)

Text: In Machen's *The Great God Pan and The Inmost Light* (London: John Lane, 1894; Boston: Roberts Brothers, 1894; Freeport, NY: Books for Libraries Press, 1970). In Machen's *The House of Souls* (London: Grant Richards, 1906; Boston: Estes, 1906; New York: A. & C. Boni, 1915; New York: Knopf, 1922; Freeport, NY: Books for Libraries Press, 1971; New York: Arno Press, 1976). In *Tales of Horror and the Supernatural* (q.v.). In Herbert A. Wise and Phyllis Fraser, eds., *Great Tales of Terror and the Supernatural* (New York: Modern Library, 1944).

"The Great Return"

Text: Evening News (London), 21 October–16 November 1915. London: Faith Press, 1915. In *Tales of Horror and the Supernatural* (q.v.). In Dorothy L. Sayers, ed., *The Second Omnibus of Crime* (New York: Coward-McCann, 1932).

The Hill of Dreams (*LL* 572)

Text: London: Grant Richards, 1907. Boston: Estes, 1907. New York: Albert & Charles Boni, 1915. London: Secker, 1922. New York: Knopf, 1923. London: Richards Press, 1954 (introduction by Lord Dunsany). London: John Baker, 1968.

"The Red Hand" (*LL* 573)

Text: Chapman's Magazine, December 1895. In *The House of Souls* (q.v.). In Machen's *The Strange World of Arthur Machen* (New York: Juniper Press, 1960).

"The Shining Pyramid" (*LL* 576)

Text: Unknown World, 15 May–15 June 1895. In Machen's *The Shining Pyramid,* ed. Vincent Starrett (Chicago: Covici-McGee, 1923). In Machen's *The Shining Pyramid* (London: Secker, 1925). In *Tales of Horror and the Supernatural* (q.v.). In *The Strange World of Arthur Machen* (q.v.). In Arthur Neale, ed., *The Great Weird Stories* (New York: Duffield, 1929).

The Terror

Text: *Evening News* (London), 16 October–31 October 1916 (as "The Great Terror"). *Century Magazine,* October 1917 (abridged; as "The Coming of the Terror"). London: Duckworth, 1917. New York: McBride, 1917. New York: W. W. Norton, 1965. In *Tales of Horror and the Supernatural* (q.v.). In Edward Wagenknecht, ed., *Six Novels of the Supernatural* (New York: Viking Press, 1944).

The Three Impostors (*LL* 578)

Text: London: John Lane; Boston: Roberts Brothers, 1895. London: Secker, 1923. New York: Knopf, 1923. London: John Baker, 1964. New York: Ballantine, 1972. In *The Strange World of Arthur Machen* (q.v.).

"The White People" (*LL* 573)

Text: *Horlick's Magazine,* January 1904. In *The House of Souls* (q.v.). In *Tales of Horror and the Supernatural* (q.v.). In *The Strange World of Arthur Machen* (q.v.). In Alexander Laing, ed., *The Haunted Omnibus* (London: Cassell, 1937; New York: Farrar & Rinehart, 1937; New York: Garden City Publishing Co., 1939).

Additional Works:

The Canning Wonder [nonfiction]. London: Chatto & Windus, 1925. New York: Knopf, 1926.

The Children of the Pool and Other Stories. London: Hutchinson, 1936. New York: Arno Press, 1976.

Dreads and Drolls [essays]. London: Secker, 1926. New York: Knopf, 1927. Freeport, NY: Books for Libraries Press, 1967.

Far Off Things [autobiography]. London: Secker, 1922. New York: Knopf, 1923.

The Green Round [novel]. London: Ernest Benn, 1933. Sauk City, WI: Arkham House, 1968.

Hieroglyphics: A Note upon Ecstasy in Literature. London: Grant Richards, 1902. London: Secker, 1910. New York: Mitchell Kennerley, 1913. New York: Knopf, 1923.

The Secret Glory [novel]. London: Secker, 1922. New York: Knopf, 1922.

Selected Letters. Ed. Mark Valentine and Roger Dobson. London: Thorsons, 1988.

Things Near and Far [autobiography]. London: Secker, 1923. New York: Knopf, 1923.

Criticism (General): William Francis Gekle, *Arthur Machen: Weaver of Fantasy* (Millbrook, NY: Round Table Press, 1949). Adrian Goldstone and Wesley Sweetser, *A Bibliography of Arthur Machen* (Austin: University of Texas Press, 1965). S. T. Joshi, "Arthur Machen: The Mystery of the Universe", in Joshi's *The Weird Tale* (Austin: University of Texas Press, 1990). A. Reynolds and William Charleton, *Ar-*

thur Machen: A Short Account of His Life and Work (London: Richards Press, 1963; Oxford: Caermaen Books, 1988). Vincent Starrett, *Arthur Machen; A Novelist of Ecstasy and Sin* (Chicago: W. M. Hill, 1918). Wesley Sweetser, *Arthur Machen* (New York: Twayne, 1964). Mark Valentine, *Arthur Machen* (Bridgend, Wales: Seren, 1995). Mark Valentine and Roger Dobson, ed., *Arthur Machen: Apostle of Wonder* (Oxford: Caermaen Books, 1985). Mark Valentine and Roger Dobson, ed., *Arthur Machen: Artist and Mystic* (Oxford: Caermaen Books, 1986).

MACPHERSON, JAMES ("OSSIAN") (1736–1796)

The Poems of Ossian, Translated [i.e. written] by James Macpherson

> *Text:* London: T. Becket & P. A. Dehondt, 1765 (2 vols.). Edinburgh & London: William Blackwood & Sons, 1870. Edinburgh: Patrick Geddes, 1896. New York: AMS Press, 1974 (2 vols.).

> *Criticism (General):* J. S. Smart, *James Macpherson: An Episode in Literature* (London: David Nutt, 1905). Thomas Bailey Saunders, *The Life and Letters of James Macpherson* (London: Sonnenschein, 1894). Derick S. Thomson, *The Gaelic Sources of Macpherson's Ossian* (Edinburgh: University of Aberdeen Press, 1952).

MALORY, SIR THOMAS (C. 1400–1471)

Le Morte d'Arthur (*LL* 591)

> *Text:* Westminster: Wynkyn de Worde, 1498. London & New York: Everyman's Library, 1906 (2 vols.). In Malory's *Works,* ed. Eugene Vinaver (Oxford: Oxford University Press, 1947; 2nd ed. 1967 [3 vols.]).

> *Criticism:* Ben F. Fiester, "The Function of the Supernatural in Malory's *Morte Darthur*", Ph.D. diss.: Pennsylvania State University, 1967. R. M. Lumiansky, "Malory's 'Tale of Lancelot and Guenevere' as Suspense", *Mediaeval Studies* 19 (1957): 108–22. Edmund Reiss, *Sir Thomas Malory* (New York: Twayne, 1966).

MARLOWE, CHRISTOPHER (1564–1593)

The Tragicall History of D. Faustus

> *Text:* London: Printed by V. S. for Thomas Bushell, 1604. Oxford: Oxford University Press, 1950 (ed. W. W. Greg). Ed. Frederick S. Boas (1932; rpt. 1966). Edinburgh, 1973 (ed. Keith Walker). In *Complete Plays,* ed. J. B. Steane (Harmondsworth: Penguin, 1969).

> *Criticism:* Muriel C. Bradbrook, "Marlowe's *Doctor Faustus* and the Eldritch Tradition", *Essays on Shakespeare and Elizabethan Drama in Honor of Hardin Craig,* ed. Richard Hosely (Columbia, MS., 1962).

MARRYAT, CAPT. FREDERICK (1792–1848)

The Phantom Ship (*LL* 593)

Text: New Monthly Magazine, 1837. London: H. Colburn, 1839 (3 vols.). London: Richard Bentley, 1847. London & New York: Macmillan, 1896, 1924. London: New English Library, 1966.

"The Werewolf" [excerpt from *The Phantom Ship;* see above]

Criticism: Maurice P. Gautier, *Captain Frederick Marryat* (Montreal: Didier, 1973). David Hannay, *The Life of Frederick Marryat* (London: W. Scott, 1889). Oliver Warner, *Captain Marryat: A Rediscovery* (London: Constable, 1953).

MARSH, RICHARD (1867–1915)

The Beetle (*LL* 595)

Text: London: Skeffington & Son, 1897. New York: Brentano's, 1901. London: Unwin, 1907. New York: G. P. Putnam's Sons, 1917. London: Grayson & Grayson, [1932?]. New York: Arno Press, 1976.

MATURIN, CHARLES ROBERT (1780?–1824)

Fatal Revenge; or, The Family of Montorio

Text: London: Longman, Hurst, Rees, & Orme, 1807 (3 vols.). London: J. Clements, 1840. New York: Arno Press, 1974 (3 vols.).

Criticism: Willy Müller, *Charles Robert Maturins Romane* Fatal Revenge *und* Melmoth the Wanderer (Weida: Thomas & Hubert, 1908).

Melmoth the Wanderer (*LL* 400, 599)

Text: Edinburgh: A. Constable & Co., 1820 (4 vols.). London: Richard Bentley, 1892. Lincoln: University of Nebraska Press, 1961. London: Oxford University Press, 1968 (ed. Douglas Grant).

Criticism (General): Syndy M. Conger, *Matthew G. Lewis, Charles Robert Maturin and the Germans* (Salzburg, 1977). John Bernard Harris, "Charles Robert Maturin: A Study", Ph.D. diss.: Wayne State University, 1965. Niilo Idman, *Charles Robert Maturin: His Life and Works* (London: Constable, 1923). Dale Kramer, *Charles Robert Maturin* (New York: Twayne, 1973). Robert E. Lougy, *Charles Robert Maturin* (Lewisburg, PA: Bucknell University Press, 1975). Willem Scholten, *Charles Robert Maturin: The Terror Novelist* (Amsterdam: H. J. Paris, 1933).

MAUPASSANT, GUY DE (1850–1893)

"Apparition" ("The Spectre")

Text: Gaulois, 4 April 1883. In Maupassant's *Oeuvres Complètes Illustrées* (Paris: Librairie de France, 1934), Vol. 3.

Translation: In Maupassant's *The Life Work of Guy de Maupassant* (Akron: St Dunstan Society, 1902f.), Vol. 4. In Maupassant's *Best Stories,* tr. Michael Monahan (New York: Modern Library, 1925) (as "An Apparition"). In Maupassant's *Complete Short Stories* (New York: Blue Ribbon Books, 1941). In Maupassant's

Tales of Supernatural Terror, ed. & tr. Arnold Kellett (London: Pan Books, 1972) (as "Apparition").

"Un Fou" ("The Diary of a Madman")

Text: Gaulois, 10 September 1885. In *Oeuvres Complètes Illustrées* (q.v.), Vol. 5.

Translation: In *The Life Work of Guy de Maupassant* (q.v.), Vol. 3. In *Complete Short Stories* (q.v.). In *Tales of Supernatural Terror* (q.v.) (as "Was He Mad?").

"Le Horla" ("The Horla") (*LL* 335, 400)

Text: Gil Blas, 26 October 1886. In *Le Maupassant du "Horla"*, ed. Pierre Cogny (Paris: Minard, 1970 [short and long versions]). In *Oeuvres Complètes Illustrées* (q.v.), Vol. 6. In Maupassant's *Le Horla et autres histoires* (Paris: Sieul, 1993).

Translation: In *The Best Short Stories of Guy de Maupassant* (Cleveland: World Publishing Co., 1944). In *Complete Short Stories* (q.v.). In *Tales of Supernatural Terror* (q.v.). In Joseph Lewis French, ed., *Masterpieces of Mystery* (Garden City, NY: Doubleday, Page, 1920), Vol. 2. In Alexander Laing, ed., *The Haunted Omnibus* (London: Cassell, 1937; New York: Farrar & Rinehart, 1937; New York: Garden City Publishing Co., 1939). In Herbert A. Wise and Phyllis Fraser, ed., *Great Tales of Terror and the Supernatural* (New York: Modern Library, 1944).

Criticism: Jacques Bienvenu, *Maupassant, Flaubert, et "Le Horla"* (Paris: Editions Muntaner, 1991).

"Le loup" ("The White Wolf")

Text: Gaulois, 16 October 1882. In Maupassant's *Clair de lune* (Paris: Ollendorff, 1888). In *Oeuvres Complètes Illustrées* (q.v.), Vol. 2.

Translation: In *The Life Work of Guy de Maupassant* (q.v.), Vol. 9. In *Complete Short Stories* (q.v.). In *Tales of Supernatural Terror* (q.v.) (as "The Wolf").

"Lui?" ("He?")

Text: Gil Blas, 3 July 1883. In *Le Maupassant du "Horla"* (q.v.). In *Oeuvres Complètes Illustrées* (q.v.), Vol. 3.

Translation: In *The Life Work of Guy de Maupassant* (q.v.), Vol. 5. In *Complete Short Stories* (q.v.). In *The Tales of Guy de Maupassant* (Heritage Press, 1964). In *Tales of Supernatural Terror* (q.v.).

"Qui sait?" ("Who Knows?")

Text: Echo de Paris, 6 August 1890. In *Oeuvres Complètes Illustrées* (q.v.), Vol. 8. In *Le Maupassant du "Horla"* (q.v.).

Translation: In Maupassant's *Useless Beauty and Other Stories*, tr. Ernest Boyd (New York: Knopf, 1926). In *Tales of Supernatural Terror* (q.v.).

"Sur l'eau" ("On the River")

Text: Sans Lieu, [1888]. In Maupassant's *Contes choisies* (Paris: P. Ollendorff, 1886). In *Oeuvres Complètes Illustrées* (q.v.), Vol. 1.

Translation: In Maupassant's *Boule de suif and Other Stories,* tr. Ernest Boyd (New York: Knopf, 1922). In *Complete Short Stories* (q.v.). In *Tales of Supernatural Terror* (q.v.). In Joseph Lewis French, ed., *Ghosts Grim and Gentle* (New York: Dodd, Mead, 1926). In Seon Manley and Gago Lewis, ed., *Shapes of the Supernatural* (Garden City, NY: Doubleday, 1969).

"Terreur" ("Horror")

Text: In Maupassant's *Des Vers* (Paris: G. Charpentier, 1880). In *Oeuvres Complètes Illustrées* (q.v.), Vol. 14.

Translation: In *The Life Work of Guy de Maupassant* (q.v.), Vol. 13. In *Tales of Supernatural Terror* (q.v.) (as "Terror").

Criticism (General): Marie Claire Bancquart, *Maupassant, conteur fantastique* (Paris: Les Lettres Modernes/Minard, 1976). John R. Dugan, *Illusion and Reality: A Study of Descriptive Techniques in the Works of Guy de Maupassant* (The Hague, 1973). Henry James, *Partial Portraits* (London: Macmillan, 1888). Georges Normandy, *La Fin de Maupassant* (Paris: A. Michel, 1927). Nafissa A.-F. Schasch, *Guy de Maupassant et le fantastique tenebreux* (Paris: Nizet, 1983). Robert H. Sherrard, *The Life, Work and Evil Fate of Guy de Maupassant* (London: T. Werner Laurie, 1926). Francis Steegmuller, *Maupassant: A Lion in the Path* (New York: Random House, 1949).

MEINHOLD, WILHELM (1797–1851)

Maria Schweidler, die Bernsteinhexe

Text: Berlin: Duncker & Humblot, 1843. Schwerin: Peter-mauken Verlag, 1954 (ed. Erich Sielaff).

Translation: Lady Duff Gordon (New York: Wiley & Putnam, 1845; often rpt.; last rpt. London: Oxford University Press, 1928; as *Marie Schweidler, the Amber Witch*).

Criticism: Josef Rysan, *Wilhelm Meinhold's* Bernsteinhexe: *A Study in Witchcraft and Cultural History* (Chicago: University of Chicago Press, 1948).

MÉRIMÉE, PROSPER (1803–1870).

"La Vénus d'Ille" ("The Venus of Ille") (*LL* 347)

Text: Revue des Deux Mondes, 1 July 1840. In Mérimée's *Colomba* (Paris: Magen et Comon, 1841). In Mérimée's *Romans et nouvelles,* ed. Maurice Parturier (Paris: Editions Garner Freres, 1967), Vol. 2.

Translation: In *Tales Before Supper,* tr. Myndart Verelst [pseud. of Edgar Saltus] (New York: Brentano's, 1887; rpt. New York: AMS Press, 1970). In Mérimée's *The Venus of Ille and Other Stories,* tr. Jean Kimber (London: Oxford University Press, 1966).

Criticism: Geneviève Biourquis, "La Theme de la Vénus fatale chez Eichendorff et Mérimée", *Revue Universitaire* 51 (1942). F. P. Bowman, "Narrator and Myth in

Mérimée's 'Vénus d'Ille' ", *French Review* 33 (1959–60): 475–82. I. Nagel, "Gespenster und Wirklichkeiten: Prosper Mérimée's Novelle 'La Vénus d'Ille' ", *Neue Rundschau* 68 (1957): 419–27. Maximilian Rudwin, "Mérimée and the Marvellous", *French Quarterly* 8 (1926): 198–214. A. W. Raitt, *Prosper Mérimée* (New York: Scribner's, 1970).

METCALFE, JOHN (B. 1891)

The Smoking Leg and Other Stories

Text: London: Jarrolds, 1925. Garden City, NY: Doubleday, Page, 1926.

Criticism: Review, *New York Times Book Review,* 2 May 1926, p. 9. Review, *Saturday Review of Literature,* 17 October 1925, p. 450.

MEYRINK, GUSTAV (1868–1932)

Der Golem (*The Golem*)

Text: Leipzig: Kurt Wolff, 1915. Munich: Langen-Müller Verlag, 1972.

Translation: Madge Pemberton (London: Gollancz; Boston: Houghton Mifflin, 1928; New York: Dover, 1976 [in *Two German Supernatural Novels,* ed. E. F. Bleiler]; separate publication 1986). Mike Mitchell (Sawtry, UK: Dedalus, 1995).

Film: Der Golem, Bioscop-Film, Berlin (first version 1914; second version 1920).

Criticism: Helga Abret, *Gustav Meyrink conteur* (Bern: Herbert Lang; Frankfurt am Main: Peter Lang, 1976). Serge Hutin, "Gustav Meyrink et *Le Golem*", *Symbolisme* 5 (1958): 281–95. Florian F. Marzin, *Okkultismus und Phantastik in den Romanen Gustav Meyrinks* (Essen: Blaue Eule, 1986). Special Gustav Meyrink issue of *Cahiers de L'Herne* (No. 30), ed. Yvonne Caroutch (1975). Siegfried Schödel, *Studien zu den phantastischen Erzählungen Gustav Meyrinks* (diss., Erlangen-Nürnberg, 1965).

MOORE, THOMAS (1779–1852)

Alciphron (*LL* 618)

Text: London: J. Macrone, 1839 (with *The Epicurean*). Philadelphia: Carey & Hart, 1840. In *The Poetical Works of Thomas Moore* (London: Longman, 1840–41; London: E. Moxon, 1870 [ed. W. M. Rossetti]; London: Henry Frowde/Oxford University Press, 1910 [ed. A. D. Godley]).

The Epicurean (*LL* 617)

Text: London: Longman, Rees, Orme, Brown, & Green, 1827. London: J. Macrone, 1839 (with *Alciphron*). Rev. ed.: New York: C. S. Francis, 1841. London: Downey, 1889. Chicago: A. C. McClurg, 1890.

"The Ring" (*LL* 618)

Text: In Moore's *Poetical Works* (Philadelphia, 1845). In *Poetical Works,* ed. A. D. Godley (q.v.).

Criticism (General): Miriam De Ford, *Thomas Moore* (New York: Twayne, 1967). Stephen Gwynn, *Thomas Moore* (New York & London: Macmillan, 1905). H. H. Jordan, *Bolt Upright: The Life of Thomas Moore* (Salzburg, 1975; 2 vols.). H. H. Jordan, "Poe's Debt to Thomas Moore", *PMLA* 63 (1948): 752–57. L. A. G. Strong, *The Minstrel Boy: A Portrait of Thomas Moore* (London: Hodder & Stoughton, 1937). Terence de Vere White, *Tom Moore: The Irish Poet* (London: Hamilton, 1977).

O'BRIEN, FITZ-JAMES (1828–1862)

"The Diamond Lens" (*LL* 335)

Text: Atlantic Monthly 1 (January 1858): 354–67. In *The Poems and Stories of Fitz-James O'Brien*, ed. William Winter (Boston: J. R. Osgood, 1881). In O'Brien's *Collected Stories*, ed. Edward J. O'Brien (New York: A. & C. Boni, 1925). In *The Fantastic Tales of Fitz-James O'Brien*, ed. Michael Hayes (London: Calder, 1977). In *The Supernatural Tales of Fitz-James O'Brien*, ed. Jessica Amanda Salmonson (New York: Doubleday, 1988; 2 vols.). In Joseph Lewis French, ed., *Masterpieces of Mystery* (New York: Doubleday, Page, 1920), Vol. 2. In Seon Manley and Gogo Lewis, ed., *Shapes of the Supernatural* (Garden City, NY: Doubleday, 1969).

"What Was It?"

Text: Harper's 18 (March 1859): 504–9. In *Poems and Stories* (q.v.). In *Collected Stories* (q.v.). In *Fantastic Tales* (q.v.). In *Supernatural Tales* (q.v.). In Joseph Lewis French, ed., *Great Ghost Stories* (New York: Dodd, Mead, 1918). In Herbert A. Wise and Phyllis Fraser, ed., *Great Tales of Terror and the Supernatural* (New York: Modern Library, 1944). In Eric Protter, ed., *Monster Festival* (New York: Vanguard, 1965).

Criticism: Francis Wolle, *Fitz-James O'Brien: A Literary Bohemian of the Eighteen-Fifties* (Boulder, Col., 1944; University of Colorado Studies in the Humanities, Vol. 2, No. 2).

T. PETRONIUS NIGER ("ARBITER") (?–A.D. 66)

Satyricon

Text: Ed. Michael Heseltine (Cambridge, Mass./London: Harvard/Heinemann [Loeb Classical Library], 1913; rev. ed. 1969 [by E. H. Warmington]; with Eng. trans.). Ed. Alfred Ernout (Paris [Budé], 1923; 7th ed. 1970; with French trans.). Ed. Konrad Müller (Munich, 1961; 2nd ed. 1965 [with German trans. by W. Ehlers]). Ed. Martin S. Smith (Oxford, 1975; only *Cena Trimalchionis;* with comm.).

Translation: Joseph Addison (London, 1736; rpt. New York: AMS Press, 1975). Oscar Wilde [?] (Paris: C. Carrington, 1902 [as by "Sebastian Melmoth"]; often rpt.). William Arrowsmith (Ann Arbor: University of Michigan Press, 1959). J. P. Sullivan (Harmondsworth: Penguin, 1965; rev. ed. 1969).

Criticism: M. Schuster, "Der Werwolf und die Hexen", *Wiener Studien* 48 (1930): 149f.; 49 (1931): 83f. J. P. Sullivan, *The Satyricon of Petronius* (Bloomington: Indiana University Press, 1968).

PHLEGON OF TRALLES (1ST–2ND C. A.D.)

Peri thaumasion (*Mirabilia, or On Wonderful Events*)

Text: In *Rerum Naturalium Scriptores Graeci Minores,* ed. Otto Keller (Leipzig: Teubner, 1877), Vol. 1. In *Paradoxographoi: Scriptores Rerum Mirabilium Graeci,* ed. Antonius Westermann (1839; rpt. Amsterdam, 1963).

Translation: Partial trans. included in Lacy Collison-Morley, *Greek and Roman Ghost Stories* (1912; rpt. Chicago: Argonaut, 1968).

C. PLINIUS CAECILIUS SECUNDUS (PLINY THE YOUNGER) (C. A.D. 61–112)

Epistulae 7.27 (to Sura) (*LL* 335)

Text: Ed. Selatie Edgar Stout (Bloomington: Indiana University Press, 1962). Ed. R. A. B. Mynors (Oxford [Oxford Classical Text], 1963). Ed. Betty Radice (Cambridge, MA/London: Harvard/Heinemann [Loeb Classical Library], 1969 [2 vols.; with Eng. trans.]).

Translation: See Radice above. Letter to Sura alone included in Joseph Lewis French, ed., *Masterpieces of Mystery* (Garden City, NY: Doubleday, Page, 1920), Vol. 2. In Julian Hawthorne, ed., *The Lock and Key Library* (New York: Review of Reviews, 1909), Vol. 2. In Alexander Laing, ed., *The Haunted Omnibus* (New York: Farrar & Rinehart, 1937).

Criticism: A. N. Sherwin-White, *The Letters of Pliny: A Commentary* (Oxford: Clarendon Press, 1968).

POE, EDGAR ALLAN (1809–1849)

[*Poems*] (*LL* 702)

Text: Poems, 2nd ed. (New York: Elam Bliss, 1831). *Poetical Works,* ed. J. H. Whitty (Boston & New York: Houghton Mifflin, 1911; 2nd ed. 1917); ed. Killis Campbell (Boston: Ginn & Co., 1917); ed. Floyd Stovall (Charlottesville: University of Virginia Press, 1965); ed. T. O. Mabbott (Cambridge, MA: Harvard University Press, 1969).

[*Tales*] (*LL* 701, 702)

Text: Tales of the Grotesque and Arabesque (Philadelphia: Lea & Blanchard, 1840 [2 vols.]). *Tales* (New York: Wiley & Putnam, 1845). *The Works of the Late Edgar Allan Poe,* ed. Rufus W. Griswold (New York: J. S. Redfield, 1850–56 [4 vols.]).

The Complete Works of Edgar Allan Poe, ed. James A. Harrison (New York: Crowell, 1902 [17 vols.]). *Tales and Sketches*, ed. T. O. Mabbott et al. (Cambridge, MA: Harvard University Press, 1978 [2 vols.]).

The Narrative of A. Gordon Pym of Nantucket (*LL* 702)

Text: *Southern Literary Messenger*, 1837. New York: Harper & Brother, 1838. New York: Wiley & Putnam, 1838. In *Works*, ed. Griswold (q.v.), Vol. 4. New York: Hill & Wang, 1960 (ed. Sidney Kaplan). Harmondsworth: Penguin, 1975 (ed. Harold Beaver).

Criticism: J. O. Bailey, "Sources for Poe's *Arthur Gordon Pym*, 'Hans Pfaal', and Other Pieces", *PMLA* 57 (1942): 513–35. Evelyn J. Hinz, " 'Tekeli-li': *The Narrative of A. Gordon Pym* as Satire", *Genre* 3 (1970): 379–99. J. Gerald Kennedy, The Narrative of Arthur Gordon Pym *and the Abyss of Interpretation* (New York: Twayne, 1995).

Criticism (General): Hervey Allen, *Israfel: The Life and Times of Edgar Allan Poe* (New York: George H. Doran, 1926; 2 vols.). Haldeen Braddy, *Glorious Incense: The Fulfilment of Edgar Allan Poe* (Washington, DC: Scarecrow Press, 1953). Vincent Buranelli, *Edgar Allan Poe* (New York: Twayne, 1961). Killis Campbell, *The Mind of Poe* (Cambridge, MA: Harvard University Press, 1933). Edward Davidson, *Poe: A Critical Study* (Cambridge, MA: Harvard University Press, 1957). Joan Dayan, *Fables of Mind: An Inquiry into Poe's Fiction* (New York: Oxford University Press, 1987). Daniel Hoffman, *Poe Poe Poe Poe Poe Poe Poe* (Garden City, NY: Doubleday, 1972). Burton R. Pollin, *Discoveries in Poe* (Notre Dame, IN: University of Notre Dame Press, 1970). Arthur Hobson Quinn, *Edgar Allan Poe: A Critical Biography* (New York & London: Appleton-Century, 1941). Kenneth Silverman, *Edgar A. Poe: Mournful and Never-Ending Remembrance* (New York: HarperCollins, 1991). G. R. Thompson, *Poe's Fiction: Romantic Irony in the Gothic Tales* (Madison: University of Wisconsin Press, 1973). Edward Wagenknecht, *Edgar Allan Poe: The Man Behind the Legend* (New York: Oxford University Press, 1963). Sarah Helen Whitman, *Edgar Allan Poe and His Critics* (1860; rpt. New Brunswick, NJ: Rutgers University Press, 1949). George Woodberry, *The Life of Edgar Allan Poe* (Boston & New York: Houghton Mifflin, 1909; 2 vols.).

POLIDORI, JOHN WILLIAM (1795–1821)

"The Vampyre"

Text: *New Monthly Magazine,* April 1819 (as by Lord Byron). London: Sherwood, Neely, & Jornes, 1819. Boston: Munroe & Francis, 1819. In Horace Walpole, et al., *The Castle of Otranto* [and other works], ed. E. F. Bleiler (New York: Dover, 1966). In Polidori's *The Vampyre and Other Works* (Chislehurst, UK: Gargoyle's Head Press, 1991). In *The Vampyre and Ernestus Berchtold; or, The Modern Oedipus: Collected Fiction of John William Polidori,* ed. D. L. Macdonald and Kathleen Scherf (Toronto: University of Toronto Press, 1993).

Criticism (General): David Lorne Macdonald, *Poor Polidori: A Critical Biography of the Author of "The Vampyre"* (Toronto: University of Toronto Press, 1991). John William Polidori, *The Diary of Dr. John William Polidori, 1816,* ed. W. M. Rossetti (London: Elkin Mathews, 1911). J. Rieger, "Polidori and the Genesis of Frankenstein", *Studies in English Literature 1500–1900* 3 (1963): 461–72.

PREST, THOMAS PECKETT (1810?–1879?)

Varney the Vampire; or, The Feast of Blood

Text: London: E. Lloyd, 1847 (3 vols.). New York: Arno Press, 1970 (3 vols.). New York: Dover, 1972.

RADCLIFFE, ANN (1764–1823)

The Castles of Athlin and Dunbayne: A Highland Story

Text: London: T. Hookham, 1789. London: J. S. Pratt, 1845. New York: Arno Press, 1972.

Gaston de Blondeville

Text: London: Harry Colburn, 1826 (4 vols.). Philadelphia: H. C. Carey & I. Lea, 1826. Hildesheim: Georg Olms Verlag, 1976 (4 vols. in 2). New York: Arno Press, 1972 (2 vols.).

The Italian; or, The Confessional of the Black Penitents

Text: London: T. Cadell & W. Davies, 1797 (3 vols.). London: Folio Society, 1956. New York: Russell & Russell, 1968 (3 vols.). London: Oxford University Press, 1968 (ed. Frederick Garber).

The Mysteries of Udolpho (LL 718)

Text: London: G. G. & J. Robinson, 1794 (4 vols.). London & New York: Dent/Dutton (Everyman's Library), 1931 (2 vols.). London: Oxford University Press, 1966 (ed. Bonamy Dobrée).

Criticism: Martha Hale Shackford, *"The Eve of St. Agnes* and *The Mysteries of Udolpho", PMLA* 36 (1921): 104–18. Celia Whitt, "Poe and *The Mysteries of Udolpho", University of Texas Studies in English* 17 (1937): 124–31.

The Romance of the Forest

Text: London: Hookham & Carpenter, 1791 (3 vols.). Philadelphia: J. B. Lippincott, 1865. New York: Arno Press, 1974 (3 vols.). In Harrison B. Steeves, ed., *Three Eighteenth Century Romances* (New York: Scribner's, 1931; abridged).

A Sicilian Romance

Text: London: Hookham & Carpenter, 1790 (2 vols.). London: J. S. Pratt, 1843. New York: Arno Press, 1972.

Criticism (General): Margaret L. Carter, "The Fantastic Uncanny in Radcliffe", in Carter's *Specter or Delusion: The Supernatural in Gothic Fiction* (Ann Arbor, MI:

UMI Research Press, 1986). Aline Grant, *Ann Radcliffe: A Biography* (Denver: Alan Swallow Press, 1951). Clara F. McIntyre, *Ann Radcliffe in Relation to Her Time* (New Haven: Yale University Press, 1920; New York: Archon Books, 1970). Robert Miles, *Ann Radcliffe: The Great Enchantress* (Manchester, UK: Manchester University Press; New York: St Martin's Press, 1995). E. B. Murray, *Ann Radcliffe* (New York: Twayne, 1972). Lee Edward Keebler, "Ann Radcliffe: A Study in Achievement", Ph.D. diss.: University of Wisconsin, 1967. Sir Walter Scott, "Ann Radcliffe", in Scott's *Lives of the Novelists* (1825; rpt. New York & London: Dent/Dutton [Everyman's Library], 1910). Ford Harris Swigart, "A Study of the Imagery in the Gothic Romances of Ann Radcliffe", Ph.D. diss.: University of Pittsburgh, 1966. Malcolm Ware, *Sublimity in the Novels of Ann Radcliffe* (Copenhagen, 1963).

RANSOME, ARTHUR (1884–1967)

The Elixir of Life

Text: London: Methuen, 1915.

RAPPOPORT, SOLOMON ("ANSKY") (1863–1920)

The Dybbuk (original in Yiddish)

Translation: Henry G. Alsberg and Winifred Katzin (New York: Boni & Liveright, 1926). John Hirsch (Winnipeg: Peguis Publishers, 1975). In *Chief Contemporary Dramatists: Third Series,* ed. Thomas H. Dickinson (Boston: Houghton Mifflin, 1930). In *Sixteen Famous European Plays,* ed. Bennett A. Cerf and Van H. Cartmell (Garden City, NY: Garden City Publishing Co., 1943).

Criticism: Review, Saturday Review of Literature, 4 December 1926, p. 396.

REEVE, CLARA (1729–1807)

The Old English Baron: A Gothic Story (LL 724)

Text: Colchester: W. Keymer, 1777 (as *The Champion of Virtue*). London: E. & C. Dilly, 1778. New York: Cassell, 1888. London: Oxford University Press, 1967 (ed. James Trainer).

Criticism: J. K. Reeves, "The Mother of Fatherless Fanny", *ELH* 9 (1942): 224–33.

REYNOLDS, GEORGE W. M. (1814–1879)

Faust: A Romance of the Secret Tribunals

Text: London Journal, 1845–46. London: G. Vickers, 1847. London: John Dicks, [1883?].

Wagner the Wehr-Wolf

Text: Reynolds's Miscellany, 1847. London: J. Dicks, 1848, 1857, 1872. New York: Dover, 1975 (ed. E. F. Bleiler).

ROCHE, REGINA MARIA (1773–1845)

The Children of the Abbey

Text: London: W. Lane (Minerva Press), 1796 (4 vols.). Philadelphia: J. B. Lippincott, 1874. Chicago: Donohue, [1912?]. London: Folio Press, 1968.

SCOTT, SIR WALTER (1771–1832)

Letters on Demonology and Witchcraft

Text: London: John Murray, 1830. London: Routledge & Sons, 1884. New York: Gordon Press, 1974.

"The Tapestried Chamber" (*LL* 313, 637)

Text: The Keepsake for 1829, 1828. In *The Supernatural Short Stories of Sir Walter Scott* (London: John Calder, 1977). In Arthur Neale, ed., *The Great Weird Stories* (New York: Duffield, 1929). In *Short Stories by Sir Walter Scott* (London: Oxford University Press, 1934).

Criticism: Coleman O. Parsons, "Scott's Prior Version of 'The Tapestried Chamber'", *Notes & Queries* 207 (1962): 417–20.

"Wandering Willie's Tale"

Text: In *Redgauntlet,* ch. 11. Edinburgh: Archibald Constable, 1824 (3 vols.); London & New York: Dent/Dutton (Everyman's Library), 1906; London: Nelson, [1951?]. In *The Supernatural Short Stories of Sir Walter Scott* (q.v.).

Criticism (General): Mody C. Boatright, "Demonology in the Novels of Sir Walter Scott", *University of Texas Studies in English* 14 (1934): 75–88. Mody C. Boatright, "Scott's Theory and Practice concerning the Use of the Supernatural", *PMLA* 50 (1935): 235–61. Mody C. Boatright, "Witchcraft in the Novels of Sir Walter Scott", *University of Texas Studies in English* 13 (1933): 95–112. John Buchan, *Sir Walter Scott* (London: Cassell, 1932). Neal F. Doubleday, "Wandering Willie's Tale", in his *Vanity of Attempt* (Lincoln: University of Nebraska Press, 1976), pp. 49–60. Walter Freye, *The Influence of "Gothic" Literature on Sir Walter Scott* (Rostock, 1902). Reginald W. Hartland, *Walter Scott et le roman "frenetique"* (Paris: Champion, 1928). Harendrakumar Mukhopadhaya, *The Supernatural in Scott* (Calcutta, 1917). Coleman O. Parsons, *Witchcraft and Demonology in Scott's Fiction* (Edinburgh: Oliver & Boyd, 1964).

SHAKESPEARE, WILLIAM (1564–1616)

Hamlet (*LL* 787–789)

Text: London: Printed for Nicholas Ling and John Trundell, 1603 (quarto). In *Mr. William Shakespeares Comedies, Histories, & Tragedies* (London: Printed by Isaac Jaggard, and Ed. Blount, 1623) [First Folio]. Ed. G. L. Kittredge (Boston: Ginn & Co., 1939). Ed. Willard Farnham (Harmondsworth: Penguin, 1957). Ed. Cyrus Hoy (New York: W. W. Norton, 1963).

Criticism: Roy W. Battenhouse, "The Ghost in *Hamlet:* A Catholic 'Linchpin'?", *Studies in Philology* 48 (1951): 161–92. Joseph Miriam, "Discerning the Ghost in *Hamlet*", *PMLA* 76 (1961): 493–502. Isidore J. Semper, "The Ghost in *Hamlet:* Pagan or Christian?", *The Month* 9 (1953): 222–34. H. M. Doak, "Supernatural in Shakespeare, Part III: *Hamlet* and *Macbeth*", *Shakespeariana* 9 (1892): 226–31. C. E. Whitmore, "The Ghost in *Hamlet*", in his *The Supernatural in Tragedy* (Cambridge, MA: Harvard University Press, 1915).

Macbeth (*LL* 787–789)

Text: In *Mr. William Shakespeares Comedies, Histories, & Tragedies* (q.v.). Ed. G. L. Kittredge (Boston: Ginn & Co., 1939). Ed. Kenneth Muir (London: Methuen, 1951). Ed. Alfred Harbage (Harmondsworth: Penguin, 1956). Ed. G. K. Hunter (Harmondsworth: Penguin, 1967).

Criticism: Terence Hawkes, ed., *Twentieth Century Interpretations of* Macbeth (Englewood Cliffs, NJ: Prentice-Hall, 1977). Marvin Rosenberg, *The Masks of* Macbeth (Berkeley: University of California Press, 1978).

SHELLEY, MARY WOLLSTONECRAFT (1797–1851)

Frankenstein; or, The Modern Prometheus (*LL* 793)

Text: London: Lackington, Hughes, Harding, Mayor, & Jones, 1818 (3 vols.). London: Routledge, 1882. London & New York: Dent/Dutton (Everyman's Library), 1912. London: Oxford University Press, 1969 (ed. M. J. Kennedy). In Peter Fairclough, ed., *Three Gothic Novels* (Harmondsworth: Penguin, 1968).

Criticism: Chris Baldick, *In Frankenstein's Shadow* (Oxford: Clarendon Press, 1987). Radu Florescu, *In Search of Frankenstein* (Boston: New York Graphic Society, 1975). David Ketterer, *Frankenstein's Creation* (Victoria, BC: University of Victoria Press, 1979). George Levine and U. C. Knoepflmacher, eds., *The Endurance of* Frankenstein (Berkeley: University of California Press, 1979). Christopher Small, *Mary Shelley's* Frankenstein (Pittsburgh: University of Pittsburgh Press, 1973). Martin Tropp, *Mary Shelley's Monster* (Boston: Houghton Mifflin, 1976).

The Last Man

Text: London: Henry Colburn, 1826 (3 vols.). Lincoln: University of Nebraska Press, 1965 (ed. Hugh J. Lake).

Criticism: Jean de Palacio, "Mary Shelley and *The Last Man*", *Revue de Litterature Comparée* 42 (1968): 37–49.

Criticism (General): Betty T. Bennett, *Mary Wollstonecraft Shelley: An Introduction* (Baltimore: Johns Hopkins University Press, 1998). R. Glynn Gryls, *Mary Shelley: A Biography* (London: Oxford University Press, 1938). Elizabeth Nitchie, *Mary Shelley, Author of* Frankenstein (New Brunswick, NJ: Rutgers University Press, 1953). Muriel Spark, *Child of Light: A Reassessment of Mary Wollstonecraft Shelley* (Hadleigh:

Tower Bridge, 1951). William Walling, *Mary Shelley* (New York: Twayne, 1972). Emily W. Sunstein, *Mary Shelley: Romance and Reality* (Boston: Little, Brown, 1989).

SHELLEY, PERCY BYSSHE (1792–1822)

St. Irvyne; or, The Rosicrucian

> *Text:* London: J. J. Stockdale, 1811. New York: Arno Press, 1977.

Zastrozzi: A Romance

> *Text:* London: G. Wilkie & J. Robinson, 1810. London: Golden Cockerel Press, 1955. New York: Arno Press, 1977. In Eustace Chesser, *Shelley and* Zastrozzi: *Self-Revelation of a Neurotic* (London: Greag/Archive, 1965).

> *Criticism (General):* Joseph Barrell, *Shelley and the Thought of His Time* (New Haven: Yale University Press, 1947). H. N. Brailsford, *Shelley, Godwin, and Their Circle* (New York: Henry Holt, 1913). Kenneth M. Cameron, *The Young Shelley* (New York: Macmillan, 1950). A. M. D. Hughes, *The Nascent Mind of Shelley* (Oxford: Clarendon Press, 1947). A. H. Koszul, *La Jeunesse de Shelley* (Paris: Bloud, 1910). John V. Murphy, *The Dark Angel: Gothic Elements in Shelley's Works* (Lewisburg, PA: Bucknell University Press, 1975).

SHIEL, MATTHEW PHIPPS (1865–1947)

"The House of Sounds"

> *Text:* In Shiel's *Shapes in the Fire* (London: John Lane; Boston: Roberts Brothers, 1896 [as "Vaila"]). Rev. ed.: In Shiel's *The Pale Ape and Other Pulses* (London: T. Werner Laurie, 1911). In Shiel's *Xélucha and Others* (Sauk City, WI: Arkham House, 1975). In August Derleth, ed., *Sleep No More!* (New York: Farrar & Rinehart, 1944).

The Purple Cloud (*LL* 800)

> *Text:* London: Chatto & Windus, 1901. London: Victor Gollancz, 1929. New York: Vanguard Press, 1930. New York & Cleveland: World Publishing Co., 1946. Boston: Gregg Press, 1977.

"Xélucha"

> *Text:* In *Shapes in the Fire* (q.v.). In *The Best Short Stories of M. P. Shiel*, ed. John Gawsworth (London: Victor Gollancz, 1948). Rev. ed.: In August Derleth, ed., *Dark Mind, Dark Heart* (Sauk City, WI: Arkham House, 1964). In *Xélucha and Others* (q.v.).

> *Criticism (General):* A. Reynolds Morse, ed., *Shiel in Diverse Hands: A Collection of Essays* (Cleveland: Reynolds Morse Foundation, 1983). A. Reynolds Morse, *The Works of M. P. Shiel: A Study in Bibliography* (Los Angeles: Fantasy Publishing Co., 1948; rev. ed. 1980 [with John D. Squires; 2 vols.]). Sam Moskowitz, "The World, the Devil, and M. P. Shiel", in Moskowitz's *Explorers of the Infinite* (Cleveland:

World Publishing Co., 1963). Carl Van Vechten, "Matthew Phipps Shiel" (1924), in Van Vechten's *Excavations: A Book of Advocacies* (New York: Knopf, 1926).

SINCLAIR, MAY (1865?–1946)

Uncanny Stories

Text: London: Hutchinson, 1923. New York: Macmillan, 1923.

Criticism (General): Theophillus E. M. Boll, *Miss May Sinclair: Novelist* (Rutherford, NJ: Fairleigh Dickinson University Press, 1973). Hrisey D. Zegger, *May Sinclair* (Boston: Twayne, 1976).

SMITH, CLARK ASHTON (1893–1961)

The Abominations of Yondo. Sauk City, WI: Arkham House, 1960. Jersey: Spearman, 1972. St Albans: Panther, 1974.

The Book of Hyperborea. West Warwick, RI: Necronomicon Press, 1996.

The Double Shadow and Other Fantasies. [Auburn, CA: Auburn Journal, 1933.] (*LL* 810)

Genius Loci and Other Tales. Sauk City, WI: Arkham House, 1948. Jersey: Spearman, 1972. St Albans: Panther, 1974.

Lost Worlds. Sauk City, WI: Arkham House, 1944. Jersey: Spearman, 1971. St Albans: Panther, 1974 (2 vols.).

Other Dimensions. Sauk City, WI: Arkham House, 1970. St Albans: Panther, 1977 (2 vols.).

Out of Space and Time. Sauk City, WI: Arkham House, 1942. Jersey: Spearman, 1971. St Albans: Panther, 1974.

Poems in Prose. Sauk City, WI: Arkham House, 1965.

A Rendezvous in Averoigne: Best Fantastic Tales of Clark Ashton Smith. Sauk City, WI: Arkham House, 1988.

Selected Poems. Sauk City, WI: Arkham House, 1971.

Strange Shadows: The Uncollected Fiction and Essays of Clark Ashton Smith. Ed. Steve Behrends et al. Westport, CT: Greenwood Press, 1989.

Tales of Science and Sorcery. Sauk City, WI: Arkham House, 1964. St Albans: Panther, 1976.

Tales of Zothique. West Warwick, RI: Necronomicon Press, 1995.

Criticism (General): Steve Behrends, *Clark Ashton Smith* (Mercer Island, WA: Starmont House, 1990). Jack L. Chalker, ed., *In Memoriam: Clark Ashton Smith* (Baltimore: Mirage Press, 1963). *The Dark Eidolon: The Journal of Smith Studies* (Necronomicon Press). S. T. Joshi and Marc A. Michaud, "The Prose and Poetry of Clark Ashton Smith", *Books at Brown* 27 (1979): 81–87. Donald Sidney-Fryer, *Emperor of Dreams: A Clark Ashton Smith Bibliography* (West Kingston, RI: Donald M.

Grant, 1978). Donald Sidney-Fryer, *The Last of the Great Romantic Poets* (Albuquerque: Silver Scarab Press, 1973).

SMOLLETT, TOBIAS (1721–1771)

The Adventures of Ferdinand, Count Fathom

> *Text:* London: Printed for W. Johnston, 1753 (2 vols.). In *Works,* ed. George Saintsbury (Philadelphia: Lippincott, 1895–1903), Vols. 8 & 9. Oxford, 1971 (ed. Damian Grant).

Criticism: Catherine L. Almirall, "Smollett's 'Gothic': An Illustration", *Modern Language Notes* 68 (1953): 408–10.

SPENSER, EDMUND (1552?–1599)

Poetical Works

> *Text:* Ed. J. C. Smith and Ernest de Selincourt (Oxford, 1909–10 [3 vols.]; 1-vol. ed. 1912). *Works,* ed. Edwin Greenlaw, C. G. Osgood, F. M. Padelford, et al. (Baltimore: Johns Hopkins University Press, 1932–49 [10 vols.]).

Criticism (General): Leicester Bradner, *Edmund Spenser and* The Faerie Queene (Chicago: University of Chicago Press, 1948). Patrick L. Cullen, *Infernal Triad: The Flesh, The World, and the Devil in Spenser and Milton* (Princeton: Princeton University Press, 1974).

STEVENSON, ROBERT LOUIS (1850–1894)

"The Body Snatcher"

> *Text: Pall Mall,* Christmas 1884. New York: Merriam Co., 1895. In *The Complete Short Stories of Robert Louis Stevenson* (Garden City, NY: Doubleday, 1969). In *The Short Stories of Robert Louis Stevenson* (New York: Scribner's, 1923).

"Markheim" (*LL* 846)

> *Text: Broken Shaft,* Christmas 1885. In *Complete Short Stories* (q.v.). In *The Short Stories* (q.v.).

The Strange Case of Dr. Jekyll and Mr. Hyde (*LL* 846)

> *Text:* London: Longmans, Green, 1886. New York: Scribner's, 1886. London: Chatto & Windus, 1895 (with *The Merry Men and Other Tales*). In *Novels of Mystery from the Victorian Age,* ed. Maurice Richardson (London: Pilot Press, 1945). New York: Limited Editions Club, 1952. New York: Bantam Books, 1967. London: New English Library, 1974.

> *Criticism:* Vladimir Nabokov, "The Strange Case of Dr. Jekyll and Mr. Hyde (1885 [*sic*])", in Nabokov's *Lectures on Literature,* ed. Fredson Bowers (New York: Harcourt Brace Jovanovich, 1980). William Veeder and Gordon Hirsch, ed., Dr. Jekyll and Mr. Hyde *After One Hundred Years* (Chicago: University of Chicago Press, 1988).

Criticism (General): Graham Balfour, *The Life of Robert Louis Stevenson* (New York: Scribner's, 1901; 2 vols.). Jenni Calder, *Robert Louis Stevenson: A Life Study* (New York: Oxford University Press, 1980). Edwin M. Eigner, *Robert Louis Stevenson and Romantic Tradition* (Princeton: Princeton University Press, 1966). Malcolm Elwin, *The Strange Case of Robert Louis Stevenson* (London: Macdonald, 1950; New York: Russell & Russell, 1971). John S. Gibson, *Deacon Brodie: Father to Jekyll and Hyde* (Edinburgh: P. Harris, 1977). Robert Kiely, *Robert Louis Stevenson and the Fiction of Adventure* (Cambridge, MA: Harvard University Press, 1964). Irving S. Saposnik, *Robert Louis Stevenson* (New York: Twayne, 1974). Roger G. Swearingen, *The Prose Writings of Robert Louis Stevenson* (Hamden, CT: Archon Books, 1980).

STOKER, BRAM (1847–1912)

Dracula (*LL* 848)

Text: London: Constable, 1897. New York: Grosset & Dunlap, 1897. New York: Modern Library, 1897. New York: Doubleday, 1899, 1929. New York: Dell, 1965. Garden City, NY: Doubleday, 1973 (with Mary Shelley, *Frankenstein*). *The Annotated Dracula*, ed. Leonard Wolf (New York: Charles N. Potter, 1975; rev. ed. New York: Penguin/Plume, 1993 [as *The Essential Dracula*]).

The Jewel of Seven Stars

Text: London: William Heinemann, 1903. New York & London: Harper, 1904. London: William Rider, 1912, 1919. London: Jarrolds, 1966. Leicester: Ulverscroft, 1967. London: Arrow, 1975. New York: Carroll & Graf, 1989. Oxford: Oxford University Press, 1996.

The Lair of the White Worm

Text: London: William Rider, 1911. London: W. Foulsham, 1925. London: Jarrolds, 1966. London: Arrow, 1974. London: W. H. Allen, 1986. Dingle, Ireland: Brandon, 1991. In *Bram Stoker's Dracula Omnibus* (London: Orion, 1992).

Criticism (General): Barbara Belford, *Bram Stoker: A Biography of the Author of* Dracula (New York: Knopf, 1996). Daniel Farson, *The Man Who Wrote* Dracula (New York: St Martin's Press, 1975). David Glover, *Vampires, Mummies, and Liberals: Bram Stoker and the Politics of Popular Fiction* (Durham, NC: Duke University Press, 1996). Phyllis A. Roth, *Bram Stoker* (Boston: Twayne, 1982).

VILLIERS DE L'ISLE-ADAM, JEAN MARIE MATHIAS, COMTE DE (1838–1889)

"La torture par l'esperance" ("Torture by Hope") (*LL* 335, 400)

Text: In Villiers de l'Isle-Adam's *Nouveaux Contes cruels* (Paris: La Librairie Illustrée, 1888). In Villiers de l'Isle-Adam's *Oeuvres Complètes* (Paris: Mercure de France, 1922), Vol. 3. In Villiers de l'Isle-Adam's *Contes cruels; Nouveaux Contes cruels,* ed. P. G. Castex (Paris: Garnier Frères, 1968).

Translation: In Julian Hawthorne, ed., *The Look and Key Library* (New York: Review of Reviews, 1912), Vol. 5. In Joseph Lewis French, ed., *Masterpieces of Mystery* (Garden City, NY: Doubleday, Page, 1920), Vol. 4.

Criticism (General): Jacques-Henry Bornecque, *Villiers de l'Isle Adam, createur et visionnaire* (Paris: A. Nizet, 1974). William t. Conroy, Jr., *Villiers de l'Isle-Adam* (Boston: Twayne, 1978). Stéphane Mallarmé, *Villiers de l'Isle-Adam,* ed. A. W. Raitt (Exeter, UK: University of Exeter, 1991). A. W. Raitt, *Villiers de l'Isle-Adam et la mouvement symboliste* (Paris: Corti, 1965). A. W. Raitt, *The Life of Villiers de l'Isle-Adam* (Oxford: Clarendon Press, 1981). A. W. Raitt, *Villiers de l'Isle-Adam: Exorciste du réel* (Paris: Corti, 1987).

WAKEFIELD, H[ERBERT] RUSSELL (1889–1965)

Others Who Returned (LL 912)

Text: London: G. Bles, 1929 (as *Old Man's Beard*). New York: D. Appleton & Co., 1929.

They Return at Evening (LL 913)

Text: London: P. Allen & Co., 1928.

WALPOLE, HORACE (1717–1797)

The Castle of Otranto (LL 916)

Text: London: William Bathoe & Thomas Lowndes, [1764] (dated 1765). London: Chatto & Windus, 1923 (ed. Caroline Spurgeon; with Sir Walter Scott's introduction). London: Constable, 1924 (ed. Montague Summers; with *The Mysterious Mother*). London: Oxford University Press, 1964 (ed. W. S. Lewis). In Peter Fairclough, ed., *Three Gothic Novels* (Harmondsworth: Penguin, 1968).

Criticism (General): Martin Kallich, *Horace Walpole* (New York: Twayne, 1971). Thomas Babington Macaulay, "Horace Walpole" (1833), in Macaulay's *Critical, Historical, and Miscellaneous Essays* (Boston: Houghton Mifflin, 1860), Vo.l. 3. K. K. Mehrotra, *Horace Walpole and the English Novel* (Oxford: B. Blackwell, 1934). Lewis Melville, *Horace Walpole* (London: Hutchinson, 1930). Tim Mowl, *Horace Walpole: The Great Outsider* (London: Murray, 1996). Leslie Stephen, "Horace Walpole" (1872), in Stephen's *Hours in a Library* (1874–79; rev. ed. London: Smith, Elder & Co., 1892), Vol. 1.

WALPOLE, HUGH (1884–1941)

"Mrs. Lunt"

Text: In Cynthia Asquith, ed., *The Ghost Book* (London: Hutchinson, 1927; New York: Scribner's, 1927).

Criticism (General): Rupert Hart-Davis, *Hugh Walpole: A Biography* (London: Macmillan, 1952). Elizabeth Steele, *Hugh Walpole* (New York: Twayne, 1972).

WARD, ARTHUR SARSFIELD ("SAX ROHMER") (1883–1959)

Brood of the Witch-Queen (*LL* 920)

Text: London: C. A. Pearson, 1918. Garden City, NY: Doubleday, Page, 1924. London: Cassell, 1932. New York: Pyramid, 1966.

Criticism (General): Cay Van Ash and Elizabeth Sax Rohmer, *Master of Villainy: A Biography of Sax Rohmer* (Bowling Green, OH: Bowling Green University Popular Press, 1972).

WEBSTER, JOHN (1580?–1625?)

[*Plays*]

Text: *The Duchess of Malfi*, ed. J. R. Brown (London: Methuen, 1964); ed. Clive Hart (Edinburgh: Oliver & Boyd, 1972). *The White Devil*, ed. J. R. Brown (London: Methuen, 1960; 2nd ed. 1966); ed. Clive Hart (Edinburgh: Oliver & Boyd, 1970). *Complete Works*, ed. F. L. Lucas (London: Chatto & Windus, 1927–28; rpt. 1966 [4 vols.]).

Criticism (General): George L. Grant, "The Imagery of Witchcraft in *The Duchess of Malfi*", Ph.D. diss.: Stanford University, 1971. Muriel West, "The Devil and John Webster", Ph.D.diss.: University of Arkansas, 1956.

WELLS, H[ERBERT] G[EORGE] (1866–1946)

Thirty Strange Stories

Text: London: Edward Arnold, 1897. New York & London: Harper, 1897. See also: *28 Science Fiction Stories* (New York: Dover, 1952). *The Short Stories of H. G. Wells* (London: Ernest Benn, 1927; Garden City, NY: Doubleday, 1929).

Criticism (General): Bernard Bergonzi, *The Early H. G. Wells: A Study of the Scientific Romances* (Manchester: Manchester University Press, 1961). Richard H. Costa, *H. G. Wells* (New York: Twayne, 1967). Stephen Gill, *Scientific Romances of H. G. Wells* (Cornwall, Ont.: Vesta Publications, 1975). Roslynn D. Haynes, *H. G. Wells, Discoverer of the Future* (New York: New York University Press, 1980). Mark R. Hillegas, *The Future as Nightmare: H. G. Wells and the Anti-Utopians* (New York: Oxford University Press, 1967). Frank McConnell, *The Science Fiction of H. G. Wells* (New York: Oxford University Press, 1981). Darko Suvin and Robert M. Philmus, ed., *H. G. Wells and Modern Science Fiction* (Lewisburg, PA: Bucknell University Press, 1977). Jack Williamson, *H. G. Wells: Critic of Progress* (Baltimore: Mirage Press, 1973).

WHITE, EDWARD LUCAS (1866–1934)

Lukundoo and Other Stories (*LL* 943)

Text: London: Ernest Benn, 1927. New York: George H. Doran, 1927.

The Song of the Sirens and Other Stories (*LL* 944)

Text: New York: E. P. Dutton, 1919, 1934.

Criticism (General): George T. Wetzel, "Edward Lucas White: Notes for a Biography", *Fantasy Commentator* 4, No. 2 (Winter 1979–80): 94–114; 4, No. 3 (Winter 1981): 178–83; 4, No. 4 (Winter 1982): 229–39; 5, No. 1 (Winter 1983): 67–70, 74; 5, No. 2 (Winter 1984): 124–27.

WILDE, OSCAR (1854–1900)

[*Fairy Tales*] (*LL* 954)

Text: The Happy Prince and Other Tales (London: David Nutt, 1888; Boston: Roberts Brothers, 1888; London: Duckworth, 1913; New York: G. P. Putnam's Sons, 1913; New York: Greystone, 1951). *A House of Pomegranates* (London: J. R. Osgood, McIlvaine, & Co., 1891; London: Methuen, 1909; New York: Dodd, Mead, 1925). [Combined:] London: Methuen, 1908; Boston: John W. Luce, 1910; New York & London: G. P. Putnam's Sons, 1913; New York: Boni & Liveright, 1918 (with *Poems in Prose*); London: Unicorn Press, 1949; London: Gollancz, 1976.

The Picture of Dorian Gray (*LL* 956)

Text: London & New York: Ward, Lock, & Co., 1891. Paris: Charles Carrington, 1901. London: Methuen, 1908. Boston: John W. Luce, 1910. New York: Brentano's, 1911. New York: G. P. Putnam's Sons, 1916. New York: Boni & Liveright, 1917. Cleveland & New York: World Publishing Co., 1944. Harmondsworth: Penguin, 1949. London: Oxford University Press, 1974 (ed. Isobel Murray).

Criticism (General): Richard Ellmann, *Oscar Wilde* (New York: Knopf, 1988). H. Montgomery Hyde, *Oscar Wilde: A Biography* (New York: Farrar, Straus & Giroux, 1975). Christopher S. Nassaar, *Into the Demon Universe: A Literary Exploration of Oscar Wilde* (New Haven: Yale University Press, 1974). Arthur Ransome, *Oscar Wilde: A Critical Study* (London: Martin Secker, 1912). E. San Juan, *The Art of Oscar Wilde* (Princeton: Princeton University Press, 1967). Rodney Shewan, *Oscar Wilde: Art and Egotism* (London: Macmillan, 1977).

YOUNG, FRANCIS BRETT (1884–1954)

Cold Harbour

Text: London: Collins, 1924. New York: Alfred A. Knopf, 1925. New York: W. W. Norton, 1968.

Criticism: J. F. S., Review, *Boston Transcript,* 12 December 1925, p. 1. Review, *New York Tribune,* 25 October 1925, p. 2.

Index

Adventures of Ferdinand, Count Fathom, The (Smollett) 26
A.E. *See* Russell, George William
Aikin, Miss. *See* Barbauld, Anna Letitia
Ainsworth, William Harrison 12, 36
Albertus Magnus 24
"Alchemist, The" (Lovecraft) 82n9
Alciphron (Moore) 35–36
"All-Hallows" (de la Mare) 57
Alraüne (Ewers) 39
Amber Wltch, The (Meinhold) 39
"Ambitious Guest, The" (Hawthorne) 48
"Ancestor, The" (Derleth) 99n50
"Ancestral Footstep, The" (Hawthorne) 48
"Ancient Sorceries" (Blackwood) 67
"'And He Shall Sing . . .'" (Wakefield) 58
Angels of Mons, The 65
Anne (Queen of England) 26
Ansky. *See* Rappoport, Solomon
Apollonius of Tyana 37
"Apparition of Mrs. Veal, The" (Defoe) 26
Apuleius, Lucius 25
Arabian Nights 33
Arthur Mervyn (Brown) 30
"Ash-Tree, The" (James) 109n56
Asquith, Lady Cynthia 10, 104n42
At the Mountains of Madness (Lovecraft) 77n6, 93n22, 101n11
Austen, Jane 31
"Avatar" (Gautier) 40
"Azathoth" (Lovecraft) 85n4

"Bad Lands, The" (Metcalfe) 58
Balzac, Honoré de 31, 89n9
Barbauld, Anna Letitia 28
Baring-Gould, Sabine 25
Barker, Clive 16
Barlow, R. H. 11
Barrett, Francis 34

Barrie, J. M. 58
Baudelaire, Charles Pierre 31, 40, 43, 45
Beckford, William 33–34
Beetle, The (Marsh) 56
"Bells, The" (Poe) 93n13
Benson, A. C. 102n31
Benson E. F. 57–58
Benson, R. H. 102n31
Beowulf 25
"Bethmoora" (Dunsany) 108n43
"Beyond the Wall of Sleep" (Lovecraft) 77n3
Bierce, Ambrose 9, 13, 14, 17, 50–52, 53, 72, 73, 98nn44–45
Birkhead, Edith 9, 12, 14, 33, 81n8
Biss, Gerald 56
Blackwood, Algernon 9, 11, 13, 66–67, 73, 90n14, 92n5, 105n3
Blake, William 26
Bleiler, E. F. 12, 14
Blessing of Pan, The (Dunsany) 11
"Blind Man's Buff" (Wakefield) 58
Bloch, Robert 17
Boats of the "Glen Carrig," The (Hodgson) 59
"Body-Snatcher, The" (Stevenson) 37
Book of Enoch 23
Book of Wonder, The (Dunsany) 68
"Books to mention in new edition of weird article" (Lovecraft) 10
"Bowmen, The" (Machen) 65–66
Braddon, Mary 12
"Bride of Corinth, The" (Goethe) 25
Brontë, Emily 9, 38
Brood of the Witch-Queen (Ward) 56
Broughton, Rhoda 12
Brown, Charles Brockden 29–30, 46
Browning, Robert 22, 60
Buchan, John 10, 11, 57
Bulwer-Lytton, Edward. *See* Lytton, Edward Bulwer-Lytton, Lord

163

Bürger, Gottfried August 26
Burleson, Donald R. 77n8, 95n4
Burns, Robert 26
Byron, George Gordon, Lord 31, 35, 38, 48, 54, 86n18

cabbalism 41, 78n3
Cagliostro 34
"Cairn, The" (Wakefield) 58
Caleb Williams (Godwin) 34–35
"Call of Cthulhu, The" (Lovecraft) 20, 90n14, 106n10
"Camp of the Dog, The" (Blackwood) 67
Campbell, Ramsey 16
Can Such Things Be? (Bierce) 52
Cannon, Peter 85n4, 100n5
"Canterville Ghost, The" (Wilde) 77n8, 100n6
"Captain of the 'Pole-Star,' The" (Doyle) 58
Carleton, William 60
Carnacki, the Ghost-Finder (Hodgson) 60
Case of Charles Dexter Ward, The (Lovecraft) 20, 80n16, 82nn9–10, 83n20, 84nn10–11, 87n32, 95n12, 99n5, 102n28, 109n60
Castle of Otranto, The (Walpole) 27–28, 82n13
Castles of Athlin and Dunbayne, The (Radcliffe) 29
Castle Spectre, The (Lewis) 31
"Cats, The" (Lovecraft) 92n11
Catullus 12
Celestial Omnibus, The (Forster) 58
Centaur, The (Blackwood) 67
"Challenge from Beyond, The" (Lovecraft et al.) 104n46
Chambers, Robert W. 10, 52–53, 73
Chamisso, Adalbert von 89n2
"Chef-d'oeuvre inconnu, Le" (Balzac) 90n9
"Chemical" (Blackwood) 10
"Childe Roland to the Dark Tower Came" (Browning) 22, 60

Children of the Abbey, The (Roche) 33
"Christabel" (Coleridge) 26
Chronicle of Clemendy, The (Machen) 61
"City in the Sea, The" (Poe) 93n15
"Clarimonde" (Gautier) 40
Claviculae of Solomon 23
Cline, Leonard 10, 15, 54
Cobb, Irvin S. 53–54
Cold Harbour (Young) 56
Coleridge, Samuel Taylor 26, 92n4
Collier, John 18
Collins, Wilkie 12, 37
Collison-Morley, Lacy 76n19, 79nn21–22
Colman, George 86n16
Colum, Padraic 60
Commonplace Book (Lovecraft) 10, 75n10, 95nn8–9, 96n14, 97n30, 99n47, 100n8, 101n14, 102nn21, 28, 107n23
Conover, Willis 11
Conrad, Joseph 60
Constant, Alphonse-Louis [pseud. Eliphas Lévi] 37
conte cruel 18, 41, 77n7
Cook, W. Paul 9–10, 100nn8, 101n14
"Cool Air" (Lovecraft) 93n20, 107n23
Cooper, Frederic Taber 51
"Count Magnus" (James) 70–71, 73
Count of Narbonne, The (Jephson) 81n5
Cram, Ralph Adams 10, 53
Crawford, F. Marion 10, 22, 52
Creeps by Night (Hammett) 18
Croker, T. Crofton 60
Curse of the Wise Woman, The (Dunsany) 11

Dacre, Charlotte 33
"Dagon" (Lovecraft) 15
"Damned, The" (Blackwood) 108n32
"Damned Thing, The" (Bierce) 51, 96n26
Dante Alighieri 25
Dark Chamber, The (Cline) 10, 15, 54
"Dead Smile, The" (Crawford) 52
"Dead Valley, The" (Cram) 11, 53

164

Death Mask, The (Everett) 15
"Death of Halpin Frayser, The" (Bierce) 51, 73
Decadents 40, 43
Dee, Dr. John 24
"Defence Remains Open!, The" (Lovecraft) 92n9
"Defence Reopens!, The" (Lovecraft) 77nn1–2, 83n3, 107n42, 109n46, 110n65
Defoe, Daniel 26
de la Mare, Walter 9–10, 13, 57, 73n3
De Quincey, Thomas 36
Derleth, August 11, 14, 18, 99n50
"Descent into Egypt, A" (Blackwood) 108n33
"Diamond Lens, The" (O'Brien) 50
"Diary of a Madman, The" (Maupassant) 41
Dickens, Charles 12, 22, 36
"Distressing Tale of Thangobrind the Jeweller" (Dunsany) 108n37
Dolliver Romance, The (Hawthorne) 48
"Doom That Came to Sarnath, The" (Lovecraft) 108nn35, 44
Door of the Unreal, The (Biss) 56
Double Shadow and Other Fantasies, The (Smith) 55
Doyle, Arthur Conan 37, 58
Dr. Faustus (Marlowe) 25
Dr. Grimshawe's Secret (Hawthorne) 48
Dr. Jekyll and Mr. Hyde (Stevenson) 37
Dracula (Stoker) 56, 100n15, 101n17
Drake, H. B. 10, 15, 20, 57
"Dream-Land" (Poe) 93n16
Dream-Quest of Unknown Kadath, The (Lovecraft) 20, 76n24, 85n4, 95n10, 104nn45–46, 106n15
Dreamer's Tales, A (Dunsany) 68
"Dreams in the Witch House, The" (Lovecraft) 20, 82n9, 94n3, 98n52
Dumas, Alexandre 85n13
Du Maurier, George 52
Dunn, Henry 83n6

Dunsany, Lord 9, 11–12, 13, 14, 16, 20, 45, 67–69, 94n26, 105n2, 107n27
"Dunwich Horror, The" (Lovecraft) 90n14, 93n17, 96n17, 106nn11, 13, 107n16, 108n28
Dweller on the Threshold, The (Hichens) 87n29
Dybbuk, The (Rappoport) 41–42

Eddison, E. R. 16
Edgar Huntly (Brown) 30
"Edward Randolph's Portrait" (Hawthorne) 48
Elsie Venner (Holmes) 22, 52
Elixir of Life, The (Ransome) 57
Epicurean, The (Moore) 36
Epicurus 77n5
"Episode of Cathedral History, An" (James) 71–72
Episodes of Vathek, The (Beckford) 34
Erckmann-Chatrian [Emile Erckmann and Alexandre Chatrian] 41
"Ethan Brand" (Hawthorne) 48
Etidorhpa (Lloyd) 75n11
Euripides 12
Everett, Mrs. H. D. 15, 58
Ewers, Hanns Heinz 10, 20, 39

"Face, The" (Benson) 58
"Facts concerning the Late Arthur Jermyn and His Family" (Lovecraft) 82n18
"Facts in the Case of M. Valdemar, The" (Poe) 44
"Fall of the House of Usher, The" (Poe) 45, 56, 92n9
Fantastics (Hearn) 55
Fantasy Fan, The 10–11
Fatal Revenge (Maturin) 31
Faulkner, William 18–19
Faust (Goethe) 26
Faust and the Demon (Reynolds) 34
"Final Words" (Lovecraft) 99n54
"'Finest Story in the World, The'" (Kipling) 55

165

"Fishhead" (Cobb) 53–54
Five Jars, The (James) 70
Flaubert, Gustave 40, 55, 99n3
Fludd, Robert 24
"Foot of the Mummy, The" (Gautier) 40
"For the Blood Is the Life" (Crawford) 52
Forster, E. M. 58
Frankenstein (Shelley) 35
Freeman, Mary E. Wilkins 53
French, Joseph Lewis 76n19, 98n47, 102n33
Fungi from Yuggoth (Lovecraft) 97n37

Galland, Antoine 33
Gaston de Blondeville (Radcliffe) 29
Gautier, Théophile 40, 55, 99n3
"German Student, The [Adventure of the]" (Irving) 25, 35
Ghost Book, The (Asquith) 10, 104n42
"Ghost of Fear, The" (Wells) 58
Ghost Pirates, The (Hodgson) 59
Ghost-Stories of an Antiquary (James) 70
Ghosts Grim and Gentle (French) 98n47, 103n33
Gilman, Charlotte Perkins 22, 53
Gods of the Mountain, The (Dunsany) 68
Godwin, William 34–35, 82n17
Goethe, Johann Wolfgang von 25, 26, 31
Golem, The (Meyrink) 10, 11, 41–42
Gorman, Herbert S. 15, 20, 54
Grand Guignol 41
"Great God Pan, The" (Machen) 62–63
Great Return, The (Machen) 65
Greek and Roman Ghost Stories (Collison-Morley) 76n19, 79nn21–22
Green Round, The (Machen) 11
"Green Tea" (LeFanu) 88n35
"Green Thoughts" (Collier) 18
"Green Wildebeest, The" (Buchan) 57
Gregory, Lady Augusta 60
Grosse, Marquis von 33
Guiney, Louise Imogen 97n36

Haggard, H. Rider 12, 37
"Haïta the Shepherd" (Bierce) 98n44
Hall, Leland 15, 54
Hamlet (Shakespeare) 25
Hammett, Dashiell 18
Hans of Iceland (Hugo) 40
"Harbor-Master, The" (Chambers) 98n46
Harris, Thomas 17
Hart, B. K. 73n1
Hart-Davis, Rupert 84n9
Hartley, L. P. 58
Hashish-Eater, The (Smith) 54
Hathorne, John 95nn5, 8
Haunted Castle, The (Railo) 9
"Haunter of the Dark, The" (Lovecraft) 20, 89n7, 94n29
Hawthorne, Julian 14, 82n19, 84n12, 90n16
Hawthorne, Nathaniel 14, 47–49, 68, 80n14, 94n1
Hay, George 79n12
"He?" (Maupassant) 41
"'He Cometh and He Passeth By'" (Wakefield) 58
Hearn, Lafcadio 55
"Herbert West—Reanimator" (Lovecraft) 86n19
Herodotus 68
Hichens, Robert 12, 87n29
Hill of Dreams, The (Machen) 61, 107n17
History of the Caliph Vathek, The (Beckford) 33–34
"Hoard of the Gibbelins, The" (Dunsany) 108n40
Hodgson, William Hope 9, 11, 58–60, 101n12
Hoffmann, E. T. A. 38, 44
Hogg, James 10, 26
Holmes, Oliver Wendell 22, 52
Homer 12
"Horla, The" (Maupassant) 40, 50
Hornig, Charles D. 10, 11
Horrid Mysteries (Grosse) 33
"Horror" (Maupassant) 41

"Horror at Red Hook, The" (Lovecraft) 93n24
"Horror-Horn, The" (Benson) 58
"Hound, The" (Lovecraft) 82n9, 90n13, 94n32, 96n25, 98n43
"House and the Brain, The" ["The Haunted and the Haunters"] (Bulwer-Lytton) 36
"House of Sounds, The" (Shiel) 56, 73
House of the Seven Gables, The (Hawthorne) 48–49, 68, 80n14
"House of the Sphinx, The" (Dunsany) 107n38
House on the Borderland, The (Hodgson) 59
Housman, Clemence 57
"How Nuth Would Have Practised His Art upon the Gnoles" (Dunsany) 108n41
"How One Came, as Was Foretold, to the City of Never" (Dunsany) 108n42
Hugo, Victor 40
Huysmans, Joris-Karl 40
Hyde, Douglas 60
"Hypnos" (Lovecraft) 89n12

"Idle Days on the Yann" (Dunsany) 108n44
In Defence of Dagon (Lovecraft) 15
In Search of the Unknown (Chambers) 53
In the Midst of Life (Bierce) 52
"In the Vault" (Lovecraft) 96n25
Incredible Adventures (Blackwood) 66–67, 107n27
"Inexperienced Ghost, The" (Wells) 77n8
"Inhabitant of Carcosa, The" (Bierce) 98n45
"Invisible Eye, The" (Erckmann-Chatrian) 41
Iron Chest, The (Colman) 35
Irving, Henry 85n16
Irving, Washington 25, 35–46, 46
Italian, The (Radcliffe) 29

Jacobs, W. W. 22
James I (King of England) 25
James, Henry 22, 52
James, M. R. 9, 13, 14, 69–72, 73
Jephson, Robert 81n5
Jewel of Seven Stars, The (Stoker) 56
Jewish folklore 41
Jimbo: A Fantasy (Blackwood) 67
John Silence—Physician Extraordinary (Blackwood) 67
Johnson, Samuel 85n6

Keats, John 26
Kilmeny (Hogg) 26
King, Stephen 16
King in Yellow, The (Chambers) 52–53
King of Elfland's Daughter, The (Dunsany) 11
Kipling, Rudyard 55
Klein, T. E. D. 16
Koenig, H. C. 73n1, 75n13, 104n44
Kwaidan (Hearn) 55

La Motte-Fouqué, Friedrich Heinrich Karl, baron de 38–39
Lady Who Came to Stay, The (Spencer) 10
Lair of the White Worm, The (Stoker) 56
Lamia (Keats) 26
Last Man, The (Shelley) 35, 101n12
Laughter of the Gods, The (Dunsany) 68
Lawrence, D. H. 47
Lee, Sophia 28
LeFanu, Joseph Sheridan 12, 37
Legends of the Province House (Hawthorne) 48
Lenore (Bürger) 26
Letters on Demonology and Witchcraft (Scott) 35
Level, Maurice 41
Lévi, Eliphas. *See* Constant, Alphonse-Louis
Lévy, Maurice 9
Lewes, George Henry 83n7

Lewis, Matthew Gregory 30–31, 33, 46, 94n33
Life and Letters of William Beckford, The (Melville) 34
"Ligeia" (Poe) 45
Ligotti, Thomas 16
Lilith (Macdonald) 57
"Listener, The" (Blackwood) 66
"Listeners, The" (de la Mare) 57
Lloyd, John Uri 75n11
Lock and Key Library, The (Hawthorne) 14, 82n19, 84n12, 90n16
Long, Frank Belknap 62, 79n12, 105n4, 106n15
"'Look Up There!'" (Wakefield) 58
Lord Jim (Conrad) 104n48
"Lot No. 249" (Doyle) 58
Louis Lambert (Balzac) 39
Loveman, Samuel 50, 96n21
Lucian 12
"Lukundoo" (White) 54
Lully, Raymond 24
"Lurking Fear, The" (Lovecraft) 82n9, 100n2, 109n55
Lytton, Edward Bulwer-Lytton, Lord 12, 34, 36–37

Mabbott, T. O. 76n25, 94n29
Macbeth (Shakespeare) 25
Macdonald, George 57, 79n9
Macdonald, Greville 102n26
Machen, Arthur 9, 11, 13, 14, 16, 20, 61–65, 72, 73, 92n5, 93n20
Macpherson, James [pseud. Ossian] 26
Magus, The (Barrett) 34
Maker of Moons, The (Chambers) 53
Malory, Thomas, Sir 25
"Man of the Crowd, The" (Poe) 17, 44, 92n19
"Man Who Went Too Far, The" (Benson) 57–58
Man-Wolf, The (Erckmann-Chatrian) 41
Marble Faun, The (Hawthorne) 47
Mariconda, Steven J. 80n17, 90n13

"Markheim" (Stevenson) 37
"Mark of the Beast, The" (Kipling) 55
Marryat, Frederick 36
Marsh, Richard 56
"Masque of the Red Death, The" (Poe) 45, 93n27
Masterpieces of Mystery (French) 76n19
Maturin, Charles Robert 9, 31–33
Maupassant, Guy de 40–41, 50, 99n3
Medea (Euripides) 12
Meinhold, Wilhelm 39
"Melmoth Reconciled" (Balzac) 31
Melmoth the Wanderer (Maturin) 9, 13, 14, 31–33, 95n12
Melville, Lewis 34
Memoirs of a Justified Sinner (Hogg) 10
"Memory" (Lovecraft) 94n27
Mérimée, Prosper 26, 40
"Merlinus Redivivus" (Lovecraft) 87n27
Merritt, A. 73
Metcalfe, John 58
"Metzengerstein" (Poe) 44, 82n12, 92n9
Meyrink, Gustav 10, 41–42
"Middle Toe of the Right Foot, The" (Bierce) 51
"Minister's Black Veil, The" (Hawthorne) 48
Miniter, Edith 101n15
Molière 31
"Money-Diggers, The" (Irving) 35–36
Monk, The (Lewis) 30, 33
"Monkey's Paw, The" (Jacobs) 22
"Moon-Pool, The" (Merritt) 73
Moore, Thomas 26, 36, 40
More Ghost Stories of an Antiquary (James) 70
More, Paul Elmer 46
Morte d'Arthur, Le (Malory) 25
Morton, James F. 107n27
"Mound, The" (Lovecraft-Bishop) 99n58
"Mr. Kempe" (de la Mare) 57
"Mrs. Lunt" (Walpole) 58
"MS. Found in a Bottle" (Poe) 14, 44
Murray, Margaret A. 78nn5–6

"Music of Erich Zann, The" (Lovecraft) 89n7
Mysteries of Udolpho, The (Radcliffe) 29, 33

"Nameless City, The" (Lovecraft) 15, 78n4, 86n21
Narrative of A. Gordon Pym, The (Poe) 44
Necronomicon (Alhazred) 79n12, 82n11, 85n7, 97n30, 98n43
"Negotium Perambulans" (Benson) 57
"Nemesis of Fire, The" (Blackwood) 67
Nibelung tales [*Nibelungenlied*] 25
Night at an Inn, A (Dunsany) 68
Night Land, The (Hodgson) 59–60, 101n12
Nitokris (Queen of Egypt) 109n49
Northanger Abbey (Austen) 31
Nostradamus 24
"Notes on Writing Weird Fiction" (Lovecraft) 19–20, 77n9, 105n1
"Novel of the Black Seal" (Machen) 64–65, 73
"Novel of the White Powder" (Machen) 65, 73, 93n20

O'Brien, Fitz-James 40, 49–50
"'Oh, Whistle, and I'll Come to You, My Lad'" (James) 71, 109n57
Old English Baron, The (Reeve) 28
Oliphant, Margaret 12
"On Reading Arthur Machen" (Long) 62
"On the River" (Maupassant) 41
On Wonderful Events (Phlegon) 25
Onderdonk, Matthew H. 19
"One of Cleopatra's Nights" (Gautier) 40
Onions, Oliver 12
Ormond (Brown) 30
Ossian. *See* Macpherson, James
Others Who Return (Wakefield) 58
"Out of the Deep" (de la Mare) 57
"Outsider, The" (Lovecraft) 82n9, 94n27, 100n4, 109n49

Outsider and Others, The (Lovecraft) 11
Ovid 12
"Owl's Ear, The" (Erckmann-Chatrian) 41

Pain, Barry 10
Paracelsus 38
Pattee, Fred Lewis 12
Penzoldt, Peter 12
Peter Schlemihl (Chamisso) 89n2
Petronius 25
Phantastes (Macdonald) 79n9
"Phantom 'Rickshaw, The" (Kipling) 55
Phantom Ship, The (Marryat) 36
"Philinnion and Machates" (Phlegon) 25
Phlegon 25
"Pickman's Model" (Lovecraft) 20, 94n30
"Picture in the House, The" (Lovecraft) 82n9, 95n3
Picture of Dorian Gray, The (Wilde) 55–56, 95n12
Place Called Dagon, The (Gorman) 15, 20, 54
Pliny the Younger 25, 107n21
Poe, Edgar Allan 9, 13, 14, 17, 27, 40, 42–46, 47, 50, 52, 56, 67, 73, 82n12, 94n1
"Polaris" (Lovecraft) 94n27
Polidori, John William 35, 86n18
"Poor Old Bill" (Dunsany) 108n45
Prawer, S. S. 76n18
Prest, Thomas Preskett 37
"Probable Adventure of the Three Literary Men" (Dunsany) 108n39
Proclus 25
"Psychical Invasion, A" (Blackwood) 67
Psycho (Bloch) 17
"Psychopompos" (Lovecraft) 79n14, 80n15
Purple Cloud, The (Shiel) 56

Queen's Enemies, The (Dunsany) 68

Radcliffe, Ann 28–29, 31, 33, 46, 78n11
Raeper, William 102n26
Railo, Eino 9
Ransome, Arthur 57
Rappoport, Solomon [pseud. Ansky] 41–42
Rasselas, Prince of Abissinia (Johnson) 85n6
"Rats in the Walls, The" (Lovecraft) 76n24, 79n17, 82nn9, 12, 93n23, 99n49
"Raven, The" (Poe) 92n12
Recess, The (Lee) 28
"Recluse, A" (de la Mare) 57
Recluse, The (magazine) 9, 10, 11
"Recrudescence of Imray, The" (Kipling) 55
"Red Brain, The" (Wandrei) 18
"Red Hand, The" (Machen) 65
"Red Lodge, The" (Wakefield) 58
"Red Room, The" (Wells) 103n33
Redgauntlet (Scott) 35
Reeve, Clara 28
Return, The (de la Mare) 57
Reynolds, George W. M. 12, 34
Rice, Anne 17
Riddell, Mrs. J. H. 12
Rime of the Ancient Mariner, The (Coleridge) 26
"Ring, The" (Moore) 26, 40
Rocca, Lodovico 91n25
Roche, Regina Maria 33
Rohmer, Sax. *See* Ward, Arthur Sarsfield
Roman "gothique" anglais, Le (Lévy) 9
Romance of the Forest, The (Radcliffe) 29
"Rose for Emily, A" (Faulkner) 18–19
Rosicrucianism 34
Rossetti, Dante Gabriel 31
Rossetti, William Michael 83n6
Russell, George William [pseud. A.E.] 60
Rymer, James Malcolm 88n36

"Sacrifice, The" (Blackwood) 108n31

St Armand, Barton L. 82n18
St. Irvyne (Shelley) 33
St. Leon (Godwin) 34
Saintsbury, George 14, 33, 84nn12–13
Scandinavian Eddas and Sagas 25
Scarborough, Dorothy 76n29
Schlegel, A. W. 92n4
Schultz, David E. 75n10
Science-Fantasy Correspondent 11
Scott, Sir Walter 26, 31, 35, 83n1
"Seaton's Aunt" (de la Mare) 57, 73n3
"Secret Worship" (Blackwood) 67
Seneca 12
Septimius Felton (Hawthorne) 48
Séraphita (Balzac) 40
"Seventeenth Hole at Duncaster, The" (Wakefield) 58
"Shadow—A Parable" (Poe) 45
"Shadow out of Time, The" (Lovecraft) 77n6, 87n31
"Shadow over Innsmouth, The" (Lovecraft) 20, 98n46, 99nn48, 52, 100n2, 108n34
"Shadows on the Wall, The" (Freeman) 53
Shadowy Thing, The (Drake) 10, 15, 20, 57
She (Haggard) 37
Shea, J. Vernon 89n4, 92n20, 97n27
Shelley, Mary Wollstonecraft 35, 100n12
Shelley, Percy Bysshe 33, 86n18
Shiel, M. P. 13, 56, 73
"Shining Pyramid, The" (Machen) 65
"Shunned House, The" (Lovecraft) 82n9, 101n15
Sicilian Romance, A (Radcliffe) 29
"Signalman, The" (Dickens) 36
"Silence—A Fable" (Poe) 45, 93n27
Silence of the Lambs, The (Harris) 17
"Silver Key, The" (Lovecraft) 20
Sinclair, May 58
Sinister House (Hall) 15, 54
"Sir Bertrand" (Barbauld) 28
"Skule Skerry" (Buchan) 57

Smith, Clark Ashton 11, 16, 54–55, 85n10, 90n12, 105n2
"Smith: An Episode in a Lodging House" (Blackwood) 66, 108n29
Smoking Leg, The (Metcalfe) 58
Smollett, Tobias 26
"Snout, The" (White) 54
"Some Notes on Interplanetary Fiction" (Lovecraft) 78n10
"Some Words with a Mummy" (Poe) 92n9
"Song of the Sirens, The" (White) 54
Sorcerer's Apprentice, The (Ewers) 39
Southey, Robert 83n1
"Spectre, The" (Maupassant) 40
Spencer, R. E. 10
Spenser, Edmund 25
Sphinx of the Ice-Fields, The (Verne) 93n22
"Spider, The" (Ewers) 20, 39
"Spook House, The" (Bierce) 51–52
Spook Stories (Benson) 102n31
"Stalls of Barchester Cathedral, The" (James) 71
Stephens, James 60
Stevenson, Robert Louis 12, 37, 64, 107n17
Stoker, Bram 56
Stories in the Dark (Pain) 10
"Story of a Panic, The" (Forster) 103n39
"Strange High House in the Mist, The" (Lovecraft) 81n9
Strange Story, A (Bulwer-Lytton) 36–37
"Suitable Surroundings, The" (Bierce) 51, 73n3
Sullivan, Jack 12, 14
Summers, Montague 12, 84n2
Supernatural in Modern English Fiction, The (Scarborough) 76n29
Symbolists 40, 43
Synge, J. M. 60

Tale of Terror, The (Birkhead) 9, 14, 81n8

"Tale of Satampra Zeiros, The" (Smith) 99n58
Tales of a Traveller (Irving) 35
Tales of Mystery (Saintsbury) 14, 84nn12–13
Tales of Terror 31
Tales of Wonder (Lewis) 31
"Tam o'Shanter" (Burns) 26
Tanglewood Tales (Hawthorne) 47
"Tapestried Chamber, The" (Scott) 35
Temptation of St. Anthony, The (Flaubert) 40, 55
"Terrible Old Man, The" (Lovecraft) 96n25, 108n39
Terror, The (Machen) 65
Thackeray, William Makepeace 31
They Return at Evening (Wakefield) 58
Thin Ghost and Others, A (James) 70
"Thing on the Doorstep, The" (Lovecraft) 20, 80n16, 87n29, 94n28, 107n22
Thirty Strange Stories (Wells) 58
Three Impostors, The (Machen) 64–65, 107n25
"Tomb, The" (Lovecraft) 20, 82n9, 94n32
"Torture by Hope, The" (Villiers) 41
"Treasure of Abbot Thomas, The" (James) 71
Treatise on Elemental Sprites (Paracelsus) 38
"Tree, The" (de la Mare) 57
Trilby (du Maurier) 52
Trithemius 24
True History (Lucian) 12
Turn of the Screw, The (James) 22, 52

"Ulalume" (Poe) 93n14
"Unbroken Chain, The" (Cobb) 99n49
Uncanny Stories (Sinclair) 58
"Under the Pyramids" (Lovecraft) 86n21, 90n10, 109n49
Undine (La Motte-Fouqué) 38–39
"Undying Thing, The" (Pain) 10
"Unnamable, The" (Lovecraft) 96n25, 97n32

"Upper Berth, The" (Crawford) 22, 52

"Vampyre, The" (Polidori) 35, 86n18
Varney, the Vampyre (Prest) 37
"Venus of Ille, The" (Mérimée) 26, 40
Vergil 12
Verne, Jules 93n22
Villiers de l'Isle-Adam, Jean Marie Mathias, comte de 41
Visible and Invisible (Benson) 58
"Visitor from Down Under, A" (Hartley) 58
Wagner, Richard 96n18
Wagner, the Wehr-wolf (Reynolds) 34
Wakefield, H. Russell 58
Walpole, Horace 26–28, 34, 58
Walpole, Hugh 58
Wandering Ghosts (Crawford) 52
"Wandering Willie's Tale" (Scott) 35
Wandrei, Donald 18, 97n40
Ward, Arthur Sarsfield [pseud. Sax Rohmer] 56
Ward, Richard 109n60
Warning to the Curious, A (James) 14, 70
"Waters of Death, The" (Erckmann-Chatrian) 41
Webster, John 25
"Weird Work of William Hope Hodgson, The" (Lovecraft) 11, 104n44
Wells, H. G. 37, 58, 77n8
"Wendigo, The" (Blackwood) 66, 90n14
"Werewolf, The" (Marryat) 36
"Were-wolf, The" (Housman) 57
Wetzel, George T. 79n9, 94n29, 95n8, 96nn14–15, 102n28, 107n19
"What Was It?" (O'Brien) 50, 90n15
"Whisperer in Darkness, The" (Lovecraft) 98n44, 99n58, 106n15, 107nn18, 20
White, Edward Lucas 10, 54
"White People, The" (Machen) 63–64, 73, 92n5
"White Ship, The" (Lovecraft) 15, 108n35
"White Wolf, The" (Maupassant) 41

Whitman, Sarah Helen 93n21
"Who Knows?" (Maupassant) 40
Wieland (Brown) 30
Wild Ass's Skin, The (Balzac) 40
Wild Huntsman, The (Bürger) 26
Wilde, Lady 60
Wilde, Oscar 16, 17, 32, 45, 55–56, 60, 77n8
Wilkins, Mary E. *See* Freeman, Mary E. Wilkins
"Willows, The" (Blackwood) 9, 66, 73, 92n5
Wilson, Colin 100n4
Wilson, Edmund 76n25
"Wind in the Portico, The" (Buchan) 57
Wind in the Rose-Bush, The (Freeman) 53
Witch-Cult in Western Europe, The (Murray) 78n5
Witch Wood (Buchan) 10, 56
"With a Copy of Wilde's Fairy Tales" (Lovecraft) 100n4
Wollstonecraft, Mary 86n17
Wonder Book, A (Hawthorne) 47
Wood, Mrs. Henry 12
Woodberry, George 14
Wuthering Heights (Brontë) 9, 37–38

"Xélucha" (Shiel) 56

Yeats, W. B. 60, 105n49
"Yellow Sign, The" (Chambers) 52–53, 73
"Yellow Wall Paper, The" (Gilman) 22, 53
Young, Francis Brett 56

Zanoni (Bulwer-Lytton) 36, 37
Zastrozzi (Shelley) 33
Zofloya (Dacre) 33

Printed in the United States
55752LVS00002BA/68